COPYRIGHT

Claimed by a KING

B. LYBAEK & SARAH JD

Guys, we're here. We're finally at the finishing line, and Zoe & Grayson have gotten their happy-ever-after. After all the trials and tribulations our Prez and Mama have been through, I don't think anyone can dispute how well-deserved that was.

After over a year of living in the head of The Cruz Kings MC, weekly calls at stupid o'clock with Sarah, I think I'm going to suffer from withdrawals. I'll sit around at 2am. And wonder why she hasn't called yet. I tell you, it'll be a whole thing. Writing with Sarah has been challenging, fun, frustratingly amazing, chaotic, surprising, and so many more adjectives. But above all, it's been an experience I'll treasure, and something that's taught me so much. Both about authoring and myself. So thank you, Sarah. Thank you for going on this wild ride with me!

It's strange to think that this mammoth project has come to an end. What started out as an idea for a short anthology piece turned into a whole series that, I'm sure Bibi would agree, has been one hell of a ride to write.

Probably for me, one of the most rewarding parts of this project was how challenging it was to bring two writers together who do things so differently and finding a way to make it work.

I have learned so much about myself while writing the Cruz Kings Series. I've learned that I'm a hot mess, that's for sure! But also I've learned more about my writing, and having eyes constantly on it has helped it to evolve.

I'm extremely grateful to Bibi for the memorable experience, the hours of video calls and conversations that steered way off path before we had to get back on topic, and for the opportunity to really create, what I think is some of my best work.

I fucking love you Grayson Black!

And I adore Bibi. She's not just a co-writer. She'll forever be my friend.

ACKNOWLEDGMENTS

Our awesome alpha and beta readers; you ladies have gone above and beyond, and we couldn't be more grateful. You have challenged us, and helped us make Zoe & Grayson's story the best it could be.

Emma — For the amazing pictures that perfectly bring Grayson Black to life.

Cady — For putting up with us, and wowing us with another incredible cover.

Our readers; you've kept us going when the going got tough. Your support and love for our characters have been the best inspiration we could ask for.

Thank you, from the bottom of our twisted hearts.

DEDICATION

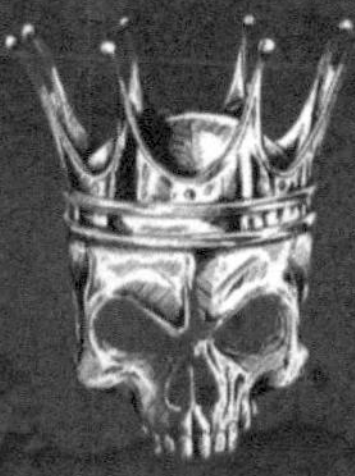

Love isn't about finding the perfect person. It's about realizing that an imperfect person can make your life perfect.

—Crystal Ball

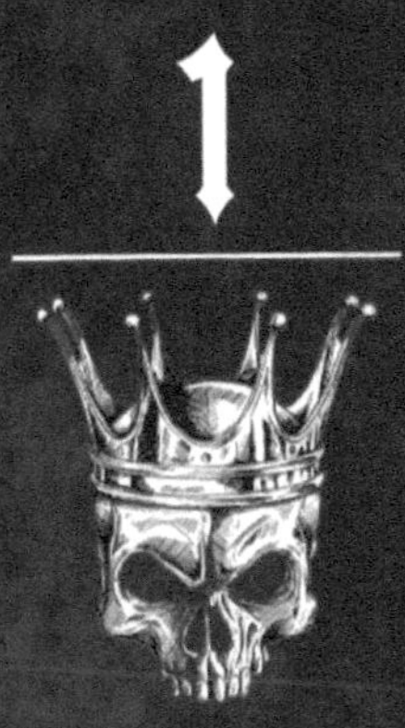

Grayson

For a moment, we're airborne, our bodies weightless as the truck launches over another fucking rise in the road. A moment later, we slam back onto the blood-soaked floor of the truck, and I instantly start compressions on our Prez again, who I fear may be too far gone to come back to us.

"How fucking long?!" I roar, not taking my eyes off Rocco's lifeless face as I pump his chest, and Tex cradles his head to keep him steady.

"One more set of traffic lights!" Titch yells from the front, where he sits jammed between Munroe and Doug.

"He has to live," Slasher mutters as he watches on, his voice almost robotic like he's talking to himself.

"I need another shirt. This one is soaked through as well." Stretch panics as he holds the blood drenched fabric of his shirt to Rocco's pelvis which won't stop fucking bleeding.

Slasher stumbles as the truck swerves, wrestling his cut off as he rights himself before he drags his shirt off too, tossing it to Stretch who immediately presses it on top of the other two blood-soaked shirts trying to stop the life from draining out of our Prez.

I count compressions, trying to focus on that as the lifeless look on Rocco's face doesn't change.

Don't fucking die on me.

"Hold on!" Munroe calls from the front before we go air-borne again.

"Fuck." Tex hisses trying to keep Rocco's head in his grip, and we all jerk with the hard thud from the truck meeting the road again before we're almost thrown sideways as we round a fucking corner.

"Come on, Rocco. Stay with us." Tex taps Rocco's cheek as I start compressions again, and my fucking eyes blur, filling with fucking tears.

This can't be happening. We can't lose our Prez. *I* can't lose him.

"Hold on again!" Munroe calls once more, and we brace the best we can as the truck comes to a screeching halt.

So many things happen at once then.

Slasher throws the rear doors open, launching out with his gun raised, ready to shoot any fucker who gets in the way of getting our Prez the help he needs.

Titch climbs through from the front cabin to help us slide our lifeless Prez across the floor of the truck toward the doors, right as Munroe comes into view holding his gun to the head of a fucking man while he pulls on the wrist of a woman, both wearing hospital scrubs.

"Help him!" he roars, and the woman whimpers as the man nods.

"Y-yes. Of course." He agrees before calling over his shoulder. "We need a gurney, stat!"

Others wearing hospital scrubs dart toward us, despite the guns we threaten them with, and as I continue compressions at the back of the truck bed, the male with the gun to his head disregards it and leaps up to join me.

"I can take over."

I shake my head. "No. I can't stop. He-he..."

The man clutches my shoulder in a firm grip of support and dips his head to get in my line of sight.

"You are the Cruz Kings, right?"

I nod sharply, and his face softens.

"Then your guns aren't needed here. We are *your* people, and we'll do everything we can to save your man."

"King." I snap, still pumping Rocco's chest. "He's our king."

The man's eyes go wide, as if realizing just who he promised to keep alive.

"This is Rocco?" he asks, and I nod as the gurney arrives at the end of the truck.

"This is our Prez."

The man barks numerous orders to his staff, and Stretch and I have no choice but to remove our bloody hands from Rocco's practically lifeless body as they lift him onto the gurney, and the man straddles him, taking over compressions as they rush him into the hospital.

Still inside the rear of the truck, my shoulders sag as a heavy weight settles over me.

There's a huge fucking chance that I'll never speak to Rocco again.

"Gray." A voice drags my eyes up from the pool of blood I seemed to be transfixed by, and my eyes meet Munroe's. "You need to get treated too."

I nod weakly as I glance down at myself, taking stock of my injuries. They didn't really seem all that important at the time, because Rocco was my top priority. Now though, he's in the hands of the medical staff here at the hospital, and I guess I should get my gunshot wounds looked at. There's no way any of us were going to be lucky enough not to at least take *one* bullet with the way the Reapers shot up the back of the truck as we got the fuck outta there. We are all bleeding, but luckily, none hit anything vital except for our Prez.

As I struggle to lower myself from the truck, my limbs start to fucking shake and more medical staff come out wearing scrubs and gloves, ready to help us.

"Do you want a wheelchair, sir?" a nurse asks as I start limping in their direction, but I shake my head.

"I'll fucking walk."

She nods quickly, her shoulders hunching a little as if she's scared of me.

I don't mean to scare her. That's not my fucking intention, but then again, if the nurse fears us, then maybe she'll make sure she doesn't make a fucking mistake while working on us.

Within minutes, the large frames of my battered men fill the ER. They didn't bother making us wait to be seen, instead making us top priority as the nursing staff start disinfecting wounds, prying out easy to reach bullets, and stitching holes closed.

This isn't how we usually handle getting shot up. Normally we have our own doc that tends to us, but we knew Rocco's only chance of surviving, if there is even a chance, was to bring him here to the local hospital.

It's no surprise to me when the cops turn up, right before those fucking annoying detectives stride through the ER like they own the joint.

"Grayson Black. We meet again." The female detective smiles like she's privy to something I'm not, and never in my life have I wanted to reach behind me and pull my gun out and introduce it to her fucking skull more than I do now.

"Detectives." I grit through clenched teeth as my nurse injects another dose of local anesthetic into my body. This one into my right thigh where she's about to stitch up my last bullet wound.

I was lucky. Mine were mostly flesh wounds that hurt like a bitch but will heal relatively quickly. Unlike Rocco whose pelvis got blown wide open.

Fuck. Rocco.

"I don't suppose you'll tell us who filled your men with bullets?" Detective Caruso asks, and I shrug at him.

"Didn't see their faces," I mutter and Detective Nelson rolls her eyes.

"Sure you didn't. Why don't you just do yourself and your men a favor and cooperate with us. We can help."

I scoff, but don't say anything.

"How about the explosion that ripped a farmhouse to smithereens outside of town?" Detective Caruso asks. "Do you know anything about that?"

Shaking my head, I eye Slasher over Detective Caruso's shoulder. He's pacing in front of the nurses' station where a couple of cops sit, keeping watch. He looks twitchy as fuck, and I wouldn't put it past him to start shooting anyone that looks at him the wrong fucking way.

"We found members of the Cali Reapers dead on that property," Detective Nelson continues as if I'm going to just start chatting.

I do love hearing that some Reapers are dead though. That's satisfying.

"We've been advised that Rochus King has been taken into emergency surgery," Caruso states, glancing at his notepad before he sighs. "Word is it's not looking hopeful."

In an instant I'm off the gurney, a fucking needle and thread hanging from my thigh as the nurse scrambles backward and I reach for my gun. The next second, two strong bodies are on either side of me holding me back, as a gruff voice whispers in my ear.

"Let it roll off you, brother."

Munroe's voice keeps me in place as the two detectives smirk, just waiting for me to threaten them and give them a reason to take me in.

"I guess that makes you number one now?" the female detective asks, lifting a curious brow up past the rim of her glasses. "I mean. If Mr. King doesn't survive."

"That's enough." The stern words come from my timid nurse as she pushes her way between the wall of Kings, and the two detectives. "I am trying to treat my patient, and you are doing nothing but making that impossible. Mr. Black and the other patients here will be available to answer your questions as soon as they've been treated. Until then, kindly leave."

The two detectives smirk down at the short dainty nurse, but snicker and turn away, leaving the emergency room, just as she'd asked.

"Damn." Munroe grins down at the woman, whose eyes are now locked on Slasher who has stopped pacing and is staring down the two cops behind the glass like he's getting ready to pounce.

"Is he going to be a problem?" the nurse asks, turning back to me. "My staff have already removed too many bullets today. I'd like to avoid more."

I want to grin at the feisty nurse, but I can't conjure the action. Instead, I grunt at Tex, who is on my other side.

"Coax Slasher down. There's been enough bloodshed today."

"On it," Tex mutters, stepping away to handle Slasher.

He hasn't been right since his brother died.

Munroe also steps away from me, and I ease back onto the gurney where the nurse sets to work on my leg again.

As Munroe hovers, his eyes more interested in the nurse stitching me up than my welfare, I let myself get lost in the words the detectives spoke.

"Word is it's not looking hopeful."

"I guess that makes you number one now."

"If Mr. King doesn't survive."

No. This can't happen. I'm not meant to step up until Rocco decides to step down. He's not meant to fucking die on me.

"I need to know how my Prez is. When will we get an update?" I snap at my nurse, and she shrugs.

"It will take time. He's in surgery, which is a good thing, but there was a lot of damage. The surgeons will need time to fix what they can."

What they can?

Shit. I don't even want to comprehend what the fuck that means.

"Has his next of kin been contacted?" I ask the nurse, not taking my eyes off the cops that have their eyes on Slasher who is still staring at them, just this time it's from a gurney in a curtained bay as a nurse patches him up.

"I believe so." The nurse admits, and my heart sinks.

Cara.

If Rocco dies, this is going to destroy her.

As my mind goes through all the fucked up scenarios, it shouldn't even be contemplating, the ache in my chest has me longing for my princess.

I want her here with me, but she's safer out of the way and hidden out of sight in Dirty Diamonds where Cain can watch over her. I should call her, but I don't want to worry her. I also can't bring myself to tell her about Rocco. I can't bear to say the words that I'm worried he's not going to make it, because if I do, then they might fucking come true.

One by one, we all get patched up, and one by one, the men make their way to my bay, standing at the end of the uncomfortable bed, looking to me for instruction.

Shit.

I'm all they have right now. With Rocco temporarily incapacitated, I'm number one. Their fucking acting President.

My mind flits back to that day all those years ago when Rocco and Cara formed the Cruz Kings.

We had our first meeting where we were all patched in. We were given our patches and titles, and it was the beginning of something big. Now as I stare at the men before me, my chest aches with the knowledge that we aren't all here. There are some missing. Some that will never return, like Gunner and Slayer.

If Gunner were here, I'd ask him to be my second, but he's not, and I'm still not sure how to feel about his death, and the confusing mess he left behind. He was the club's Sergeant at Arms, and the natural progression for that role is VP.

Tex is our Treasurer. Munroe is our Secretary. Stretch is our Road Captain. And Slasher is our Tail-Gunner and Enforcer, a role he shared with his now dead brother. I'd make him acting VP in an instant if his head were in the right place, but it's not.

Shit.

I don't know how to fucking do this.

"Tell us what you need." Munroe offers, seeming to pick up on my indecision with the whole fucking situation.

"I need to know what's happening with Rocco," I state, and they all nod, feeling the same.

"I can take you to a lounge in the surgical waiting area. I'll make sure the doctors come to find you there when they finish."

Glancing at the small framed nurse, I nod, thankful for the support she's offered us here today.

Even though they couldn't refuse to treat us, I was half expecting sneers and rough hands as they patched us up, not the welcoming treatment they actually gave us. Rocco was the only one that I was thinking of when we brought him here.

We make our way through the hospital and up two floors to the surgical suite. Apart from our bloody clothes and surgical patches, most of us aren't wearing shirts, since we used what we could to try to stop Rocco's injuries from draining him dry. Our chaotic state draws the eyes of everyone in our vicinity, but most already know who we are and what we represent, so they don't stare too long.

We take over the small lounge area, some of the guys taking up the two sofas while others sit on hard plastic seats. I can't sit. I can only pace, mimicking Slasher, who can't seem to sit still as well.

This is fucking torture. I should just call Zoe, but I hold off, not wanting to call her until I have news on Rocco.

"Please tell me he's going to be alright?"

The pained familiar voice makes me spin to the door as Cara comes into view, her cheeks wet and stained with trails of black tears.

Munroe, who's the closest to her, darts his head in my direction, his dark eyes pleading at me to answer her, so he doesn't have to.

Shit. This is part of the role. Being President means answering the tough questions. Making the hard decisions. And for the first time, I struggle with self-doubt that I'm not the right man for the job.

"Gray?" Cara pleads as a sob escapes her, and I know what I have to do.

I have to be the man they need.

"Come here," I say even as I take a step toward her, and she rushes forward, wrapping her arms around my middle in a death grip.

"Please tell me he's going to be okay, Grayson. I need him to be okay." She sobs, and I hold her head to my chest remembering the words Rocco asked me to tell her only moments after getting shot.

"Tell Cara I'm sorry."

"Tell Cara I never stopped loving her."

Fuck.

How can I tell her that he's going to be okay, when everything in me is screaming the opposite?

So I don't. I just hold her and whisper that we'll know more soon, and fucking hope that will be enough for now.

It feels like days have gone by, but the clock says a couple of hours when the doorway fills with a male surgeon, and the same man that took over CPR from me out in the truck.

Still standing with Cara in my arms, where she's refused to move from, she must feel the way I stiffen, because she pulls back to look up at me, and my gaze flicks down to hers before returning to the door.

"Mrs. King?" the surgeon asks, and Cara releases me, spinning quickly to face him.

"Yes. How's my husband?"

He has a fucking good poker face, because I can't tell if the news is good or fucking bad, but then he steps into the room and gestures to an empty chair.

"You should take a seat, Mrs. King."

And just like that, I know the news is bad.

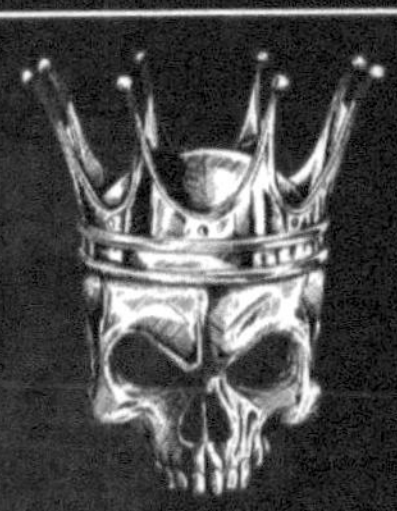

Grayson

"**I**f you don't start talking, I'm going to cut your balls from your body right fucking now."

Cara's words aren't shocking to me, but they sure as shit shock the surgeon who visibly flinches backward.

His fearful eyes dart to me for help, and I shake my head.

"You heard her. Start talking."

"Uh, okay." He stumbles over his words a little. "Mr. King sustained extensive internal damage due to the bullet fragments. We've had to remove one of his kidneys, and his spleen. We repaired his liver and the damage to his large intestine, but uh..." He clears his throat, his feet shuffling on the spot as he takes stock of all the brutes glaring back at him. "Unfortunately, the bullet fragments that nicked his spine have left him in a state of paralysis."

My. Whole. Fucking. World. Stops.

Did he just say what I thought he said?

I must be imagining it. Surely, he didn't just tell us that our King is paralyzed.

"W-what?" Cara stutters through her tears. "Did y-you say that my husband is... p-paralyzed?"

The surgeon nods slowly. "We won't know for a while how permanent it is. It could have been worse, and we managed to remove all the fragments, so that's positive, but you need to prepare for the possibility that Mr. King may not regain use of his legs."

A choked sob escapes Cara before she crashes to her knees, clutching her chest as she screams.

"NO!"

I fall to my knees beside her, dragging her to me as I contemplate putting a bullet between the surgeon's eyes.

"When can she see her husband?" Munroe asks, and the surgeon looks grave.

"He's not out of the woods yet. There were some other complications."

"What sort of fucking complications?" I growl as Cara tries to listen past her sobs.

"He lost a lot of blood. His heart was in great distress and failed twice during surgery. He is at high risk for a heart attack over the next twenty-four to forty-eight hours from the anesthetic and stress his body endured, so we've placed Mr. King in a medically induced coma to let his organs heal without further distress during the most critical stage."

"C-coma?" Cara stutters, and the man who helped at the truck speaks up.

"Medically induced. It's just to help him heal. We expect if he has no further complications that he will come out of it okay."

"But he won't be able to walk?" she asks and the man who helped shrugs.

"We won't know that for a while. His body needs time to heal."

I don't fucking like what they're saying, but it's better than him being dead, so for now, this is something positive.

"Is that everything?" I snap, and they both nod. "So, when can she see her husband?"

"As soon as he's moved out of recovery and into a room. The nurse will get you as soon as that happens, Mrs. King."

Something crashes out in the hall and raised voices float down the hallway as the surgeon steps out of the room to take a look at what's happening.

"Can I help you?" he asks, his body stiffening as if he's preparing for an attack.

"We are here for our Kings."

Even though the surgeon stiffens even more at the words, we all breathe a sigh of relief at hearing Cain's overdramatic voice before he appears in the doorway.

"Ah-ha. Here are thy men returned from war." He sing-songs as he steps in the doorway wearing a grin. It only lasts momentarily when he sees our expressions, and his face drops. "What the fuck happened?"

Not a second after the words pass his lips is he shoved aside by the horde of women trailing behind him. Darting into the room first, Alana's eyes lock on Slasher, ready to go to him until she spots Cara huddled on the floor with me.

"Cara?" she asks, her face morphing with pain as she takes in Cara's tear-stained cheeks.

Dropping to the floor with us, Alana wraps her arms around Cara while the other Cruz Cunts file in, all silent, their eyes darting around to take in the men, finally realizing who's missing.

My eyes remain on the door as I wait for my princess to appear, but after a long beat, I realize she isn't here.

"Where's Zoe?" I ask, releasing Cara into the care of her Cunts before standing.

"She's coming with Rhiannon." Rose answers as she hugs Cara.

"Rhiannon?" I frown, fucking confused.

"Yeah, when I overheard on the police scanner that a bunch of Cruz Kings turned up at the hospital, I knew I had to get the girls here to you fellas. Zoe had been napping or some shit, so Rhiannon offered to bring her, so we didn't have to wait."

Frowning, I glance at Tex who offers me a shrug, and we all listen as Munroe fills them in on what happened with Rocco.

Something about Rhiannon driving Zoe here doesn't sit well with me.

Rhiannon is... different. She's rarely charitable, and last I knew, she wasn't that keen about my princess. They've never hung out like Alana and Zoe have, but I guess under the circumstances, it would be normal for Rhiannon to step up and help.

I pace as I wait for the girls to arrive. After ten minutes have passed, I snatch Alana's phone off her and call Zoe's, but it goes straight to voicemail like it's not even switched on.

"What's wrong?" Cain asks, coming to stand before me.

"Something's not right. Zoe should be here by now."

Cain looks down at his watch and frowns too. "Let me call one of the Diamonds and get them to check the club."

I nod, pacing again as Cain steps out into the hall and makes the call, which is when a nurse steps into the room.

"Mrs. King?" she asks, looking amongst the women in the room, and Cara stands from the floor, quickly.

"Yes. I'm Mrs. King."

The nurse smiles warmly. "We have your husband set up in his room now. You are welcome to see him."

Nodding quickly, Cara steps forward, but she halts, spinning until her eyes meet mine. "Grayson. I need you to come with me."

"Yeah. Of course." I nod, moving to her side, and together, we follow the nurse out.

Passing Cain in the hallway, I shove my finger into his chest.

"Come and get me when Zoe arrives."

"Yeah, man. Consider it done." Cain smiles, but fuck. Why does that smile not reach his eyes?

Cara and I follow the nurse to a room that isn't a typical hospital room, the sign by the door saying, Intensive Care Unit.

"Mr. King will be monitored in this room until we rouse him from sedation in a couple of days." The nurse explains in a soft and soothing tone. "I'm sorry it's not a more comfortable space for you, but it is the required space for your husband right now."

Cara nods at the nurse, more tears springing from her eyes as she stares at the closed door, before pushing it open.

Following behind, I nearly run into her when she stops abruptly, her hand slapping over her mouth as a choked sob escapes her, and my eyes follow her line of sight to fall on my friend.

Rocco would look like he's sleeping if it weren't for the tubes protruding from his mouth and nose. Aside from that, he looks more lifelike than he did earlier, lying on the ground beside the Reapers' barn.

"You can talk to him." The nurse suggests as she moves around us to glance at a machine beeping at the top of the bed.

"Can he hear me?" Cara asks, and the nurse offers her another one of her warm smiles.

"It's possible, and if he can, your positive words will help encourage his healing."

Cara starts crying again as she steps closer to the bed, and I stay by her side, offering my support until she picks up Rocco's limp hand and presses her lips to it.

"Te amo," she whispers, her tears falling to his wrist.

Shit.

I can't fucking help it. I choke up too.

If there were ever the right people to fall apart in front of, it's Rocco and Cara.

Not that Rocco can see me right now, but that doesn't matter. He's family.

The only person missing right now is Zoe.

I need her here so fucking bad. I feel like I'll be able to breathe better once I have her in my arms. Shit like this puts everything into perspective, and I know more now than ever that Zoe and the club are my whole fucking world.

As Cara sobs quietly, I stare at my lifeless friend in the bed, his skin pale and looking all wrong wrapped in the crisp white sheets.

Looking around, I see a bag under the bed in a basket, and rummage through it to find what's left of his bloody clothes. They are all ruined. All except his cut, and I take it out and move over to the hand basin on the wall where I start cleaning the dry crusty blood from it.

His name and title patch, which were once white, are now tinted pink, and no matter how much soap and water I use on them, I can't clean the stain of blood from them.

Deciding it will have to do, I use half the roll of paper towels on the wall to dry the cut, before returning to Rocco with it, and I lay it across his body.

Cara's red-rimmed eyes meet mine, and she offers me a small smile.

"Thank you."

I go to speak, but a weird fucking squeak comes out as my words stay lodged in my throat.

Cara shakes her head and places a hand on my arms.

"It's okay. You don't need to say anything. He knows you love him."

Shaking my head, because apparently I'm lost for fucking words, I watch as Cara releases Rocco's hand and engulfs me in her arms.

"It's okay, to be freaking out right now," she says quietly, offering me the chance to let go.

I don't.

I fight. I fight hard.

Sure my eyes burn like a bitch as I blink any fucking wetness from them. I will not fucking cry for Rocco because he's not fucking dead.

Besides, right now, Cara needs me to be strong.

"He'll be okay," I rasp into Cara's dark hair, and she nods against my shoulder, rubbing my back.

"He will be. He's a strong son of a bitch. Nothing will stop him."

The conviction in Cara's words is reassuring.

She knows Rocco better than anyone. She knows how hard he'll fight.

"I don't know how to do this," I admit as Cara pulls back, her dark glassy gaze meeting mine.

"Do what?" she asks, and my eyes flick to Rocco in the bed.

"To fill his shoes."

Slowly, a warm smile morphs Cara's expression.

"Yes, you do, Grayson. He chose you all those years ago for a reason. The men already look up to you. Just make sure you lean on them. That's what they are there for, and what they also need."

Nodding, our attention is drawn to the door when there's a tap on it and the nurse from before pokes her head in.

"Ah, Mr. Black?" she asks, and I nod. "There's a gentleman out here that insists on speaking with you. I've sent him back to the main hallway as we can't have people wandering around the ICU."

Sighing, I nod and eye Cara. "Will you be alright?"

She nods back, lifting Rocco's lifeless hand in hers again. "Yes. Don't worry about me. As long as I'm here with Rocco, then I'll be okay."

Offering her a smile, I lean forward and peck the top of her head before giving my Prez one last glance.

"You'd better fucking fight. Cara's not the only one that needs you."

I don't say the words out aloud. I keep them to myself, hoping Rocco has suddenly gained the ability to read minds while he's in a comatose state, and then I leave the room.

Blowing out a breath, I straighten my cut as I walk down the hallway and out into the main hall before coming face to face with Cain.

"Is she here?" I ask, fucking more than ready to feel my princess in my arms, but when I see the way Cain's lips turn down and his eyes fucking appear to be frantic, my gut twists.

"She's not here. She's not at the club, and one of the Diamonds picked up on the police scanner that there was a car accident on the west side."

My chest is rising and falling quickly, my fists balled as I wait for him to get to the part I want to fucking know.

"They called Lola to see if she could go and check out the scene since it was a block away from where she lives."

"Cain. Why the fuck does this matter? Where's Zoe?"

He shuffles nervously, something I'm not fucking used to seeing.

"The car wreck was Rhiannon's car."

It takes me a fucking second to put two and two together. Zoe was driving here with Rhiannon.

"What?" I snap, wanting to make fucking sure I heard him right.

"I don't know what she was doing driving west, man. But the car rolled, and Rhiannon is dead. Not from the car wreck, though."

"What the fuck do you mean? Where the fuck is Zoe?!" I roar, and Cain takes a wise step back.

"Rhiannon was shot in the head, execution style, and Zoe is missing."

I stumble back as ringing fills my ears, my hand reaching out to brace the wall as I try to shake away the fucking panic sweeping through me. Because if Rhiannon was executed, it means that her killer probably has my princess, and I know without a doubt that my worst nightmare has just come true.

The Reapers have Zoe, and I can't bear to think about the cruel things they are likely doing to my princess as we speak.

A metal cart goes flying, crashing to the wall as all the medical equipment it was holding follows. I can feel the roars of anguish leaving my body, feel the way I'm vibrating in rage, yet I can't hear a fucking thing but the incessant ringing in my ears.

Zoe!

"Calm down, man." Cain's voice breaks through the ringing, and I spin on him, fisting the neck of his shirt before slamming him against the wall.

"How can I calm down when you fucking let them take her?!" My roar echoes through the baron halls of the hospital, and through my red haze, I see Cain's eyes widen right before my fist crashes into his nose.

Strong arms tackle me from behind, and the ground meets my fucking cheek as the weight of two men pin me down.

"Not here," Slasher growls against my ear, but his words mean nothing to me as unbearable thoughts flicker into my head of the horrors my girl might be meeting right now.

Just the thought of it pumps more adrenaline through my veins. Slasher and Munroe's attempt at subduing me fails and I rise with them still latched on to me, and charge for Cain again.

The sick fucker stands tall as I rush him, holding his arms out wide like a fucking invitation as he closes his eyes looking more like he's fucking meditating than about to be hit with a mack truck of rage.

It doesn't slow my pace, and I collide with him, sending us both back into the wall again before I use his face as a fucking boxing bag.

People are yelling, both male and female. Some women screech, and I know I'm causing havoc in the hospital in front of innocent Santa Cruz citizens, but right now, I don't fucking care.

"Grayson Black!" The scold comes right before claw-like fingers dig into my fucking ear, and forcefully pull, making me cease my wrath on Cain and come face to face with Cara. "What the hell are you doing?!"

Slapping Cara's hand away I round on her, furious that she dare touch what belongs to Zoe.

"Zoe's been taken by the Reapers, and Cain let it fucking happen!" I roar, and if it were anyone else, I know she would've flinched.

But not Cara. She's not scared of me.

Cara's harsh glare shoots to Cain, who peels himself off the wall and nods.

"I admit, I shouldn't have taken Rhiannon's word and let her arrange to bring Zoe here. I should have been the one to drive Zoe. I shouldn't have taken my eyes off her."

Cara's glare returns to me. "How do you know she's been taken?"

"Rhiannon's car has been found in a wreck, with her dead body from a headshot. Zoe's nowhere to be found," I explain, as fear courses through me.

"Have the Reapers reached out and said they have Zoe?" she asks, and I shake my head.

"Not yet."

"Well, then how do you know she hasn't run off, scared? Gone into hiding?"

Shit. I hadn't thought of that.

"Gray." Cara says my name quietly, leaning in closer. "Don't forget your duty here. You're the President now—"

"Acting President." I interrupt her, and she rolls her eyes.

"Fine, acting President. It still means the men are looking at you for guidance. I know Zoe missing isn't a good sign, but don't turn on those who care about you because of your misplaced anger. This isn't Cain's fault. It's all on the Reapers. Focus on who deserves your wrath and rally your men and go out and comb the streets until you find her."

"What if I can't find her?" I whisper, admitting my fear.

Cara scoffs. "You may not find her tonight, or tomorrow, or even the next day. But you're Grayson fucking Black. You won't rest until she's safely in your arms, and your men will fight that fight with you, and for you. Don't forget the power of our family."

Fuck.

Our family.

The Cruz Kings.

It's exactly what we are, and even though Cain isn't a King, he's still family. Diamond Crew family.

My hard gaze moves back to Cain, and I shake my head in regret. "Sorry, man. I—"

Cain cuts me off by launching at me with a bro hug, slapping me on the back.

"You punch like a sissy." He chuckles, and my lips quirk up as we pull back from each other.

I'm fucking angry, but the red haze of rage has ebbed for now, and I turn in the wide hallway, my eyes falling to my club brothers who are waiting for instruction, already prepared to fight with me. For me.

"We got you," Munroe rasps. "And Zoe."

I nod, turning back to Cara. "I can't leave you." She waves me off.

"Nonsense. I'll let you know if anything changes. Rocco's going to be out for the next few days, anyway. Hopefully, you find Zoe before then, and you can be here when he wakes."

Shit. My heart sinks at the thought of him waking and realizing he can't walk.

"Are you sure?" I ask, feeling way too fucking emotional today.

"Yes. Go find your girl."

I nod before pulling her in for a hug and when I release her, I notice the Cruz Cunts gathering at the end of the hall.

"Cain." I snap, and he jumps in my line of sight like I didn't just beat him moments ago.

"Sir, yes, sir." He salutes me, and I roll my fucking eyes at his antics, even as the bruising and swelling around his nose makes me want to beg for forgiveness. Like what the fuck. Grayson Black doesn't beg for forgiveness.

"Question the Cunts. See if they know anything about Rhiannon that can help us. And keep your Diamonds on the scanner. I want to know the moment the police do if there's anything going down on our turf."

Cain nods, saluting me again and giving his foot a stomp like he's about to fucking march off, but then he turns and swaggers away.

Turning to my men with my need to find Zoe fuelling me, I instruct each of them with a different task from ditching the truck, and finding us new wheels so we can split up, and within minutes, we sneak out a side exit to avoid the detectives who are most likely still waiting to question us, and we hit the streets of Santa Cruz to find my girl.

3

Zoe

I startle awake as something burns across my body. It's my calves... no, my thighs. Fuck, it's everywhere. With a yelp, I try to push myself up from where I'm laying, but nothing I do helps.

Even though it's awkward and hurts my neck, I force my head from one side to the other while I look down. My hands are fucking tied, making it impossible to sit up.

Closing my eyes, I count to ten, then I look around again, but no matter how many times I've done it, the room I'm in doesn't change. It remains dank, dirty, and it smells awful.

"I'm so glad to see you're awake, Zoe," a woman sing-songs.

No matter how much I crane my neck, I can't see her. But now that I know she's there, I can hear her breathing—it's deafening.

"Y-you have to help me," I stutter. "Please. I need to get to the hospital. I have to see him—" I cut my words off as another yelp breaks free. More fire licks along my legs, making my stomach churn.

The woman cackles, and her hold, I'm only now noticing, on my ankle tightens. "You're not going anywhere, Zoe. Do you know how much trouble we've been through to get a hold of you?"

I feel like I'm choking on the fumes of whatever it is she's rubbing over my legs. The smell is overwhelming. It's making my nostrils burn, my eyes sting, and... wait a fucking second. What did she just say?

"W-what?" I cry out. "What do you mean? Where am I? Who are you?" The questions burst from me in rapid succession.

"No." That's all she says. I cry out again as her nails dig into my skin. "You're right where you belong." With a swift slap to my injured legs, she turns, taking the light with her as she leaves me in complete darkness.

"This can't be happening," I chant to myself.

Repeating the words does nothing. The restraints binding my hands in place don't magically loosen. No amount of pulling or twisting helps. If anything, it's making it worse. My wrists ache almost as much as my shoulders do from being tied down in this awkward position.

I do my best not to panic, which isn't easy with the lights off and nothing or no one to talk to. Everything happened so quickly, I never got the chance to really process it.

Rhiannon is dead.

Gray's injured... or worse...

Or is he? Did Rhiannon make it all up?

When I close my eyes, I see the shock still marring her face after they shot her. Bile burns the back of my throat at the memory, and I dry heave in the darkness.

I shake my head and pick up my efforts to free myself. I don't know how long I keep trying, but it's long enough that I've soaked the pillow under my head. More sweat runs down my back, and since I'm lying on my front, it's quickly getting cold.

"Help!" I scream. "Somebody fucking help me. I'm in here. Help!"

I continue to scream until my voice becomes hoarse, and that's when I hear it. Skittering across the floor. My arachnophobia flares to life, and I feel like a woman possessed, as I feel something run across my exposed legs.

"You fuckers!" My voice fails me, making the intended screech sound like nothing more than a croak. "He'll come for me. You're all going to die."

In my heart, I know Gray isn't dead. He can't be. As much as he tormented me when we first met, he's also been my protector, my savior. I *know* he'll come for me.

Despite the nasty voice in the back of my head telling me I don't know if Gray's alive, I hold on to the small spark of hope with everything I have. He has to be.

Just as I'm about to shout out again, the door opens, and the woman strolls back in. "Oh dear," she mutters when she switches the light on.

"What?" I snap, not sure I want to know, but I ask anyway.

It hurts turning my neck to look at her, so I let my head fall into the smelly pillow beneath me. Her hand swooshes across my back, and I feel more than see something being swatted away.

Fear holds me in a chokehold, and I know it's irrational that I'm more scared of the creepy crawlies in here than the fact I'm tied down. But that's the thing about fear, isn't it? It's irrational at best, insane at worst.

I once read in one of my psychology books that all phobias take root in the same fear. So whether you're afraid of clowns, spiders, holes, heights, snakes, or even balloons... it's really just different faces for the same fear. Death.

"Who are you?" I croak. "Why am I here? Why won't you help me?"

"You know," she says as she starts to untie me. "I've heard so much about you, Zoe."

I grit my teeth, ignoring the smile in her voice, since I don't want her to change her mind until I'm free.

"And I've heard nothing about you," I say, doing my best to keep any malice from my tone.

As soon as my wrists are free, I turn to my back and push myself up. My legs scream in protest when I try to fold them, so I keep them straightened.

"Yeah, sorry about the pain," she says, and she sounds sincere. "You weren't meant to get hurt. Brian isn't happy about that at all."

"Brian? Dad?"

Wait... that's right. How could I forget? The man hiding in the shadows who...

"Got any last words?"

The terror on Rhiannon's face as he spoke was real. Whatever she was up to, that's not the ending she expected.

"Thank you for your service."

I can still hear the crack of the gun as he pulled the trigger and shot her. It wasn't until her lifeless body hit the ground and he stepped out of the shadows that my brain caught up with the facts in front of me.

"What have you done to my dad?" I ask, my tone getting more and more shrill. "Is he tied up somewhere as well?"

It's a stupid question, and I wish I hadn't asked it. At the mention of his name, the memory of him shooting Rhiannon comes to the forefront of my mind. He never flinched, or even looked remorseful that he'd just taken a life.

Whatever's going on, I don't think dad is an unwilling participant.

"Brian's fine," the woman says. There's something in her tone that I can't quite decipher. "He's more than fine, actually. It's all thanks to him that you're finally where you belong."

"B-belong?"

She nods. "Yes, Zoe. You belong here with us."

Although I will my mouth not to ask, the question still rushes out. "Who the hell are you people?"

The woman smiles, showing off her perfect teeth. "Don't you already know?" she asks softly, sounding almost friendly. "That's disappointing. I expected more from someone who wants to go to Harvard."

Ridiculous as it is, her words feel like a slap across my face. I shouldn't care what this woman thinks. And the fact that it's taking me longer than normal to piece things together doesn't make me stupid. Yet, I fucking feel it with the look she's giving me.

"Reapers," I whisper, like I'm scared to say the name out loud. "You're part of the Cali Reapers."

She nods and pats my head. "Well done, Zoe."

My head swims and I'm reeling from all the information I've received in such a short amount of time. My head feels like it's ready to burst, and unable to cling to anything, but... "Is Gray still alive?"

Shaking her head, she softly says, "I don't know, Zoe."

Tears gather in my eyes, and I'm unable to stop them from falling. I hate that the woman—whoever she is—gets to see me like this. So weak, so scared. But I can't contain any of it. I'm helpless, and so far out of my depth that I don't even know which way is up.

"How long?" I croak, pausing to clear my raw throat. "How long has it been? Days? Weeks?"

The woman gives me a smile. "Does it matter? You're here now, Zoe. And you're not leaving us."

"I want to see my dad," I demand. "Take me to him."

"All in good time," she sing-songs. Then she gets up from the small stool next to me she's been sitting on. "But first, we need to get you some food. Do you want me to leave the lights on?"

Concern mars her features, and she sounds nice. But I'm not that easily fucking fooled. I've been around the Kings, Cunts, and Mama C long enough to recognize power when I'm staring it right in the face.

I might not know who this woman is yet. But she's not a Cunt, or whatever the Reapers call their women. She could be the Mama. Or maybe she belongs to the Prez. Either way, I need to be careful about how I behave.

I watch as the woman walks over to the door. She bangs on it once before it opens, then she disappears from my view, once again leaving me with nothing but my thoughts.

Running my hands down the back of my legs, I feel the cuts and grazes she was treating when I woke up. There are more than I noticed right after Rhiannon crashed the car, and they're not only on my thighs. There are multiple spanning the length of my legs.

Rhiannon... Why the hell would she do something like that? Even though I'm sad she's dead, I'm more angry she died without giving me any answers. I have so many whys and not a single explanation.

As I'm left with nothing but my thoughts, I mentally go back to when she entered the room I was holed up in at Dirty Diamonds. Why did I follow her? When she said Gray was injured, all reason left me, and I willingly followed her.

Maybe I was stupid for not reaching out to Alana or even Rose to double-check. But I dare anyone in my situation to act that rationally when their worst fear has just been laid out in front of them.

Sure, if I was watching that scene play out in a movie, I'd be screaming at the screen. Calling the woman too stupid to live, especially if it was a horror. But watching or reading about something is nothing like living it. In real time, you have split seconds to make your move, not multiple pages or scenes.

While I mentally do my best not to berate my past self for acting before thinking, I get out of the bed and walk around the dusky room. It's small, filthy, and there's a foul smell permeating the air. I try my best to ignore the many cobwebs and what looks like... nope. As I said, I'm ignoring it.

To keep myself occupied in the windowless room, I walk back and forth, counting my steps. It's ten paces wide and fifteen long. In other words, it's small.

I don't even know why I focus so much on it. Because regardless of size, it's clear it's a cage—my cage. One I'm not getting easily out of.

Gray, where the hell are you?

The more I think about him, I can almost feel him. As I lean against the filthy wall and close my eyes, I swear I can hear him rasp, "Princess," and see his cocky smirk in my mind's eye.

Please be okay. I need you to be okay.

For all the time I've spent defying him, plotting against him, and yeah, at times, even hating him, I crave his nearness on a soul deep level.

My heart has long known what my mind's refused to entertain. I love him. I love him so much it's like I'm missing a vital part of myself.

I don't know when the tall, dark-haired, kinky biker wormed his way into my heart, but he did. And he's there to stay.

Taking a deep breath, I force my thoughts back on the danger at hand. The problem is that I don't know fuck all about what's going on. Too many questions to count run rampant in my mind. Like why did Rhiannon trick me and serve me up to the enemy? Why is my dad with the Reapers? Why am I here? Why-oh-fucking why?

And what about the other Kings and the Cunts... are they okay? For all I know, they're all gathered together, having a good old time and not in danger at all. No, if they're safe, they'll know I'm missing, and Gray and Alana will definitely be looking for me. Possibly even Rocco and Cain.

Cain... wait, didn't Rhiannon say he was meant to meet us at the car? I know I can't trust anything she said. But it still grinds on me that I don't know if he was part of the trap.

No, Gray trusts Cain, so I have to...

"Here we go," the woman chipperly announces as she kicks the door open while holding a tray of food. "Aren't you hungry?"

Forgetting my earlier mantra about biting my tongue in her presence, I scowl. "How long have I fucking been here?"

Rather than answering me, she tuts. "Don't forget your manners, Zoe. I know you were raised better."

I ball my hands into fists and meet her blue eyes head on. "Don't you fucking dare speak about how I was raised," I hiss.

Her smile grows like she's entertained by my thinly concealed anger. "Do you want the food or not?"

As I eye the bowl of food that looks like it's already been eaten and thrown back up, my stomach growls. Reining in my temper, I nod, and sit back down on the bed.

The first mouthful proves that the food doesn't taste any better than it looks. It's cold and lumpy, and I honestly don't even know if it's meant to be a stew or a soup.

Once I'm done eating, the woman urges me to get back on my feet. "We have to get you cleaned up," she says, scrunching up her nose. "You can't be there for the punishment, while looking like that."

My blood runs cold, and I stop mid-step. "P-punishment?" I stutter. The eager bob of her head is the only answer I get.

When we reach the door, she knocks like the other times she's exited. As she links her arm with mine, she immediately digs her nails into the soft skin on my inner arm.

"I know it'll be tempting to run. Hell, it would make my week if you try. But for your own sake, don't."

With those ominous words, she drags me through rooms where men are lying passed out on the floor. If I thought my little cell smelled bad, well, let's just say the rooms we walk through don't have a better odor clinging to them.

"Watch your step," the woman says as I almost trip over a girl that barely looks old enough to be legal. Her eyes are rolled back in her head, a needle sticking out of her arm, and she's mumbling something about fudge.

As we finally make it to the bathroom, the woman holding me pushes me inside. "Strip," she commands, holding her hand out for my dirty clothes.

"I can shower by myself," I snarl, ignoring the danger lurking in her cold, blue eyes.

"Glad to hear it," she says dismissively. "Now strip. If you don't, I'll do it for you. And I can get very handsy."

At her words I quickly rip the clothes from my body. With each piece I remove, I become aware just how dirty I am. Dried blood clings to my legs, front and back, and I'm covered in dirt and grime.

"What now?" I ask once I'm fully naked.

The woman rolls her eyes. "I thought you said you could shower yourself. Usually, one turns on the water and gets under it. Then—"

"I get it," I snap.

Despite the alarm blaring in my head, I turn my back on her and walk over to the rusty shower. As I turn the tap for the hot water, ice cold, reddish water comes from the showerhead. I quickly jump back, narrowly avoiding the spray.

The woman laughs. "Aww honey, this ain't the Ritz. There's no hot water. Hell, I'm not even sure we have clean water."

"W-what?"

"Yep. So if you want the good, clean stuff, you have to beat everyone else here. But since it's late at night, we've all used this shower today." Her eyes sparkle with laughter, and her tone is downright condescending. "Oh, and watch out for the white on the floor. Some of the Reapers like to rub one out while they're in here."

Refusing to give her more to laugh about, I roll my shoulders back and straighten my spine. Then I mentally count to three before I dive under the filthy spray. Closing my eyes I tilt my head back, letting the ice cold water run down the length of my body.

As I reach for the soap bar, I do my best not to think about who else has used it, and instead run it over my body. Once I'm clean, I look around for some shampoo, but of course there isn't any.

During the walk from my cell to the bathroom it became clear that these people—the Reapers—don't live like the Kings. While the Kings aren't wealthy, or living like it, they're posh compared to the squalor the Reapers live in. So yeah, I suppose something as simple as shampoo isn't available.

I rub the soap in my wet hair, doing my best to spread the suds to the strands. I don't think I'm doing a good job, but at least it's enough.

As soon as I'm done, I take the towel from the woman's hand, and use it to pat my hair somewhat dry, before wrapping it around my body.

"You know," the woman says, her eyes glued to my chest. "I'm not sure you need the towel any longer."

I eye my filthy clothes, and make a move for them when she throws her head back and laughs menacingly.

"You don't need that either. Why hide a body as perfect as yours." Before I can react, she snatches the towel from me, and kicks open the door. "Let's go find your dad," she says, smiling evilly at me.

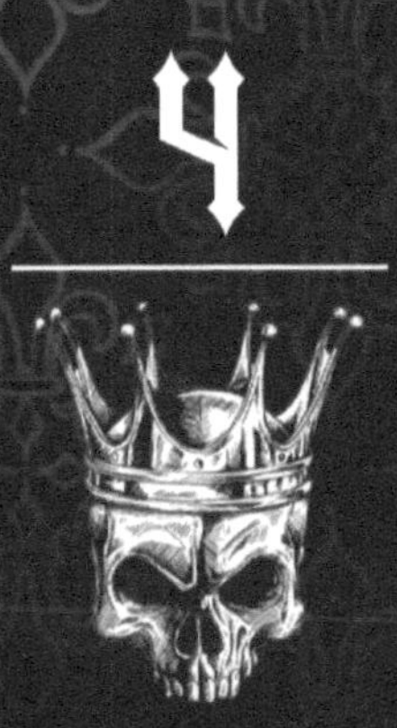

Zoe

Hope stirs to life in my chest. Yes, she's taking me to see dad. He'll help me. We can leave together, and once we're safe, he can explain everything to me—and I'm sure there's a rational explanation for his behavior. For... shit, I don't know.

He did leave me with the Cruz Kings without trying to rescue me, and then he killed Rhiannon in cold blood. But he's my dad, so I just know there's more going on than I know of. Because my dad isn't a bad person. He's the one who taught me that family sticks together, so of course we'll do that.

Spurred on by my thoughts, I make my strides longer. I try not to pay attention to the Reapers who gather to watch me.

"Look at that ass!"

"Nah man, I'm a tits guy. And hers would look so good painted in my cum."

"I hope the Kings haven't broken in her ass. That's my favorite thing to do. Especially when they bleed."

"There are other ways to make them bleed," a man guffaws, making all of them laugh boisterously.

A coldness runs down my spine, making me shudder. Despite my newfound hope, I try to cover myself up. It's pretty much impossible to do, as the woman at my side isn't letting go of my other arm.

"Pfft, is that her? The Kings' toy? She's nothing special."

My head snaps to the side, and I glare daggers at the woman who spoke up. Or rather, girl. It's the one I stepped over earlier, only now she's on her feet. She's swaying as she holds on to the door frame for support, and her eyes are glassy.

"You're just jealous because her tits are better than yours," another woman sniggers.

Despite my shower, I feel dirty. Like their taunts and insults are adding a layer of grime to my skin, coating me in their vileness. A sob works its way up my throat, but I press my lips together, refusing to let it escape.

I refuse to show them how terrified I really am.

As we enter the next room, my eyes immediately land on my dad. "Dad!," I cry, relieved to finally see him.

He's sitting next to the Prez of the Cali Reapers, at least if the badge on his cut is to be believed.

"Oh, dad." I try to shake the woman off me, but her nails dig further into my skin. I feel blood pebbling at the cuts left behind by her nails.

Bitch!

As Dad glances my way, it's with a look that resembles the one from the lawyer's office after he found out mom left all her money to me. There's no emotion in his eyes as he looks at me, causing me to shake.

Not from the cold, or being naked in a room full of strangers. No, it's my dad's indifference that causes the shiver.

"Dad," I call out to him again, hoping my voice will spark some—*any*—emotion on his face. There's no such expression when he keeps looking at me like I'm a nuisance and not his daughter. His last fucking living relative.

I've never felt more alone and vulnerable than I do right now. I can feel the looks and hear the taunts from the Reapers who followed in the wake of my walk of shame.

"Ahh, Irina," dad practically coos and his gaze softens as he looks at the woman next to me. "I've missed you, darling."

Darling? What the fuck is going on here?

"And I've missed you, Brian," she says seductively. "But you know business comes first."

I swear I'm about to throw up when my dad beckons her forward with his finger, and she swings her hips exaggeratedly as she walks to him. Once she reaches him, they kiss like they're sucking the oxygen from each other's lungs.

The best part about their shocking display of... whatever the hell to call it, is that I'm forgetting about my nudity. My mind is working overtime as I try to make sense of the scene playing out in front of me.

Mom hasn't been dead long enough for dad to act like this, has she? I mean, sure, there's no exact rule on how long one should grieve. And I guess he can get his dick wet if he wants to. But that isn't what this is. The looks he gives Irina aren't those of lust. It's more akin to him actually feeling something for her.

"That's enough," the Reapers' Prez calls out in a booming voice. "Irina, why the fuck is Zoe naked?"

The woman laughs and rolls her eyes. "Because I didn't feel like waiting for her to get dressed," she quips.

"Careful," the Prez warns. "Remember the orders of our new VP."

Irina immediately stops laughing. "Sorry, Prez. I forgot myself."

Before I can stop myself, I scoff out loud at her acting, which is all it is. The truth is right there, in her eyes, for all to see. She isn't sorry at fucking all, and she definitely doesn't care about not following orders.

"Got something to say?" the Prez asks, turning his gaze on me.

It's hard not to falter under his penetrating stare, but I manage to keep my spine straight. "I have plenty to say," I shoot back, faking bravery I don't feel. When he waves his hand in a 'go on' motion, I do. "What the fuck is the matter with you?" I hiss, looking straight at my dad.

If I thought speaking directly to him was going to... I don't know, shake him out of whatever spell he's under, I was dead fucking wrong.

"Don't talk to me like that," he barks. "Actually, don't talk to me at all."

I recoil as his words hit me like a fist. "W-what? You don't mean that."

Shaking his head, he pulls Irina onto his lap. He wraps his arm around her middle as he begins to kiss her neck. The bitch gyrates her hips, and it's all too clear what she's doing.

Anger like I've never felt before roars to life inside me, demanding I let it go. And I do. Without thinking about the consequences, I lunge at Irina.

She turns her head just as my fist connects with her nose, and I laugh like a lunatic as blood spurts from her nostrils.

"Who the fuck do you think you are?" she screeches like a banshee.

"Your worst fucking nightmare," I hiss as I tangle my fingers into her long, red curls and pull until she hisses in pain.

"Zoe!" My dad's booming voice isn't enough to break my focus. "Get the fuck off her."

Those words do the trick. When he's looking at her and not me, it shatters something inside me. I don't even feel the slap as Irina's hand connects with my cheek, or the guy tackling me to the ground from behind.

All I can do is stare at my dad, who doesn't even spare a look in my direction.

"Dad," I croak, pathetically. "Why won't you look at me?"

Indescribable pain makes me choke on my breath as my heart breaks into a billion jagged pieces.

"Brian!" the Prez says, and despite not raising his voice, he easily gains the attention of everyone. "She's your daughter and you'll fucking treat her as such."

It's only when I try to shake my head that I realize it's being pushed against the dirty floor. I taste blood in my mouth, and now that I'm aware of my surroundings, the hand I slammed into Irina's nose throbs painfully.

When the Prez gets up and walks toward me, I pick up my efforts to get free. I try to kick the guy holding me down, but since he's almost on top of me, I can't reach him and he just laughs at my weak attempts.

"Get up!" he orders when he's in front of me.

I try again, but I can't.

Lightning fast, the Prez grabs the guy holding me down. I don't see what he does to him, but seconds after the pressure from my back disappears, the guy is on his back, with the Prez's foot on his neck.

"Now, get the fuck up." His tone makes it clear he doesn't like waiting, so I scramble to my feet. "Follow me."

Without another look in my dad's direction, I follow the Prez as he takes me to a room and hands me some clothes.

They don't fit, and they smell dirty, but I'm so glad I can cover my body that I'm beyond caring. "Thank you," I say, my voice hoarse.

He shrugs. "You don't belong to us, so it's not right to parade you around naked."

"No, I don't. I belong to Gray. Please, you have to help me—"

Before I can finish speaking, he wraps his hand around my throat and pushes me forcefully back against the wall. My breath is forced from my lungs, and my eyes start to water as he flexes his hand, making it impossible to breathe.

"Listen carefully," he spits. "I'm not your fucking get-out-of-jail-free card, and I'm not your friend. I'm Rusty, the President of the Cali Reapers. When I said you don't belong to us, I meant the people in the room. You've already been claimed by one of us."

"Gray's claimed me," I force out. "I don't belong to anyone but him."

Rusty lets go of my throat and moves his hand to the top of my forehead. Before I can act, he slams my head back against the wall while roaring in my face. "Don't mention that fucking dick in this house, little girl. My patience only goes so far. If you keep it up, no one can save you. Not even our new VP."

My vision swims, making it so I see two or three of him. Even though I claw at his hands, he doesn't loosen his hold on me.

"The faster you learn your place, the easier things will be for you, little girl. Are you ready to play nice?"

"Fuck you," I spit.

My words cause him to throw his head back and let out a booming laugh. "Only if you ask nicely," he grins with a wink. "You're so uptight, your cunt might just cut my dick in half. But if you insist, I'd be happy to teach you a thing or two."

I immediately stop fighting him, forcing my body to become limp.

"See, that wasn't so hard," he grins. "I will be if you keep it up, though. So keep that in mind." His grin sickens me, and I have to inhale deeply to stop my stomach from churning at the mere prospect of having his hands on me.

As I notice his expectant look, I realize I have to say something. "Fine," I spit. "I'll behave." It pains me to give in, but I'm not stupid enough to think fighting will get me anywhere.

Rusty claps his hands together. "Let's talk about your duties—"

"I'm not your fucking slave," I hiss, unable to keep my mouth shut.

With a shrug, he continues. "Everyone here has to pay their own way. That's how we work. Especially after your precious Kings shot up our clubhouse."

My ears perk up as he mentions the Kings. I desperately want to ask if they're okay, specifically Gray. But I can't just come out and ask. No, I have to get him to give me answers of his own volition.

"Oh?" I say, forcing myself to sound bored. Despite the one word, I don't do a good job. I sound too eager, luckily that doesn't stop Rusty from going on.

"Fat good it did them," he chuckles. "They no longer have a VP."

At his words, my heart drops to my stomach and pain webs through my chest. "Y-you're lying," I cry. "Gray's their VP."

Rusty shrugs again. "No, little girl. Not anymore."

"But I—"

"Your precious Gray isn't around anymore. If you believe nothing else, believe that."

As my anguish grows, so does his smile. I'm vaguely aware that my legs give out and I fall to the floor. An inhuman wail bubbles up my throat and I'm powerless to stop it as I pull at my hair like a crazy person.

"You're lying," I scream. "Gray isn't dead. He's coming for me, I know he is."

Rusty leaves me without another word, but I'm painfully aware of his merry whistling as he walks out of the room.

I don't know how long I'm left alone, only that it isn't long enough to pull myself back together. I'm still a mess when my dad walks through the door.

"Get up." His words crack like a whip.

Ignoring him, I pull my knees up and rest my head on them, refusing to look at him.

"Don't make me repeat myself, Zoe."

I laugh scathingly and wipe tears from my eyes. "Or what? Who even are you?"

As his arm shoots out toward me, I try to dodge him but to no avail. My dad all too easily wraps his hand around my upper arm and hauls me to my feet with no effort at all.

"Don't embarrass me," he spits.

I wipe the spittle that hit my cheek away. "Why? Are they going to give you a daddy of the year award?" I taunt. I almost hope he's going to hurt me because if he does, my stupid heart will have to stop trying to force my head to make excuses for him. "You fucking disgust me." Not only do I put as much venom into the words as I can muster, I make sure spit flies from my mouth on purpose.

There's a fleeting look of disappointment and hurt in my dad's eyes, but I ignore it. I have to. It's too late for him to change my opinion of him now. He's nothing but a... wait a second.

"You cheated on mom!" The words fly out of my mouth as soon as the thought registers.

It's the only logical reason for the PDA I saw between him and Irina.

"We don't have time to discuss that now, baby girl." Regret coats his words.

I hold my hand up. "There's nothing to discuss. It's a simple yes, or no. Did you cheat on mom?"

Anguish dances in his eyes as the hand he runs down his face lands on the shoulder of the leather cut he's wearing. Fucking traitor.

"I did," he confirms.

Just as I decide to rip into him, Irina joins us. "It's time for the punishment, and Rusty says Zoe has to be there."

When she mentioned the punishment earlier, I thought I was the one who had to be punished. But now it sounds like it's someone else who'll be on the receiving end.

My dad avoids Irina's attempts at holding his hand as we walk back. I know it's because I'm here and I kind of want to tell him it doesn't matter. There's no way I could think less of him than I do right now.

As we return to the room I stood in naked not too long ago, Rusty calls my name and points at the chair next to him. "Since you belong to our new VP who isn't able to be here right now, you'll take his seat." His boom brooks no room for discussion, so I do as I'm told.

Once everyone is seated, all chatter dies out, and a heavy silence falls across the room. As I look around, I spot Adam, the guy I lost my virginity to. When our eyes lock, he gives me one of the most sinister smiles I've ever seen, and mouths, "Fuck you, Princess."

I shouldn't be surprised after our run-in at the cemetery, yet I am. There's indifference, hatred, and then whatever feeling Adam harbors for me. A chill spreads across my skin, and my hair rises at the reminder of just how far outside my comfort zone I am.

"Bring in the prisoner," Rusty shouts.

His words cause a stir among the other Reapers. They start chanting his words, some even bang their fists on the tables.

One of the Reapers I saw the night they took me drags another guy into the room. His hands are held together by zip ties that look to be digging into his meaty wrists. Every step he takes makes chains rattle, and when I look down, I discover why. His feet are shackled together by a metal chain. His face is swollen and completely covered in bruises and cuts, most still leak blood.

It's not until he comes closer that I think I recognize him as the guy who pulled me from the wrecked car, and dropped me onto the glass shards littering the asphalt.

"You don't look too good, Johnny," Rusty says gleefully. "Why don't you take a seat? You must be tired."

As the Prez points at a chair, one of the women scurries over to help Johnny. Or so I thought. The moment he goes to sit down, she pulls the chair away from under him. The man groans in pain as he falls on his ass.

"There we go," Rusty laughs. "Now you're sitting."

The room erupts into laughter as everyone else joins in. They sound like a pack of hyenas to me, and I guess that's a fair comparison, considering they're getting a kick out of preying on someone who's defenseless and weak.

I don't feel sorry for Johnny, far fucking from it. He deserves everything he's getting.

"Our new VP isn't too happy with you, Johnny," Rusty says conversationally. "You made his girl bleed without his permission. So now she gets to make you shed some blood."

The words don't sink in until everyone turns to look at me.

"What's your weapon of choice, Zoe?" Rusty asks. When I don't answer quickly enough, he decides for me. "Since women belong in the kitchen or on a cock, we'll give you a fork."

I frown in confusion, not sure I heard him right until Irina hands me a fork. "There you go," she says, wearing a shit-eating grin. "Have fun."

"Is this necessary?" dad asks, but one look from Rusty silences him, making him cringe away from the Prez.

I look down at the cutlery in my hand. It's not the weapon I would have chosen if I'd thought quicker, but it's a weapon all the same. Maybe I can use it to escape. That thought is squashed as I glance at Rusty, who shakes his head and tuts at me.

When the Reapers grow impatient and shout for me to get to it, I step over to Johnny on unsteady legs. My hand shakes so much I can barely keep the fork in my grasp, and as I look down at the already beaten Reaper, I know I can't do it.

I let the fork fall from my hand and onto the floor. "I won't do it," I say. My voice cracks, giving out just like my bravado. "You can't make me."

The Reapers shout their disappointment, calling me weak and pathetic, and they might be right. But that's not going to change my mind.

As Rusty raises his hand into the air, they all fall silent again. "So be it," he says. "It was a present from our VP, but not one you had to accept."

He waves me back to my seat, and I quickly sit down next to him again.

"Now, since you won't dole out Johnny's punishment, you get to decide what it should be."

Fuck!

As much as I don't want to do that, something tells me I can't refuse a second time, so I ask, "What are my options?"

"The Kings taught her well," Irina says, earning a glare from Rusty.

"Don't mention those bastards in this house," he roars, acting much like he did when I brought up Gray. "Your options are death by stoning, death by stabbing, or removing his hands."

Double fuck!

Those options are barbaric. There's seriously none of them that seems less severe. Death is one thing, but I'm pretty sure it won't just be one blunt force blow, or one stab. No, they're so sick they'll undoubtedly drag it out, maybe even make a sport out of it. And taking his hands... that means he can't ride again, effectively kicking him out of the MC, and then they'll probably kill him, anyway.

What the fuck do I do?

"I'll need time to think about it," I say, trying my best to sound nonchalant. "It's an important decision, and I want to make the right choice."

With a sardonic bow of his head, Rusty agrees to give me until the VP's back so he can help me decide. Even though I know I'm only postponing the inevitable, I'm relieved.

"I'll take you back to your new room," Rusty grins. "You might as well get familiar with your new digs."

He pulls me to my feet and practically pushes me all the way into the room he took me to when I got dressed.

"Sweet dreams, Princess." He sneers at the last part before pushing me into the room. Then he slams the door shut behind me, locking it.

Exhausted and on the brink of losing what little is left of my sanity, I throw myself down on the queen-sized bed. At least it smells clean and somewhat fresh. It might be the first thing I come across here that doesn't make my stomach churn just at the smell.

As I close my eyes, Rusty's words about Gray come back, haunting and taunting me. I know he's wrong, there's no way any of the Reapers are man enough to kill my Gray.

Grayson Black will come for me, and when he does, he'll kill them all.

Gray's tongue sliding between my folds is what wakes me up. His stubble burns against my throbbing sex, a delicious contrast to the licks, nips, and sucks at my cunt. Two fingers are already inside me, stretching me as he pumps leisurely.

"Yes," I moan.

I knew Rusty was lying and that Gray would come to my rescue.

"More," I demand, huskily. "I need you inside me."

When he adds a third finger, I almost come. My eyes roll to the back of my head, while primal sounds, only Gray can get me to make, fall from my lips.

I pull at his hair that feels longer than I remember it. Huh, I must have been gone longer than I realized. That doesn't matter right now, though. I'm eager to get him closer, to get him deeper.

"Do you like that?" he rasps against my soaked entrance. "Do you like my fingers inside you, Sugar?"

I arch and moan.

Wait... Sugar? Not Princess?

I lose my train of thought as he sucks my clit between his lips, the edge of his canines grazing the sensitive skin.

"Fuck," I cry out when he curls his fingers inside me. "Don't stop. P-please... I need more. I'm going to... so close..."

His answering chuckle vibrates against my soaked folds. "I'm far from done with you, and we have all night."

He pumps his fingers harder, and within minutes I writhe in pleasure, screaming out my orgasm.

Grayson

My boots thud loudly on the linoleum floor, echoing up the halls of the hospital as I run with Slasher and Munroe on my heels. The hospital staff and locals visiting patients move quickly out of our way, already used to our presence since we brought Rocco here a few days ago.

As I round a corner, my feet slip a little, and my blood-caked hand grips the corner of the wall to keep myself upright. I make a mental note to send one of the Cunts to clean the evidence off the wall before the cops find it.

"Where?" I yell as Tex and Alana come into view up the hall, their eyes going wide as they take us in.

"He's been moved down there." Alana points down yet another fucking hall. "Room 304."

I don't stop. I keep running. My feet carrying my exhausted body as I round another corner and see the doors for the ICU up ahead.

They aren't accessible unless you get let in by a staff member, but it wasn't hard to pay off one of the nurses to accidentally lose her swipe card, of which I tug from my back pocket as I near the doors, and quickly use it to give me the access I need.

No staff question my sudden presence in the ward, the doors closing behind me leaving Slasher and Munroe on the other side for now.

I see room 304 straight away since there are only six glass rooms surrounding the nurses' station. It's still in the ICU, but the fact that Rocco has been moved to his own glass room now is good.

Right?

Rushing forward, I see Cara's back as she leans over the bed, and I step into the glass box, but suddenly my feet can't move any closer.

My heart thrashes in my chest as I hear Cara's voice talking quietly, her body angled toward Rocco's head, blocking my view.

My emotions are completely fucked right now. I've spent the last three fucking days trying and failing to find Zoe. It's like she vanished from the fucking earth. Wherever the Reapers are hiding, they are doing it too fucking well, but they will slip up, eventually. Or someone will talk. And when that day comes, I'll fucking wreak havoc on those motherfuckers.

"Gray?"

The raspy deep voice is what makes my feet move again, and as Cara turns to look over her shoulder at me, I get my first look at Rocco.

"Fuck," I whisper, feeling relieved to see the tubes that kept him breathing over the last few days are gone, and his dark eyes are open and blinking, staring back at me.

I slowly round the bed, coming to the opposite side of Cara, all while his eyes stay locked on me.

"I—"

I can't speak, so he does.

"I guess I'm not so easy to kill."

I blow out a fucking breath as my shoulders relax and a smile tugs at my lips.

"Fuck no, you're not. I told you, you weren't gonna die." I manage to tease, and he snickers a little, but then winces in pain.

Cara moves forward to try to fix his pillow, but he stills her hand with his in a lazy fashion and shakes his head at her.

"Killer, stop fussing over me."

She rolls her eyes. "I'll fuss over you all I damn well like. I'm still your wife and the only way to get rid of me is to divorce me, so until you grow big enough balls to do that, I'll fuss over you every minute of every day as I see fit."

"My balls will never grow that big." He grins, and Cara returns it.

"I know."

Fuck. It's nice to see them like this. Back together after he banished her. I'm sure she'll make him pay for that, eventually.

After Cara presses a kiss to his forehead, she excuses herself to leave us alone.

"I thought you were better at following instructions." Rocco grumbles, frowning at me, and my brows shoot up in confusion.

"What are you talking about?"

"I was very fucking specific when I was lying on the ground with my gut blown open. I told you to take my wedding ring and give it to Cara. I told you to tell her that I was sorry and never stopped loving her, yet she never got that message."

I shrug. "And I told you, old man, that you can tell her yourself, because you weren't gonna fucking die."

He grunts, rolling his head on the pillow like he's trying to get comfy. "You know your problem? You always have to be right."

I snicker. "I'm Grayson Black. No more needs to be said."

"Jesus fucking Christ." He whines, rolling his eyes at me, and for the first time in days, I start to relax a little.

I'll never admit this to him, but I wasn't so fucking sure he was going to wake up. The notion of him not being in this world was too unbearable to even consider, yet it kept hounding my thoughts along with the possibility that I'll never see my princess again.

I have Rocco back now, so that's a start, but my princess...

"I take it your bloody knuckles are a result of your subtle search for Zoe?" Rocco asks, eyeing my busted-up knuckles, and I nod.

"There's nothing subtle about it." I admit.

"No, I don't suppose there is."

Rocco sounds disappointed. Is he unhappy with my methods?

"What's bugging you? Should I not be kicking down doors?" I ask him, and he stares at me, his face a little thinner than it was this time last week.

"You should, but you have a club to run now, so you need to remember that you and Zoe aren't the only people that matter."

Anger heats my face and I ball my fists at his words, and I keep my mouth shut until I know I'm not going to go off the fucking rails like an obsessed maniac.

"The club is always my priority. The Reapers need to pay. We need to wipe those fuckers off the face of this earth for what they've been doing to us for years. Not just the stuff they've been doing since Zoe's family got dragged into it. Enough is fucking enough."

Rocco nods. "I agree. But remember the club needs money to survive. The men need a reason to stay devoted to us, and seeking vengeance on the Reapers isn't enough. For now, it will keep their anger fuelled, but eventually, they'll need more. The clubhouse needs to be restored. The runs need to keep happening. The Cunts need to keep their beds warm. As weird as it sounds for a bunch of brutes, they need stability. A home."

I understand everything Rocco is saying. It's not new to me. I know how the club operates and I know what the men need. What I don't know is why he's reminding me.

"You know I know all of this, man. What are you really trying to say?"

I watch as emotion battles to contort his expression, and his lips thin as he stares up at the ceiling for a long beat.

"The club is yours now, Gray." He rasps before he sucks his lips in like he's trying not to fucking tear up.

"What? What are you talking about? You're okay. You survived. I'll keep running it for you until you get better, man."

"I won't get better!" he roars, his head rising off the pillow as he glares at me with rage. "I'm a fucking cripple! I can't even move my fucking toes, let alone ride a bike! I'm fucking done!"

As his harsh words sink in, air gets trapped in my lungs, and I fight to push my words out.

"It might not be permanent. The doc said it's still too early to tell." I counter, but he chuckles harshly.

"I can fucking tell, Gray." He flops his head back on the pillow. "I can fucking tell I'll never walk again. I'll never be able to run away from my enemies. I'll never be able to dance with my wife." He chokes up then, and I fail at keeping the hot tears in my fucking eyes. "What if I can never fuck her again? I can eventually come to terms with all the rest, but that..." He shakes his head as tears stream from his eyes. "That I can't live with."

"Don't fucking say that," I hiss, lurching forward and fisting the neck of his hospital gown. "It's early days, man. You have a long road ahead, but you're a fucking fighter. You've got this. You and Cara can get through fucking anything."

A choked sob leaps from his dry lips, and he weakly fists my cut. "Don't let me walk off that cliff, brother. Don't let me turn into a bitter self-loathing ass."

I shake my head. "Never." I promise, pressing my forehead to his. "That's not how your story ends. You're gonna be an old grumpy fucker sitting on a porch next to your old grumpy wife pointing guns at the fucking mailman and passersby just for fucking kicks. And when you take your last fucking breath, it'll be because you're old as fuck, your skin sagging with wrinkles, and your dick hard from the blue pills that help you fuck your wife until your fucking heart stops. You hear me!?"

A choked laugh rips from Rocco's lips as his lips turn up. "Yeah, I fucking hear you."

I lift my head from his, releasing his gown before I thump my hand over my fucking aching heart.

"With honor we ride, side by side." I straighten, keeping my voice strong as I chant the words that bind us for life as club brothers. "Brothers by choice. Brothers by heart. Brothers with pride." I watch as he tears up again, even as he balls his own fist and thumps it lazily over his own heart. "In this life and the next, together we fly." He nods, like he's letting my words pick him up from the dark hole he's fallen into before he chants the last sentence with me.

"We are the Cruz Kings, ride or die."

He nods frantically at me like he's making me a silent promise to stay strong, and it's then that I see movement from the corner of my eye.

Cara stands in the doorway, tears wetting her cheeks as she takes us in, her own hand pressed to her chest as if she felt every single word in the chant.

"Get your sexy ass over here," Rocco rasps, and Cara obeys, hurrying forward to her man.

I step back to give them some space as they hug for a few minutes, and when they pull apart, both of them turn their gazes to me.

"What?" I ask. Should I have left already?

"I meant what I said before, Gray. The club is yours now. Even if I do recover someday, it'll be a long road, and the club needs a President. That's you, brother."

Rocco's words really hit fucking home. I know it's always how it was meant to be, but I thought he'd be older. I'd be older. I never imagined doing this without him.

"I... What if I fail?" I ask, revealing my fear to two of the three people I trust most in this world, and my heart fucking aches from not having the third here with me.

Zoe.

Releasing her hold on Rocco's hand, Cara rounds the bed to come to me and straightens my cut, much like I imagine a woman would straighten a man's suit jacket and I notice how she's careful not to touch me.

"You've always been a cocky bastard, Gray. Use it. Fake it until you make it and stop letting the fear rule you. You're one of the strongest people I know, and if we didn't think you had it in you to reign, then we wouldn't insist on you doing it." She taps her hand over my cheek and gives me a wink. "Don't forget. Mama knows best."

I chuckle at her words as she returns to Rocco's bedside, knowing she's the closest thing to a mother I've had in years.

"So how do we do this?" I ask, unsure how the baton gets passed since it's the first time our club has changed leadership.

"We'll have a ceremony," Cara explains, and I realize she's already memorized the rules for this part. "Since Rocco is standing down, he will present you with the President's patch, and you will present him with a Founder patch."

A smile tugs at my lips as I glance at Rocco. He'll still be part of it then. Not as involved but acknowledging him as Founder means he'll still be there if I need an ear. He'll probably come to some of our events like the Fourth of July. It doesn't mean goodbye. It just means he's retiring.

I blow out a relieved fucking breath. I can run this club. I know I can. But I can't handle the thought of severing all ties with Rocco, and this means I won't have to.

"It'll be my honor to present you with that patch," I tell him, and he grins.

"Just like I'm not easy to kill, I'm not easy to get rid of either."

We all laugh at his words, before I remember the monumental task I have ahead of me.

Find Zoe. Obliterate the Reapers. Survive to tell the fucking tale.

Rocco's right with what he said before though. Zoe isn't the club's only priority. She's definitely mine, but I can't make my men put themselves in danger to save her.

We need to regroup, and I need to consider who my VP will be. And then, we will paint the town, the state, hell, the fucking country red with Reaper blood until every last one of them is dead.

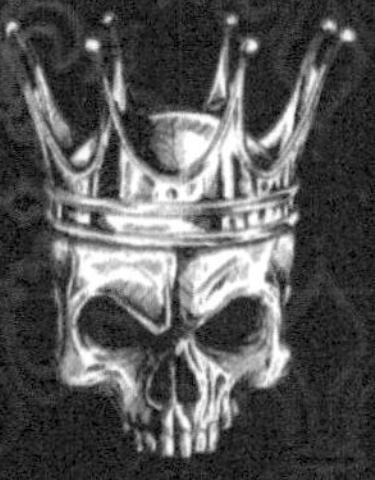

Zoe

*G*ray's scruff scrapes against my inner thighs, and my pussy is impaled on his tongue.

He pins my legs to the mattress, holding me in place as I writhe in the pleasure he's giving me. I whimper as the pressure on my legs turns painful, but not in a bad way. I fucking love it, thrive on it.

I let out a guttural moan when he throws my legs over his shoulders.

"Smother me in your cunt," he groans, nipping my clit.

Then he palms my ass and lifts me higher. His tongue licks past my pussy and grazes my... "Fuck!" I cry. "That's so... so..." Words fail me as he licks the rim of my ass.

"All your holes are mine," he rasps.

"Yes," I moan. "Yes. Yes. Yours." My words sound like a chant.

My hands flail to the sides, searching for something—anything—I can hold on to as Gray makes me unravel.

He slides his fingers into my drenched sex, making my pussy tighten around the digits. "Gray!" I cry. I undulate my hips in an attempt to get him deeper. "Why won't you fuck me?"

I don't understand the game he's playing. He won't let me touch him, and he refuses to fuck me.

"Oh! God!"

When he scissors his fingers deep inside me, I forget everything but his name.

"All in good time," he says, his tone husky with lust. "For now, I want to eat you until the sun comes up."

"Let's make the most of it then," I purr.

As he continues to lap at my opening, my legs begin to shake. I tighten them around his face, practically suffocating him with my thighs and cunt as I grind against his mouth.

"Gray... oh! Shit... I'm so close."

He uses his tongue to roll my clit as his fingers work my hole. "Come for me, Sugar."

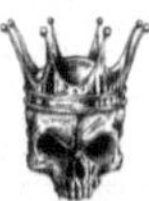

Like every morning I've woken up here, I started my day washing my arousal from my pussy and inner thighs. My dreams of Gray feasting on my cunt and fucking me mercilessly with his fingers are beyond vivid.

Each night, I think I wake up to him giving me pleasure, but when he's nowhere to be seen in the morning and I'm still in this hellish dump, I know it's nothing more than a dream.

I'm ashamed to admit how addicted I'm getting to my dreams. So much so that I sleep longer and go to bed earlier. Yet, he only shows up in the middle of the night, and once he's had his fill of pleasuring me, he leaves.

But while he's with me, even if it's only in the land of dreams, everything is better. Not only because of the pleasure we share. But he makes me feel treasured and loved. Unlike the Reapers, who are best when they ignore me.

No one will tell me how long I've been here, and it's starting to get on my nerves. I know several days have passed since I woke up here, but I don't know how long I was out. Minutes? Hours? Surely it can't have been days, can it?

"Watch it, bitch."

I jump out of the way of the mean-looking woman headed in my direction. She's carrying a tray of food, for one of the Reapers, of course. God forbid they get off their asses and grab their own food.

After sitting down next to Rusty, I look across the room. The way the Reapers treat their women makes me realize just how much freedom the Cruz Cunts have.

Here, they punish every mistake with a beating. Well, the minor mistakes get corrected with the Reapers' fist or belt. The bigger ones... I shudder as I recall watching one of the women getting whipped bloody for sneezing into the line of drugs the guy they call Noose had just lined up.

When he was done, and she had passed out, the other women took pictures on their phones while cackling like a group of witches. No one tried to help her.

I went to bed before I saw what happened to her, and the next morning she was gone. There was still blood on the floor, making her imprint hard to miss. I haven't asked any questions because I'm pretty sure I don't want the answers.

Swallowing down a yawn, I force myself to take another bite of the disgusting food we're served. Well, I say served, but that's a fucking joke. We're the ones doing the serving while the Reapers do nothing but drink, fuck, smoke, and snort whatever they can get their hands on.

"How long are we going to stay here?" Noose asks, leaning over the table to look at Rusty. "It's a fucking dump."

I try to look like I'm not listening intently.

"What the fuck did you expect?" Rusty growls back. "We lost our clubhouse in the fight. This is what we have for now."

Noose swipes his plate of food off the table. "This isn't fucking living, Rusty. It's something we shouldn't have to go through again. Especially not when we have the money to—"

Rusty leaps out of his chair, kicking the woman who was sucking him off out of the way. "One more word," he threatens, wagging a finger at Noose. "I fucking dare you to continue your whining."

Doing his best not to lose face, Noose folds his arms over his impressive chest. "Or fucking what? You're our Prez, so fucking act like it. Why are you hiding us like cockroaches instead of waging war on the few Kings who survived?"

"Noose!"

Ignoring his Prez's warning, Noose carries on, growing more heated through his tangent. "We're fucking split, man. Instead of being under one roof, you have us in different safe houses. What if the Kings come back? We're sitting fucking ducks."

With an angry growl, Rusty jumps over the table, punching Noose square in the face. "Show some fucking respect," he bellows. "Do you think I don't know all this? I'm waiting for the next shipment of girls. Once we sell them, we'll have enough money to fix our living situation."

What the fuck? Do the Reapers sell women? Oh, God, I think I'm going to be sick.

"Yeah?" another Reaper interjects. "And when is that going to be? I'm sick of fucking the same overused holes and eating the same disgusting food."

Empowered by the two Reapers who were first to question their Prez, more start voicing their disagreement.

"And then you fucking have this grade A cunt walking around, but we're not allowed to touch her. This is bullshit!"

I cringe and try to make myself smaller at the mention of me. The last thing I want is to draw attention to myself.

"She's not yours to touch," Rusty says smoothly. "You know the consequences if you do."

I pray the conversation isn't going where I think it is, because I'm still not ready to choose Johnny's fate. Fuck, I don't think I'll ever be ready.

Rusty turns his evil eyes on me. "No, that's right. You don't know, do you? Because the VP's Old Lady hasn't decided yet."

Fuck!!

"No time like the present, sweetheart. Tell us your final decision."

"I-I..." Words fail me as ice spreads in my stomach. "I was going to wait for the VP. Because... umm... I wanted to make sure he's pleased with my decision." The words spill from my lips like verbal diarrhea. I don't know where they come from, but it sounds good—plausible, even.

Rusty laughs heartily, and I know I've lost when Noose and the others join in.

"Sweet words from a sweet girl," Rusty says. "But since he already said it's *your* decision, there's no way around it."

Closing my eyes, I pray for the earth to swallow me whole. When that doesn't happen, I pray for the ceiling light to fall down and hit me in the head. Of course, nothing happens.

How the hell am I meant to pick whether they stone him, stab him, or cut off his hands? There are no good scenarios, not even a lesser evil. It's so fucked up.

"Stab," I whisper, cursing my voice for failing me. I repeat the word, louder this time. "Death by stabbing."

Every time I think my soul or conscience, or whatever it is, can't be damaged further, I'm proven wrong. My throat closes up, and I feel sick from having to speak the condemning words.

"So be it," Rusty grins. "Grab your knives, Reapers. Let's show the former King Cunt that the Reapers are men of their word."

Noose chuckles and reaches into his pocket. Tears form in my eyes, blurring my vision, as he pulls a pocketknife out. A fucking pocketknife.

Not a big, scary-looking blade that could finish the job in seconds. Nope, I was right in my assumption the other day. The Reapers are going to drag it out, inflict the maximum amount of pain before Johnny tastes the sweet relief of death.

"Irina," Noose calls out to the redheaded woman, who's busy sucking my dad off. "Finish our treasurer off, and then go get Johnny."

She pouts. "Can't someone else do it?" Without waiting for his answer, she continues what she's doing.

I force myself to look up at the dirty ceiling, counting the spots of mold. That's preferable to watching my dad get... yeah, no. Just hell fucking no.

"Irina," Rusty growls.

I wish I didn't hear the sloppy sounds and my dad's groans.

"Fine," Irina snaps haughtily. "Brian, dear. You'll have to wait until later." There's laughter in her tone, and I'm tempted to join in. Not because it's funny, but because I like the thought of him being robbed of something he wants.

Fucker!

"I'll come with you," dad says, slapping her ass as they walk out of the room.

As I watch a blond Reaper force his cock down the throat of a crying girl that barely looks older than sixteen, I'm reminded of the BBQ the Kings had on the Fourth of July. The outrage I felt watching them paw at the Cunts without permission is laughable compared to what's going on here.

The Reaper who said he'd like to fuck my ass bloody did just that a few days ago. Not to me, but I was forced to watch as he did it to... I don't know her name. Apart from road names, there aren't a lot of names being thrown around. It's mostly bitch, cunt, and more to that effect.

"What the fuck?" the blond Reaper roars, bringing my attention back to him.

It all happens so quickly that if I'd blinked, I would have missed it. One second the crying girl is sucking him off, the next he lifts her into the air by her hair.

"You fucking bitch." His voice sounds extra loud as everyone else goes quiet.

"What did she do?" The words are out of my mouth before I can tell myself to stay out of it.

He doesn't look my way, as he sneers, "She fucking bit me."

"I-I d-didn't mean t-to," the girl hiccups. "I-it was an a-accident."

The Reaper shakes her hard and the girl screams even harder. Then he throws her against the wall while ordering two other women to hold her down. They scramble to the crying girl and force her arms back.

A third woman joins them, she's wearing a wicked smile as she walks behind the girl and takes her head between her hands, holding her in place.

The blond Reaper walks over to a shelf and grabs something I can't see. Then he returns to the girl, and when he shoves what looks like a dental gag into her mouth so she can't close it, I see red.

"What are you doing to her?" I shout. I don't even notice that I'm out of the chair until I'm next to the guy. "She said she didn't mean to."

Laughing, he pushes me away. "That's none of your business, little girl."

The words Rusty has called me so many times I've lost count grind on me. Mostly because I am a little girl. I'm weak, outnumbered, and completely alone.

I ball my hands into fists and repeat the question. "This little girl is making it her business," I snap. "Tell me what you're going to do."

He doesn't spare me as much as a glance or a word. Instead, he lifts the pliers in his hand and moves toward the girl who thrashes harder when he comes closer.

The entire thing is making me sick. From the women who help the Reapers, to the fact he's going to remove her teeth for something that could happen to anyone.

I look around between the women present. Not a single one looks like she's willing to help. "Why are you just standing there?" I accuse. "She needs your help."

As the Reaper removes the first tooth, the crunching sound reverberates around the room. Or maybe it's just me.

"Stop it!" I scream. "Let her go. She didn't mean to."

I ignore the mental warning bells going off in my head. I know I should let things play out and not get myself involved, but how can I live with myself if I just sit back?

"Do you want to take her punishment instead?" Rusty's voice cuts through the noise. "Is that what you want, Zoe? To take her place?"

"N-no," I stutter.

He nods. "I didn't think so. Sit the fuck down and stay out of shit that's nothing to do with you."

Everything in me balks at the order, and I don't heed it. "No," I spit.

"You have ten seconds to get your ass back here, or you're taking her place," he demands.

I don't move.

"Ten. Nine."

I quickly look at the girl. Blood and drool spill from her mouth that's still forced open.

"Eight."

Shit, I don't want that to be me.

"Seven."

But I also don't... another snap sounds as the blond Reaper removes the second tooth.

"Six."

My shoulders slump as I return to my seat next to Rusty. Shame and fear course through me, and if I'm honest, disgust at myself for taking the cowardly way out.

"Good girl," Rusty praises, and it makes me sick.

I force my eyes shut as the girl loses another three teeth. Sadly, I hear it all, and I know the sound of the teeth being ripped from her gums is going to haunt me for a very long time. Possibly forever.

"There," the blond Reaper announces, smirking at me. "I'm done." He gestures for the women to let her go, which they do. One even removes the gag. Then the Reaper turns to one of the prospects and tells him to take the girl to his house as she's no longer welcome here.

If I thought the girl was hysterical before, it's nothing compared to now. As soon as she learns she's being moved to another house, she crawls to the Reaper that just took her teeth.

"P-please... I-I want to s-stay."

He doesn't spare her a glance as he kicks her away.

I'm not aware I'm crying until one of the women taunts me. "Look at her, she's crying like a fucking baby. Boohoo, bitch. Boo-fucking-hoo."

Though the words light a fire on my temper, it mostly makes me feel sad. I miss the Cruz Cunts. Their camaraderie and loving banter. I especially miss Alana, who I'd gotten really close to. The fact that she's a fair bit older than me, probably around Gray's age, never seemed to matter. We bonded, and that's all there is to it.

If she was here right now, she'd tell me to keep my head down, and when I didn't, she'd be there, ready to hug me and tell me that everything would be okay. But the longer I'm here, the less I believe that.

The room erupts into cheers when my dad and Irina return with Johnny in tow. His face is covered by a smiling cartoon mask, which just adds to the creep factor.

"What took you so long?" Rusty barks, impatiently.

Irina smirks and makes a big show of daintily wiping the corners of her mouth with her index finger. "No reason, dear brother," she sing-songs.

Brother? Wait... are Rusty and Irina siblings? I narrow my eyes and study them, but when I don't see any similarities, I decide it must be a club thing.

Rusty gets up and walks over to Johnny. "Circle, boys," he calls out.

The chosen Reapers quickly create a circle around the poor guy I've condemned to be stabbed to death. Each of them hold a pocketknife in their hand.

"Any last words, Johnny?" Rusty asks.

Johnny makes garbled noises behind the mask.

"Oh, that's right," Noose sniggers, slapping one of his brothers on the back. "Cat got your tongue."

They laugh boisterously.

"That I did," the guy Noose slapped grins.

"Cat! Noose!" Rusty barks. "Focus."

I don't know why my mind chooses to dwell on the unconventional road name. But, Cat? There has to be a story behind that.

Out of the corner of my eye, I notice my dad and Irina sitting down next to me. I deliberately don't look in their direction as they take the seat one of the Reapers abandoned.

Not Rusty's, the guy who's been sitting on my other side. I bet it's because they want a better view.

Rusty is the first to stab Johnny, and predictably, it's not fatal. Rusty sinks his knife into the hand closest to him, causing Johnny to stagger and howl in pain.

Noose stabs his left shoulder.

Cat picks his calf.

Once everyone has stabbed the poor guy at least once, Rusty cuts off one of his ears. They continue to mutilate and torture him, all while praising each other and trading ideas.

I feel lightheaded as I watch them, yet I can't look away from the horrific display. My eyes are glued to them as they dance around the man who's now fallen to his knees, unable to get back up.

"Let's do the next one together," Rusty says.

Each Reaper lifts their hand, and as one, they bring them down simultaneously. This time the wounds are more severe. Blood oozes from the many stab wounds, covering the dirty floor in a blanket of blood.

I gag and retch, trying my best not to throw up what little food I have in me. But I'm not sure I can remain that strong.

"Why's your daughter so weak? Isn't it embarrassing?" Irina asks, looking between me and dad.

I hate that I still hold a small amount of hope that he'll help me. Maybe if I could get him alone, I could find out what they have on him. Because... there has to be something.

"She's not my concern," he says, sounding like he really means it.

"Still," Irina presses on. "If that was my daughter, I would disown her if she was that weak."

I make the mistake of turning my attention back to the... slaughter just as the blond Reaper from earlier jams his pocketknife into Johnny's left eye.

My own eyes throb with phantom pain, and I scream. I didn't mean to, but the sight... oh God. No. I can't take this. Just as I think that, my stomach revolts and I only manage to turn my head to the side before I throw up.

"You fucking bitch," Irina screeches. "You disgusting—"

"Irina," dad interjects. "Let me look at you."

"No, Brian." Her tone is shrill. "Your daughter fucking threw up on me. I'll show her some manners."

Before I can react, she pushes me off the chair and forces my face down in the pool of my own vomit. Even though I claw at her hand, she doesn't let go.

"How do you like it?" she laughs like a fucking maniac. "I should make you lick it all up."

A door slams against the wall, then hurried footsteps sound like they're coming closer. The next thing I know, the pressure on the back of my head disappears.

I scramble backward while wiping my eyes clean with my hand. As I open my eyes, I look straight into a pair of blue eyes.

"Sorry I couldn't be here until now, Sugar."

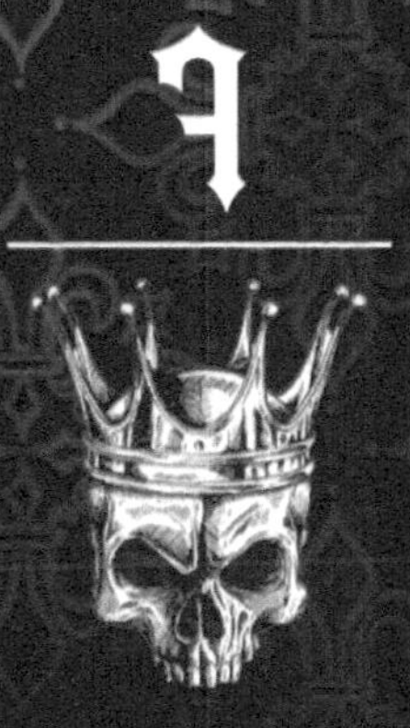

9

Zoe

I completely forget about the vomit clinging to my skin and hair as I look at the man I thought to be dead. My lips open and close so many times I lose count. Words fail me as I gawk at...

"Breathe, Sugar," he urges.

I think I nod, but I can't be sure. I feel like I'm in a stupor. My mind's racing to figure out if this is really happening, or if I passed out. Maybe I'm dead... having an out of body ghostly experience. That would make so much more sense than seeing Gunner here—alive and well, I might add.

"Am I dead?" I finally whisper.

Gunner laughs, his eyes sparkle with mirth and for once, his bushy beard doesn't hide the corners of his lips as they turn up. "No, Sugar. But Irina is." The last part comes out as a growl.

He moves so quickly I have to blink several times before my vision clears enough that I see him throw her down on the ground. She lands in the pool of my vomit, and like she did to me, he holds her down.

"How do you like that?" he growls, fisting her wild red curls. "Maybe I should make *you* lick it up for daring to touch what's *mine*."

"Gunner," Rusty says, admonishingly. "Settle down. You can deal with Irina later. For now, let us welcome you back home."

Even though they speak in English, it might as well have been a foreign language for how little sense the words make. I open my mouth again, intending to ask some of the many questions filling my mind, but again, nothing comes out.

"Look, I know she's your sister and the Mama of our club. But what she did..." Gunner breaks off when Rusty shoves him out of the way and pulls Irina up.

"I know," Rusty says. Then he looks at Irina. "Apologize, now."

She folds her arms across her chest and cocks her hip. "No."

"Irina!" Rusty growls her name. "If you won't, I'll send you to one of the other houses."

The words have the desired impact. Irina drops her bitch stance and says, "I'm sorry, Gunner. My temper got the better of me."

He shakes his head. "It's not me you need to apologize to." Pointing at me, he adds, "Say sorry to Zoe. And you better fucking mean it."

Irina takes a shuddering breath and turns toward me. "Sorry," she says, not sounding it at all.

"I said you need to mean it," Gunner warns, taking a step closer to her.

"I'm so sorry, Zoe," Irina blurts out. "I lost my cool. Please, can you forgive me?"

When our eyes meet, I'm glad looks can't kill. If they could, she'd slice me open with the daggers in her glare.

"No," I say, refusing to play any games.

Gunner laughs heartily. "It's good to see you still have your spark." He winks like this is all some big elaborate joke, and not... not...

Fuck.

While my mind breaks and my brain plays the Jack-in-the-box song on an endless loop, Gunner's being greeted by the Reapers. They slap each other on the back, smile, and share a few laughs. The way they interact makes it clear that they know each other. That they're close.

Some of the women saunter up to him, but he doesn't pay them any attention—even pushes a few of them away when they get too close.

I choke on my breath as my eyes land on the VP badge on his cut. My hand flies to my throat, and I think I claw at the skin, but I can't feel anything apart from the overwhelming dread unfurling in my stomach.

Gunner is the fucking VP of the Reapers... that means... why can't I think straight? Every time I pull at a memory, it slips further away, and the fucking song in my head blares louder.

I barely feel my body moving as I stand up and walk toward the door. As my feet automatically carry me, I feel like an outsider—an intruder—looking in. Like it isn't my body, but someone else's.

Fuck, I wish it was all happening to someone else.

"Go clean your girl, then we can discuss business."

Gunner nods. "Got it. See you then."

While being dragged out of the room, I hear the Prez instruct Noose and Cat to gather the Reapers from other safe houses for church in a couple of hours.

Gunner doesn't speak as he pulls me into the bathroom and starts running the shower. And when he reaches for my clothes, I avert my gaze. I want to fight him. Shout, scream, kick, and claw him until he leaves me alone, but I don't. I just stand there like a fucking statue.

"Lift your arms above your head, Sugar," he rasps.

A shudder is the only outward sign I'm struggling, yet I still do what he says.

"I know this is a big shock, and I promise I'll explain every-thing once you're clean." Even though he almost whispers, he might as well have been shouting for the way I jump in surprise.

"Y-you w-will?" I stammer.

"Later," he vows. "For now, let's get you clean. Step into the shower while the water's hot, Sugar."

Like a robot, I obey his command and walk under the hot spray of the rusty showerhead. Although it's the fourth or fifth shower I've had since being here, it's the first that isn't ice cold. The water is even clean, not the disgusting brown substance I've come to expect.

Gunner holds out a bottle of shampoo, and when he squirts the coconut-smelling goodness into my palms, I almost cry with relief. It's the smallest thing, but it means so much more than I can explain.

"Thank you," I sob as I massage it into my roots. Fuck, I lather my long strands in the suds, desperate to smell of something other than the decay this house reeks of. "Thank you so much."

He chuckles softly. "You're very welcome, Sugar. Want some conditioner as well?"

"Y-yes, please."

I don't know why I'm getting so emotional over hair products, and if I cared to examine it further, I'm sure there's another reason. But I can't do that, I refuse to. I'm afraid that if I look too deep into the recesses of my mind, the things I've seen and heard will swallow me whole.

When my fingers are pruned and the water turns cold, I turn it off and willingly step into the clean towel Gunner's holding. I let him wrap it around me while rubbing my arms dry. I even let him run another towel up my legs, drying them in the process.

My mind screams at me to jerk away, to do anything other than let him touch me like this. As I try to move, nothing happens. I remain unmoving, forced to feel hands I don't want caress my inner thigh.

"G-Gunner." It doesn't come out how I intended, instead of sounding angry, I sound breathy. "P-please."

He looks up at me from where he's crouched, and whatever he sees on my face makes him sigh. "You're not ready yet, Sugar. I promised that you would be ready for me when it was time."

At his words, I'm vaguely reminded of something he said at the Kings' Fourth of July BBQ.

"I know you're not ready for me yet, so I'll wait."

"You've been planning this for a long time, haven't you?" I ask, as the words that made little sense at the time do now.

"I have," he admits, sounding almost... proud. "It was never meant to be like this, though. But fucking Gray ruins everything."

My heart skips a beat as Gunner mentions Gray. I want to ask if he's really dead because I still don't believe it. Though, I can't deny the voice in the back of my head, the one that warns me not to mention Gray, is right.

Scared to say or do the wrong thing, I keep still. Even when Gunner stands up so abruptly a whimper makes its way past my lips, I don't move a muscle.

"Let's get you dressed," Gunner says, softly.

I follow him back to the room I now assume is his—ours—and dress in the clothes he pulls out of his back-pack. It's not until I'm fully dressed in the washed out band tee and jeans that I realize who it belongs to.

"You've been to my house," I gasp. "These are Leslie's clothes."

Gunner nods and puffs out his chest. "Your dresses are no good here, Sugar. This will help you fit in."

He says it like he's done me a huge favor rather than the ugly truth. He's been rummaging through my sister's room, a place he had no business being.

"Come sit down," Gunner says while patting the space next to him on the bed. "You must have a lot of questions for me."

I gulp. "Just a few," I say timidly, wringing my hands in front of me.

Despite the open invitation to voice my questions, I know I have to be careful. I can't risk angering him by asking about Gray or any of the Kings—probably not even the Cunts. But...

"Why did Rhiannon serve me up to the Reapers?" I ask, unable to hold my anger back as I say her name.

Gunner gives me a sly smile. "Because I asked her to, of course." He boops my nose like I'm a fucking kid.

"O-okay." Anger makes my voice shake, making it sound like I'm stammering.

With a sigh, Gunner shuffles closer so our legs touch. "If it helps, she didn't want to. She was promised the attacks on the Kings would stop if she delivered you."

"Oh..." With no idea of what to say to that, I trail off.

It shouldn't matter, but if that's really the reason, then she didn't betray the club. Only me. It doesn't make me feel better, not by a longshot. But at least it makes a twisted kind of sense. And right now, I need all the sense I can get.

"Any more questions before I go to church?" Gunner asks, kindly.

The way he's acting messes with my head big time. He's easygoing, like the Gunner I thought I knew. He isn't threatening me, or... well, treating me badly—unless you count the fact he's the reason I'm here against my will, obviously.

"Where does my dad fit into all of this?" I ask, hesitantly. "Why is he here? Why's he wearing a fucking MC cut? And just fucking why didn't you tell me he was cheating on my mom?"

The more I talk, the more worked up I become. I don't know how to temper my feelings when it comes to the man who was supposed to protect me, but instead served me up to the Kings. All while hiding here with his fucking whore.

"Your dad is... well, I didn't want to tell you, Sugar," Gunner says, putting his hand on my denim-clad thigh and squeezing. "Look, the deal was for Brian to pretend to work for the Kings. He was always meant to funnel the money to the Reapers."

"But if that was the deal, why threaten my life?" Gunner looks at me like I'm being stupid, and I guess I am. Because now that I say it out loud, it's all too easy to spot the lie. "That never really happened, did it?" I ask, crestfallen at the revelation.

"No, Sugar. It didn't," Gunner says. There's laughter in his tone. "Brian played his part perfectly. As for his mistress, I didn't really want to be the one to tell you."

Unable to sit still, I jump off the bed and start pacing the room. I begin biting the nail on my thumb, a nervous habit I haven't indulged in since I was a kid.

"Why not?" I ask when I can't suppress the need for more answers.

"Because," Gunner says, solemnly. "Your dad's demand for stealing from the Kings was that we killed your mom."

There's something wrong with my ears because Gunner clearly didn't say what I just thought I heard. There's just no fucking way. Dad isn't that kind of person... what a fucking joke I am. He's exactly that type, isn't he? He shot Rhiannon in cold blood.

It wasn't self defense or even because of something she did. He did it to tie up loose ends. So clearly my dad is capable of more than I would ever have thought possible.

"B-but why?" I croak. The hoarseness of my voice isn't caused by overuse. It's the emotions clogging up my throat that's making it hard to talk.

"He wanted to be with Irina," Gunner says with a shrug. "So this was the arrangement we came up with."

We... Gunner keeps saying we. Was he the one to shoot my mom? Or Leslie? Shit...

"And Leslie?" I force the words out, needing to know where my sister fits into all of this.

"That was an accident," Gunner replies. "Your dad didn't want you or Leslie to be harmed. But shit went south when Gray showed up. I told you he ruins every-fucking-thing."

Although it isn't funny at all, I burst out laughing. Tears form in my eyes, and I clutch my stomach as I laugh so hard it's hard to keep standing. Unable to keep my balance, I fall to my knees, barely registering the jarring pain that follows.

"Y-you..." Laughter steals my words. "I-I..." Then I'm no longer laughing, I'm sobbing my heart out.

I'm barely aware that Gunner pulls something from his backpack until he throws something soft toward me. When I look to the side, I immediately reach for the stuffed unicorn. I hug it tightly to my chest as I roll to my back.

It's not just any unicorn... this is the one I brought from my house to the Kings' clubhouse. The one I thought was destroyed when the Reapers attacked.

Grayson

My fist slams into some guy's face, blood spraying from the way his lip splits, as Gertie screams in the background.

"Stop! Gray! Please stop hurting him!" she screams, over and fucking over, and it's grating on my fucking nerves.

Most of the patrons, except for Loretta's whores, vacated the Sleep-Eazy Motel the moment I started kicking down fucking doors. The businessmen, and even the fucking cops who frequent this seedy fucking motel on the edge of town took off, and no authorities have returned to stop my wrath.

"I'll fucking stop, when you tell me what I want to know, Gertie." I point a blood-soaked finger in her direction before pointing back down to the guy she's been dating. "Until then, this motherfucker is going to learn what it's like to be associated with the likes of you."

My fist crunches his nose next, his cries almost as high pitched as Gertie's as he tries to scramble away from me.

He's wasting his fucking energy. He can't run from me. No one can.

"I haven't seen any Reapers. I swear. If I had, I would have told you."

I curl my lip at her. "I didn't fucking ask if you'd seen any Reapers. I asked if you heard anything about them. Anything about Zoe. Stop fucking wasting my time."

"Adam Perry was in here bragging about getting one over on the Kings."

My head darts in the direction of the voice to see Loretta standing in the doorway, taking a drag of her cigarette. She's as classy as a whore turned pimp can be with her satin nightie hanging off one shoulder, and her nipple nearly showing.

"Lori!" Gertie scolds as Loretta shrugs at her.

"What? It's no skin off my nose to tell Gray about his visit. That fucker roughed up Erin and didn't pay extra for it. As far as I'm concerned, he's not worth protecting."

Crossing my arms over my chest, I eye Gertie. "You're willing to let your boyfriend get beaten to death. Why?"

She shakes her head, looking fucking terrified as her mascara smeared eyes dart to the doorway like she's thinking about fleeing. Or trying to, anyway.

She won't get far.

And won't live long if she tries that.

"I need to protect my guest's privacy." She lies and Loretta scoffs.

"You talk so much shit, Gertie. You had no problem ratting me and my girls out to the cops last month when they offered you a Benjamin Franklin. It cost me three fucking grand and a blow job to clear those fucking charges. You're not protecting anyone but yourself."

When Gertie lurches for Loretta, I pull my gun and stop her in her tracks, my barrel digging into her double chin as a gasp leaves her pink smoke creased lips.

"Start fucking talking, Gertie, or I'll paint this ceiling with your brain."

"Gertie. Just tell him." The loser boyfriend moans from the floor where he huddles in a pool of his own fucking blood.

I hope that fucker breaks up with Gertie after this. If she's still alive, that is.

"A-Adam Perry was here last week. H-he was bragging about stealing the Kings' most prized possession, but he was pissed that he wasn't allowed to have a go at her cunt. Said he borrowed some cash off his parents to buy a whore for the night, so he didn't have to fuck the club's whores and the slops left behind from the other Reapers."

I roll my tongue in my mouth, trying to keep my fucking composure at hearing Adam's desire about my princess. But fuck. This is the first intel I've had that actually confirms the Reapers have her and that she's alive. We were going off speculation, and since the Reapers are known for laying claim to their attacks, I was beginning to worry something else had happened to Zoe since the Reapers have gone into hiding and remained quiet.

Shoving Gertie away, I spin to face Loretta. "Get your girl. Erin, was it? I want to fucking talk to her."

Loretta shrugs, stubbing out her cigarette on the door-jamb. "It'll cost you."

My hand is around her throat before she can even take another breath, and I spin her, slamming her back against the open door.

"It'll cost *you* if you don't fucking do as I ask!" I roar in her face, and she flinches back, the calm, relaxed pimp vanishing before my eyes. "Get your fucking girl here now or it'll be your fucking brain all over the ceiling."

Nodding as much as she can with my hand around her throat, she waves to another whore hovering outside the motel office door.

"Get Erin," she rasps, hardly able to speak past the squeeze of my fingers.

The woman nods, running across the parking lot to the other side, and I watch as she runs up two flights of stairs and enters a room on the second floor.

"Is there anything else I need to know?" I ask, talking to both women, and while Loretta shakes her head, Gertie whimpers. I swing my gaze to her and raise a brow, and this time, I don't need to threaten her with my gun. This time she's forthcoming.

"A-Adam made a booking again for a room. Next month. The first Saturday in September." She shrugs. "He's done that before and not shown up since it's his daddy's money he's paying with, but he's booked room sixty-nine."

I lift a single brow. "Really? Sixty-nine?"

She nods. "He thinks it's funny."

"Fucking immature cockhead," I mutter before turning my sights across the parking lot as two of Loretta's whores hurry across in the dark.

"This her?" I ask Loretta and she rasps a yes before I release her neck and she tumbles to the floor.

The slim girl looks no older than Zoe, her blonde hair pulled up in a mess on top of her head, and the shiner bruising her left eye shows she's still healing from Adam's visit.

Fucker.

Her doe eyes look up at me with an air of innocence not typical with one of Loretta's whores that tells me she's extremely fucking new in this business.

Fuck. She kind of reminds me of Zoe. So much so that they could be sisters.

"Everyone out." I order, turning to the small office and raising my brows impatiently as Gertie helps her boyfriend up off the floor. He shoves her away as soon as he's on his feet and tells her to stay the fuck away from him, and I fucking grin.

Bitch deserved that.

As Loretta stumbles out of the room too, I gesture to the innocent-looking whore to enter the office and step in behind her, closing the door before slipping my gun in the back of my jeans.

"What's your name?" I ask to see if she tells me the truth, and she clears her throat, her head tilted down as her eyes lift to meet mine.

"My name is whatever you want it to be, sir."

My lip twitches. Loretta has taught her well.

"I'm not your sir, and I'm not a client. I'm Grayson Black. President of the Cruz Kings MC." I widen my stance and cross my arms over my chest. "Do you know who I am?"

"Yes, sir. I mean, Mr. Black. I've heard of you and your club."

"Call me Gray. Mr. Black makes it sound like I'm a gentleman. And I'm no gentleman."

She nods quickly keeping her eyes trained on me even as her anxious hands wring together in front of her.

"You had a client last week. His name was Adam. I believe he's the one who did that to you." I gesture to her eye with a finger and she nods.

"Yes, sir—Gray. He's booked me again for next month."

"So he's booked you and room sixty-nine for next month? How do you feel about that?"

She clears her throat, shifting anxiously on the spot. "I'm happy to serve my clients."

Sighing, I step forward and tilt her chin up, so she looks less submissive.

"Stop talking to me the way Loretta has trained you to. I'm not a client, remember. I want to speak to the real you. I want to speak to Erin. That's your name, isn't it?"

She nods again.

"Okay, Erin. How do you really feel about Adam booking you again next month?"

Slowly, I watch as the innocence falls from her face and her top lip curls. "I hope he gets hit by a bus on his way here."

I chuckle. "Much better." I remove my finger from her chin, happy to see that she doesn't drop her chin again. "When Adam was with you, did he mention the Cruz Kings, or the Reapers, or a woman named Zoe?"

When she hears Zoe's name, she flinches.

"Tell me," I demand, and she flinches again.

"He didn't say anything about the Cruz Kings or Reapers, but he wanted my name to be Zoe. He kept calling me that and told me I deserve everything I get. Then he beat me as he..." She shakes her head, not able to finish, but I get the fucking gist.

I spin, giving her my back as I fight the urge to smash up everything in my fucking sight. That sick fucker used a whore to pretend it was *my* Zoe. Fuck him. He's going to die a slow and agonizing death. I'll make fucking sure of it.

Turning back to Erin abruptly, she whimpers taking a step back like she's waiting for me to hit her, and while I'm vibrating with rage, I don't fucking hit innocent women.

"Are you here on your own accord?" I ask her and she frowns in confusion. "Are you whoring for Loretta by choice?"

"Oh... yes." She nods. "I need to pay for nursing school."

My brows shoot up. "You're studying to be a nurse?"

She nods. "Just starting, but it's expensive. I don't have parents to support me."

"They don't live around here?"

She shrugs. "I wouldn't know. I grew up in the system. I'm trying to make a life for myself now."

Blowing out a breath, I step back from her taking her in. She's definitely a lot like Zoe, just not as curvy. Her hair is blonde, although a little brassier than my princess' hair, and she doesn't have the same blue eyes as Zoe. Erin's eyes are a golden brown.

It could be because she reminds me of my princess, or simply the fact that she's obviously been dealt a bad hand most of her life and is trying to change her path, but whatever the reason, I offer her something I don't normally.

"If you ever find yourself in trouble, I want you to go to Dirty Diamonds and ask to speak to Cain. You tell him to call me, and I'll come and help you." When she nods, I add, "Allowing yourself to be beaten while you're being fucked isn't part of your job. Don't let anyone lay a hand on you again. I'll make sure Loretta knows, but if she lets it slide, you fucking reach out to me, okay?"

She nods again. "When Adam comes for his booking next month, do you need me to do anything?"

I smirk and shake my head. "He won't make it. That bus is gonna run him down before that."

Erin's shoulders drop in relief, and she returns my smirk. "I hope so."

Chuckling, I turn and leave her in the office, focusing my attention on Loretta to ensure she fucking protects her women better in the future. By the time I leave, I gather by the smell of piss that Loretta understands very fucking clearly where I stand on the issue.

It's been a long fucking night.

Hell, it's been a long fucking few weeks.

Rocco has been moved to a rehabilitation unit in the hospital to start therapy in the hopes that as the inflammation around the spine goes down, that he'll hopefully learn to walk again.

I haven't been officially sworn in as the new President yet, still walking around telling everyone I'm the acting President until Rocco is ready to be part of the ceremony.

I've stepped up though. Taken the role with two fucking fists and as of last week, our runs started up again, without incident from any Reapers trying to block our way.

Cain is still putting up with us living at Dirty Diamonds, but I got word just today from the fire investigation that we can go back onsite at our clubhouse as soon as next week to start repair work. It won't be ideal, and security will be an issue, but we'll make it work until the front of the building can be rebuilt.

Each day I delegate jobs to my men and the Cunts, and each day, after my work is done for the club, I go off on my own, kicking down door after fucking door in search of any small bit of information about Zoe.

Today is the first day I got something.

I rub the center of my chest that never stops fucking aching as I slip into the small girly car belonging to the Cruz Cunts. It's inconspicuous, and fucking quiet compared to a Harley, so it's been my mode of transport around Santa Cruz lately, as I turn this fucking place upside down in search of answers.

The need to kill something is fucking pulling at me, but I push it down, letting it fester with the rest of my rage, keeping it for the day I slaughter the Reapers.

And Adam.

At least I know Zoe is alive, and I now know that the Reapers definitely have her. What Gertie said about Adam being pissed about not being allowed to have a go at Zoe's cunt confuses the fuck out of me. The Reapers aren't known to be fucking nice. I've spent sleepless night after sleepless night trying to push away images of what the Reapers could be doing to my princess. Especially since they are known for their love of a fuck train when they get a new piece of meat. So why hasn't Adam been permitted to have a go at her?

Maybe because he's still a prospect? Maybe they haven't patched him in yet?

Fuck!

I don't know, but what I do know is, he's just become my number one target. He has a standing booking next month at the Sleep-Eazy Motel, and I made Loretta confirm the date with me, so if I haven't found my princess before then, well, let's just say, Adam isn't going to get the fucking happy ending he'll be hoping for.

9

Zoe

"**F**uck, Zoe. Even like this, you feel fucking amazing," Gunner groans.

My eyes are squeezed shut as I try to imagine doing anything but being here. The mascara and eyeliner I applied earlier is undoubtedly smudging, and I know I'll have to correct it as soon as possible.

When Gunner showed me what other things he'd taken from the Kings' clubhouse, some clothes and makeup, he made it clear he always wants me to look my best for him.

"I'm so close, Sugar. So fucking close." He begins to move faster, tightening his grip on my ass cheeks as he thrusts his dick in the crevice.

Luckily, I'm on all fours so he can't see my face—can't see the revulsion written all over it as he chases a pleasure I don't want to be the one giving him.

Gunner moves so he's covering my back, and his mouth quickly finds my shoulder. The moment he comes, he bites down so hard I scream in pain. It fucking hurts.

"That's it, Sugar. I love hearing you scream for me."

I shudder, but keep my mouth shut. If my time with him has taught me anything, it's that I need to say as little as possible, and don't look at him unless I have to.

The first few days after Gunner rose from the fucking dead, he was somewhat normal, like the guy I thought I'd gotten to know, but then I had a dream about Gray and said his name. That's when Gunner flipped a switch and has spent the last couple of weeks "training me" as he likes to put it, for our future together.

"I almost miss you fighting me," Gunner rasps as he gets off me. He lies down on his back and pulls me with him.

"Do you?" I ask while I move onto my side, letting him hold me like I know he wants.

"I miss punishing you." I suppress a shudder when he winks at me.

I fought him at first, and I have the bruises and teeth marks to prove it. But then came the point where self-preservation took over, and now I'm his obedient toy. When he wants to use my body to grind himself into an orgasm, I willingly bend over for him.

Though I hate every minute of his touch, I can endure it if it means I don't have to return it. I know I'm living on borrowed time, and it's only a matter of when he'll want me to be a more active participant.

And when that time comes, I don't know if I'll be strong enough to fight him, or if I'll end up betraying what I had with Gray even more.

So, as sick as it is, I tell myself this is for the best.

"Do you know what day it is?" Gunner asks.

I peek up at him, and the look in his eyes tells me that it's not something to be thrilled about. Well, he's clearly excited, which can only mean it's bad for me.

"No," I say. He frowns, and I curse myself for not being more pliable. "Will you tell me, please?"

Adding a simple word like please might not seem like a big deal, but it's causing me a lot of pain to tag it on when all I want to do is spit in his face.

"It's exactly one week before Harvard starts."

"That... but... are you sure?" My mind is spinning out of control, making it hard to believe what he's saying. "How long have I been here?" I ask, not for the first time.

As the other times I've asked, Gunner just laughs and shakes his head. "That doesn't really matter, does it?"

I suppose he's right. My constant need to find out how long I've been here is a fight that's not worth taking. What difference will it make? None, absolutely none. Yet I have a burning need to find out.

People are so obsessed with time, and our perception of its passing all depends on the circumstances. If you're happy, it flies by. If you're miserable, every minute feels like a year. Which is why I can't let it go.

Fuck, I don't even know the date the Kings attacked the Reapers. Everything's blurred together, and the last time I was really aware of the date was on the Fourth of July. But since then I'd been busy wanting Gray to pay, and... irrevocably falling for him.

When I don't answer Gunner quickly enough for his liking, he wraps his hand around the nape of my neck and squeezes until I gasp.

"I asked you a question, Sugar."

"N-no," I mutter through the pain slicing my insides. "You're right, Gunner. It doesn't matter at all."

He nods, pleased with my answer. "Of course it doesn't. You're here now, and you'll never get to leave. Not even in a body bag."

Though I know I shouldn't, I ask, "What do you mean?"

"Did you know Cat is really good at taxidermy? He reckons he can even do it to humans." Gunner's blue eyes light up with a cruel excitement that makes it impossible to misinterpret the underlying implication of his words.

Schooling my features, I do my best not to give an outward reaction to the sick words. Instead, I snuggle closer and hide my face against his skin.

When I was lying like this with Gray, I loved every minute of it. The smell of his sweat wasn't revolting to me. It was a part of him I grew to love, just like everything else about him. But with Gunner, I have to breathe in through my mouth so I don't gag. He smells as rotten as he is.

After a while, Gunner gets up and gets dressed. Unsure of what to do, I don't move a muscle. Unlike when I first came to the Kings' clubhouse, I haven't been given any duties here.

And I'm too scared to walk around by myself to take any initiative.

"You've been good lately," Gunner says, like he's carrying on a conversation.

"Thank you," I say as I force a smile.

He takes Leslie's unicorn from the floor, placing it next to me on the bed. "One of the times Gray and I had lemonade with Leslie, she told us about getting you a graduation present she wanted you to have for when you moved away to go to Harvard."

Breathing is always hard when my mom or sister is mentioned, and it feels like my heart breaks all over again. But this time, I feel a rush of excitement. I'd completely forgotten about the present her horse riding trainer mentioned at the memorial.

"I know she hid it at the stables so you wouldn't find it, and I assume it's still there?"

Nodding, I say, "Yeah... I-I never picked it up."

Gunner beckons me over to him with his finger, and I quickly move to his side. When he hands me a pair of booty shorts and a crop top, I automatically put them on.

Once I'm dressed, he circles me, letting out a low whistle. "Your ass really is magnificent," he groans. As he cups his junk and swats my ass, I suppress the need to roll my eyes.

"Thank you," I say again, happy I manage to actually sound grateful this time.

"I've decided to take you to get the graduation present next week. You deserve a treat."

At first, I'm not sure I heard him correctly. Then I grow suspicious, because Gunner isn't my fairy fucking godmother. "Really?" I ask, not daring to believe him.

"Absolutely," he grins. "You've earned it, Sugar."

Even though I know I should appease him by smiling back and thanking him for his benevolence, I can't make myself do it. I'm too scared to take him at his word. He's dangling a priceless carrot in front of me, and I'm terrified he'll rip it away before I can grasp it.

"I'm serious," he says, reading the distrust on my face. "We'll make a day out of it. You need a change in scenery."

A day of it... a day in public... if I play my cards right, I might be able to use this for my benefit. If I can find a way to warn Chris, he can call the cops for me and I can go... home. Wherever that is. No, focus, damnit. That's a problem for later. Freedom is within my reach, so close I can taste it on the air, and that's all that matters.

Spurred on by the thought of getting the hell out of here, I jump into Gunner's arms, quickly wrapping my legs around his waist.

"You're too good to me," I purr, peppering his neck in kisses. "Thank you so much."

At first he seems surprised by my outburst, and honestly, so am I. Neither of us questions it, probably for very different reasons. I don't because I'm willing to do anything to get out of here. And him... I don't even want to guess his reasons.

When Gunner beams as he puts me down, I'm reminded of the guy I thought I was friends with. It's his easy-going smile, the one that puts you at ease and makes you lower your guard.

Never fucking ever again.

"I shouldn't have to tell you this," Gunner says, pulling me from my thoughts. "But if you displease me in anyway, I'll burn the fucking present in front of you."

As soon as the words leave his mouth, I want to slap myself for being so fucking stupid. I was right with the carrot analogy. He did indeed dangle it in front of me, and I'm the idiot who jumped and fell for it.

I don't think he ever doubted how much I wanted it, but now he'll never have to. I inadvertently showed him just how much I want it. Which means that for the next week, he can make me jump through rings of fire, and I'll do it to get Leslie's present—and for a chance at my freedom.

Though he doesn't know about the last part, I can't be sure he isn't suspecting it. So I'll have to make him think I'm starting to warm up to him, without being obvious about it.

I'm so busy trying to plan how best to go about it, when there's a knock on the bedroom door. Gunner crosses the room in a few strides, throwing it open so hard it bounces off the wall.

"What?" he barks.

"Is Zoe here?" my dad asks.

I suck my bottom lip between my teeth and bite until I taste blood. This is the first time he's come to see me, and I'm not sure how to feel about it.

Since Gunner told me that my dad is the reason mom and Leslie are dead, I've been torn between wanting to confront him, and wanting absolutely nothing to do with him at all. So far, the latter have won out.

"She is," Gunner drawls. Then he takes a step forward, so he's filling most of the opening. "But I don't recall seeing your name on the guest list." Though the words on their own might sound teasing, the bite in his tone makes them anything but.

"Listen up, Gunner. Zoe's my daughter and I have a right to see her," my dad insists.

"Says who?"

I can hear the smirk in dad's voice when he says, "Rusty."

Gunner shrugs. "Then he can come tell me himself. Until he does, I see no reason to let you into my room."

As they bicker back and forth, I eye an opportunity to show Gunner I'm on his side. I inhale deeply and mentally count to twenty before moving to his side.

"In case anyone wonders what I want, I don't want you in here," I hiss as I point an accusing finger at my dad. "And before you can even think of suggesting it, I'm not going anywhere with you either. I don't belong to you. Hell, as far as I'm concerned, I'm an orphan."

Seeing the stricken look on my dad's face is a bittersweet victory, because it tears at me to even say the words. It's not that I don't believe them, I very much do. But just because he's a dick unworthy of anything from me, doesn't mean I can just shake him off like an unwanted bug.

He's the man who raised me, who drove me to my tutor sessions. Every year since I was thirteen, he took me to Harvard's Visitor Center, and he always bought me a new keychain to add to my collection.

Despite my now ambivalent feelings about the man who feels like a stranger as he stands in front of me now, there's history between us. I've known him for my entire life... well, not really. I thought I knew him. Now...

"You don't mean that," dad pleads. "No matter what, you're still my daughter. And I have a right to spend some time with you."

Steeling myself, I take the opening. "Do you? You fucking served me up to the Cruz Kings without looking back. You left me—*literally.* Just because I come from your sperm doesn't give you the right to anything."

The shocked look on my dad's face spurs me on, and I'm unable to stop the toxic words on the tip of my tongue.

"If it wasn't for Gunner, the Kings would have eaten me alive. And you never even cared, did you? No, you were too busy screwing around with your mistress..." I hiss the word. "To care about what I was going through. If whatever fucking game you were playing backfired, that's not my problem."

"Baby girl—"

I let out a scream of outrage. "Don't fucking call me that after you sold me like a fucking brood mare. *Me!* Your daughter. How fucking dare you stand here right now and demand to spend time with me."

The only good thing about the things my dad has done is that I don't have to fake my outrage and anger, it's very much the way I feel about him. He did those things, and in the beginning I had to buy protection with my body. So technically, nothing I'm saying is a lie.

Almost nothing... the part with Gunner's involvement isn't exactly the truth. He didn't protect me, but since he also didn't directly add to my suffering while Gray tormented me, it's close enough.

Gray... fuck. I need to stop thinking about him. He can't save me from beyond the grave.

I didn't believe them until Gunner showed me a newspaper with a chilling headline on the frontpage.

COMMUNITY LIVING IN FEAR AFTER THE NOTORIOUS REAPERS TAKE OUT THE LEADERS OF THE KINGS.

I only got to read some of the article before Irina snatched it from me while cackling about the only good King being a dead King.

"The roads of Santa Cruz that the self-appointed Kings have kept safe for years are now a playground for the infamous Cali Reapers.

The Kings and Reapers' rivalry dates back longer than both clubs have existed. Though there's never been any hard proof, many speculate that the Cruz Kings were created as a means to keep the Reapers at bay, and if that was the plan, they've now failed their community.

While their President fights for his life in the hospital, it seems they no longer have a VP.

We've tried to get a comment from Santa Cruz PD regarding the ongoing investigation of the vicious attacks on first, the Kings' property, then later on the Reapers' property, but the detectives involved and Chief of Police refuse to comment.

All we know is..."

The date of the newspaper was washed out, so I don't know how new it is. Just as I don't know if Rocco survived whatever happened to him. I hope he did.

While I don't personally care all that much about the Prez of the Kings, I know his club needs him. Alana, Rose... all the Cunts will be in danger if they don't have the protection of the Kings. And the Kings... fuck. I don't even know what would become of them without their Prez.

I don't realize I've completely spaced out, not even noticing my dad leaving until Gunner spins me around.

"Earth to Sugar," he says, snapping his fingers in my face.

"S-sorry," I stutter. I don't bother pretending I wasn't lost in my thoughts since it's obvious this isn't his first attempt at getting my attention.

"That was impressive," he grins. "I think you almost made him cry."

The sinister smile gracing my lips isn't faked. "Good." Venom coats the one word.

Still grinning, Gunner takes me into his arms. He nuzzles into the crook of my neck, licking my skin before blowing cold air on it until the skin pebbles.

"You look fucking beautiful wearing my marks," he rasps.

Another memory stirs to life. The time Gray let me cut him, and how adamant I was in wanting to leave a scar behind. I even went as far as picking the scab while smothering the remnants of Mama C's punishment in healing lotions so hers would disappear.

Closing my eyes, I tilt my head to the side. On the outside, it'll look like I'm being pliable and giving Gunner better access. In reality, I need him to hurt me to chase the memories of Gray away.

Some day when I'm safe and this is nothing but a nightmare from my past, I'll treasure my time with Gray. I'll mourn him, and hate myself for not enjoying our time together more. Fuck, I'll always regret not telling him I loved him.

For now, I can't allow my subconscious to cling to all the times I shared with the man I went from hating to loving.

I once read in one of my psych books that the more you think about something, especially something unresolved, the more it'll plague your subconsciousness. I can't take that chance, which is why I need to bury Gray in my mind.

Zoe

"**A**re you ready, Sugar?" Gunner asks.

I'm so excited I can't stand still, and instead keep shifting my weight from one foot to the other. "Yes," I announce. The smile I give him is one thousand percent sincere.

This last week has been worth every demeaning moment since we're now on our way out the door.

Gunner makes a big show of revealing the gun he's carrying. "Remember what I said," he warns, looking me right in the eye. "Don't try any bullshit. It won't end well for you."

I know he means it, but it's not enough to squash the impending feeling of freedom I'm high on. Today's the day I get the fuck out of here.

As we leave, I turn around and grin at Irina. Then I flip her off just because that bitch is half my torment. She never lets a chance to come after me slip through her fingers. God, I hope she dies a painfully slow death.

Before opening the door, Gunner turns and gives me a once over. I know he's probably looking for any signs of whether or not I'm up to something.

With the promise of Leslie's present and some fresh air, I've been giddy most of the week. A model captive all week. Every single thing he's demanded, I've given without once complaining. So when he looks at me now, I'm sure it's the same happiness he sees.

And yes, part of it is the present. The bigger part is my freedom. I already know that the first thing I'm going to do is return to Dirty Diamonds. If the Kings aren't there anymore, Cain will know where they're hiding, and can take me there. I need to see the Kings and Cunts for myself, otherwise I'll never believe they're okay.

If Gray was still alive, I'd stay with them forever. But without him around, I might move to another country to get a new start. I'll ask Alana if she wants to join me, but since she's been a Cunt forever, I already know she won't want to leave. Plus, she has Slasher to think about.

Whatever I decide, it'll be what I want to do. Not something orchestrated by someone who has no business forcing me to do anything.

Freedom, here I come.

The sun blinds me as soon as I step outside. I close my eyes as they slowly get used to the natural light. A laugh escapes me as I feel the warm rays on my skin.

Living in Santa Cruz I've never given the sun much thought. It's another part of my life that I've taken for granted. Right now I can feel it like never before. Feel my skin absorb the rays and the warmth that follows.

"Move your ass, Sugar."

Eager to get to the stables, I follow Gunner while promising myself I'll move somewhere sunny and never again take the sun for granted. I'll take up outdoorsy activities or something. Yes, maybe I'll get a big garden and fill it with beautiful flowers. Or get into hiking so I never again have to just sit and twiddle my thumbs inside.

I'm surprised when Gunner leads me over to a yellow school bus. He doesn't offer me any explanation as he knocks on the door, and it swings open.

"Ready, Noose?" Gunner asks the guy at the wheel.

He smiles widely. "Born ready, VP." He does this weird kind of salute that draws attention to the stupid hat he's wearing. "Even dressed the part," he deadpans.

I've never seen another school bus driver wear a hat, but since I've only taken the bus a handful of times, I wouldn't know if it's out of place. Maybe it's specific for the local school here, in which case he'll fit right in.

The logo on his chest reads Santa Cruz Elementary, the white standing out against his black short-sleeved shirt.

"Right," Gunner says, interrupting my staring. "Take us toward the school, and then swing left at—"

Noose growls under his breath. "I know the fucking drill, man. Just get in the back so we can get going."

After telling Noose exactly where to stick his attitude, Gunner drags me to the back and tells me to lie down across the seat. He then stretches across the floor, so we can't be seen from outside the windows.

During the drive, he keeps a hand in my hair like he's making sure I don't pop up and... well I don't fucking know what I could even do. It's not like armed or special forces are looking for me, stopping every vehicle to see if I'm hidden in the backseat. So even if I banged enough on the window to get someone's attention, they wouldn't know who I am.

The drive takes about an hour and a half, which I'm sure involves multiple detours. Once we pull to a stop, Gunner slides up next to me.

"Empty your pockets," he rasps.

I roll my eyes, immediately knowing that was stupid. To cover my slight, I playfully bump my shoulder against his. "Why don't you just cop a feel to see if I'm hiding something?" I deliberately make my tone sultry.

Taking the bait, Gunner pushes me to my feet. He wastes no time sliding his hands along the denim skirt I'm wearing, squeezing my ass hard as he searches the back pockets. Of course there's nothing there, which is very much on purpose.

Not trusting his lack of findings, he moves his hands under my top. He stiffens when he reaches my bra, specifically the front clasp holding the cups together.

"What's this?" he growls as he rips the red lipstick from where I hid it.

"Gunner," I scold. "Be careful with that. It was expensive."

My offensiveness works like a charm, making him blink in surprise. "Ehh..." He trails off, swallowing harshly before speaking again. "Why are you hiding it?"

"Hiding it?" I scoff. "Look at this skirt, Gunner. I can't fucking walk around with a lipstick bulge when it's so tight. That would look stupid, and you know I want to look my best for you."

The words taste sour on my tongue, but they work like a charm. He nods to himself and gives me back the lipstick, the only thing I brought.

All week I was agonizing about what to do, how to get a note to Chris without tipping off Gunner. I knew he'd search me, and find whatever I might try hiding. That only left me one option, be disarmingly obvious so he wouldn't do more than scratch the surface.

A guy like Gunner will never think of a lipstick like a tool, or realize it can be used to write a note. Not a long one and definitely not prettily, but that hardly matters. It's enough to scribble a few words on some toilet paper.

Moving on to the next part of my plan, I use the back of my hand to pat my forehead. Then I make a big show of fanning myself, even moving closer to the window so I can press my head against it. Even though it's September, the days are still hot, and today is even warmer than usual.

"Do you have any tissues or something?" I ask Gunner sweetly.

With no windows in the rooms I'm allowed in, I've had no way of knowing the weather. If it'd been raining, it could still work, but if it was windy and overcast, I'd have no reason to ask for tissues.

Gunner walks to the front of the bus and talks to Noose before returning. "No," he answers gruffly.

I send a silent thank you to the powers that be for the reprieve. Now it won't look out of place when I excuse myself to use the bathroom. I can claim I need cooling down.

"It's okay," I say. My eagerness makes the words come out in a rush. "I'll just ask Chris for some. Don't want to ruin my makeup." I gesture to my face.

Gunner's eyebrows shoot up his forehead, and his face morphs into a mask of anger. Several moments pass in an agonizing silence before I realize my mistake. By calling him by his name instead of just referring to him as Leslie's trainer, I've made it seem more personal—intimate.

"I think that's his name," I muse while doing my best to appear aloof. "Maybe it was something else. No, I think Chris is right. I wonder if that's his actual name or if it's short for Christopher or possibly Christian."

In my attempt to cover up my mistake, I'm turning into a rambling lunatic with a heavy bout of verbal diarrhea.

Noose chooses that moment to shout for Gunner. "Yo. The last car just left, so we should be alone now."

My heart thunders in my ears, and my blood feels like it's boiling while I wait for Gunner to say something—anything. I need his reaction to know how badly I fucked up. When he just shakes his head and hauls me toward the door, I breathe a sigh of relief since it seems I didn't completely ruin my chance at freedom.

Noose parked the bus so it's hidden among the trees lining Chris' property. If we'd been in a normal car, he wouldn't have been able to see the parking lot. But thanks to the height on the vehicle, he could watch them without being seen—even in a yellow fucking bus.

Gunner takes my hand as we walk toward the stables. I hate the way his hand feels in mine, but shoot him a forced grin anyway.

I'm so close to being free it's all I can think about. Once I give Chris the note I've yet to write, I know it's just a matter of time. I've already prepared myself to do anything it takes for us not to make it back to the hellhole Gunner calls home.

Even if I have to... to touch him, I'll do it.

I spot Chris as soon as we make it to the enclosure Leslie's preferred horse grazes on. "Chris," I shout and wave at him.

He turns his head in our direction, doing a double take as he sees us. It's probably more because of Gunner than me. Instead of dressing down and being incognito, he's wearing his Reaper cut, proudly displaying his VP badge as he puffs his chest out.

It doesn't matter, though. Gunner isn't really the type you can easily overlook. Not with his bulking frame, long hair that's pulled into a man-bun, and long beard. If that isn't enough to make people turn their heads, he's completed it by sleeking his usually bushy beard into a beard-ring with the Reapers' logo on it.

"Zoe," Chris asks as we get close enough to make shouting unnecessary. "Is that really you?"

"It is," I confirm, smiling at him.

When he takes a step toward me, Gunner growls menacingly. "Keep your distance."

Chris looks bewildered between me and Gunner, and I can't say I blame him. He's probably wondering who the hell I'm with, and... nope, definitely not wondering anymore. I see the exact moment he notices the Reapers' logo. It's when all color drains from his face.

"S-Sorry," he mumbles. "What brings you by?"

Gunner rolls his eyes. "You have something that belongs to my Old Lady."

Though hearing him call me that makes me want to throw up, I keep a smile plastered on my face. Then I giggle girlishly, as though I liked hearing it. "Oh, you," I laugh good-naturedly. "I haven't quite earned that yet."

Every time I have to betray my true feelings to play Gunner at his own game, I feel dirty—vile, even. Hearing him call me that is one of the worst things he's said, and I hope I never have to hear it again.

I keep reminding myself that before the day is over, I'll be free. That's the only thing that'll get me through putting up with him.

"Oh, yes. I wondered when you would come for it," Chris says. "Let me just go get it—"

Gunner interrupts him. "We'll come with you."

Chris pales and I wish I could say something—anything—to make him at ease. But how can I when I don't know what Gunner's thinking.

"Lead the way," I say, getting us back on track when Gunner continues to stare the other man down like his very existence is offensive.

"I had to move it out of the locker since someone else is using it now," Chris explains, sounding extremely apologetic. "But being out in the stable probably wasn't good for it, anyway." He smiles half-heartedly as he walks us to the annex he lives in.

When he goes to open the door, Gunner pushes him out of the way and kicks the door down—literally. I ignore the way Chris looks at me, but I see it out of my peripheral vision. There's distrust and fear written all over his face.

"Sorry about that," I offer lamely.

Neither of the men pay any attention to me as Gunner stomps into the other man's home. He doesn't even care that he knocks a vase from the table, or that it shatters on the floor.

Knowing that the only way to get this over with is to move on with my plan, I ask, "Do you mind if I use your bathroom?"

Gunner spins around, eyeing me through narrowed eyes. Once again acting like I'm oblivious, I swipe my fingers under my eyes, trying my best to smudge them through the mascara on my lower lids.

"I'd like to freshen up," I say innocently while holding up my digits, showing the men the black on the pads.

Chris is smart enough to look at Gunner, and only when he nods, does he point toward his bathroom. "Yeah, it's just through there." His voice shakes the tiniest bit. "I'll go find the present while you get cleaned up."

Yes!

This is exactly what I hoped for. I mean, I had no way of knowing if it would play out like that, but as it turns out, luck is on my side today.

With us splitting up and Gunner being the only one here, he can't keep an eye on both of us. And I know he won't call Noose to come, because his club brother is keeping an eye on everything, making sure we aren't spotted.

"Remember what I said, Sugar," Gunner growls at me.

"Of course," I reply sweetly. "I'll just be a couple of minutes."

Without waiting to see if he follows, I spin on my heel and make my way to the bathroom. My shoulders sag with relief as I close the door and he isn't right there to stop me.

As soon as I've locked the door, I spring into action. I rip toilet paper from the roll and pull out my lipstick. By now it's practically melted, something I hadn't anticipated or even thought about.

"Fuck!" I curse in frustration as the tip breaks off.

I immediately slap my hand over my mouth, scared to breathe as I listen to see if Gunner heard me. When he doesn't come barging in, I quickly look through Chris' things, but as a bachelor he's infuriatingly low on makeup products. There's not even a pencil next to the crossword puzzle next to the sink.

Knowing I'm running out of time, I flush the toilet for good measure. With shaking hands, I do my best to write with the ruined lipstick.

→ CRUZ KINGS

HELP!

REAPERS!

X ZOE

The letters are hard to make out, and I had to think on my feet when it became impossible to write full sentences. Hopefully, Chris and the police will know the arrow means the note is to the Cruz Kings.

When I originally planned this, I meant to warn the Kings of Gunner being alive. That was when I thought I'd be able to write at least one full sentence. Now I'm not sure his name will do anything apart from confuse people, so I leave it out.

I quickly fold the toilet paper as much as I dare, all while hoping I'm not smudging it more than it already is. Then I wash my hands, blasting the water so they can hear it from the other side. As soon as the blackness is gone I quickly check my reflection to make sure I look presentable.

As I open the door, I come face-to-face with Gunner, whose fist is raised like he was about to knock.

"Took you long enough," he grumbles. "What were you doing in there?"

I quirk an eyebrow and give him my best are-you-fuck-ing-kidding-me stare. "I wasn't that long, was I?" I force myself to sound upbeat and unbothered. "I had to pee as well."

Chris stands right behind Gunner, and when I look at him, he quickly hands me the square wrapped present.

I eagerly take it and tear the paper away. "Oh," I gasp as I look at the Tiffany framed picture of me and Leslie.

The rare captured moment of us where we're having fun, is from last Christmas morning. We're covered in flour after baking our annual Christmas cookies and laughing together.

"Thank you," I sob. "Thank you so much for keeping it safe."

I turn it over and read what she's written on the back.

Something to remember me by when you're gone.

Love you.

Leslie

My vision turns blurry, making it impossible to read through the tears that won't stop falling.

"Are you okay?" Chris asks, concern palpable in his voice. "Do you need anything?"

Ignoring him, I show Gunner the picture and the note on the back. Rather than looking indifferent, heat flares to life in his blue eyes.

"Your sister didn't deserve to die like that," he says, his voice thick.

I'm so stunned by the emotion in his voice I can't think of anything to say. Gunner clears his throat and blinks a few times until there are no remnants of the... whatever that was.

"Time to leave," he says, brusquely.

As he turns and heads toward the door that's now upright and leaning against the wall, I throw caution to the wind and hug Chris close. Using the hand that's hidden from Gunner, I fish the note out of my pocket and push it into Chris'.

"Call the police as soon as we leave," I whisper, urgently. "I need you to help get me free—"

My words are cut off when a click sounds just seconds before Chris becomes limp and his body crashes to the floor. In shock, my fingers lose their grip on the frame and it falls to the ground, shattering in the pool of blood from the bullet Gunner put in Chris' chest.

I whip my head to Gunner, who's holding his gun. "I told you not to do anything stupid," he snarls. "Look what you fucking made me do."

My body freezes in place as I take in the anger twisting his face into an unrecognizable expression.

Fuck...

He saw me give Chris the note.

Fuck!

"G-Gunner I-I..." My teeth chatter so hard it's impossible to speak.

"Don't!" he roars. "I've been patient with you, Sugar. I've been lenient and generous even. And this is how you repay me? By fucking touching another man."

The sound of my blood coursing through my veins almost drowns out his words—*almost,* but not quite. He didn't see the note... I think.

"No more!" Gunner thunders, continuing his tirade. "I'm done taking it slow."

Throwing his gun to the floor, he advances on me. Since my body still refuses to move, I just stand there, terrified of what he's going to do.

Gunner grabs my hair and pulls until my scalp screams out in pain. "It's time to make you completely mine."

Using his foot, he shoves the broken glass to one side before kicking my legs until I fall to the ground. Then he spins me around and forces me on all fours, hoisting my skirt up. It's the sound of his pants being opened that finally unfreezes me.

"No!" I scream, kicking and clawing at the ground. "I'm sorry... I didn't think... Gunner, please. Not like this. Let me... PLEASE!"

He laughs at my weak attempts of explaining myself, and the sound is woven from the sounds of nightmares. It sends a shiver down my spine, and I thrash harder, trying to break his hold.

"Don't make it worse for yourself by fighting," Gunner growls. He yanks at my underwear until it breaks, then he roughly shoves two fingers into my dry pussy. "You better find a way to get wet, Sugar. Otherwise this is going to hurt."

I whimper as he retrieves his fingers, but it turns to a scream when I feel the tip of his cock against my opening.

There's no time to prepare myself before he thrusts into me, all the way to the hilt. My insides feel like they're on fire, and I open my mouth to scream again but no sound comes out.

I can't breathe.

I can't scream.

There's nothing but pain, so much fucking pain.

"To think I wasted all those nights making you come in your sleep," he groans, punctuating each word with another thrust. "I should have known you weren't worth the effort."

His words... the dreams... Fuck! Those dreams weren't because... because... fuck.

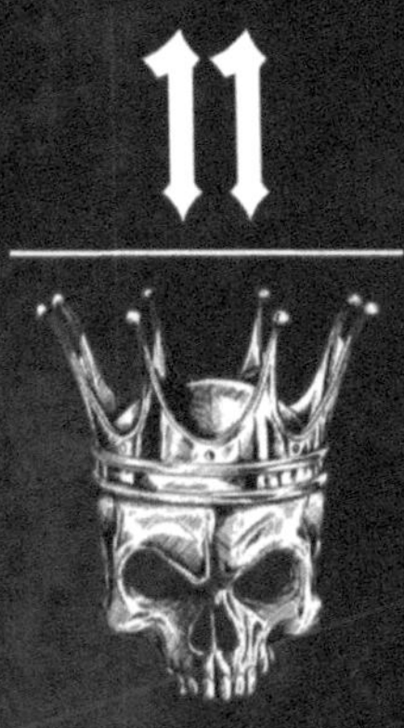

11

Grayson

Crunching glass sounds under my heavy boot as I storm through the ruins of the front of our clubhouse, my eyes wild with anger after coming from the Sleep-Eazy Motel empty fucking handed.

Adam fucking postponed his appointment. Gertie received a call just before I got there. Apparently, Adam had club business to attend to, so he rescheduled to next fucking month.

I can't wait another fucking month to find my girl. I'm going to go out of my fucking mind.

The things they must be doing to her.

"Where are they?" I snap at Stretch who's standing by the hallway that leads to the back of the club and the staircase up to the apartments.

"Up in Gunner's room," he states, his expression grim.

I want to ask him what the fuck is going on, but I'm here now and I'm about to find out why Alana called me so distraught when I was in the middle of trying to find Adam.

Taking the stairs three at a time, I round the corner to see Rose lingering outside Gunner's door. Her eyes go wide when she sees me, and points into the room.

"You need to see this."

I don't bother speaking and step through the door of the room my dead best friend used to sleep in.

I stop abruptly, my feet feeling like they are in cement blocks as the familiar space slams me with memories.

We used to take turns hosting the Super Bowl each year. It was usually only the two of us, sneaking away from the rowdy main room and locking ourselves away so we could enjoy the last game of the NFL season in peace. I hosted it this year, and he was meant to host next year, but I guess that'll never happen again.

"Gray, I'm sorry that I interrupted your... ah... work." Alana approaches from Gunner's bedroom, and it takes me a moment to respond while I push back the fucking memories of Gunner.

"What the hell were you so upset about?" I snap, and she flinches, picking up that I'm in a fucking mood.

The things they must be doing to my princess.

Gesturing her thumb over her shoulder, Alana's eyes fill with tears. "You need to see it for yourself. It's in there."

What the fuck is going on?

Somehow making my heavy feet move, I storm to the bedroom and Alana jumps out of my way with a squeak to avoid getting bowled over.

The first thing I notice is the smell. I was expecting the familiar scent of Gunner, but instead it's a lot like the rest of our clubhouse now. Smoke.

Even though it doesn't smell like Gunner, his things are still here. There's a t-shirt draped over the end of the bed. A pile of dirty socks in the corner which was his self appointed laundry basket. A porn magazine face down on his bedside table. It still looks like he lives here, and it makes me feel like he's still here with me.

That thought should be calming, but it's fucking not. My best buddy changed at some point, and even though I only noticed some odd behavior over the last few months, what we learned at his memorial from the Cruz Cunts has fucking thrown me. They were scared of him.

My gaze darts around the space, frowning at what the hell it is I should be looking at, but then the open door of the closet catches my attention and I move to it, pushing it open wider.

My heart fucking stops.

What. The. Fuck.

I blink a few fucking times, making sure my eyes are seeing right, and each time, they see the same fucking thing.

There, lining the back of Gunner's closet door are hundreds of photos, and in each one is Zoe.

Anger surges in me and I step closer, looking at my princess, most photos showing her naked flesh, her expression in different states of contorted ecstasy. Some pictures are cut in half, like I've been cut out of them, and others where you can see my face, but have my eyes scratched out with crosses.

"Where the fuck did he get these?" I all but whisper, and Alana's voice comes from behind me.

"I don't know, but Tex is trying to get into Gunner's laptop."

I nod, still fucking stunned at what I'm seeing.

As my eyes dance from picture to picture, I start recognizing some of the still images. Leaning in closer, I examine one. It's of Zoe, kneeling, my cock deep in her mouth and it's not hard for me to pick up where this photo was taken.

It's from that night when I got her to suck my dick after she came home drunk. The bet Gunner and I made is still fresh in my mind and I remember how determined I was to win.

The next day, both Zoe and I received a video of our time out behind her pool house. We didn't know who had sent it, but now, as I find another still image from another one of the videos we received, I'm left with no other conclusion but the sender was my best fucking friend.

What the fuck, Gunner.

Fuck!

I wish that motherfucker was still alive. I want to beat the ever-loving shit out of him right fucking now. I feel cheated that he's already dead. He fucking deserves to die by my hand.

"Where's Tex?" I hiss, spinning to face Alana who is still wiping tears from her eyes.

"In the back room." She steps out of my way, and I barge past her.

"Take the pictures down and burn them."

She rushes out an "okay", but I'm already halfway out the door, my mind set on seeing what Gunner has on his laptop.

I don't know what good it will do other than torture me some more, but I need to know for sure the person sending the videos was him. Then, at least, I can be sure it's over and done with.

Some of the men are here starting to clean up the rubble and tossing the trash in the dumpster I ordered. Our insurance has approved to cover the cost of the repairs, so contractors will start work in a few days, and soon enough, we'll have our clubhouse back.

Pushing to open the door to the back room that doubles as our poker room, Tex glances up from an open laptop as his fingers fly across the keys.

"That Gunner's?" I ask and he nods.

"Wasn't hard to get into. The password was easy."

My eyes darken and my lip curls. "What was it?"

"Zoe69," Tex mutters like he doesn't want to be the bearer of that fucking sick joke.

With my fist balled, I spin and slam it into the plaster, reveling in the pain that shoots through my knuckles and up to my wrist on impact. "FUCK!"

"You need to see this," Tex states, not the least bit concerned about my outburst, so I take a moment to get my fucking breathing under control before I turn and march his way.

Looking over his shoulder, I see the file folder open on the screen, and in it are an array of videos and photographs.

"Open the first video," I snap, and Tex follows my order, clicking on it before it starts playing.

There, on the screen is me on stage at Dirty Diamonds, looking murderous as I snarl at Zoe.

Shit. This is the video of me forcing Zoe to suck me off at gunpoint.

My fucking gut rolls with disgust at myself, and I slam the fucking laptop shut.

Why would he do this?

I'm so fucking confused. All I want to do right now is get lost in Zoe, and I fucking can't.

What are they doing to her?

What if she's dead?

I spin, giving Tex my back as my emotions threaten to break me.

"Hey, man. Try not to let this shit get to you. We'll find Zoe."

I nod, even though I don't believe Tex's words. I get the sinking feeling that I'll never see Zoe again.

It's an unbearable fucking thought, and even though I have my club men around me, with Rocco on the outs, and Zoe MIA, I feel so fucking alone. Just like I did that day in the alley after my dad was killed.

I've been visiting Rocco every morning, and every morning I leave feeling guilty that he's suffering the way he is. He puts on a brave face for Cara, but I can see it in his eyes. He's struggling with all the physical therapy that doesn't seem like it's making any difference yet.

I fucking hope it does. I feel like each day I see Rocco, the light has faded in his eyes a little more.

Needing a fucking minute, I charge from the room and go back upstairs, this time beelining for my apartment.

The moment I close myself in, all I can smell is the faint remnants of smoke that still lingers from the fire when all I want to smell is Zoe.

"Fuck. Princess..." My whispered words meet no one's ears, my apartment so devoid of life with Zoe gone that I feel like burning the whole fucking building down.

But needing her scent I find my feet leading me to the bedroom where I pick up the pillow she claimed as her own from Cain's fort and press it to my face breathing her in deep.

I'm so fucking glad Alana brought the few things Zoe had claimed from Dirty Diamonds today. There are so many emotions swirling through me right now, but her scent starts to calm the raging storm brewing, and I turn, dropping my ass to the bed we used to share.

It's been too long. Five fucking weeks since we retaliated against the Reapers. Five fucking weeks since Rocco nearly died. Five fucking weeks since my princess was taken.

"I don't want to fucking do this without you," I whisper again, letting myself pretend that Zoe is here with me.

My eyes fall to the bag on the floor that Alana must have left. Without a second thought, I unzip it and grab a handful of Zoe's clothes, bringing them to my nose to smell her scent on them too.

One day, the scent will fade. What the fuck will I do then?

Letting her clothes drop to the floor at my feet, a pair of her panties gets hooked on my thumb, and I lift my hand to study them.

They are so fucking small. I remember these ones on her, the pink lace a temptation she knew I couldn't fucking resist.

I bring them to my nose and breath in, the scent of her cunt shooting currents straight to my dick which hardens in a matter of seconds, standing to fucking attention.

Fuck.

It's been weeks since I've been hard. I've tried on numerous fucking occasions to get myself hard in the shower, hoping to relieve some fucking stress, but nothing has worked, my mind always too fucking chaotic to let myself enjoy anything.

Now though, I'm fucking hungry. Starved. And all I fucking want is to sink into Zoe's tight hot heat and fucking lose myself forever.

I have my pants open and my cock in my fist before I know it, my eyes trained on the crotch of Zoe's panties, and the dried white substance she left behind.

I start pumping my dick, pressing the crotch to my nose and letting the smell of her cunt control me as I picture my princess here with me.

"Zoe," I rasp, pumping faster before dragging my tongue over the crotch, wanting to taste her.

That's what fucking undoes me, in a matter of seconds I yell into the empty space as pleasure sweeps over me and hot cum shoots from my cock onto my fucking lap and t-shirt, narrowly missing my cut.

Fuck.

I'm fucking panting as the shrill of my phone ringing snaps me out of my Zoe daze, and I hit accept.

"What!" I snap at Slasher, who doesn't take my attitude personally.

"Pigs are here. They want to speak to you."

Motherfuckers. I wish they would fuck right off. I don't want to deal with those pricks right now, but since I'm the man in charge, I have no fucking choice.

"Be down soon." I hang up, not waiting for a response and take one last inhale of Zoe's panties before slipping them under her pillow and finding myself some new fucking clothes to wear.

I take my sweet fucking time, and the inconvenience is written all over Detectives Caruso and Nelson's faces when I finally grace them with my presence.

"Apologies for interrupting your very important work," Detective Nelson snarls, and I shoot her a wink and a fucking cocky grin.

"Think nothing of it."

Detective Caruso rolls his eyes but gets straight to the point.

"We are here about a murder across town. At the stables."

Frowning, I flop down in one of the few chairs that wasn't destroyed in the attack.

"What the fuck does that have to do with me?"

"Does the name Chris Brooks mean anything to you?" Caruso asks and I shake my head.

"Should it? Who's Chris Brooks?"

Caruso and Nelson give each other a look before glancing back at me, and this time, Detective Nelson speaks.

"Chris Brooks is a riding trainer. One of the best in the state."

"Do I look like someone who takes fucking pony lessons?" I snap, and Nelson shrugs.

"Not you, but maybe Zoe."

My brows hitch and I shoot up from my seat. "What about Zoe?"

Once again, the two detectives share a look, and Caruso shrugs. "Do you know if she used to get horse riding lessons?"

"No." I shake my head. "Zoe wasn't the rider. Her little sister was."

Caruso nods, like that's the answer he wanted, and I fucking lose my patience.

"Would you tell me why the fuck you are asking about this?"

"Chris Brooks was Leslie's riding teacher. Do you know why Zoe would have gone to see him?"

"What?" I ask at the same time Alana does, and she steps up to my side quickly.

I didn't even know she was lingering.

"When did Zoe go to see him?" I snap, balling my fists as I try to hold myself back from shaking the information from the fucker.

Detective Caruso's gaze darts between me and Alana briefly before he fucking answers.

"We believe she was there to see him last night."

For a moment, air gets trapped in my lungs, and it's Alana who fucking speaks for me.

"Zoe was seen last night? Why didn't you tell us? We told you she's been missing. Where is she now?"

"We don't know where Zoe is." Detective Nelson explains, pulling out a clear sealed bag with something white in it. "But this was found at Chris Brooks' house, in his pocket, where he lay in a pool of his own blood after being shot in the chest."

Loud ringing fills my ear canal as lightheadedness makes me dizzy, yet I don't take my eyes off what Detective Nelson has in her hands as she holds up what looks like tissue or toilet paper sealed in the bag and angles it toward us to see words written in something red.

→ CRUZ KINGS
HELP!
REAPERS!
X ZOE

"What the fuck!" I yell, lurching forward to grab it, but Nelson steps back, moving what appears to be a note in the bag, out of my reach.

"This is evidence. You can't take it."

"Show it to us again," Alana snaps, and the detective does as she asks.

The message is clear.

It's to the Cruz Kings, asking for help from the Reapers, and it's signed by my princess.

Zoe.

Fuck.

Hope surges through me.

She's still fucking alive. That's fucking good.

"Oh, my god. She's alive." Alana starts to cry, slapping a hand over her mouth as her emotions get the better of her, and it fucking aches that she's saying out loud what I thought.

I'm not the only one that considered Zoe might be dead.

The detectives had said Zoe went to see the trainer, but that didn't mean shit until the evidence was right before my eyes.

"Look, I'll level with you. The scene we found suggests there was a struggle. There was a broken picture frame on the floor. It has a photo of Leslie and Zoe Miller in it, and there's a message on the back from Leslie to Zoe." Caruso gets his phone out and keys something on the screen. "As far as we've been able to put together, we think Zoe went there to see Mr. Brooks, and he gave her a gift. We found torn wrapping paper at the scene and forensics have been working overtime for us and have been able to assess that it was wrapped around the picture frame. Something went wrong after that. We can't be sure, but it's obvious given the note, and other factors at the scene that Zoe wasn't alone." He holds his phone up for me, and I look at the image on the screen.

"You can see the broken glass and the pattern it's in shows it's not resting where it fell. You can also see a smear of blood. Forensics have determined the blood is not Mr. Brooks' blood."

My eyes dart up from the screen to lock on the detectives. "It's Zoe's?"

"It's still to be confirmed, but that's the theory we are running with right now. She was clearly under duress. She managed to sneak a note to Mr. Brooks either before or after he was killed."

Fuck.

I rake my hand through my hair seeing Alana still hovering in my peripheral. She's just as worried about Zoe as I am, and it warms my heart to know that Zoe has built friendships within my circle.

I have to get her back.

"Do you know where the Reapers are?" I ask the detectives, and they both shake their heads.

"We were hoping you could help us with that." Caruso suggests and I scoff.

"As if I'd tell you. Besides, don't you think if I fucking knew, I'd already have my girl back?"

They share another look.

"Word on the street is that you've been kicking down enough doors. We'd hoped you would have found out more by now." Nelson points out and fuck, I want to kill that bitch.

"Look. We know you guys like to handle things in house and have sworn an oath not to share with the police, but we can help, if you let us."

Caruso's words mean nothing. He can't fucking help us. No one can. This is our war, and only we can win it.

I spin away for a moment, needing to compose my-fucking-self when Nelson's words prick at my ears.

"You should tell him."

I spin back, eyeing the female detective. "Tell me what?"

Caruso sighs, shooting his partner a glare before rolling his shoulders back.

"I shouldn't be telling you this. It'll likely just fuel your fucking rampage even further, but Nelson, here, is of the belief that you'd want to know."

"Tell me fucking what?" I snap, and Nelson is the one to answer.

"We found semen at the scene. Near the blood smear on the floor."

Once again, my fucking breath leaves me. Why the fuck are they telling me this?

A growl slips past my lips as I eye Caruso and the smirk he's trying to hold back.

Motherfucker!

He knew his partner would say something and now he's trying to gauge my reaction, otherwise why the fuck would they divulge information like that? I'm not Zoe's fucking dad, so there would be no reason why they should tell me that. But they aren't dumb. They know Zoe means something to me. So either they are trying to provoke me into losing my shit and spilling information, or it's a warning. Perhaps they think it was me after all.

Thank fuck Alana has her wits about her before I lunge for the smug prick, because she steps in front of me and asks the questions I can't seem to summon.

"Was it the riding trainer's jizz?"

"No." Nelson answers as Caruso still smirks. "Forensics have already ruled him out as the owner of the semen. They are still working on finding a DNA link."

"Are you suggesting that Zoe was raped?" Alana asks quietly, and I fucking stumble back at hearing *those* words, only to run into Slasher's chest.

Fuck. How long has he been behind me?

Any smugness quickly falls from Caruso's face, and the look the two detectives share is answer enough, and as red-hot rage sweeps through my body, igniting the monster in me, Alana herds the detectives out of our crumbling clubhouse as my men try to contain me.

Grayson

Dragging myself out of the bed Zoe and I shared each morning is a form of torture. Maybe coming back to sleep in the clubhouse was a bad fucking idea. Everywhere I look I'm reminded of the one person who was put on this earth to save me from myself.

Every fucking morning, I consider if perhaps I should just go back to Dirty Diamonds and sleep in Cain's office which is where I took residence after Zoe was taken. Even though I'd fucked her on his desk, it didn't smell like her in there, and I realize now that was easier. Because her scent is like dangling a fucking drug in front of me, that's just out of reach.

Fuck.

Nothing feels right anymore. Everything is fucking wrong. Getting out of bed feels wrong. Showering feels wrong. Taking my dick in my hand and obsessing over Zoe's panties feels wrong.

The worst part is, I don't know how to make it right again. Each week that passes, the hope that I'll get Zoe back fades a little more. It's nearly been two fucking months since everything went to hell. And it's been four fucking weeks since the cops came to me with Zoe's note. A cry for fucking help.

A lot of good it did. We are still no fucking closer to finding the Reapers. It's like they vanished off the face of the earth.

I go through the motions of preparing for another day in hell, and when I show my face down in the main clubhouse, I find my brothers waiting for me.

I feel like an imposter. They look to me for leadership, and all I want to do is burn everything to the ground. If they only knew the thoughts consuming me, they wouldn't want to follow me.

Maybe I should leave.

"You gotta get out of your head," Slasher grunts as he comes to stand in front of me.

"Why? What does it matter?"

He stares at me, long and hard before he fists the front of my cut and jerks me forward until we are nose to nose.

"My brother died for this club, Prez. He fucking died for each one of us. Don't let his death mean nothing."

A ragged breath escapes me as I let Slasher's emotions tangle with mine.

"I can't think clearly. Not with her gone, man. Every fucking thought I have is about her. How can I run this club when I'm only thinking of myself?"

I tug free of his hold and go to move past him, but he clasps my shoulders, halting my steps.

"Don't you get it? The club is you. The club is me. Hell, the club is Zoe. She's part of this family, brother. You don't think if Slayer was still alive and taken prisoner I wouldn't fucking turn this earth into a living hell until I got him back?" He gives me a shake before getting in my face again. "Stop trying to do this on your own and let us help. The money is coming back in steadily now. The repairs on the clubhouse are well under way and it's secure again. The fucking cartel is happy with our work. But you..." He releases me and steps back, gesturing to our club brothers all standing behind him, "Me, and the guys are fucking empty right now. We gotta do something meaningful, and right now, all any of us want is to get your princess back, and massacre the Reapers. You just have to stop trying to do the hunting all on your own."

A thick ball of emotion lodges in my throat, and I nearly choke on the fucking thing as I try to clear it.

Can I really ask them to take on my battle? My need to find Zoe?

"Slasher is right, Gray." Munroe steps forward and claps Slasher on his shoulder. "Let us help. We need this too."

I study Munroe's hard, yet sincere expression.

Can I really ask them to put their life on the line for Zoe?

"Are you sure?" I ask, leaning to the side before addressing the others. "Are you all sure?"

"Yes." The say in unison, and fuck my heart squeezes.

"It's taking a toll on you doing it alone." Tex speaks up. "Let us carry the burden with you."

Well, fuck.

They must see the moment I wane because their faces all light up with smirks.

"You fuckers really sure you're ready to have me officially as your President?"

A round of hell yeahs fill the space, and I shake my head, feeling the glimmer of something like hope for the first time in weeks.

"Well, don't say I didn't fucking warn you." I grin and they chuckle as I head for the door.

Fuck.

We are really doing this.

Rocco had been putting off the changing of the guard, so to speak, at my request. But a couple of days ago during my visit, he declared that it's time.

I'd been stalling, and he knows it. He knows I feel honored to take on the role, but he also knows I don't want to take it from him.

When we go outside, the Cruz Cunts are waiting, standing on either side of the path, offering warm smiles as we pass by.

I feel like shit that I haven't made more time for the women. I'm still trying to figure out how Rocco balanced all of this stuff, making sure everyone was happy or doing okay. I tried to talk to Alana and Rose about the shit Gunner put them through after I calmed the fuck down after finding his shrine of Zoe, but they insisted it could wait, their need to find Zoe on the forefront of their minds too. I hope they don't think I'm gonna forget. I need them to know that the things that happen to them matter too.

As I give Alana a nod at the end of the path, me and my men pile into the two borrowed vans we've been using to fly under the radar of the Reapers in case they are around watching and waiting to strike again.

The trip to the rehabilitation center, which is Rocco's temporary home, takes around twenty minutes to get to. It's out of the main bustle of Santa Cruz on a property with a long tree-lined driveway which divides off to three structures that offer different private specialty services.

Security was good here, which is why we had Rocco moved to this location for his therapy. Not only were the medical staff the best in the region, but we knew he'd be safe here.

Having prearranged our large visit, Cara booked the dining room on Rocco's floor for us to use, and had Rocco already there waiting for us when we arrived. My eyes travel over him sitting in the wheelchair, and like every time I see him, my gut twists with regret that I couldn't do more to save him from this fate.

He's lost weight. His face is thinner than a few months ago, but his hair is longer. The cut he wears almost looks too big for him now.

Maybe I should get him a new cut. Would he like that or would it be weird?

Fucked if I know.

The guys clammer around Rocco, making a big production of seeing him again, and the smile on his face looks close to genuine as they shoot the shit with him for a bit.

"You ready for this?" Cara asks, coming to stand by my side.

"I don't have much choice." I shrug, not taking my eyes off Rocco. "Are you sure he's okay with this?"

Cara sighs. "He's doing better than I thought about handing over the club to you. It's the whole not being able to walk stuff that's getting to him."

I glance at Cara then, taking in the exhaustion darkening the area under her eyes.

"Has he felt the twinge again?" I ask, referring to his temporary moment of tingling down his legs last week.

"No. Nothing. I think that's what's eating at him right now. He's trying to figure out how to make the tingles come back."

Turning back to Rocco, I nod. "It's still hopeful. The doctor said it was a good sign."

"Yeah, they did." She agrees before adding. "It's time Gray."

My heart speeds up and I don't know if it's from excitement or dread. I don't know how to feel about this.

The room falls silent, and my gaze lifts to meet Rocco's across the room. He gives his head a lift, a nod of approval and I take in a calming breath before I close the distance between us.

The men all disperse, standing in an arc around us as Rocco clears his throat.

"We are here today to acknowledge and celebrate a change in leadership in our club." He wheels closer and my eyes fall to the book on his lap. It's the Cruz Kings' book of bylaws.

That book.

I was there when the first patching in happened. I was there to see everyone sign the register and pledge themselves to the Cruz Kings. I was there the first time the chant was called.

Now, I'm here to see the first time the Presidential role changes.

"I am Rochus King, and I am standing down as President of the Cruz Kings MC," he announces. "In my place, I name Grayson Black as my successor, to wear the patch of Cruz Kings' President."

It's a shock to hear Rocco say the words, even though I knew they were coming. I think what really hits me is the conviction in his tone, almost like he is proud.

Rocco holds up the book, his dark eyes locking with mine as he places his hand on it, and gestures for me to add my hand too.

"Do you, Grayson Black, accept the role as President of the first chapter of the Cruz Kings MC, otherwise known as the mother charter?"

"I, Grayson Black, accept the role as President of the Cruz Kings MC with honor," I rasp, my voice husky with the honor I speak of before Rocco gives me a nod and removes his hand from the book of bylaws, presenting it to me.

Accepting the oversized book, I see that it's open on the registry page. Inside, the new patches are resting between the pages, and my heart speeds up as I see the President patch on top.

Rocco, Cara and I went through the process of this ceremony last night, so I know what has to be done. I didn't think I'd be this damn emotional though, and I fucking wish more than ever that Zoe was here by my side, just like Cara was for Rocco the day this all began.

With the pages open, I lower the book in front of Rocco, watching as he takes the President patch and holds it out to me. I turn and place the open book on the table next to me before stepping closer.

Slowly, I lower to one knee, and I can see by the way Rocco's eyes widen that he didn't expect that, but I refuse to do this looking down at him. For this part, we need to be eye to eye.

I hold my hand out, and he places the patch in my open palm, and I don't miss the slight tremble in his hand showing me how much this is affecting him.

With the patch now in my hand, I close my fingers around it and thump my fist over my heart, already knowing the words I must recite.

"As President I swear my allegiance to the Cruz Kings MC and its members, and swear to uphold the club values with honor, and protect each one of my members with my life."

A round of hoo rahs sound with thumping fists onto chests as Rocco gives me a glassy eyed nod before I stand. I slowly turn to look each of my club brothers in the eye, noting their support in their smiles.

Even Cara looks happy.

Pressing my new patch to my cut, the double-sided tape holds it in place which is a temporary fix until one of the Cruz Cunts stitches it on properly later.

Fuck. A sharp pain slices through my chest at that thought. I don't want the Cruz Cunts to stitch on my patch. I want Zoe to, and if she were here, I just know she'd fucking insist on being the one to do it.

Fuck, Princess. I'm coming for you.

Bending, I sign the registry, writing my name under the President section and today's date, before drawing a line through my name under the VP role.

With that done, I scoop up the Founder patch and hold it out to Rocco.

"Rochus King, former President of the Cruz Kings MC and our founding father, please accept this patch acknowledging you as the Founder of this club, and your lifetime membership that will be honored for generations to come."

This time when Rocco reaches out, his eyes are truly teary, and he gives me a nod of thanks, unable to speak.

Thumps sound around the room as each member once again beats the place over their heart, showing Rocco that he will forever be the true King.

Knowing there is still one more patch to be presented, I hurry on, eager to finalize the formalities and resume the search for my princess.

Taking the Vice President patch, I turn to my men, eyeing each one. They all have an important role but I can only choose one VP, and it's something I've been stewing over for weeks.

There are reasons why each man deserves this role, and also reasons why each man doesn't, but at the end of the day, I have to choose someone I trust with my life, and who I know will do right by this club if something should happen to me.

It was meant to be Gunner. I never imagined it would be anyone else as my second. At least not until finding out he's a fucking creepy motherfucker who's been frothing at the mouth for my princess. I'm still fucking shocked to my core about what we found in his room and on his laptop.

Then there's the fact that the Cruz Cunts have been scared of him for fucking years.

You think you know someone…

Shaking that shit off, I turn to Slasher.

"Slasher Long," I announce, and his eyes widen in surprise. "Do you accept the Vice President patch?"

"Yes," he rasps, nodding quickly. "I accept with honor."

I hand him the VP patch before he fists it and thumps his chest, and I gesture to the registry, where he steps forward and signs his name under his new role.

When he returns to his spot, the guys slap him on the back, offering their congratulations before they fall quiet, knowing what comes next.

"With the change of leadership, I ask that each man here declare your allegiance." I announce, and in unison, one last time fists are thumped over hearts as my club brothers speak in unison.

"I swear my allegiance to our President, Grayson Black, and the Cruz Kings MC and its members, both patch, and pussy. I swear to uphold the club values with honor and protect each member with my life."

Fuuuuck. It's official. I'm now the President of the Cruz Kings MC.

I give a sharp nod, not knowing what the fuck else to do, and everyone relaxes, giving bro hugs.

I close the registry, and Rocco wheels closer, giving my ankle a nudge with his chair.

"You've got this, Gray. I wouldn't have handed it over if I didn't think you could handle this."

Raking a hand through my hair, I sigh out a breath. "Things just don't feel right."

He nods. "They will. Give it time. And for fuck's sake use the men and find your girl. Stop trying to do everything on your own."

My brows shoot up. "Why does everyone keep saying that?"

Rocco chuckles. "I fucking wonder."

"You sure you don't want to celebrate with us?" I ask and he shakes his head.

"Nah. My goal for the rest of the night is to make Cara come as many times as possible."

"What the fuck." I gape at him, because he doesn't usually tell me that stuff. He chuckles.

"What? Just because my dick isn't working right now doesn't mean I can't make her scream with my tongue."

I chuckle. "Dude. TMI. You're like my dad."

"Like fuck." He smirks, but then it drops as his words are nearly a whisper. "I gotta do something. What if I can't get it up ever again and she leaves me?"

Fuck it's hard to see Rocco like this. Never have I seen him so fucking unsure of himself and as much as I feel for him, it pisses me off. He's better than this.

Leaning over, I cage him in his chair. "Now you listen here. That woman loves you. You banished her and yet she's still fucking here. If you think for one minute that your dick is the reason she is around, then you are fucking mistaken." I shift, gripping his chin as I breach his personal space, continuing to keep my voice low so only he can hear. "She loves you. The decent man you are. Not your body. Get that shit out of your head right fucking now."

He tries to nod, but I'm gripping his chin too tight. "See. I told you, you've got this."

A laugh bubbles up escaping my lips, and I shove back from him as he smirks. Everyone around us is busy talking, all except for Cara.

Rocco can't see her a few feet behind him, but I see her and the tears she bats away, and she gives me a nod of thanks.

She heard everything.

We are about to leave to head back to the clubhouse for the small celebration the Cruz Cunts were arranging when a member of staff opens the door to the dining room and ushers a man in I recognize.

It takes me a moment to place him, and when I realize he's the doctor that helped me get Rocco from the truck and took over CPR for me, my brows shoot up.

"What are you doing here?"

"I'm sorry for intruding, but I knew this is where Mr. King had been taken, and I have some information he needs."

"Information I need, or the President of the Cruz Kings needs?" Rocco barks, wheeling up to my side.

The doctor looks confused for a moment, but then his eyes land on my patch. "For the President. Is that you now?"

"Yes. What information?" I bark this time, and he steps closer.

"The other motorcycle club, the Reapers, is it?"

Frowning I nod. "Yes. What about them?"

"There are some living in the house next door to my mom. Three or four of them. She lives in Watsonville."

My heart stops beating momentarily before it bursts to life in anticipation.

"Watsonville? Since when?" I snap and he pales a little, but doesn't back down.

"A couple of months. They come and go, but she started complaining about the noise from the new neighbors, and I thought they just had their music too loud, but when she told me earlier today that the noise was motorcycles, I drove over there to see for myself." He looks between all of us, certain with what he's saying. "They have the Reapers' logo thing on their vests."

"It's called a cut," Stretch snaps, but the doctor shrugs. What the fuck does he care what it's called.

My eyes find Slasher's as this information settles in. This is the first lead we've gotten of their whereabouts. Three or four Reapers isn't their club, but it's a start, and if they aren't the ones who have Zoe, then we'll fucking make sure they tell us who does.

13

Zoe

I hiss in pain as Gunner, none too gently, applies antibacterial to the fresh bite mark on my shoulder. It stings like a motherfucker, which only serves as a reminder that I'm still alive and living my days as his fuck doll.

He takes a step back, admiring the scars and indents he's littered all over my flesh. "Such a pretty sight," he groans. "If you're a good girl, I'll carve my name into your skin one day."

A wave of disgust slams into me when I notice his cock thickening again. I don't know how much more of this I can take.

"You would like that, wouldn't you, Sugar?"

I don't have it in me to answer him, so I remain quiet.

Since he raped me the first time, it's become an almost daily activity. The bad days are when it's more than once per day, the good is when it's only once, and the perfect ones are when Rusty sends him on club errands, which is the only thing that keeps him away.

For once, Gunner doesn't demand a reply, and just laughs as he leaves the bathroom. As soon as he's out of sight, I lean behind the toilet and use my fingers to erase the number I'd drawn in the dirt and grime on the floor.

As I write "40" I let out a sigh.

That's how many days it's been since Gunner killed Chris in cold blood. Guilt makes my stomach clench so hard it feels like a cramp. Chris did nothing wrong, it was my need for freedom that killed him. I touched him without thinking about what Gunner would do, and Chris paid for that with his life.

As though feeling my inner turmoil, my hand throbs with a phantom pain I should no longer be feeling. Remnants from the glass of the frame I deliberately cut myself on, leaving my DNA in Chris' house. A desperate attempt to leave something more than the note. Fat good it did me.

Though I'm sad he had to die, all I could think on the drive back home was that no one was coming for me. In my mind, I'd already tasted the freedom I craved so badly, but Gunner snuffed that spark of hope out with a single bullet.

After we returned from the stables, he raped me again. Then, Gunner took me to the room I woke up in when I first got here, where he tied me naked to the bed. On his way out, he made a big production of telling me it was my own fault, and that I had no one to blame but myself.

He left me in the dark with spiders and insects biting and crawling all over me for three days. Three fucking days without food, water, or even access to a toilet.

The first day, I screamed until my vocal cords felt like they were bleeding. When that didn't help, I cried myself to sleep, only to constantly be woken back up by the creepy crawlies.

I shudder and try to bury the memories that I'd prefer not to dwell on. I've learned my lesson now.

I know now that this is it—my life will never change. I'm alone, living with people who either hate me or want to use me.

With each passing day, I feel less like the person I once was. I have no hopes or dreams. No ambitions or desires. Most days, I'm not even sure I want to go on living. I'm like an abused animal starving for affection. Though, unlike most animals, I'm too stupid to show my master complete obedience.

Maybe there are still some remnants of the brat Gray accused me of being inside me.

After getting dressed, Gunner tells me that I have to help Irina and the women today. "I'm going out with Rusty and Cat. But Noose and the others will be keeping a close eye on you, Sugar. So don't do anything stupid."

"I won't," I dutifully agree.

"You know what happens if you do," Gunner says in a conversational tone that doesn't hint of the warning I know it to be.

As soon as I'm dressed, Gunner pulls me flush against him. "Listen to Irina and do everything she says." There's an urgency to his tone that I can't quite make sense of.

"Okay," I say.

"I'll be gone for a few hours. But she'll take care of you."

Instead of asking pointless questions, or pointing out that I don't want whatever care Irina has in store for me, I just stand there, barely reacting as he kisses me goodbye.

Less than half an hour after Gunner left, locking the door after him, I hear a key being slid into the lock.

"Are you in there, Zoe?" Irina asks seconds before opening the door.

I roll my eyes at the stupid question.

"There you are," Irina beams. "I bet you'd love to see some different walls, so let's get you out of here." Her relaxed tone and posture puts me on edge. It's so different from the hateful looks I've become used to, and I don't like it.

If Irina notices the suspicious glances I throw her way as we walk to the main room, she doesn't let on. She's busy pointing at things and telling me funny stories. Like I'd ever let my guard far enough down to laugh with her.

What in the hell is going on?

"Now we're all here," Irina announces as we enter the room.

Most of the other women are already busy doing... it looks like they're busy doing some kind of arts and crafts.

Before I can decide if I'm curious enough to ask, Irina explains, "The Reapers only have one patching event a year, and it's coming up in two weeks."

When I notice everyone looking expectantly at me, I clear my throat. "Oh?" I don't bother to feign curiosity.

I only ask because they look like I should, and I'm terrified of angering Gunner. Just because he isn't here doesn't mean he won't find out if I've somehow behaved wrong.

"Yeah," Irina continues. "It's on Devil's Night."

"Devil's Night?" I ask.

One of the women sniggers and looks up from the pumpkin she's slicing into. "Bet the high-class cunt doesn't know what that is."

Once upon a time, her words would have offended me—maybe even pissed me off. I'd feel like I had to defend myself by explaining that of course I know, I just hadn't fully realized it's October.

Sure, I have my day count, but this is one of those situations where knowing and realizing is very different.

"Watch your mouth!" Irina snaps, surprising the fuck out of me. "You all know how Gunner's been treating her. Plus, who the fuck amongst you ever took the time to answer her when she asked for the date? Cut Zoe some slack or I'll fucking cut you. Understood?"

They all cringe and wear matching expressions of fear under the heat of Irina's temper.

That all pales in comparison to the shock I feel at having her come to my rescue. That just doesn't... nope. Irina isn't Alana or Mama C. She might be Mama Irina, as she wants to be called, but her morals are as skewed and rotten as any of the Reapers. She's definitely not the kind to defend me just for the hell of it.

"Sit down," she urges, softly. Without waiting for my answer, she gently pulls me over to a chair and pushes me down. "Do you want something to eat?"

I don't trust my mouth not to spew shit, so I keep my jaw clamped shut and shake my head.

"Sweety," Irina laughs. "You have to eat something. Or do you prefer a smoothie? I have this amazing recipe for a strawberry and coconut one that I swear by. I was just about to make myself one so I'd be happy to make you one as well."

Feeling very much on the spot, I nod once, but still don't verbalize my answer.

While Irina goes to make the smoothie, I watch the women work. Some are busy carving pumpkins, and others look like they're making some kind of posters. I can't see them properly from where I'm sitting.

I could get up and move closer, but that would mean getting up from the chair that's perfectly placed. It's against the wall, and I can see all the exits from here. Which means no one can sneak up on me. So, yeah, I don't move. Hell, I barely breathe.

When Gunner mentioned spending time with Irina, I was fully prepared for her brand of abuse and nastiness. This... whatever game she's playing at, I hate that I think it might work. With each nice word, my body relaxes a little more—completely ignoring my mind screaming to keep my guard up.

"Here you go," Irina says, again sounding kind as she hands me the glass with the pink drink. Not trusting her at all, I sniff it, which makes her laugh. "Do you want to swap glasses?"

I'm just about to say yes, but then I realize she could be counting on that, and maybe did something to the glass she's holding.

"That won't be necessary," I mutter. "As long as you drink from both."

There's begrudging respect in her eyes as she takes the glass I'm holding and sips from that and the one in her hand in quick succession.

"Happy now?" Her tone isn't accusing, it's teasing.

"I wouldn't go that far," I quip before I can think better of it. "I mean—"

"It's okay, Zoe," she says softly. "I know what you meant, and I know you're not happy. I've talked with Rusty about your situation—"

"You have?" I blurt out.

She moves closer and lowers her voice. "I have. We both know that Gunner's being... well, what he's doing to you isn't fucking okay." At the expression of complete and utter disbelief on my face, she cringes slightly. "Okay, so I'll never claim that I or any of the Reapers are good people. But even we have limits."

Now that's a fucking laugh. They sell people just for money. Actually, there's little they don't do in the name of the almighty dollar. So why would Gunner raping me be the line they won't cross?

"Look, Rusty's sorry he hasn't stepped in until now. But he feels responsible, and that's why he's taking Gunner away for the afternoon."

"Right," I mumble. Now I definitely don't believe her.

Irina grabs a chair and pulls it flush against the one I'm sitting on. Then she turns in her seat, so she's facing me directly. "The reason he didn't do anything until now has nothing to do with the club, it's personal. You might not know this, but years ago, they worked for Mama C's mom—"

"What?"

"Yeah. It was messy and not a good situation at all. Anyway, that's a story for another time. And it doesn't really matter except it's why Rusty's having a hard time being objective when it comes to the Kings." She points at me. "And therefore you. It's just too personal for him."

I give her a sarcastic smile. "But you talked to your brother and convinced him to do something about it. So you're my knight in shining armor?"

Irina lets out a laugh. "Oh, God, no. I'm not that good. I just won't stand for what you're going through. That's all there is to it. You don't have to believe me, just know you're going to get a reprieve."

Sagging in the chair, I mull over everything Irina just said. It's a lot to grasp, and I'm honestly not sure I even understood all of it. Like the stuff with Mama C... is that even true? Out of all the Kings and Cunts, I only really know Gray's and Alana's backstories. Yet, I have no trouble believing that most of them have tragic backgrounds.

The thought makes something crack inside me, and I begin laughing hysterically. I feel everyone's gazes on me, but I can't stop. Not when I drop the smoothie, or when I fall off the fucking chair.

Without warning, the laughter turns to full-blown and heart-wrenching sobs. What are the odds that the one person who didn't have a tragic upbringing turned out living in a nightmare? If I was any good at math, I'd carry the fucking one and work out the odds.

"Are you okay?" Irina asks, bending to help me up.

I slap her hand away and get up by myself as I swipe at the tears wetting my cheeks. I need to pull myself together damn it. I can't fall apart in front of these people. They'll just use it against me.

"Never better," I bite as I sit back down.

Fuck, how I wish that I was some kind of robot so I didn't have to worry about stupid shit like feeling. Yes, a feeling-free existence would be perfect.

"Why isn't she fucking helping us? Is she too good to get her hands dirty?"

The whispers among some of the women cause me to stiffen.

"No idea why they even keep her scrawny ass around. She isn't even fighting with us in the brawl—"

"Silence!" Irina shouts. "The Zoe hate stops now. She's your VP's Old Lady, so you'll fucking treat her with respect. If she wants her toes cleaned, you should hope she'd ask you to lick them clean."

I almost throw up at the mental image those words conjure up.

"But why?" One of the women, Lu I think she's called, challenges. "She isn't one of us."

Irina glares at her. "She's not one of *you,* no. But she's like me. Which means our asses are way above your ungrateful ones."

The more Irina defends me, the more suspicious I get. It's one thing to go from cruel to indifferent, that I could believe. But defensive and nice... nope. She's up to something.

"Looking good," Adam drawls as he walks through the door. "Nothing like seeing a group of bitches on the floor. The only thing that would make it better was if someone offered to suck me off."

As he grabs his crotch his eyes lock with mine and I have to suppress the disgust I feel so it isn't showing on my face.

"Hi Adam." Irina greets him and walks over to where he's standing. "Unless you're here to pick, leave my women alone."

"Hmm," he says, still looking straight at me. "Have you changed your mind about including Zoe in the draft?"

I stiffen, my spine becoming ramrod straight as I listen intently.

"Nice try," Irina scolds. "You know Zoe is way above your paygrade, so to speak. And if you value your life and intend to live to become a full member, don't speak like that about your VP's Old Lady."

I hate the way she uses that title to refer to me. I'm no one's Old fucking Lady, least of all Gunner's. Yes, I'm aware it's inevitable, but until the day it's official, I wish I'd never have to hear the words.

"W-what draft?" I ask. It's probably stupid to insert myself in the conversation, but the lack of answers is getting to me.

"It's for the Brawl," one of the girls says.

Irina sighs audibly and points at the girl who spoke up. "I've just about had enough of you, Max. Go to the kitchen and wait for me there."

"But I—"

"No," Irina snaps. "If I want you to explain anything, I'll fucking ask you to. Now go wait for me. And strip naked so I don't have to waste my time."

Adam grins widely and waggles his eyebrows. "Can I go—"

"No," Irina snaps again. "You know you're not allowed to touch anyone but your draft pick, which can't be Zoe. So who's it going to be?"

Adam makes a show of walking around the room, asking different women to stand up, bend over, show him their tits... you get the classy picture.

"I pick Mani," he says. "With nails like that, she'll surely be able to defend herself."

"Excellent," Irina says. "Until the ceremony at the Devil's Night Brawl she's the only woman you're allowed to touch."

"Sure, Irina." The smug expression on Adam's face disappears the second Irina turns her head in his direction.

She frowns and taps her cheek with the long nail on her index finger. "There are no loopholes, Adam," she says, reading his expression perfectly. "When I say she's the only one you can touch, it isn't an invitation to make others touch you. Mani's it. End of."

"I understand," Adam says, looking like he just got called out.

"Good," Irina says. "I'll remove Mani from the list so the others can't pick her."

The way they're talking about the Brawl is both confusing and... scary. I'm pretty sure I've figured out what the women's roles are, yet I need someone to spell it out for me.

"What are the women going to do?" I ask.

Irina sends Adam on his way, promising she'll personally bring Mani to him later, before answering me. "The Devil's Night Brawl is a tradition Rusty started many years ago. Back then, I was his pick, and I won him the title of President."

I gasp but manage to keep my words to myself.

"The men have already proven themselves, otherwise they wouldn't get the needed votes to have a chance to move from prospects to members. But knowing how to control and use a woman is a big part of it."

She talks like the words coming out of her mouth make all the sense in the world and aren't disgusting, archaic, and just fucking wrong.

"If the woman picked to fight for the Prospect loses, he can't become a member. If he's a good Prospect, he might get another chance the following year. But no one gets more than two attempts."

"What happens to the women?" I ask, though I don't think I have to.

The coldness I'd come to know and hate is back in Irina's eyes and voice as she says, "They fight to the death, Zoe. If they lose, that's it. It's a big honor to get picked."

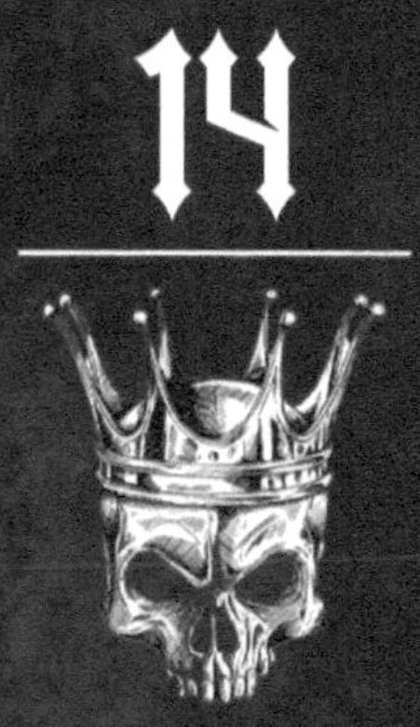

14

Grayson

For more than three fucking weeks we've stalked the Reapers living in the shitty beat up house in Watsonville. Doc Lawson, whose name I now know, moved his mom, Maude, out of her house for a bit so we could use her property. I also think he was concerned about the violence that might erupt if we get noticed by the Reapers, which is a smart fucking move.

I was ready to go in guns blazing when we first found out there were some Reapers living there, but my new VP, Slasher, managed to calm me down enough to remind me that killing them won't lead us to Zoe, and fuck him. He was right.

The four Reapers living in the house are young, which makes them a good target, because young assholes like that slip up, and we were waiting for the moment they did.

I just didn't think it would be three fucking weeks.

"Look who I found." Tex announces, carrying a box as he steps in through the back door of Maude's house with a familiar face on his heels.

"Fuck. Tido." My brows shoot to my fucking hairline at the sight of the Santa Cruz Police Department's surveillance guy. "Where the hell have you been?"

Chuckling, Tido steps into the old kitchen looking a little uncomfortable as he shoves his hands in his pockets and shrugs his shoulders.

"I kind of got myself into a bit of trouble."

"What kind of trouble? Who do we have to kill?" I snap, my smile dropping from my face.

Tido may be a cop, but he's been on our side since day one, and we didn't even have to threaten or bribe him.

"Nah, nothing like that..." He rocks back on his heels nervously, and the preppy looking officer blushes. "I got hitched. In Vegas. To a stranger."

The room is eerily silent for a beat before we all throw our heads back laughing, and it's Munroe's *shhh* that shuts us up, reminding us that we are trying to remain hidden from the Reapers next door.

"Fuck, man." I step forward and clap Tido on his shoulder. "You had me fucking worried."

"So what's your wife like?" Munroe snickers and Tido blows out a breath.

"She's not my wife anymore. As soon as my pops got wind of it he had a team of lawyers working on an annulment."

We all chuckle again, and I turn and scoop a beer out of the sink filled with ice and hand it to him. "Sounds like you need this."

Nodding, he takes it from me and gestures to the box Tex carried in.

"I'll get this equipment set up and you'll be able to hear what's happening inside that house."

"Fuck, man. Thanks for this. Titch nearly got busted last night trying to hear through their back window." I clink my beer against his before we both take a swig.

We all settle in sipping on our beers as Tido gets his equipment set up on Maude's table that looks like it came from a nineteen-seventies sitcom.

I can't stop fucking pacing. The need to find Zoe is all-consuming, and each day that passes makes me feel like I'll never fucking get to her.

Assuming she's still alive.

Fuck.

When we can, we've been following the Reapers inside the house. There's only one day a week all four of them leave and go off together, and some-fucking-how, we've lost them each time.

I've considered snatching one, but we don't want to alert Rusty that we are on to them, but fuck it's trying my patience.

Tido shows Titch how the equipment works, and they start their surveillance, and I eventually hit another fucking low and pass out on the couch, wanting to sleep my existence away.

For the next few days, the surveillance equipment picks up chatter about a Devil's Night celebration. They never speak of where it's going to be, but since we all know Devil's Night is October thirtieth, we start preparing.

Not wanting to leave our women vulnerable ever again, I arrange some extra reinforcements at the clubhouse with Cain and Dante supplying some Diamond Crew men, with clear instructions that no matter what happens, unless the order comes directly from me or Slasher in person, they aren't to leave the premises.

Tex, Tido and Doug stay hidden in Maude's house while the rest of us leave early on the day of Devil's Night so we aren't spotted and position ourselves in different locations in inconspicuous vehicles around the area.

Thanks to Munroe's convincing ways, we have an array of basic white cars at our disposal from a local used car dealership, and have them located along the roads between Watsonville and Santa Cruz with the trunks packed full of anything we might need near their locations.

We aren't fucking around anymore. We mean fucking business, and right now, our top priority is getting Zoe back. Every Reaper that dies in the process is nothing but a bonus.

Their time will come and they will wish they never fucked the Cruz Kings over.

Sitting in a shitty old Datsun just off the highway on the fringe of Watsonville, my fucking leg won't stop bouncing with nervous energy as I wait for the call that the Reapers have left the house next door to Maude's.

It's getting close to five in the afternoon when the shrill of my phone makes me jump, and I frown as I take in the number I don't fucking know.

"What?" I snap, accepting the call to hear feminine ragged breathing down the line.

"Grayson. He's here."

"What? Who is this?"

"It's Erin. I'm Loretta's girl from the Sleep-Eazy. Adam has just pulled up on a motorcycle. He's here."

"What!? I thought he canceled his appointment again this month." I snap, starting up the shit box and shoving it into drive.

"He doesn't have an appointment, but I can hear him yelling at Loretta. He wants to see me now. Something about getting in an early Devil's Night fuck."

"Fuck. Refuse. Don't let him in your room. You know he'll rough you up again." I honk my horn at a car going too slow as I enter the highway, heading north toward Santa Cruz.

"Can't you come here and stop him?" she whimpers and I fucking plant my foot to the floor, trying to make this fucking tin can go faster.

"I'm on my way, but it'll take me at least twenty-five minutes to get to you."

"Twenty-five?" she screeches. "Shit. He's walking across the lot."

"Don't open the door," I yell, but she hangs up.

"Fuck!" I slam my fist on the steering wheel before juggling my phone in one hand and calling Slasher.

"Prez?" He answers after the first ring.

"Who do we have near the Sleep-Eazy?" I ask, overtaking every fucking car I can.

"Sully is near there," he answers quickly.

"Call Sully. Tell him to get over to the Sleep-Eazy. Tell him to remove his cut and look like a fucking civilian. Loretta will give him a room number, and I want him to pretend he's drunk or fucking on something and get into that room. Tell him to act like he's there for his appointment."

"Okay. What's he really there for?" Slasher asks as I punch the horn again trying to get people out of my way.

"Adam has just turned up. I told you what he did to Erin last time."

"Yeah. I remember." He growls like the prospect of it happening again pisses him off.

"Well he's back to see her. I need Sully to run interference so he doesn't rough Erin up. Tell him to take Adam's punches if he has to, but he can't let on that he is a Cruz King. I need him to keep Adam busy until I get there, and I need him alive so I can follow him."

"Got it." Slasher hangs up and I call Loretta next, giving her a physical description of Sully so she knows she can trust him when he gets there.

I make it to the Sleep-Eazy in about twenty minutes, breaking almost every fucking traffic law there is on the way. Pulling up outside the office, Gertie comes to greet me casually like I'm just a regular customer, and from inside the car, I watch in the rearview as Adam beats up my man.

"Want me to stop it now?" Gertie asks and I nod.

"Yeah. Tell him the cops are on their way."

Giving me a sharp nod, she pushes back from the car and calls across the lot.

"Cops are on their way! Best you clear out!"

I watch as Adam heaves a breath, swiping some blood from his nose where Sully obviously took a shot at punching him, then gives him one last kick to the gut before swinging around and pointing to Erin and Loretta standing in the open doorway of the motel room.

"I'll be back to collect."

Loretta snarls something that I can't hear from my open window, and Adam throws his head back laughing as he moves to his bike and throws his leg over.

"Is Erin alright?" I ask Gertie, not taking my eyes off Adam.

"Yeah. I think so." She huffs. "You do know all of this drama is bad for business."

"Whose? Yours or Loretta's?" I scoff and she rolls her eyes.

"If business is bad for Loretta, then it's bad for me. How do you think I pay the bills around here?"

I chuckle. "Do me a favor. Make sure Sully is looked after." I insist, holding up a wad of cash.

"Of course." She smiles, more than fucking happy at seeing the roll of Benjamins.

As Adam's bike roars to life, and he pulls out of the lot, I reverse the shitty Datsun, and follow.

I call Slasher as I drive, not taking my eyes off Adam for longer than a second as we leave the streets of Santa Cruz and head back toward Watsonville on the highway.

Slasher fills me in that the Reapers next to Maude's have just left too, and Munroe is tailing them while Stretch and Tio follow the general direction on surrounding streets, ready to take over the tail should Munroe lose them.

I've ordered them to remove their cuts just as I did Sully, hoping that as long as they don't come across a Reaper that knows them well, they won't be recognized. I need this to fucking work. We've already decided that tonight is nothing more than a rescue mission. If we have to spill blood, then so be it, but I can't risk an all out war while Zoe could be in the firing line.

No. Tonight is just about getting Zoe back.

Adam speeds up on the Cabrillo Highway, going way too fast as he follows the road around the outside of Watsonville, only to turn off the main road on the other side, heading toward the farming region.

Slasher sends an update that they are in that area too, and fuck, my heart nearly leaps from my chest. We have finally found them.

I keep well back as Adam pulls onto another road lined with some sort of crops, and a quick glance over the field shows me a single house sitting alone, packed with cars and bikes.

Fucking got them.

I drive a little further up the road and take a side street, only to have another white car pull up alongside me, and Slasher leans across the passenger seat and winds the window down.

"We fucking found them." He grins, and fuck, I can't remember the last time I saw that light in his eyes.

"Fuck yeah, we did. Now I just have to figure out how to get inside and not get spotted."

"It's fucking Devil's Night, man." He holds up a tub of something and shows me the label.

"Face paint?"

He nods, all too fucking pleased. "Let's cover that pretty fucking face of yours so you can't be recognized."

Laughing, I nod, turning the engine off and getting out.

Munroe pulls up a minute later, explaining that the others are doing the same fucking thing a few streets over and I smirk.

"Why wasn't I made aware that this was happening?"

"Dude. No way were you gonna let us talk you into wearing fucking makeup." Munroe chuckles.

"We also didn't know if this was going to be a dress up thing." Slasher adds. "It was Alana's last-minute idea to take this stuff just in case."

"Huh. Well I bet she's gonna be pleased to know she was right." I grin and Slasher rolls his eyes.

"She's gonna want payment."

"Bro. Like you don't want to fuck her every fucking hour of the day, anyway." Munroe punches Slasher's shoulder before they set to work painting our faces.

Slasher paints mine all black, even my fucking top lip, with red covering my lower lip and a red wavy line coming from each corner.

It's feels tight and sticky, and I'm so fucking tempted to scratch the stuff off, but I don't, and in the end, Slasher and Munroe have their faces painted the same as me too.

"Did you pre-plan this?" I point to my face, and then theirs, and Munroe nods. "That was Tido's idea. As long as we stay apart, we can recognize each other, but no one will recognize us."

"Also, the black is a good disguise, don't you think? I found a picture online and copied it." Slasher holds up his phone to show me the picture and I try to raise a brow, but the fucking thing is stuck in place by the sticky paint.

"It's actually concerning that you're so into this. I'm second guessing making you my second."

That wins me a weird-looking smirk from Slasher and I realize he can't fucking move his cheeks.

Jesus, I hope this works because I really want to tease him about his makeup skills later.

Getting back in our cars, Munroe parks his just near the corner of the street we are on, while Slasher and I take ours closer into the fucking lion's den.

The street where the house sits is lined with more cars than before, and I can see that the people in attendance aren't just Reapers, which will make it easier for us to go unnoticed.

Slasher parks his car about halfway up the road, but I continue on, trying to get as close as I can.

When I find a spot, I leave the car unlocked and the keys in it, and head toward the driveway that has people spilling into it dressed in costumes, masks and face paint.

My nerves pick up again and I let them come, needing them to fuel my determination, because I have no fucking idea what I'm about to walk into.

Hang on a bit longer, Princess. I'm not leaving without you.

15

Zoe

"*I* *t's an honor to get picked.*"

Irina's words from two weeks ago still echo through my mind. Even when I'm asleep, they creep into my dreams. They're always present, and I know it's because there's a deeper meaning to them. Something my subconscious has picked up on, but that I haven't deciphered yet.

Or maybe it's just because she's with me day and night. Since the prospects made their picks for tonight's Brawl, Irina and I haven't stayed at the mold infested house the Reapers call home. Instead, she moved us into another house which doesn't run out of hot water, and isn't dank and dirty. In fact, it's clean, spacious, and reminds me so much of the house I grew up in.

"All yours," Irina says. She comes strutting out of the bathroom without a stitch of clothing covering her naked body. "Don't rush it. We have plenty of time." The last part is added when she notices me eyeing the timer on the flatscreen TV in the bedroom.

I take my time soaking in the large tub. It's big enough that I can stretch my legs without touching the edge. I moan in appreciation as the scorching water soothes my limbs, making me feel relaxed, like only a bath can.

My head is resting against the edge, and when I close my eyes, I can almost imagine I'm anywhere but here. Or that I had better company... ha! Irina isn't company, she's my new warden.

I haven't seen Gunner since Irina told him he wasn't allowed to see me, and that was almost a week ago. Of course, he didn't take that well. But when Rusty showed up with some of the other Reapers in tow, he relented and left while I watched from the bedroom.

While I've been forced to spend more time with the woman my dad picked over his family, I've been working overtime trying to find something—anything—likable about her. The best I got is that she doesn't smell and has nice teeth.

Sure, I could mention that she's been nothing but kind, even making sure I eat a healthy meal three times a day. But that's exactly why I don't trust her. There are cracks in her armor, glimpses where I see her behavior for the mission it really is.

I just wish I fucking knew what she's cooking...

Tonight, I'll find out one way or another, I'm sure of it. It's Devil's Night, or Mischief Night, as some call it, and I have a strong feeling that it's going to be worse than what I'm imagining. I can feel the foreboding in every fiber of my being.

With a sigh, I begin to wash my hair, finishing off with the lemon scented conditioner on the edge. Despite knowing I shouldn't, I lavish enough for three turns into my hair. No matter how many times I've used it, I feel like I can still smell the stink from the Reaper house all over me.

Although I know it's all in my head, I can't get rid of it. My mental berating and pep talks do nothing to alleviate it.

When I'm done, I towel dry my hair and gather the long locks in two braids. Then I get dressed in the outfit Irina gave me. It's a ridiculous French Maid costume, which includes a white petticoat, and thigh-high fishnet stockings.

The neckline is so low I'm worried my tits will fall out if I move too quickly. Then again, since I haven't been given any underwear, it's clearly meant to showcase my most private areas.

I don't bother looking in the mirror before I exit the bathroom, almost walking right into Irina. "Sorry," I mumble, like it's my fault. Which it wasn't since she was almost right in front of the door.

"Don't worry," she sing-songs as she corrects the latex halter top she's wearing. "Are you ready for me to do your makeup?"

As I take in her already made-up face, I just nod and dutifully follow her to the kitchen, where all her makeup is already laid out on the table.

"So are you excited for tonight?" Irina asks as she hands me a headband. "I bet you are. I remember my first Devil's Night Brawl. But a girl never forgets her first, does she?" She shoots me a wink.

"I guess," I half-heartedly answer her.

After instructing me to tip my head back and close my eyes, she carries on her tale of reminiscence. "You're lucky you get to see the Brawl now and not back before the Reapers were this big. In those days, the women never got any drugs, so they weren't suffering withdrawals on top of everything else."

"Really?" I force myself to say.

I get the urge to open my eyes and watch her when I feel a wet makeup brush against my skin. But I fight it.

"Oh, yeah. Now everyone's hopped up on one thing or another. Even those who didn't want to get forced on them."

As soon as she says that, I'm reminded of the girl who got her teeth removed. She seemed... well, they all fucking looked and acted like they were on a trip all the time. But there was just something about her that made it seem out of character. Now I'm wondering if she was forced to take whatever was handed to her.

"But for the last two weeks, they've been forced off the drugs. And the Prospect who's chosen them has been in complete control of everything from their training, food, and all that stuff."

The more she explains, the sicker it all sounds. I'm not going to pretend I like those women, or that I'd ever go out of my way to help them. But that doesn't mean I wish this upon them—or anyone, really.

"So like..." I pause and swallow when my voice cracks. "What kind of training are they going through?"

Finally finished with what I assume is foundation, Irina moves on to my eyes. The featherlight touch of the brush tickles as she swipes it across my eyelids.

"Everyone does things differently," Irina says. Her tone sounds different, serious, with a hint of ominous undertone. "Some play mind-games. Others refuse them food. It really depends on the Prospect."

The words she spoke weeks ago sound in my mind like warning bells, but I push them down and focus on what she's saying now.

"When it was Noose's turn, he pretty much starved his girl. All he allowed her to eat was a carrot every other day."

I straighten in my chair. "How did she win if she was malnourished?"

Laughing, Irina explains, "The body and mind are capable of the impossible. Hey, weren't you going to study human behavior or some shit like that? You should know that nothing is impossible if you set your mind to it."

She's right. Oh, my fucking God! It's as though I'd forgotten that. Nothing is impossible if you just want it enough. Since Chris died, I've been treating my situation like it was a done deal. But nothing is set in fucking stone. And I owe it to Chris and myself to get the hell away from the Reapers.

"So how many rounds is each fight?" I ask, desperate to get more info and see if I can use it to my advantage. Maybe I can sneak away while everyone else watches the fights. "Or is it just until one of them dies?" Since Irina is still busy working on my makeup, I do my best not to cringe at my callous words.

"It depends," she answers. "Rusty can stop the fight if he wants to. But there's never been a need to do it. It's not like there's a shortage of crack whores and desperate women."

Before I can come up with another question that doesn't sound like I'm digging, Irina tells me to sit completely still.

Then I feel something wet being painted on my lips and, much to my horror, outside the seams.

The more I focus on the feeling of what she's doing, the more certain I am that she isn't giving me a traditional look. With my luck, she's probably exaggerating or giving me a clown makeover.

I kind of hate that I care because it shouldn't matter what I look like. But it's not my vanity that's stirring, it's worry. The more I stand out, the harder it would be to slip away unnoticed.

"There!" Irina finally announces after what feels like an eternity. "Go have a look in the bathroom mirror."

As soon as I make it to the bathroom and look at my reflection, I gasp. "What the hell?"

"Right? It looks fucking awesome," Irina says, misreading my stunned expression.

I blink once, twice... but the Halloween inspired makeup doesn't go away. My face is painted white, and with the dark contouring she's added, I look even thinner than I've become. My lips are blood-red, completing the macabre look . She's added some black at the corners of my mouth, so when I open wide, it looks like my lips are cracking.

The same cracking effect is made on my forehead and under one eye. There's even some black painted to look like stitches. It's eye-catching and macabre, yet I can't deny Irina knew what she was doing.

"So what do you think?" she asks.

At the same time, I say, "Am I an undead maid?"

She laughs and hip bumps me like we're friends, which we're not. "I don't know. You can be whatever you want, I just think—"

Before Irina can finish talking, the room goes dark. With the lights out, it's so dark I can't see anything at all.

"The hell—"

"Shh!" Irina snaps. There's a lilt of fear to her tone, which instantly puts me on edge.

We hold our breaths and wait for what feels like an eternity. Then I feel the familiar metal around my wrist and hear the click as Irina puts the handcuffs into place. It's just like what she's done every night. Cuffing us together so I can't go anywhere without her.

"What did you do?" Irina hisses. "What the fuck did you do, Zoe?"

Her questions baffle me. "Me? I didn't do any-fuck-ing-thing," I hiss back.

Not only is it a stupid accusation, it's an impossibility. The only times Irina's given me any privacy is when one of us has been in the bathroom. But even then, I was never alone. Not really. The Reapers guarding us might stay out of sight, but they're there. Silently watching us and guarding the exits.

"Then who—"

I stiffen as Irina lets out a blood-curdling scream that threatens to bust my eardrums.

"Irina?" I whimper.

She screams again and again. Until her voice is raw, barely more than a whisper. Then there's a sudden weight added to the handcuff like she's pulling on it. The pressure forces me to my knees, and I use my free hand to search for her.

When she stops screaming, there are footsteps. They sound like they're... fuck. I can't tell where they're coming from or where they're going.

Fuck.

"Irina?"

Who would... Oh, my God. It's them. The Kings. They've come for me.

"I'm in here," I scream at the top of my lungs. "Help. I can't... I can't get out."

My hand lands in a warm, wet, and sticky substance, and I immediately cringe back from it. Then I force my hand back into it, following the trail until it connects with...

"Irina," I breathe.

As my eyes grow used to the heavy, all-consuming darkness I can almost make out the shape of her body. If what I'm seeing is to be trusted, she's lying completely still... too still.

"Irina?" She doesn't stir.

Shuffling around, I reach for her hand that's cuffed to mine. I'm not sure exactly what I'm searching for, or what I think I can do. I don't have the fucking key. And in the darkness there's no way I'd be able to find the key.

As I call out for help again, cackles echo through the house.

"It wants help."

I turn my head in the direction of the distorted voice.

"It doesn't even want to help itself."

This time it comes from another direction.

> *Trick or treat*
> *Tonight you'll get beat*
> *Trick or treat*
> *Tonight you'll feel the heat*
> *Trick or treat*
> *Trick or treat*
> *Trick or treat*

As the voices sing the words over and over, I feel like I'm losing my grip on reality, and my fucking sanity. What the hell is going on?

> *Trick or treat*
> *Tonight you'll get beat*
> *Trick or treat*
> *Tonight you'll feel the heat*
> *Trick or treat*
> *Trick or treat*
> *Trick or treat*

When there's a pause in the singing or chanting or whatever the fuck it is, I hear a clanking sound from something landing on the bathroom tiles.

I use my free hand to search for it, and it doesn't take long before my hand closes around a wooden handle. I let my fingers dance across the handle, all the way to... fuck. It feels like an... ax?

"Freedom must be earned."

The voices pick up volume, urging me to get free, and berating me for being so slow.

"It doesn't know how to get free."

"It's scared."

"It should hurry."

"It's not worthy."

My stomach churns at the thought of what it'll take to free myself from Irina's limp body. I know what must be done, but that doesn't mean I'm reveling in the thought.

Counting backward from ten, I mentally steel myself. Then I use one hand to move Irina's wrist so it's outstretched, while I clutch the ax with the other.

Three...

Two...

One...

I swing the ax, bringing it down on what I think is her wrist.

The sounds that follow are sickening, and I know they'll stick with me for a very long time—if not forever. Yet, I don't stop. I keep swinging until I can pull my hand away without resistance.

I try very hard not to think about what I've just done, and instead, I clutch the ax against my chest as I crawl out of the bathroom and toward the front door.

The voices haven't spoken up since I hacked off Irina's hand... or part of her arm. I don't want to examine how much I took, and I'm doing my best to pretend I can't feel the weight of it as I awkwardly make my way across the house while crawling.

When I reach the door I slowly stand, unsure of what to expect since it's already wide open. I hold my breath and listen as intently as I can, but I don't hear anyone.

The area is lit up by wooden torches that are placed in a circle. Something's burning in the middle, but I don't stick around long enough to see what it is.

I don't make it far before the hammering of my heart is drowned out by the loud roar of bikes revving their engines. "Fuck!" I scream, dropping the ax as I veer to the right.

With the sense of urgency spurring me on, I don't pay attention to my surroundings as I pump my arms, running as fast as I can. My lack of focus costs me when I trip over a branch and crash to the ground.

Getting back up, I finally take a moment to look around while I try to get my breathing under control. I'm heaving and my lungs feel like they're on fire. I'm too unfit to run for my life. Months of being holed up, and only getting decent meals for the last two weeks, has left me weak.

As I look over the crops on either side of me, I get flash-backs of some of the horror movies I used to enjoy watching on Halloween. I'm sure some of them involved teens getting hacked to fucking bits in a field of crops.

That's *not* going to be me. Nope.

The problem with running aimlessly is that I have no idea where I am. I've been turned around, and I don't even know what direction I came from.

Fuck.

I didn't even know I was near... crop fields.

When Irina drove us to the house, I was blindfolded, and the journey took hours. I don't fucking know if she drove in circles to mess with me, or if we're no longer in the same area.

Double fuck.

Trick or treat
Tonight you'll get beat
Trick or treat
Tonight you'll feel the heat
Trick or treat
Trick or treat
Trick or treat

The voices I haven't heard since... since... nope, not thinking about what I did in that bathroom either. And I'm definitely not looking down. Just hell to the fucking no.

"What do you want from me?" I scream into the darkness.

I know it's stupid. I should focus on getting the hell out of here, and not let stupid, distorted voices bait me.

Taking my own advice, I run into the field closest to me. I try my best to look where I'm running since I'm only wearing stockings that aren't doing a fucking thing to protect the soles of my feet.

> *Trick or treat*
> *Tonight you'll get beat*
> *Trick or treat*
> *Tonight you'll feel the heat*
> *Trick or treat*
> *Trick or treat*
> *Trick or treat*

The rustling nearby could be from the wind, but with the voices following, I'm not willing to bet on it. So I pump my arms even faster, not even stopping as I put more distance between myself and whoever is following me.

As I reach the end of the field, a startled scream is ripped from me as a spotlight—or farm light—casts its unforgiving and harsh light on me, momentarily blinding me.

"There she is. Our main entertainment of the evening." I recognize Rusty's voice. "You all have your betting slips and can cash them in after the last Brawl is over."

Arms close around me, pulling me forward until I'm thrown into the middle of a ring with people gathered around it.

"Let me go!" I scream. I kick, claw, and spit at the men holding me down, but it's no fucking use.

In my desperate attempts at getting free, I unintentionally look down and see the limb attached to the other end of the handcuff. It's a grotesque sight, especially since I took more than the hand, and I wish I hadn't seen it at all.

The fingers are... and there's... some of the nails are missing... no. No. Don't think about it. Just look away and pretend it isn't there.

As the hands holding me haul me to my feet and spin me around, I come face-to-face with Gunner.

"Have you missed me, Sugar?" He waggles his eyebrows suggestively. "I've fucking missed you. I can't wait to fuck you again tonight."

"But... w-what?" I can't make sense of what's happening.

Ignoring my question, Gunner moves closer and reaches for my hand with the handcuff. He pulls a key from his jeans pocket and unlocks it. The chopped off limb at the other end falls to the ground with a sickening thud.

"Let me go," I demand, my voice sounding strong. "Irina said I wasn't going to fight, and—"

Gunner cuts me off with an eerie laugh. "No," he corrects. "She said you weren't fighting them." He gestures toward a heap of bodies at the other end of the ring.

Doubling over, I retch and gag as I realize it's the bodies of the women who lost their fight tonight.

"You'll still be fighting," Gunner prattles on. "Why do you think we've treated you so nice the last few weeks? No one wants to see the VP's Old Lady lose because she's hungry. But now that you've had a taste of the good life, you should be able to put on a show."

I feel the color drain from my face, and I feel dizzy as I right myself too quickly. Fuck. I knew Irina wasn't my friend, and I always suspected there was more going on. But this... fucking fuck. I fell for it when she said I didn't have to fight.

"It's an honor to get picked."

Her words from weeks ago sound in my head again, and now I finally understand why I haven't been able to shake them. She was telling me, it was there, and I didn't see it—or rather hear it for what it was.

"Why? You're already VP so you don't need me to fight for you."

Gunner moves his hand to cup my face. "Sweet, innocent, naïve, Zoe," he croons. "The women were never fighting for the prospects to become members. That was something Irina made up for your benefit. The truth is, they fight because we want them to, and because its good entertainment."

I really should have fucking seen that coming. The Reapers are sick enough to take women in and treat them... well, not nice... but just to use them as lambs for slaughter.

Rolling my shoulders back, I meet his gaze head on. "Who am I fighting?"

Some of the amusement falls from his face, which I take as a win. A nonconsequential one, but it still counts.

"Me!"

Irina's voice rings out as she struts across the ring.

The surprise I know I should feel never registers. It's not like I suspected that she was alive and well, obviously in on the elaborate scheme to trick me. I'm just so far beyond exhausted and overwhelmed that nothing feels real anymore.

I look down at the hand I'd been content on ignoring, and before I can stop myself, I ask, "Who?" It's not a full sentence, but the one word is all I can manage.

"Mani," Gunner chuckles. "Adam was all too happy offering her up when we asked."

Rusty's enhanced voice sounds just as Gunner opens his mouth as though he had more to say. "Let's get to it!"

"Don't let me down, Sugar," Gunner says with a wink. Then I watch as he walks to where Rusty, Noose, and Cat are gathered.

"For the last fight, it's our very own Mama versus our new VP's Old Lady—"

A fight breaks out to the left of me, interrupting Rusty.

"No!" my dad bellows. "You fucking promised me, Rusty. And Irina... you said she was safe, and that—"

He's cut off by a punch to the jaw. Several Reapers jump him, kicking, punching, and even spitting at him.

"I lied," Irina replies smugly, doing a little twirl. "Just like when I said I loved you."

The moment those words leave her lips, my dad stops fighting. My heart aches for him, but at the same time, I'm sickened by him.

He threw everything away to be with this woman. Me. Leslie. Mom... we were all casualties in his... fuck. I don't even fucking know.

"What I really should have said was that I loved your money. But that well has dried up, hasn't it, Brian? Your beloved daughter is the one with all the dough."

I give Irina a scathing look. Not because of how she's treating my dad, because a sick part of me is almost gleeful at the fact they're turning on him. Yet another part is enraged that my mom and Leslie died for nothing.

"I'll fucking kill you!" I scream at Irina, who just laughs.

"Aww, coming to daddy's rescue?" she taunts, and some of the Reapers chuckle.

Turning my head, I look at dad as Noose and another Reaper drag him over to Rusty. "No," I say, forcefully. "For being so fucking basic it's disappointing. Money... really?"

I don't know where the words are coming from or why they keep coming.

"I expected more from you, Irina. Going after a married man with a family for money is nothing more than a common gold digger. You're not even worthy of being the Mama."

The crowd all inhales sharply as I stop talking. That tells me I've acted differently than what they expected, and I can only hope that's good.

"Basic?" Irina laughs, but it's a forced sound. "I'll show you fucking basic when I fuck up your pretty face." She pulls a knife from behind her back and makes a big show of licking the blade.

Despite the trepidation I feel, I roll my eyes. "Whatever you say."

"Well, it looks like our women are hungry to fight for glory," Rusty shouts. "And what are the Reapers if not accommodating? Let's give Zoe a weapon to even the fight."

Turning my head, I watch him get up, kick my dad as he passes him and makes his way over to me. "Here you go," Rusty says. I take the pocketknife from his outstretched hand.

"She's your sister," I hiss, unexplainably feeling outrage that he's arming me in a fight against his own flesh and fucking blood.

Rusty just shrugs. "She could take you with both her arms tied behind her back. This is just for show so make it a good one."

On his way back, he kicks my dad again, and this time I swear I hear bones break.

"S-she's my d-daughter," dad cries out in pain. "Let me take her place."

I should feel relieved he's finally remembering who I am to him, and that he's meant to protect me, but I don't. All I can muster up is pity as I look at the man who's responsible for everything bad that's happened to me.

How I fucking wish I could get inside his head and figure out what went wrong. If he wasn't happy with mom, why not just divorce her? What fucking drives a man to want his wife dead? In this case, it seems the answer is greed and orgasms.

"What do you say, Zoe?" Rusty's question pulls me from my thoughts. "Do you want your old man to fight in your place?"

I should say yes, shouldn't I? Take the way out I'm being offered and see him get his comeuppance.

"No," I say, fisting the pocketknife harder. "I don't want anything from him." With those words, I turn my back on them and face Irina.

"Let's dance," she sing-songs.

The Reapers begin to chant the creepy Trick or Treat shit again, though without distorting their voices this time.

Irina does another fucking twirl before skipping toward me, closing the distance between us. Her fist shoots out, but I manage to duck just in time to avoid the punch.

"Ooh, baby got moves," she croons.

I'm not quick enough to move out of the way of her leg, and she kicks me right in the stomach. My air comes out in an "oof" and I double over, wheezing.

Taking my eyes off of her even for a split second turns deadly when she kicks me again, sending me crashing to my knees.

"This is hardly any fun," she pouts. "Get back up and try again. I promise to stand still."

Although I know I'm playing into her hand, I swing my arms, but she dodges me like she knows my move before I can carry it out.

After dodging another punch I tried to land, she retaliates with one to my face. My head snaps to the side from the impact, and I feel blood seeping from my nose. Motherfucker it hurts. Tears gather in my eyes, and I angrily swipe them away, refusing to even let one fall.

"I drew first blood," she cackles.

I'm stunned as she swipes a finger below my nose. She holds it up as if to show the audience the proof, and then she fucking licks it clean.

My limbs feel too heavy to move, and I've dropped the fucking knife. I don't know when or where, only that it's a monumental task to even stay on my feet. My head feels heavy, my movements sluggish, and...

"Down you go," Irina gleefully announces as she kicks me down again.

My fingers dig into the dirt, and I don't waste any time in throwing some into her face. When she staggers back and blinks rapidly, I use some of my last strength to get back up.

This time I go on the offensive. I rush her, flailing my arms and raining down blows on her until she screams. But it's not in pain, it's like a fucking war cry of epic proportions.

"Yes! That's it, Zoe. Fight for your fucking life."

I don't need her words when that's exactly what I'm doing. But unlike her, I don't have the strength or breath to talk while fighting.

As I continue coming at her, Irina backs up. I'm so blinded by my hate for this woman that all I see is her face in a haze of red.

"I hate you!" I scream.

Punch.

Punch.

"I fucking hate you."

Irina successfully uses her arms to parry most of my punches, but it still feels good to let my anger out.

She takes another step back, and I blindly follow.

Then another.

And... as I kick out at her, she moves to the side. I don't have time to right myself as the edge comes into view.

There's no stopping my momentum as I fall, rolling down the hill. I immediately wrap my arms protectively around my head, but I still feel the impact of the branches and stones.

16

Grayson

Seething anger vibrates through my veins at what I'm seeing. I can't believe my fucking eyes, and I can tell as I glance at my club brothers spread out around the fucking weird arena the Reapers have set up, that they too have seen the ghost.

Gunner.

He's not fucking dead.

He's alive and fucking well, and apparently the new VP of the Reapers.

Now, everything fucking makes sense.

His behavior leading up to his fucking fake death. The growing anger he had with not just me but Rocco. And fuck, his obsession over my princess, who he declared as his Old Lady.

Like fuck!

Perhaps the only thing keeping my feet in place from going off the rails right now is seeing Zoe for the first fucking time in nearly three fucking months.

Her face has been painted to suit the theme of the night, so I can't get a good read on her health, but fuck, she is skinnier than the last time I saw her. There's barely any meat on her bones, and as she tries to fight Rusty Hunt's lunatic sister, I can see how weakened she is.

Have they even been feeding her?

My top lip curls and my fists ball as my chest heaves with boiling anger. My monster is here. He wants to be unleashed, and fuck I want to set him free, but even he knows now isn't the right time.

For once, I need to think with my head.

Getting Zoe out of here is top priority.

My men all know what they have to do. Their job is the same as mine. Whoever can get Zoe out, hopefully unnoticed, although I don't know fucking how, then they do that. Others can try to run interference if needed, but the Kings are here tonight to rescue our princess, and nothing will stop that from happening.

Instinctively I step forward when Rusty's sister kicks Zoe down, the sinister grin on her face doing nothing to calm my beast.

Brian is still balled up on the ground where the Reapers left him. I'm not sure why he doesn't stand the fuck up and fight for his daughter, but Zoe declared she didn't want anything from him, and trying to piece things together from what was said before the fight started, I get the feeling Brian was lured in by the Reapers' Mama.

Fuck. Poor Zoe. This shit will kill her on the inside. I just know it.

My heart leaps with anticipation as Zoe tosses a handful of dirt in Irina's face before launching her bony frame from the ground and flailing on her opponent.

"I hate you!" Zoe screams before swinging another couple of punches. "I fucking hate you!"

Rusty's sister manages to parry most of Zoe's punches, and as she steps back and Zoe follows, consumed by rage, it looks like the Reapers' Mama is leading my princess some-where.

My eyes catch on Slasher's who's closer to where Hunt's sister is, and we use our fucking eyes to communicate, and somehow, it works. Slasher gives the slightest nod and starts to weave through the crowd, to get closer.

Suspecting something is up, I ease back out of the thick of the crowd, and make my way toward the treeline closest to Irina.

It wouldn't surprise me if they have some Reapers on standby near that treeline to grab Zoe and haul her off.

I can't fucking let that happen. If they take her away again, I may never get her back.

The crowd cheers as something happens, and just as I reach the treeline which I now see lines a steep embankment, I hear a scream before a body falls over the edge and disappears into the darkness.

I'm already rushing down, hoping no one fucking spotted me, while trying to be as quiet as possible.

Twigs snap and I hear a faint thud, but with the roar of the crowd at the top of the hill, I'm pretty fucking certain they can't hear what's going on down here.

My heart thrashes in my chest as I force my eyes to fucking acclimate to the sudden darkness, and I hurry in the direction I heard the thud.

Chants up on the hill float into the night air. Some are chanting "Gunner. Gunner. Gunner." While others are chanting, "Trick or Treat. Trick or Treat."

Fuck.

I get the feeling this isn't over.

Up ahead, my eyes just make out a lumpy form on the ground, and fuck I hope it's my princess and not a fucking log.

I hurry forward, seeing the silhouette of a figure closing in from the other side.

No.

My knife is in my hand a second later, and as I near the form on the ground, the figure puts his hands up.

"Gray. It's me."

Fuck.

I breathe out a fucking sigh of relief at hearing Slasher's whisper before we both come to stop at the figure sprawled on the ground.

There she is.

My princess.

"Trick or Treat, Sugar! It's time to fuck!"

The harsh tone of my former best friend sounds around us coming from speakers somewhere in the dark and we both lurch around, ready to fucking defend what we came here for.

The buzz of a phone silently ringing gains Slasher's attention, and he makes sure the screen brightness is down before he answers it.

Ignoring him, I spin back to Zoe and drop to my knees, my fucking hands trembling as I reach out to touch her.

"Princess?"

She doesn't rouse at my whisper, nor does she react to my touch and I press my palm to her painted face which looks like she has nothing but black fucking pits for eyes in this light.

"Fuck. We gotta get her out of here now." Slasher growls, and I glance up at him. "That was Munroe. The next part of the night is starting and Zoe is Gunner's prey. He's coming after her."

"Fuck." I hiss, not bothering to even check if Zoe has a pulse. I sweep her up in my arms and haul ass deeper into the trees.

"Stretch and Munroe are going to run interference. A distraction." Slasher mutters on my heels. "There's a stream up ahead. It leads back toward the main road. Let's follow that and I'll get someone to pick us up."

I grunt in agreement, and do nothing but focus on getting my princess out of there as she bounces lifelessly in my arms as we run through the dark.

We manage to find the stream Slasher referenced, and I notice he's using his phone map to guide us.

The cheering up on the hill fades the further we get, but now and then Gunner's voice sounds on the speakers and I'm fucking glad Zoe can't hear his words. I just know they would terrorize her.

"Are you ready for me, Sugar? Tonight I'm going to rail your ass so hard your shit will be leaking out for a week."

"Fuck! Give me permission to hunt him now." Slasher snarls, skidding to a stop, and I shake my head.

"Not now. Don't forget our mission." I snap, and Slasher's eyes fall to my face and then to Zoe's slack form in my arms. "He did all of this. He's the reason my brother is dead."

Fuck. I know this now too, but we can't let our emotions get caught up. Not tonight.

"Head in the game," I snap. "I need my VP here tonight. Revenge will come. I promise you that. But not tonight."

Thank fuck Slasher nods, gesturing for us to keep going as Gunner's taunts keep coming but thankfully start getting quieter the more distance we put between us.

A loud explosion sounds back up on the hill, and then fireworks start erupting. Slasher and I don't stop running, but the distraction Munroe and Stretch have made where the Reapers are helps us see a little better as the reds and greens of the fireworks filter through the trees.

Gunner's taunting has stopped, and yelling takes its place up on the hill, and I hope like fucking hell my men are alright.

Following the stream, the trees start to thin and the bank starts to narrow as the crop fields pop up on either side of us. Up ahead is an old bridge, and a moment later, the taillights of a car pull up on it before two figures jump out.

"Hurry!"

Relief washes over me at hearing Munroe's voice, and some fucking how, my legs move faster as we near our escape.

Slasher half drags me up the embankment to get up on the road, and Stretch is standing with the back door open, his eyes trained back toward the Reapers' ruckus in the distance. I slide into the backseat with Zoe in my arms, and Slasher joins me on the other side, squeezing in with us.

As soon as Stretch and Munroe are back in the car, Munroe plants his foot on the accelerator and gets us the hell out of there.

We are all silent as we drive, like none of us are ready to believe we are safe just yet.

My eyes drop to my princess in my arms and with a shaky hand, I brush some dirt off her forehead, noting the graze on her temple and the scratches on her face.

"Is she okay?" Stretch asks, turning his head to glance at me from where he sits in the front.

"I don't know." I rasp, my voice scratchy as I drop my gaze to Zoe again, and my eyes lock on the rise and fall of her chest. "She's breathing."

Three audible sighs of relief fill the car, and finally, I let myself acknowledge that it's actually her in my arms. I have my princess back.

"Did the others get out?" Slasher asks whoever might know, and Munroe answers.

"Yeah. They are following behind us."

Slasher glances over his shoulder out the back window. "I didn't even notice them."

"They kept to the shadows just up the road while we waited on the bridge, ready to help attack if needed."

Slasher and I make eye contact then and he offers me a slight nod.

We are silently in agreement. Our men are good.

"Clubhouse or Dirty Diamonds?" Munroe asks as we speed up the freeway back toward Santa Cruz.

"Clubhouse. I want her to be surrounded by the familiarity of my apartment," I state before dragging my gaze from Zoe's face to Slasher's. "Call Alana. She needs to be there. I get the feeling Zoe's going to need her friend."

Slasher nods and does as I ask, and for the rest of the drive I drown everyone out.

I can't stop looking at her. I can't stop running my hand over her scraped knee, or watching her breathing for signs of it changing.

Three fucking months.

My fucking chest aches.

What the fuck have they put her through for three fucking months?

Guilt slams into me for not finding her sooner. Why the fuck didn't I do a better job?

Never fucking again will someone hurt what's mine.

Unbearable need to have her close consumes me, and I lift her higher in my arms while leaning closer and pressing my nose to the crook of her neck.

Big. Fucking. Mistake.

The scent I was searching for to calm my raging nerves is not fucking there, and I jerk back as my heart drops to my gut.

She doesn't smell like my princess anymore.

Suddenly, Zoe stiffens in my arms, her lids flying open before a blood-curdling scream rips from her lungs and she starts clawing at my face.

Grayson

"**D**on't fucking hurt her!" I yell over Zoe's screams as Slasher tries to pin her arms down to stop her from attacking my fucking face.

"I won't fucking hurt her!" Slasher yells back as the car swerves off the road a little, the rear fishtailing in the gravel.

"Keep the car on the fucking road!" I demand, this time to Munroe whose frantic eyes meet mine in the rearview mirror.

"Sorry," he mutters only just loud enough to hear, meanwhile Stretch leans through the center console to grab Zoe's flailing legs.

"Zoe!" I yell, trying to get her to register my voice over her screams, but it's like she's trapped in a nightmare and can't wake up.

Each time the car passes under a street lamp, I get a glimpse of her crazy eyes and her bared teeth as she snaps them when she takes a breath to restart her blood-curdling screams.

"Princess! Stop! It's me! Gray!"

It's no use. My voice booms in the small space, and yet, it doesn't even fucking register.

What the fuck have they done to her?

We all resign to the fact that she's not going to stop screaming and thrashing, so Slasher keeps her wrists in his grip, and Stretch keeps his arms wound around her knees, his body half hanging from the front seat, while I keep her as close as I can, my arms around her middle as the three of us try to stop her from hurting herself.

Munroe speeds off the highway and into Santa Cruz, barely slowing as he hits the suburban streets. When he starts thumping on the horn, I know we are close to the clubhouse, and he slows as Doug opens the gates to let us in.

The moment we pull to a stop, Alana, Rose and Beth come rushing out of the building but skid to a stop the moment Munroe opens his door to get out.

Zoe's screams float out into the night, shocking everyone, and I realize none of us were prepared to get Zoe back in any other version than how we saw her last.

What a bunch of fucking fools we are.

Munroe tugs my door open, his frantic eyes meeting mine as if to ask me what to do.

I don't fucking know.

I shuffle my ass off the seat while trying to keep my hold on Zoe and somehow manage to get my feet planted on the ground while still holding her in the car.

"Let go of her," I tell Slasher and Stretch, and while Stretch's eyes widen, Slasher curses.

"She's gonna go fucking crazy and claw the fuck outta you."

I shake my head. "Doesn't matter. I just have to get her up to my apartment," I grunt as Zoe rears back, nearly smashing the back of her head into my nose.

Zoe's screams are too loud for me to elaborate and tell the others that I'm hoping once Zoe sees the familiar space of the room we shared that she might calm down.

Slasher and Stretch take that moment to count down from three before they release their hold on her, and the moment they do, I'm back to trying to hold her to me while she thrashes wildly, kicking my shins, and reaching back to claw at my head.

Alana and the other Cruz Cunts lead the way, clearing the path on the way to my apartment so Zoe doesn't hurt herself on anything.

Navigating the stairs is fucking tricky with my princess reaching out to grab anything and everything within arms' reach as we go, and at one point as she somehow manages to press her fucking feet to the wall, she nearly pushes us back as she screams like a wild woman.

Slasher is the reason we don't end up in a heap at the bottom of the stairs, his hands firm as they press into my back, helping to keep me fucking upright.

The door to my fucking apartment finally comes into view, and Alana is there, opening it, her eyes filled with concern and tears streaming down her cheeks as she takes in the monster unleashing from her friend in my arms.

"Bedroom door!" I yell over Zoe's piercing shrieks, and Alana runs to it, throwing it open as I try to pry Zoe's grip from the doorjamb as I move to step inside my apartment.

"How the fuck is she so strong?" Slasher grunts from behind me, helping to peel Zoe's fingers from the timber frame. "There's nothing left of her."

I want to say it's just adrenaline. But what if it isn't? What if they've been forcing drugs into her and now she's hopped up on something?

Fuck. I don't want to even imagine that, yet it's something I need to consider as a possibility. After all, that's how the Reapers roll.

They use drugs to force submission, getting their women hooked and using it to control them. Fuck, there's a real possibility my princess will have to suffer through withdrawal.

That shit is brutal. I've seen it before and fuck, it's so cruel. I don't want Zoe to have to endure that.

Finally getting her fingers unclasped from the doorjamb, I lurch forward, hurrying and ignoring the kicks to my shins, managing to get Zoe through my bedroom door without her grabbing hold of something.

Once we are over the threshold, I release Zoe, letting her tumble onto our mattress, and like a scared stray cat, she scurries over the other side, tumbling to the floor as she presses herself into the furthest corner.

Fuck.

Her screams die off then, her blue eyes frantic as she trembles, locking eyes with me.

"No. No. No. No. No. No. No. No. No. No." She starts rambling, over and over, her head shaking like she is having trouble making sense of things, yet her eyes remain on mine.

"Zoe," I say quietly, lifting my hands in a calming gesture as I take a step further into my bedroom but the action causes my princess to try to scurry further away, even though she's pressed as far as she can go in the corner.

Her hands fist in her hair while her head continues to shake, and she pulls at the roots. "No. It's not real. Stop fucking with me."

"Zoe?" Alana's voice jerks Zoe's attention over my shoulder before I see Alana step up next to me in my periphery.

"W-what?" Zoe releases her hold on her hair and starts swiping at her eyes like she's trying to make them work. "No... no... They have her too. They have my Alana too. No. No." She shoots to her feet, still swiping at her eyes, her gaze dancing between me and Alana at my side.

"Zoe. It's alright—" Alana starts, but Zoe cuts her off with a loud shriek.

"GET THE FUCK AWAY FROM HER!"

Flinching back, I'm barely prepared for Zoe to run toward me like a protective lioness, her teeth bared, her fingers held like claws as she skirts over the bed and grabs for Alana.

Alana is too slow to react in time as well, and before we even know what the fuck is happening, Zoe has Alana pressed into the corner she just lurched from, her body in front of her friend as she holds her arms out as if to protect the Cruz Cunt from me.

"She is not yours!" Zoe hisses, and my eyes dart from my wild princess to Alana standing behind her, who shoots me wide eyes and shrugs.

"You're right, Princess. Alana isn't mine. You are."

It's meant to be reassuring, but it just provokes another scream from her lungs.

"Do not call me that! You have no right to call me that!" Zoe roars before a sob lurches from her throat. "Only *he* can call me that," she says quieter.

She fists her hair again, her whole body trembling. "You're not him."

I can't tell if she's talking to me or herself. Maybe both.

"Zoe. It's okay." Alana offers quietly from behind her, reaching up to place her hand on Zoe's shoulder.

The action causes Zoe to flinch, leaping around, her fists raised ready to fight, but the moment she sees Alana, her shoulders drop.

"I'm sorry they got you, too. I promise I won't let him... let any of them do those things to you."

"Things?" Alana asks, tilting her head as she plays along with Zoe's ramblings.

Zoe shakes her head like she can barely let herself think of "*those things*".

"I will kill you myself before I let you endure that."

Fuck.

Those words.

Zoe doesn't have to say anything else. Just the way she's acting, and the meaning behind the few words she's spoken tell me she has suffered unimaginable things while at the hands of the Reapers... And Gunner.

I'm going to fucking kill him.

It won't be quick.

I will draw it out for days. Weeks. Maybe even months. I'll make him wish he was never born, and just when he thinks I'm about to put him out of his misery, I'm going to let him heal and start all over again.

No one hurts what's *mine*.

Fucking. No. One.

"Zoe," I rasp, taking another step toward her and Alana, and she spins to face me, hissing like a feral cat. "It's me. Gray."

She shakes her head. "No. I know what you've done. I know you've given me something to make it seem like you're him..."

A sob lurches from her again as a pained expression contorts her face.

"Like who?" I ask, going along with the conversation to try to figure out what the fuck is going through her head.

"You're not him," she whimpers, her hand slapping her chest like it hurts there too. "You'll never be him."

"Who?" Alana whispers in Zoe's ear, and a round of tears spring from Zoe's eyes.

"Gray," Zoe whispers before spinning to face Alana. "Please tell me he wasn't in pain when he died. That it was quick, and he didn't suffer."

Alana's eyes go round, her gaze darting to me in question as my own eyes turn to slits.

"What do you mean?" Alana asks, returning her focus to Zoe. "Gray isn't dead, Zoe. He's right there."

She points in my direction, and a choked sob escapes Zoe as she shakes her head frantically, too.

"No. No. No. They must have drugged you, too. That's not Gray. That's Gunner."

Alana's face pales, her lips dropping open to form an O as she slowly drags her gaze from Zoe to me.

"No. Zo. You're mistaken. Gunner was the one that died. He's not here."

Nodding frantically, Zoe starts pacing in front of Alana, her gaze darting from me to the floor, to Alana, and back to repeat the process again.

"It's hard to believe I know." Zoe points to me, a look of sheer disgust morphing her expression. "You had us all fooled, didn't you?"

"Zoe, that's not Gunner—"

"Stop!" Zoe sneers at Alana, cutting her off. "He told me all about it one night when he held my head into his mattress with one hand and used his fucking beard ring to brand my shoulder blade as he raped me." She scoffs and all the air leaves my lungs. "The Reapers tracked down a long-lost sibling from his dad's side he didn't know about, kidnapped him and held him until the time was right," she laughs then, still shaking her head, but there's no humor to the sound, "and then killed him right before Gunner staged the explosion, leaving his long-lost sibling in his place to burn and leave his DNA. They were the same height and build and everything." Her eyes snap back to me. "Isn't that right?"

Fuck. She really thinks I'm Gunner. She thinks I'm actually dead. And she admitted that Gunner raped her.

Primal rage unfurls from me as I spin and slam my fist into the wall.

One hit isn't enough, so over and over I abuse the fucking plaster, not once feeling my skin split open as I hammer my way through to the other side.

Screams fill the air as rough hands grip my shoulders and arms, trying to force me to stop. I see nothing but Gunner's face as I lay into anything that gets in my way, and it's the slam of a door and the change of light in the room that drags me back to reality enough to see I'm no longer in my bedroom.

"Calm down, brother!" Slasher gets in my face, his hands on my upper arms, as he gives me a shake.

"You heard what she said. What he did to her," I snarl and Slasher's dark eyes pierce mine as he nods, before pressing his forehead to mine.

"I fucking heard. I fucking heard it all, but she needs you right now, man. You gotta stay calm."

"She doesn't even think I'm me!" I bellow, and he nods.

"Give her time. They've obviously been playing mind games with her. She doesn't know what's real and what isn't right now. But she will. You just gotta be patient."

My shoulders sag as I accept the truth he's telling me.

One minute, she was at the Reapers' Devil's Night, physically fighting against Irina, something Zoe isn't accustomed to having to do. Then she was tumbling down a fucking steep incline into a dark forest, only to wake up in a car with three dark shadows restraining her.

No wonder her reality is out of whack.

Drawing back from Slasher, I turn to see my apartment filled with crying Cruz Cunts and my men looking fucking forlorn. Everyone is here, and they just witnessed that.

"So Gunner is alive?" Rose dares to ask as my eyes pass by her, and I know her courage to ask while I'm so fucking highly strung stems from her fear of the man I thought was my best friend.

"Yes." I nod, addressing them all. Well, all but Alana and Zoe who are still shut away in my bedroom. "Gunner is still alive. It seems he was our rat, working with the Reapers the whole fucking time."

"But... Why? It doesn't make sense." Rose asks the question we all want to know the fucking answer to.

"I don't know the details yet, other than Gunner is now the Reapers' VP, and I'm pretty sure he claimed Zoe as his Old Lady."

Whimpers and gasps sound throughout the room, and I squeeze my lids shut for a moment, digging fucking deep for some calm so I don't fly off the handle again.

When my lids snap open, I find Munroe there with a wet towel, holding it out to me.

"Your face is still painted. No wonder she doesn't recognize you."

My brows shoot up.

I'd forgotten that my face is painted all black with red lips. I can't believe I forgot about that, even while looking at the paint smeared across her face, some washed away from her tears.

Taking the towel, I mutter a thanks and use it quickly to wipe off as much of the sticky dried paint as I can before returning to Zoe.

I march back to my bedroom door and open it slowly, not wanting to startle her. She's sitting on the end of the bed this time, her arms wrapped around Alana as they embrace each other and cry together.

"Zoe," I say quietly, and notice the way she stiffens in Alana's arms.

"Why does he sound so much like Gray?" she whimpers into the crook of Alana's neck. "Why won't he just let me mourn him in peace?"

Alana's tear-filled eyes lock with mine over Zoe's shoulder, right before she pulls back to wipe away Zoe's tears.

"I need you to listen to me, okay?"

Zoe nods, keeping her eyes locked on Alana, and I wonder if she even remembers that I've stepped back into the room.

"I know you're not going to believe what I tell you, but please try to remember I would never lie to you, and I'm trying to help."

Zoe nods again as Alana brushes back some wisps of blonde hair near Zoe's temple.

"You're not with the Reapers anymore." Alana starts, and Zoe stiffens, but Alana starts rubbing her hands up and down Zoe's upper arms, trying to keep her calm. "Tonight, the Kings came and got you back. I don't know the details of where you were or how they got you, because I wasn't there, but..." Alana's eyes flick to me again, before she cups each side of Zoe's face, making sure she is focused on her. "Whoever told you that Grayson died was lying to you."

For a moment, Alana studies Zoe's face as she lets her words sink in, and fuck, I wish I could see Zoe's face right now.

"No," Zoe finally whispers. "They showed me a newspaper article. It said something about the Kings no longer having a VP or something..." Zoe shakes her head. "I—"

"Well, technically, for a while there we didn't have a VP, but not because Gray died." Alana explains, and when Zoe doesn't speak, she continues. "Rocco got badly injured, so Gray had to be the acting President, and now... well Rocco's injuries left him unable to continue leading the club, so he stepped down and Grayson was sworn in as the new President of the Cruz Kings."

"W-what?" Zoe stutters. "H-he's not d-dead?"

Alana shakes her head, dropping her hold of Zoe's face and sitting back to look at me.

Then, slowly, Zoe's gaze follows, peering over her shoulder to lock eyes with me.

"Princess."

Zoe flies up from the bed, pressing herself against the wall, not really like she's scared so much as shocked.

Her frantic blue eyes dart from me to Alana and back again, probably about ten fucking times. All I want to do is go to her and hold her in my arms, but she's still like a caged animal right now, and she's just been delivered some news that goes against what she thought was real for who knows how long.

Shit. Maybe she was glad to hear that I'd died.

"Princess," I say again, taking a step closer but she holds a hand up to stop me.

Her eyes drop to the floor where my feet stop moving toward her, and she scrubs at her eyes again like she's trying to wake them up or something.

Her eyes flick back up to mine, and her lips part as she takes a breath to speak.

"Gunner wouldn't have stopped just now," she whispers. "He would have disregarded my gesture and kept coming, ready to take what he wanted."

Fuck me. I can barely stand to hear those words fall from her lips and the only reason I'm not flipping out is because I know she's starting to see that it's really me here in front of her.

"I may be a prick, Princess, but I won't take anything from you unless you're willing to give it."

Her lashes flutter as my words register and then even through her tears, she juts up her chin. "Except if you hold a gun to my head."

"Fuck. No. Never again. You know I'm not that monster now. Right? You remember that time at Nirvana when I gave you my gun, and you held it to *my* head, right?"

She nods slowly. "No one else knows about Nirvana," she whispers, and I nod.

"No one but you," I rasp, taking another step closer.

"Oh, my god." A sob lurches from her lips. "It's really you." She slaps her hand over her mouth and a guttural cry escapes and she slides down the wall until her ass hits the floor, and not once does she take her eyes off me.

I rush toward her, falling to my knees, but before I get close enough, she flinches away, scooting closer to the corner again.

Shit.

"Zoe." Alana's voice registers then, and fuck, I forgot she was here. She just heard us speak about Nirvana. Come to think of it, I left the fucking door open. Everyone probably heard us bring up my secret place.

Alana stands from the bed and moves to squat in front of Zoe, handing her some tissues. "Gray won't hurt you, Zo."

My princess shakes her head, not speaking as her gaze darts between me and Alana again, and I can tell the whole situation is too much for her to handle right now.

Fuck, I'm barely handling it.

"You don't trust me?" I ask her, still on my knees near where she had been slumped before.

Zoe nods, but then shakes her head, only to rake her hands into her hair again to start tugging at the roots.

"Maybe we should sedate her. Let her sleep it off and give her mind time to heal a bit."

The suggestion comes from Rose just outside the door, and while it is a good idea, the way Zoe stiffens, and the sheer terror that contorts her expression tells me it's not a good idea to her.

"No. No." Zoe shakes her head, finally scurrying right back into the corner. "No. No. No."

"No sedation," I growl. "No drugs of any kind unless Zoe asks for them. And even then, I will be the only one dealing with that. No one is to come into my apartment until further notice. No one is to touch Zoe," I snap, even as Alana and Zoe hold hands, so I add. "With the exception of Alana."

My words have the desired effect, and work to ease Zoe's mind as I watch her shoulders relax and the fear fall away from her gaze.

"I won't lay a hand on you, Princess. Not if you don't want me to, but all I ask is that you stay here with me." My eyes flick to the bed we shared before the explosion and Reapers attack months ago. "I've been searching for you for months and I..." Shaking my head I take in a steadying breath before I admit, "I don't want to spend another moment without you, even if I need to stay on the other side of the room."

She regards me for a few long beats, and I think she's going to tell me to get out when her words say the opposite.

"Okay."

"Okay?" I ask to confirm, and she slowly nods.

We stare at each other for another few long moments before Alana's voice breaks our spell.

"Zoe, do you need a shower or anything? You have some scrapes on your legs and stuff."

Zoe's eyes drop to her legs as if only just noticing, but she shakes her head.

"I'm tired. I want to go to sleep."

Alana's gaze softens, and she nods. "Let's get you into bed then."

"Y-you won't go though? Right? Y-you'll stay with me?" She starts shaking her head again, her breathing increasing like she's terrified. "Please don't leave me."

Alana's concerned gaze darts to me and then back to Zoe as she rubs her arms in comfort. "If I'm not in this room with you, then I'm not far, okay? You only have to ask and Gray will message me and then I'll be right here. I promise."

Seeming to accept that, Zoe's head shaking turns into nods and her breathing slows down.

Alana moves to help Zoe stand then, and I excuse myself when she offers to help Zoe change out of whatever the fuck costume outfit the Reapers had her dressed in.

Back out in my living area, I ask everyone to leave, all except for Slasher. He remains with me while we sit on the couch, listening to Alana and Zoe move around in my bedroom.

Alana comes out and goes to my bathroom after a few minutes before returning with a handful of things and then closes herself back in with my princess again.

"You okay?"

I glance up to see Slasher regarding me, and I flop back on the couch, sighing.

"Not one fucking bit."

He nods. "Focus on the fact that she's back. I can man the fort for a few days so you two can... figure shit out."

"Thanks." I offer him a half smile, but then let the fucking thing drop away because the last thing I feel like fucking doing is smiling. "Prepare the men for the fact our war is about to be stepped up ten fold. And give Dante and Cain an update on what's happened. I want to meet with them this week."

Slasher nods, raking his hands through his long dark hair as he pulls it up into something that resembles how some of the Cruz Cunts wear their hair.

"The men are already prepared to walk through hell with you, brother. We are all ready to end this war once and for all."

He slaps a hand on my shoulder then, and I give him a thankful nod, just as my bedroom door opens, and Alana slips out.

"She really didn't want a shower, so I helped her clean up her legs a bit and washed her face and hands." Alana's gaze darts to Slasher before returning to me. "She's still skittish. I'm not sure how close she'll let you get."

Standing from the couch, I move to stand before Alana, and clasp her shoulder. "Like I said. I'll stay on the opposite side of the room if that's what she wants." When Alana nods, looking relieved, I thank her and watch her fall into Slasher's side as they leave my apartment, locking me in with my princess.

Turning, I stare at my bedroom door for too long, before I quickly use the bathroom to clean up a bit more, and then retrieve a bottle of water and a couple of energy bars from the kitchen.

When I open the door and step back inside my bedroom, the light is dim with only the faint glow from the bedside lamp, and Zoe's big blue eyes staring back at me.

"I brought you this. If you want it." I hold the water and bars out and gesture to the bedside table next to her. "I'll just leave them there."

She nods, watching my every step as she peeks up from the blankets, and once I've placed them on the table, I move back to stand near the door.

"Would you like me to stay over here?"

At first, I don't think she's going to respond, but then she shakes her head, and my gut twists.

"Do you want me to sleep out there?" I ask, pointing my thumb over my shoulder toward my door.

This time she shakes her head frantically.

"Can I sleep in the same bed as you as long as I don't touch you?"

She nods again, and this time I hear her sniffle, like she's crying again.

Fuck.

I nod and move through my room, leaving my clothes on but kicking off my boots and socks before I slowly ease under the blankets next to her.

I lie on my side to face her, and she does the same as she swipes at the tears still falling from her reddened eyes.

Fuck it's so good to lay eyes on her again, although now that her face paint has been removed, I can see just how sickly she looks. She's definitely not been fed well. Her cheekbones are too prominent now, and her eyes look almost sunken in.

There will be hell to pay for every single person who had a hand in doing this to my princess.

"Promise me this isn't a dream, and I'm not going to wake up back in that hell with those monsters?"

I drag my hand out of the blankets and hold up my little finger. "Are pinky promises still a thing?" I waggle it in front of her face and a small smile tugs at the corners of her cracked lips as she nods. "Well, then I pinky promise that you will never wake up in that hell ever again, Princess. I lost you once. I'll never let it happen again."

More tears burst from her eyes but I keep my pinky up, waggling it, hoping like hell she'll cross this small line to touch me.

Her blue eyes dart from my finger to my eyes and back again before she shifts and her hand appears with her pinky ready.

"You know you have to touch me for me to make the pinky promise to you, right?"

She nods. "But just that."

For the first time in what feels like fucking forever, the grin that tugs at my lips is real.

"Deal. Just our pinkies." I agree, and I let her close the distance between our fingers to let her have all the control.

The moment her fragile finger hooks with mine, my heart fucking stops and my breath gets trapped in my lungs for the sheer relief it is finally to touch her again, even in this small way.

I never want it to end, so I'm relieved when she doesn't pull away, and instead lets our hands come to rest on the mattress between us as her lids start to drift closed.

There are so many things I want to say to her. So many ways I want to show her how much I've missed her. So many ways I want to conjure up of making every Reaper pay.

There will be time for all of that.

Now, it's time to help my princess heal, if that's even possible.

18

Zoe

Stirring into a semblance of being awake, my eyelids feel too heavy to even attempt to open. Slowly, I still try to peel them back, only to shut them immediately as the stark light feels like it's burning my retinas.

"Princess!"

As I hear the word, I ignore my aching limbs and curl into a ball, making myself as small as possible. This is the first time in months I've heard that word. It doesn't bring about the comfort or wrap me in a feeling of being desired like it used to. Instead, it makes my heart beat faster as I wait to see what Gunner's going to do to me next.

"Are you awake, Princess?"

Wait, no. That's wrong. I heard that name a lot last night, or was it this morning? I don't know the exact time and it doesn't really matter.

The whimper I try hard to keep inside breaks free, and I mentally curse myself for making a sound.

"She needs something to eat. Come on, Zoe, try to sit up."

"Alana?" I croak.

The moment her name registers, I remember seeing her as well.

"Yes, it's me. Can you sit up for me?" she coos, sounding like she's talking to a wounded animal.

Ever so slowly, I stretch and open my eyes, coming face-to-face with the friend I've missed so much. "It's really you," I breathe. For a moment, I allow myself to be happy, but then I remember where we are and it quickly falls away. "How did they get you?"

Her brows furrow. "Get me? No one got me, girl. You're home, remember. You're back with us and you're safe."

Tears distort my vision, making her blurry. "No," I whisper. "That's what they want you to believe. Listen, Alana, you need to do what they say. Please don't fight them. They... they'll break you so much harder if you do. Promise me—"

"Enough!"

At the thunderous boom, I let out a squeak and bury my head in the sheets that smell nothing like the sickly and heavy scent of mold, sweat, and smoke I've gotten used to from Gunner's room. They also don't smell anything like the over-the-top lemon fragrance Irina prefers.

"No one will ever fucking touch you again, Princess. I fucking pinky promised."

Ignoring the urgency in his voice, I squeeze my eyes so hard that white dots dance behind my eyelids.

Wait... yes. Gray's alive, and it's him talking to me. He pinky promised that the Reapers would never get me again, and I believe that's a promise he'll keep with his life.

Fuck, why is my head so messed up? I go from thinking and believing one thing to another. My thoughts are murky, and I can't quite make sense of it, which might be why I'm so easily confused.

"Leave her alone," Alana snaps. "Sit your ass back down or get the hell out."

"Alana," he says, a warning clear in his voice.

"No," she hisses. "This isn't about you. Zoe needs time and you're going to fucking give it to her. Don't make me make you."

I whimper again, scared of what Gunner will do to her. "Don't make him angry," I beg. "Just..."

"Shh, it's okay, Zoe. Please try to sit up for me." I feel her hand on my arm, brushing up and down my skin in a soothing motion. "You need to get something to eat or you won't be able to wear my clothes anymore."

My lips twitch as though they're trying to form a smile but have forgotten how to.

"And I know you love my shorts, but right now you don't have the ass to fill them out. So how about we get some food in you, hmm?"

I don't understand how she can sound so calm, or why she isn't scared out of her mind. None of this makes sense at all.

While I try to sort through the myriad of thoughts and onslaught of emotions inside me, Alana strokes my hair.

"Do you remember that story I told you about my mom the last time we sat like this?" she asks, a smile lilting her tone.

"Y-yes."

God, it feels like another lifetime when I was lying on the floor in the storage space. Alana was stroking my hair, telling me about her horrible mom while I was panicking after Gray forced me to suck him off at Dirty Diamonds.

"I knew back then that you were stronger than you let on, Zoe. So I need you to use some of that strength now."

Without meaning to, I snort. I'm not strong at all. I haven't put up much of a fight, or even been strong enough to fight Gunner off. All I've done is play his game and let him use my body.

"You don't believe me?" Alana asks, reading my snort perfectly. "The fact you disagree just proves my point. You're still in there, Zoe. I just need you to break free of whatever is holding you down. Sit up and at least have something to drink."

As soon as she mentions it, I can feel how dry my throat is. And my head is pounding in that way that tells me I'm dehydrated.

I wordlessly try to pull myself up, but my entire body hurts so badly I can't do it without Alana's help. I don't need to ask for it. The moment she sees what I'm trying to do, she moves with me, and wraps her arms around me to assist.

Keeping my focus on her, I ignore the rustling and movement I hear. Despite knowing that we're not alone, I'm beginning to relax. For the first time in months, my brain doesn't sound alarm bells, and I don't feel as much on edge.

"Here," Alana says as she hands me a bottle of water.

Grateful, I take it from her outstretched hand and gulp most of it down before removing it from my mouth. "Thank you," I breathe.

She nods and hands me a roll with so much butter it glistens. My mouth salivates at the thought of butter, so I'm quick to take a bite, and before I know it, I've eaten three.

"Do you need the bathroom? A shower? Do you want some other clothes?" Alana fires questions at me so quickly I barely have time to process them.

I look down at myself, surprised to see I'm now wearing a tee that looks—and smells—like one of Gray's. It's way too big on my small frame, but it's hiding all the ugly scars I've collected.

Yawning, I scoot down the bed and lie down, making myself comfortable. "I'm good," I say.

Taking my time, I look around and I'm not sure I dare believe what I'm seeing. This isn't the room I was forced to share with Gunner. It looks like... Gray's. Well, mine and his. *Ours.*

My throat thickens, and swallowing becomes difficult as I really take in Alana's words from earlier. "Am I really free?" I ask, scared to hope.

"You're free, Princess."

This time I don't ignore the voice. I turn my head and look toward the corner where Gray's sitting. At least I'm almost positive it's him... a darker, unkempt, and wild version of him. But him all the same.

"Gray?" I squeak. I try to reach for him, but my arm just kind of flops back down. "But you're... they said... I read..."

I trail off as memories of attacking him, seeing him, and being held by him floods back. He stood up for me when Rose wanted to sedate me. And the pinky promise once again comes to the forefront of my mind.

My eyes grow heavier as I just lie there looking at him. His intense gaze burns into mine, and I'm unable to break the contact.

"It's... it's really you," I slur, almost delirious as I try to fight the need to sleep. "I'm... I'm..."

The last words I hear before sleep once again claims me are, "Sleep, Princess. I'll watch over you. I'm not going anywhere."

19

Zoe

Tears fall in a steady stream from my eyes as I startle awake.

The room is dark, but I immediately feel the presence of other people near me. "Alana? Gray?" I call out, though my voice cracks as sobs wreck through me.

Oh, God, was it a dream? Are they not really here?

"Gray?" I cry, desperately.

"Shh. I'm here, Princess."

His deep rasp soothes my frazzled nerves.

"Where?" I demand, reaching for him in the darkness. "Where are you?" My voice takes on a shrill quality as I repeat my question.

"You need to wake up, Princess."

The words make little sense since I'm already awake... aren't I?

"Come on, Zo. Open your eyes for me." As I peel my eyes open—for real this time—I look straight into his dark orbs. "Hi."

Despite the darkness of the room, which wasn't just in my dream, I can make his shape out perfectly. He's lying on his side, facing me. We're so close we almost touch—almost.

"Hi yourself," I reply, lamely.

I have so much bundled up inside of me, so much I want to say. Yet, words fail me as I really take in the fact that he's here. I'm here. And we're both somehow alive.

Needing to obliterate the nagging voice at the back of my head that tells me this isn't real, I tentatively reach out and ghost my fingers across his upper arm.

The moment our skin connects, I feel tingles spread from the tips of my fingers, all the way to my toes. It's an electrical current that I can't explain, but that I've only ever felt around him.

"What are you doing, Princess?" he asks, amused.

At his words, I realize I've stopped moving my fingers, and instead dug my nails into his skin. "Oops," I murmur. "Sorry."

He makes a strangled noise at the back of his throat, and his voice sounds hoarse as he says, "Don't ever fucking apologize for touching me."

"Okay," I agree.

Sadness makes my heart contract as I'm unable to return the sentiment. But it's more than that. I crave his touch as much as the idea terrifies me. I want to be cocooned by his big, strong arms so badly the absence of the motion hurts. But the thought of being caged in, held, and yes, even touched a little makes my breathing labored.

"What were you dreaming about?" Gray asks.

I get the sense that he knows I'm wrestling with something and wants to pull me out of my inner turmoil.

"Umm..." I begin, hesitantly. "It was like one of those dreams in a dream. I was dreaming that I woke up, but then I wasn't really awake... I think."

"You called my name," he says, sounding pleased. "You've done that a lot over the last few days."

"Days?" I ask, immediately clinging to the fact that I must have been out of it more than I thought.

Gray shifts, careful to keep the distance between us. "Yeah, Princess. It's been five days since I finally fucking found you."

Even though it's dark, I nod.

"I'm so fucking sorry it took me so long to find you." He pauses and takes a shuddering breath. "Zo, you need to know I've looked for you everywhere. I never stopped looking—"

Interrupting him, I say, "I know."

He doesn't need to explain himself, or give me excuses for why we've been apart for three fucking months.

Though my brain is slow at piecing things together, I feel like I'm getting there. That's not important. No, the poignant thing is that we're together again, and that, unlike me, Gray never gave up hope. Where I believed he was dead, he never entertained the idea that I was. So if anyone has a reason to apologize, it's me.

Without thinking, I lean closer to him. "I read a newspaper article," I say, urgency coating my words. "It said the Cruz Kings no longer had a VP. I never believed Gunner or Rusty before that article... but..."

"But once you read it, you thought I was dead," Gray interjects, saying the words I can't get across my lips.

"Yes," I squeak, feeling embarrassed I gave up on us so easily. "I'm sorry—"

"No!" Gray almost shouts. "You have nothing to be fucking sorry for, Princess. God, I'm the one who needs to apologize. Now... forever... me, and not you. Fuck, Zo. I lost you, and it was all because of someone I thought was my friend and a woman we let into our club."

Not able to talk about Gunner, I focus on the Rhiannon part of it all. "She didn't betray you," I say, needing him to know this.

"The hell she didn't," he says through clenched teeth. "She fucking took you from me."

I shake my head again. "No, Gray. I went with her willingly. That was my fault. I should have insisted on waiting for Cain, or... I don't know. Called Alana or something."

Gray grumbles something that sounds like him agreeing with my fuckup, which is fair.

"But Rhiannon was told the attacks on the club would stop if she handed me over," I say, determined to tell him the truth. "She didn't betray the club. Only me."

He lets out a humorless and wry chuckle. "Only you, Princess? Is that right? What about the fact I'd claimed you and that you're mine? Or the fact you're the fucking Mama and she handed you over to the enemy? Or just—"

"Gray, it wasn't like that—"

Ignoring me, he carries on. "If you don't want to take any of that into consideration, then there's the fact she broke the club code of conduct about loyalty. Spin it however you want, Princess. She was a fucking traitor."

As I open my mouth to reply, I sense movement from the floor. Before I can stop myself, I let out a high-pitched scream and roll off the bed, crouching with my back against the wall.

"Who's there?" I hiss. I ball my hands into fists, ready to take a swing at whoever just snuck up on us.

"Hey now, it's just me, girl," comes Alana's surprised voice.

Straightening, I let my arms fall to my side. "What the hell are you doing here?" I ask, surprised that Gray let her into our bedroom like this.

I remember talking to her... it must have been yesterday. But beyond that, everything's blurring together. I'm still so fucking tired that even talking to Gray is draining me.

"You wanted me here," Alana says, sounding a little hurt. "Don't you remember begging me not to go?"

As she mentions it, I kinda do recall something like that. I think. It's so hard to keep things straight, and the dream within a dream didn't help at all.

"Sorry," I mutter, feeling bad for upsetting her.

Alana makes a tsking sound. "Fuck off, Zoe. You have nothing to apologize for, and if you want me to leave, I'll go cuddle with Slasher instead of your floor."

Do I want to be alone with Gray? Yes... but also no. Fuck, I don't know what to do here. I know he'd never hurt me, that's not even a question. So why are my legs shaking and my teeth chattering so badly?

"I-it's okay," I stammer, which doesn't really say much.

Taking a deep breath, I try to center myself. When I woke up, I didn't know Gray and I weren't alone, and I was fine. So...

"Go find Slasher," I say, trying to sound like my insides aren't in knots. "We'll be fine."

Now that my eyes are completely used to the dark, it's easy to see as she stands up and moves around the bed toward me.

"For what it's worth, girl. Gray's right. Rhiannon betrayed us all, and not just you. Or do you think I haven't fucking missed you? Dreaded what..." She trails off and shakes her head. "All of us, Zoe. I'm glad she's fucking dead, because what she did was unforgivable."

I swallow, getting emotional as Alana's tone thickens. "I know," I whisper. Then I reach my hand out to her, and she's quick to pull me into a hug. "I've missed you so much."

Tears gather anew as we hug each other tight, like neither of us wants to let go.

It's not until she's left and I'm back on the bed that it occurs to me that Alana's touch didn't bother me, not at all. In fact, I welcomed it.

"Do you want something to eat or drink?" Gray asks, and a half-smile plays across my lips at the concern in his voice.

"Something to drink would be nice," I say.

Now that he's mentioned it, I do remember waking up every now and then, and both him and Alana had food and water ready. Hell, forcing me to accept it more often than not.

The mattress dips as he gets up, and I sit up, readily taking the water he returns with. While I slowly work my way through the bottle, he makes himself comfortable, and when I'm finally done, his breathing is deep, almost like he's asleep. I can't take my eyes off of him, scared that he'll disappear if I do.

It's still hard to wrap my head around the fact that I've gone months thinking he was dead, to now lying in bed with him. It all seems too good to be true, which is why it's so hard for me to believe it.

At the same time, it's not perfect—far from it. In an ideal world, I'd let him hold and comfort me. I want it badly. Almost more than I fear it.

"Gray," I whisper, unsure if he's still awake.

"Yes?"

As I lie down, I inhale deeply, preparing myself for what I want to try. "Can you... ahh..." Unsure of how to word it, I trail off.

"Anything, Princess," he rasps.

"I... I want you to touch me. But not like... I mean... what if... fuck." The words are harder than I thought, and I'm making a fucking mess of it. "Can you put your hand on my arm?" I ask, forcing the words out despite my voice cracking.

"Are you sure?" he asks, not commenting on how inelegantly I asked.

"Yes," I say. "I'm sure I want to try."

So slowly that I can follow the movement, Gray moves his hand to my elbow. His warm skin barely ghosts mine as he gauges my reaction. When I don't jump away from him or start screaming, which is what I'm assuming he's worried about, he gently wraps his hand around my upper arm.

"Like this?" he asks.

Closing my eyes, I savor the touch. Yes, my heart beats faster and sweat coats my forehead. But it's not enough to make me flinch away or ask him to stop.

"Just like that," I say almost dreamily as my lids grow heavier. "Please don't let go."

He's quiet for so long I almost fall asleep, and when he speaks, I'm not sure if it's real or another dream.

"I'm never fucking letting go again, Princess. Where you go, I go."

20

Grayson

It's been a week since I've had my princess back, but we haven't even scratched the surface on the trauma she's suffered since she was stolen from me.

She does little else but sleep, which doc says is her body and mind trying to heal and that it's a good sign, because she's likely been in flight mode for months and now that she's back, she finally feels safe enough to let herself sleep properly.

I don't know much about any of that stuff, but I guess it makes sense.

I'm not sure how to help her. At times she screams in her sleep, and it takes so much to drag her from the nightmare trapping her there.

I try not to touch her, scared she will flinch away from me again, but each time she rouses, she wants something more from me.

Sometimes she simply wants to hook our pinkies together again.

Sometimes she wants me to touch her arm.

Earlier when she woke briefly, she let me gently sweep the blonde strands that were plastered to her cheek with sweat back off her face.

I never knew I had such fucking patience in me, but I realize now that for Zoe, I'd change the skin covering my bones if that's what she wanted.

I can tell you, it's a weird fucking thing to feel.

Propping myself up on my elbow, I study my princess in the soft daylight filtering through from the edges of the blinds.

Her skin has a little more color in it now that Alana and I have managed to get her hydrated and get some nutritional food into her, but it's not enough to fill out her cheeks yet. I will make it my mission to plump up her skin again, even if I have to cook the food myself.

Actually, scratch that.

I'm not the best cook. I'll make sure the Cruz Cunts prepare a smorgasbord for her every fucking day if that's what it takes.

Shifting carefully so I don't disturb her, I gently peel back the sheet covering her to reveal her torso and the tops of her thighs.

My t-shirt she's been living in has ridden up a little to show the lilac triangle of the panties she's wearing, and I can't help it, I think of *him* there.

Gunner.

Zoe spoke of him raping her while searing the brand from his beard ring on her shoulder blade.

I can barely let myself imagine it, yet even when I fight it, images engulf my mind, tormenting me with her cries for help, her begs for him to stop, as he holds her pressed to his bed like she described.

He slid his cock into *my* princess.

He took something that she wasn't willing to give.

He inflicted pain that she didn't welcome.

He fucking touched what's *mine*.

My top lip starts fucking twitching with the snarl that wants to rip from me but I hold it in. I'm bottling all that shit up, because his day is coming, and I'm going to unleash fucking Armageddon on him, not for me, but for my princess.

Zoe.

Eddie fucking Gunn, watch your back. I'm fucking coming for you.

21

Zoe

For the first time in months, I don't feel scared or confused as I wake up. I know exactly where I am, just like I recognize the snores coming from the man next to me. The one who made me a pinky-promise, something I never thought I'd see him do.

I try to ignore the ache in my heart as I lazily stretch my limbs. But it's no use, there's no ignoring the heaviness I carry with me. I know it's something I have to learn to cope with eventually, I'd just hoped for... I don't know. A reprieve? More time?

Gah, even an eternity wouldn't be enough, that much I know. But what I don't know is how to navigate everything. I've spent so long treading the treacherous waters of the men who have laid claim to me.

First, it was Gray when he took me from my home and forced me to come here and live with him at the Kings' clubhouse. A place I, against all odds, started to think of as home, and with a man that I've come to love so deeply.

Then Gunner ripped all that away from me, but not in one swoop. Oh, no. That wouldn't be his style. He may not have intended to force me out of my new home and into Dirty Diamonds, a place I had nightmares about. But it happened whether that's what he wanted or not.

And then... just as I got comfortable there, he had me delivered to him and the Reapers. A place that truly taught me what nightmares are made of.

But now, when my thoughts are clear and I know I'm safe, what's left? I feel like a broken husk of my former self. No, that's not entirely correct. Now that the dust has settled, and I have time to really think and breathe... who am I?

Should I go back to fighting Gray at every turn? Should I submit to him like I did to Gunner? I don't know the right answer because I'm having trouble understanding what I truly want.

"Good morning, Princess."

Shit, I've been so lost in my thoughts, I didn't notice Gray waking up. Turning to my side, I look at Gray as he slowly blinks his eyes open.

"Morning," I answer, trying to force my voice to sound less doomy and gloomy than I feel.

"What's wrong?" he asks immediately, shattering all hope that I'd be able to keep it to myself.

As I lick my dry lips, I consider simply not answering him, but I quickly push those enticing thoughts aside. Because I might be naïve and rash at times, but I'd like to think I learn from my mistakes.

The biggest mistake Gray and I are both guilty of is not talking. It's not like we misunderstood each other, we just simply didn't talk about things we should have. At the time, they never seemed all that important to me, but now they do. Hindsight really is a bitch.

"I don't know who you saved," I admit in a low tone.

He props his head up on his elbow. "What do you mean?"

That's a good question, one I'm not sure I'm able to explain.

"I don't know who I am anymore," I say. When he looks even more confused, I let out a sigh. "I can't recognize the girl I see in the mirror, Gray. I know it's me, but I don't feel like it. Hell, I don't even feel like I'm in my own body."

A strand of his messy waves falls into his eyes as he cants his head to the side. Slowly, so slowly it has to be deliberate, he lifts his hand and moves it out of the way. The action makes my heart contract because I know it's for my benefit he's slowing down.

"You've been through hell, so it's only natural you need time to get used—" He stops talking when I shake my head vigorously and make a sound that resembles a growl.

"I know that," I spit. "What I mean is that I don't remember who I was before you kidnapped me, Gray. I used to like Pop Tarts and Reality TV. But now I don't even know if I like that."

Though he tries to hide it, I glimpse the guilt in his dark eyes at the mention of him kidnapping me. Fuck, I'm not trying to be cruel, but it's the truth. That's how far back it goes.

"I used to have what I thought was a picture fucking perfect family, and now I know that was a lie. My dad was cheating on mom with Irina. Fuck! He's the reason mom and Leslie are dead. He wanted mom dead, and Leslie was just a casualty in his fucked up plans."

The more I talk, the easier the words come. Each of them unfurls something inside me, something dark that's wrapped itself around me like a security blanket. But now it's loose, and I don't know how to control it.

"Did you know that?" I ask, ignoring the shock marring Gray's features. "Did you know that my dad had my mom and sister killed? That becoming a fucking widower was his payment for cleaning out your bank accounts for the Reapers?"

My voice grows louder and louder. I'm practically shouting at him as I push myself off the bed and begin pacing the length of the bedroom.

"No, Princess. I didn't know any of that."

I nod sharply to show him I heard his answer. "What about Gunner?"

As soon as I mention his name, Gray lets out a feral snarl. "What about him?"

His tone is unlike anything I've heard from him before, and it makes goosebumps spread across my skin.

"Did you know he's alive? And that he... that he... he fucking wanted me to be his Old Lady, Gray. You have to have known that."

I have no idea why I say that, because I don't actually believe it. I'm just so fucking angry that I don't know how to contain it.

"Yes," I say, mostly to myself. "You had those fucked up bets. Why did you think he wanted to do those?"

Gray's feet hit the floor with a thud, he's moving so quickly I barely notice it. His eyes shine with thinly veiled malice, and anger rolls off him. Yet, I'm not scared, and I know in my heart that it isn't aimed at me.

"I fucked up, okay?" he roars. "You're right, Princess. The signs were right fucking there, but I was too lost in you to fucking look closer."

The potency of his words is almost choking me as I feel them burrow beneath my skin, muscle, and bone, taking root in my fucking core.

"You're not the only one," I admit, my tone softer now. "He gave me hints. Saying shit like I wasn't ready for him, and I never paid it much attention." I throw my hands up in the air in pure frustration. "I thought it was just Gun-him being... well, him."

We stare at each other for so long my legs begin to shake, but I don't move or look away. There's so much more I need to say, and need to know.

Clearing my throat, I say, "Alana told me to talk to you about the night mom and Leslie were killed. She even said it was important. But I never fucking thought much about it. I don't know why, and it seems stupid now. But I..." Trailing off, I swallow the lump of emotions clogging my throat.

Gray uses my silence to close the distance between us. Despite the anger in his eyes and sneer on his lips, he still manages to move slow enough I have time to stop him if I want to. But I don't want to. Not now.

"Princess."

The way his tongue rolls around that one word is enough to cause my breath to saw out of me. My shoulders sag, and instead of angry, I feel lost. So fucking lost.

He lifts his hand and gently runs his thumb down my cheek, keeping his touch so light I can barely feel it.

"You should feel angry with me," he says. "I fucking failed you, and I'm sorry."

"No, I—" Before I can finish my interjection, he slides his finger to my mouth and presses it against my lips.

"It's my turn to talk now."

When I look up at him, there's a hint of a smile on his lips. It's enough to make me relent, so I nod to show him I agree.

"On the surface, the bets were two bored assholes passing time. But Princess, it was more than that. I'm not going to give you pretty lies or ridiculous excuses, because I won't fucking lie to you. But I wanted you before I fucking knew it myself."

Pausing, he runs a hand through his messy waves. He closes his eyes for a brief moment, like he's steeling himself for what he's going to say next.

"So you're right." There's so much pain in those words that I unconsciously shift closer to him, our bodies now touching everywhere. "I should have fucking known there was more to it for Gunner as well. I should have asked why he was so interested in you. There are many things I should have demanded answers about but never did."

Nodding, I ask, "Like what?"

He lets out a humorless chuckle. "Like how come your dad knew to run just before we showed up after he drained our accounts completely?"

Before he can continue, I cut in. "You already told me that he said a laser was pointed at me..." Trailing off, I shake my head. Because that wasn't true. "But that was a lie. We didn't know that at the time, Gray." I'm sickened by the lengths my dad's gone to and the way he used me.

"Doesn't matter what he said or didn't say. I shouldn't have been that quick to believe Brian," Gray growls.

"What other things do you feel like you should have gotten answers to?" I ask, wanting to get us back on track.

"Why did Brian want you with us, the Kings? Now I fucking know he wanted you with Gunner," he spits out the last part like the words are physically causing him pain.

My breath hitches, and I want to slap myself for not having thought about that. But now that Gray's said it, it's so painfully obvious that getting me here, to the Kings' clubhouse, was part of his and Gunner's plan.

Fuck. I really was just a commodity, not even treated or thought of as a person by my own fucking dad.

Oblivious to my turmoil, Gray goes on. "How come the Reapers have been able to thwart so many of our attempts at getting them? The list of questions goes on and fucking on. Rocco was so busy being suspicious of you, and I was so busy chasing you, neither of us saw what was right in front of us."

Unable to stand any longer, I move over to the bed and sit down. Then I pat the empty space next to me, but Gray shakes his head. Instead of sitting next to me, he drops to his knees in front of me.

I try to open my legs so he can move between them. Not in a sexual way, but just so we can be closer. I can't. I physically can't fucking do it, and instead end up squeezing my thighs tighter.

A sob breaks free, and my entire body is shaking. I'm so fucking broken I can't even... no. Fuck, no. I refuse to be this version of myself. Whoever I really am, it can't be a broken down shell.

I. Fucking. Refuse.

Seeing my fight, Gray shuffles back until he's out of reach. I can see my own pain reflected in his features, and it breaks my fucking heart that I'm like this.

He swallows thickly before asking, "What did Gunner do to you?"

I shake my head vehemently, denying him the answers I know he's burning for.

"Please, Princess. I need to know. I... I have to know," he begs.

Averting my gaze I look down at the floor as thoughts of my time with Gunner assault my mind. Now that I've gained some distance to the hell I was living, it all seems like a bad dream. Yet, as soon as his name is brought up, every scar he's given me throbs with a phantom pain.

"Please don't make me say it," I plead, looking up at him from beneath my wet lashes. Tears cling to them, distorting my vision. "I don't think I can."

Sighing deeply, he gets to his feet and holds his hand out to me. I hesitantly take it, and let him pull me back to my feet. Then he bends so we're eye-to-eye.

"I won't force you to tell me," he vows with so much intensity in the words that I feel it wrap around me. "But you need to tell someone, eventually. I don't want it to eat you up."

My lips twitch as a smile breaks free. "Someone?" I ask, deflecting the words I know to be true.

"I don't fucking know," he says. "A shrink? Alana? Fuck if I know. I just know it helps to talk about it."

He looks away as though lost in thought for a moment.

"Gray?" I prompt, wanting to know what he's thinking about.

"Okay, don't get upset," he says. "But someone once convinced me to open up, and it fucking helped. I swear it did."

My brows furrow in confusion. "Why would that upset me?"

It's weird the way he shifts his weight from one foot to the other, like he's nervous. What does he have to be nervous about?

"Ahh," I say, as the truth hits me. "Mama C."

When he nods, I get it. I haven't exactly been giving her character glowing reviews, and yes, I was pissed that she punished Gray for a crime he didn't commit against her.

"It was before I met you," Gray's quick to say. "Back when we were all part of the Diamond Crew. I was so fucking messed up when she came into our lives, and she helped set me straight. If it wasn't for her, I don't know if I'd even be alive today."

As I listen to him talk about her, I wonder if I've misjudged the woman who's clearly been taking care of all of them. Which is fucking impressive considering the shit she suffered at the Reapers' hands as well.

"She was always Rocco's," he adds, like that's an important clarification. And honestly, it is. "She's never been anything but like a sister to me."

The soothing feeling the clarification brings doesn't last long. "Why like a sister?" I ask, needing him to elaborate.

"What do you mean?" he sounds confused, and I can't say I blame him since he doesn't know the thoughts I'm having.

My palms grow clammy, and sweat palpitates on my forehead. Fuck, how do I ask what I really need to know?

"I-I..."

Pulling my hand out of his, I sit back down on the bed. Then I do my best to gather the courage.

"What made her like a sister to you, Gray? Is it because she was Rocco's and so it was never physical between you? Because if that's—"

"No!" He cuts me off with an angry growl. "You can forget about that shit right fucking now."

His tone has me flinching. Not from fear, but from the sheer intensity.

"I don't know how else to fucking say it, Princess. But I know that Gunner raped you, and I fucking know I might never get to touch you again."

He knows? Fuck. How does he know? I didn't want to tell him that I'm basically damaged goods—broken by another man.

"You told Alana while I was here," Gray reminds me. "And I had a visit from the detectives after your trip to the stables. So, yes, Princess. I fucking know. But that's not important right now. I want you to fucking hear me when I say that even if I never get to touch you again, it changes nothing. Do you understand me?"

My throat burns with unshed emotions, and I'm shaking again. His words are so fucking perfect it's making me cry anew.

"I-I understand," I sob. "Thank you."

Gray gets on his knees again, and this time he rests his head on my knees. He keeps his arms at his side, careful to touch me as little as possible. I move my hand through his wavy hair, reveling in the feel of the soft strands between my fingers.

For now, this is all I have to offer. But with the way he's responding and acting, it feels like enough, which in turn makes me feel better about our situation.

Our moment is ruined when my stomach lets out a loud growl.

"Time to feed the princess," Gray chuckles as he gets up. "Do you want to eat here? Or maybe you'd like to come downstairs?"

I take my time pondering his question. On the one hand, I'm happy being secluded here in our room. But on the other, I want to see everyone else, and at least try to create a new normalcy.

Sighing, I get up as well. "Downstairs," I think. Then I frown as I look down at myself. "But I need a shower."

Gray smirks. "I wasn't going to say anything, but yeah, you do. Alana can't keep giving you sponge baths like she's done all week."

I pretend to be outraged by his words, and mock frown at him all while smiling so widely it hurts. It's a short reprieve from all the fear and negativity, but a welcome one. To act like we're back to normal, even for a short time.

After making sure I'm ready to leave the bedroom, Gray opens the door. "I should have known," he grumbles as he walks into the living area.

"Known what?" I ask. Since I'm behind him, I don't know what he's talking about.

"There you are," a female voice says. "I was wondering if we were going to have to smoke you two out."

Stepping around Gray, my eyes fall on Mama C as she sits on the couch, acting like she owns the damn thing.

"For fuck's sake, Cara," Gray says. "Ever heard of knocking?"

She just shrugs. "I have, but I can't say I'm fond of doing it in a house I helped renovate and decorate," she says pointedly at Gray. Standing, she puts down the magazine she was flipping through. "Anyway, this isn't about you. I'm here for Zoe. So if you could give us some space, I won't have to kick your ass."

Ignoring her, Gray turns to me. "I did not set this up, I swear," he murmurs for my ears only. "And if you want her gone, I'll tell her to fuck off. You and me, Zo. Don't forget that."

"No, it's okay," I whisper back. "It's good that she's here."

By now, exhaustion and vertigo is hitting me hard. I know I need a shower, but I'm honestly not sure I can do it by myself. And since she's here, I'll welcome Mama's help. I would prefer Alana, but I've already laid enough claim on her time. Besides, anyone but Gray would do. I can't let him see my scars. Not yet, and maybe not ever.

A shiver runs through me, making me tremble at the thought of what I'll see in the mirror. While I stayed with Irina, I did my best not to look too closely at the countless marks Gunner made on my body.

Teeth marks, and the branding... fuck, the branding.

As Mama comes closer, Gray moves over to the couch and sits down. Despite the space separating us, I know he's watching me like a hawk, which makes me feel better.

"How are you doing, Z?" Mama C asks, concern coating her tone.

Rather than answering her question that doesn't have an easy answer, I state, "I need a shower."

"Okay," she says. If she's confused by my change of topic, she isn't letting on. "I take it, you want my help with that?"

"Please," I whisper.

She nods and rolls her shoulders back, a look of determination flashing in her eyes. "Your bathroom has tiles, right?"

Before I can answer, Gray speaks up. "Yes. But the one downstairs—"

"No, it's fine," she says, cutting him off. "I can do it."

I look between them as they share a look. Though I hate feeling left out, that's not why my eyes dance from one to the other like I'm watching a ping-pong match.

"Do tiles bother you?" I ask, trying to piece it together.

She forces a smile that doesn't quite reach her eyes. "Not as much as they used to. You won't believe how much a good dicking and earth-shattering orgasms help turn the worst shit in your mind into pleasant memories."

I get the feeling that she's chosen those words specifically for me, like she's trying to tell me something without saying it outright. But just the thought of sex has my stomach churning.

"So you'll help me?" I ask, eager to get off the subject of dicks.

Rather than answering me, she links her arm with mine and we walk into the bathroom. Mama leaves the door open and immediately walks over to the shower and switches the water on. At first I think I'm seeing things, but the longer I look at her, the more visible the tremble in her hands becomes.

"Are you sure you're okay?" I ask.

She avoids my question and calls out to Gray. "We need some clean clothes and fresh towels."

"I can—"

"No," she says through clenched teeth. "I need you to stay here with me, Zoe."

The longer I look at her, the more I see the toll it takes on her to be here with me. I don't know what it is about the tiles, and I'm determined not to ask. That's for her to tell me if she wants to.

"Here you go," Gray says, joining us in the bathroom. Mama is quick to take the towels and clothes from him, before shooing him back out. "Are you sure you're okay?" he asks me, not budging until I nod.

"I'll be fine," I whisper.

As soon as he's gone, I whip the tee over my head before I have time to second-guess myself. My panties are next to go, and once I'm naked, I gather my long hair over one shoulder and hurry under the scalding water.

I moan as the water soaks my hair, and I don't waste any time reaching for the shampoo. Wanting to get rid of the lime stench still clinging to my nostrils, I use the entire bottle. Once I'm satisfied that all I can smell is coconut, I reach for my loofah and run it all over my body.

"Why are you helping me?" I ask, looking over at Mama who's sitting on the closed toilet.

She moves one leg over the other and runs her fingers through her dark hair. "Why wouldn't I?"

I huff. "You once told me you only help those who help themselves. I haven't done that."

She tilts her head to the side, not bothering to hide the way her eyes track every inch of my naked body. "Did Gunner do all that?" she asks, gesturing to the skin that he used as a canvas for his twisted and perverse entertainment. "Or did the other Reapers also..."

There's no need for Mama to complete her sentence since we both know what she's really asking. Did they take turns or was I exclusively Gunner's?

"Only Gunner," I say, my voice monotone. "He claimed me as his Old Lady. Aside from him, only two other guys touched me. There was the guy who pulled me from the car after Rhiannon got us into the car crash, and he met a grizzly fucking death."

Bile creeps up my throat, and I shudder as I remember having to make the choice of how Johnny met his end. It's just one of the many thoughts plaguing me, but this one is different. Even though I know I never had a choice, I can't shake the guilt I feel at being the one to choose his death.

"Then there was my sister's riding trainer." I squeeze my eyes shut as all-consuming guilt makes my breath hitch. "I was the one who touched him. I stupidly hugged him, and Gunner shot him right in front of me. Then he... he... fuck. That was the first time he raped me."

My mind is warring with itself. Unable to decide whether the guilt or the pain of having yet another thing taken from me weighs the heaviest. Lost for words, I slide down the tiles until I'm sitting on the bottom of the shower while the water cascades around me.

I pull my knees up and rest my head on them, facing Mama who never looks away from me. Even though our eyes meet, it's like we're both seeing something different. Unimaginable horrors playing in our mind's eye, threatening to pull us down.

Mama is the first to shake herself out of it, literally shaking her head. "Did you know my dear mom worked with the Reapers?"

"I heard something when I was with them," I answer.

She nods. "Rocco bought me when I was sixteen and married me that day. He and the Diamond Crew wanted to rescue me, and that was the best way to draw my parents out. I killed my dad that day, and that landed me in jail for three years."

I make a strangled sound as I listen to her horrific story.

"So trust me when I say that I get trauma, and I know firsthand what it's like to feel like a fucking hippo is sitting on your chest."

The comparison has me barking out a laugh. Not because it's funny, but because that's exactly what it feels like.

"If it wasn't for Rocco, I don't know what would have become of me." She says it so flippantly, like she's repeated the words so many times she's detached from them. "Loving a King isn't easy, especially not *the* King. They're stubborn, proud, and damaged bastards. But they're also loyal to a fault, and love with their entire being."

Though it's obviously Rocco she's talking about, the words fit Gray to a fucking T.

"Gray loves you, Z. You're his *it,* and I want you to understand that what you've been through changes nothing. He'll understand if you can't ever love him back—"

"But I do love him," I say, needing to set the record straight. "It fucking broke something inside me when I thought he was dead." My voice cracks at the end, and I finally allow myself to feel the emotions I've had to bottle up for months.

Mama doesn't interrupt me, or offer any more words of wisdom. She just watches me as I break down, sobbing under the water that's turning colder by the minute.

Once I'm no longer ugly crying, Mama asks, "What do you want, Zoe?"

I blink, staring uncomprehendingly at her.

"Do you still want to be free and go to Harvard? Or do you want to stay here?"

Without hesitating, I blurt out, "I want to find out who I am."

"But beyond that—"

"And then I want revenge," I seethe. The words surprise me so much I fall quiet.

The thought of making Gunner, Irina, my dad, and Rusty pay is like an alluring siren call, one I can't ignore.

"I want them to fucking pay."

Mama stands abruptly and comes over to switch off the water. Then she holds her hand out to me, hauling me to my feet as soon as I take it.

"See," she says, smiling widely. "You are helping yourself."

I can't help returning her smile as I realize she's taken us back to where the conversation began. Fuck, she's good.

As I stand in front of the sink and brush my teeth, Mama comes up behind me. Without asking permission, she runs a finger across the indent in my skin left from Gunner's teeth. She runs it all the way across to the other one where he branded me.

I cringe involuntarily, but force my spine to remain ramrod straight. I refuse to fucking crumble.

"When I came to live with Rocco, I never even knew a man's touch could bring anything but pain. He's the one who took care of me, and now the roles are reversed," she says, almost wistfully.

I'm not sure if she's talking to me or herself.

"When you came here, you took care of Gray, even if you didn't realize it. You taught him what it's like to love, and to be loved. You showed him so many things, but maybe now it's his turn to help you."

As I mull over her words, I can't stop wondering if I'm talking to the wrong person. If everything is as she says, then her and Gray are in somewhat similar positions, which means Rocco's and mine aren't all that different.

"How's he doing?" I ask, remembering Alana and Gray caught me up on what happened to him, and that he's no longer the Prez of the Cruz Kings.

Mama shrugs, trying to appear aloof, but I see the worry in her eyes. "He's... hanging in there," she says, her voice thick.

Spinning around, I ask, "Can I see him?"

She immediately narrows her eyes. "Why?"

It's a good question, and I'm not quite sure of the answer. Rocco has always scared me, and he's never been shy in voicing his dislike for me.

"I just kind of feel like I have to," I whisper, offering her the only explanation I have.

Mama hands me my clothes, and it's not until I'm dressed in jeans and a long-sleeved shirt that all feels too big on me, that she answers.

"Maybe one day, but not now. He needs to focus on his recovery. But if it helps, I'll let him know you asked."

I thank her before we leave the bathroom, and walk back into the living area where Gray and Slasher look deep in conversation. Alana is sitting on the edge of the couch, engrossed in something on her phone.

"Zoe!" she squeals as soon as she sees me. "You were in there so long I almost came barging in."

Gray chuckles. "Almost? It was only me stopping you that held you back."

She sticks out her tongue at him before bouncing to my side. "How are you feeling today, girl? You look better."

I shrug, not able to form words. I don't know how I feel right now. Better in some ways, more confused in others, and equally miserable and trapped in thirds. So a shrug is the best I got.

"Are you ready to go downstairs?" Gray asks. Though his tone is low, I hear him perfectly.

With Mama's words of wisdom fresh in my mind, I reach out for him and take his hand. It's a small gesture, tame compared to what we've shared in the past. But right now, it feels like a big step.

As surprise flicks across his face, I feel more certain that I need to fight. I need to claw my way out of my mental coffin and find out who I am, and what I really want out of life—but I don't have to do it alone.

The only thing I'm certain of right now is that I belong to Gray. I never want to be without him again, and I need to tell him that.

Grayson

The smell of fresh paint is thick in the air, the renovations in their final stages, thank fuck. Zoe takes the new space in with more curiosity than she had when she ventured out of my apartment for the first time yesterday. I can imagine it was all quite overwhelming for her, realizing that while she was held captive things kept moving forward.

I hate that.

Everything should have fucking stopped. The entire fucking world should have stopped spinning until Zoe was safe back with me. I'd wanted to stop everything, not think of a damn fucking thing but my princess, but I couldn't. This club is more than me and her, and it fell on me to lead everyone.

Sometimes I think it was probably a blessing, because I was sure to have gotten myself killed trying to find her long before I ever found her, and then, she'd still be there, living the hell she has nightmares of every night as she thrashes next to me in bed.

I want to spill so much fucking blood that the creeks and rivers flow red, tinting the ocean beyond the Santa Cruz shoreline.

"I like the new bar." Her words are quiet as she breaks little clumps off the bread roll on her plate and nibbles on them.

Zoe is stick thin, and as hungry as she is, it doesn't take much to fill her now, her stomach having obviously shrunken from being near starved.

Dragging my eyes from studying every expression she makes, I take in the new bar and Tex as he lines up new bottles of whiskey on one of the shelves behind it.

"Tex is pretty happy with it." I grin, catching her small grin in return.

"Happy is an understatement." Alana scoffs as she pulls out a chair and flops down in it. "The man is obsessed. Have you seen the fridges behind there? They are glass front drawer fridges and he keeps getting pissy at me every time I open one like I'm gonna break it."

The small giggle that leaps from Zoe's mouth shoots warmth to the center of my chest.

Fuck I've missed hearing her laugh.

Alana starts rambling about Tex insisting on a new rule of no bar top dancing as my attention gets stolen by Slasher pacing at the back of the room, his hands in his pockets, head bowed and his dark hair falling over his face.

I already know what's got him so anxious, so I lean in close to Zoe's ear.

"Princess, I'm gonna go have a chat with Slasher. I'll stay in this room and won't take my eyes off you. Okay?"

As I lean back, Zoe turns to look over her shoulder to where Slasher is still pacing and then nods, her blue eyes locking with mine.

"Okay. Don't leave without me," she murmurs quietly, fidgeting with the piece of bread in her fingers.

"I'll never go anywhere without you again," I promise and her pink lips, looking less cracked and dry today, quirk up slightly at the corners.

Standing from my chair, I reluctantly leave Zoe's side and take the twelve steps to the back of the room to stand in front of Slasher, forcing his pacing to stop.

"Why are you so nervous?"

He blows out a breath, some of the dark strands of his hair that had fallen in his face lifting away briefly. "I dunno. It just feels weird to be a part of the inner circle and that I'll be meeting them today."

Them.

He means Dante Hayton and Barrett Marx, also known as Baz.

The Marx family are considered a family you don't want to mess with in Australia, having ties to the Australian Mafia, and Baz is like an international liaison for the family, securing deals all across the globe while helping Dante in the background.

He and Dante used to be surfing buddies, and somewhere along the way they turned into business associates of the organized crime variety.

"You've met them before." I point out but he shakes his head.

"Not like this. To be in the room with them for discussions and planning..." he rakes his hand roughly through his long dark hair. "What if I say something dumb?"

And there it is.

Slasher is still getting used to the fact that I wanted him to be my right-hand man, and any minute now, Dante and Baz are going to walk through our clubhouse doors to meet with the new leadership of the Cruz Kings for the first time. Officially.

If anyone should be feeling nervous it should be me, but I've been in these meetings with them before. Hell, I was once part of Dante's Diamond Crew before Rocco formed the Cruz Kings, so I already have history with him and Baz, but Slasher has only ever been standing on the outside of this particular circle.

Now he's on the inside.

Clapping him on the shoulder, I lock eyes with his dark ones and give him a reassuring squeeze. "You won't say anything dumb, brother." I ball my fist and tap it over his heart. "Your head and heart are why I chose you to stand beside me. You're the best man for the job."

His lip curls. "I want revenge. Are they gonna have a fucking problem with that?"

Shaking my head, I smirk. "Fuck no. As long as it serves the community, there won't be a problem."

A bell chimes, and we all glance over to the bar where Tex moves to a panel and looks at a screen.

Part of our new security measures is a camera and motion detector at the front gate. Now, in addition to having a couple of men man the gates, we get notified when someone is there, and the men manning the gates aren't permitted to open them until me, Slasher, Tex or Munroe give the all clear.

Once the Reaper threat is eliminated, we will loosen those rules, but for now, this place is Fort-fucking-Knox.

"It's Dante," Tex calls over his shoulder, and a hush falls over the room.

"Let them through," I call back, my eyes shifting back to Slasher. "You and me, brother. These men are relying on us now. Are you with me?"

A low growl rumbles in Slasher's chest before he claps me on the shoulder this time. "Fuck yeah, I am."

Gesturing my head toward the back room, I instruct my second in command. "Head on through to church. Rocco and Cara are in there already. I'll be in soon."

Slasher nods before his eyes drift across the room to where Alana and Zoe sit. When my gaze follows, I see Alana's sights locked with Slasher's like they are having a silent conversation before he turns and leaves the room.

Dante and Baz enter the club like they fucking own it, but I actually don't hate that. If it wasn't for Dante, we wouldn't have this club, so even though he's not a member or a founder, it was with his support that Rocco started the MC, and he has worked alongside us to try to keep the community safe, and in our control.

"There he is. The new ruler of the kingdom," Dante smirks, his boots heavy as he strides through the room.

As he passes Zoe's table, I don't miss the way she flinches as he nears and shrinks in on herself.

I fucking hate seeing how much she's affected by the presence of other men. Especially the good ones.

I manage to drag my eyes from her in time to accept Dante's hand in a shake right as the gate bell goes off again.

"What's that?" Dante asks, looking around but not spotting where the bell sounded from, so I gesture to Tex, who is again, checking the monitor.

"Security measures."

"Cain is here," Tex calls this time, and I nod as Dante's brows dart high.

"Let him in," I respond and Baz joins us, giving me an approving nod.

"Impressive. Now we just have to line the roof with sharp shooters and rig up some booby traps."

Dante and I laugh at Baz's suggestion and he smirks, reaching his hand out for a shake, too.

"Head on through. Slasher and Rocco are already there," I tell them, and they make their way through as well.

Moving back over to Zoe, I give her a wide berth so I don't startle her, making sure her eyes find me as she drags them away from Alana.

"You ready, Princess?"

Her lips thin as she glances over her shoulder to the back passage that leads to church.

"Are you sure it's okay for me to be there? Because I'll be okay here with Alana if it's easier."

Dropping down to my haunches, her blue eyes follow me, watching as I slowly hook my pinky with hers. "I've already told you, Zo. Where I go, you go, and where you go, I go. I lead this club now, and if I say my princess is to sit by my side during church or any sort of discussion, then that's just the way it is. If someone doesn't like that, then they know where the door is."

Her blue gaze softens as her lips tip up in a small smile, giving me a nod right as Cain enters the clubhouse.

"It's alright my minions. Cain is here. You can worship the ground I walk on now."

Snickers sound through the room from the few Cruz Cunts sitting nearby, and Munroe and Stretch who have taken a seat at the bar with Tex.

I'm about to remind Cain that he's on my turf now as I stand, but Zoe beats me to it.

"You're not the king here."

His face lights up at hearing her voice, his arms spreading wide as he strides in our direction.

"Ahhh, here she is. My princess."

I growl as he gets closer, stepping in front of him so he can't get to her.

"Don't you mean *my* princess?" I lift a brow and he frowns and nods.

"That's what I said. *My* princess."

Zoe giggles behind me, halting any more of my words. "It's good to see you, Cain."

He beams, standing on his toes and eyeing Zoe over my shoulder. "It's good to see you too. At least the half of your face I can see." He glares at me then. "You're not made of glass, Gray."

"I know I'm not fucking made of glass. Keep your distance."

A slow sinister smirk spreads Cain's lips wide. "Ooooh you're so possessive."

I glare harder and he rolls his eyes. "Relax. I know the situation, man." He fake punches my shoulder. "I won't touch my princess until she asks."

"She's not your fucking princess," I snap, and Alana snickers.

"I think what Cain is trying to say is that Zoe is all of our princess." She shoots Zoe a smile before bending at the waist to bow and Zoe laughs again.

Okay. This is good. She's laughing more. That's a good sign.

I hope.

"In the back." I snap at Cain and he bows too, in a fucking extravagant way, and when I huff and turn to Zoe, my annoyance falls away as I see the brief lightheartedness in her face.

She's in there somewhere. Even though she told me she doesn't know who she is anymore, I can still see my princess behind her haunted eyes. It doesn't matter what version of herself she settles on when all this is over with, I'll still love her, anyway. How could I not?

Gesturing for Zoe to follow Cain, she trails behind him and my eyes naturally fall down the length of her body as she walks. Her frail frame is a reminder of some of the cruelty she suffered, but what hurts the most to see is the way she curls her shoulders forward as she walks, her arms wrapped across her chest like she can close herself off to the world.

I fucking hope that one day, I see her with her shoulders back, her chin up, and that sassy mouth stirring my temper. I don't want to see that for me. I want to see that for her.

Entering church, I gently press my hand to the small of Zoe's back, leading her to the head of the table. The chatter between everyone falls silent as I pull a seat out for Zoe, all eyes falling to us as we sit.

"Thanks for coming," I announce, picking up the pack of cigarettes on the table and tapping one out before offering one to Slasher.

After lighting the smoke, I glance at everyone sitting around the table.

With Zoe directly to my left, Rocco and Cara take up the seats next to her, and Dante and Baz at the far end. To my right, Slasher blows out a lungful of smoke, with Cain sitting to his right, pouring himself a whiskey.

Dante's frown catches my attention, and I hitch a brow in his direction.

"Problem?" I ask and he leans forward to rest his forearms on the tabletop.

"I'm not trying to be rude. This is your kingdom, after all, but I'm just wondering why Cara and Zoe are in here with us."

I stare Dante down at the other end of the table as I drag in another lungful of nicotine, holding it in for a long beat before releasing it.

"I seem to remember a time we were on your turf, Dante, and you insisted on your girl, Storm, being present."

He nods. "True. But she's family, and yes, I know Cara and Rocco are husband and wife. I was there when that happened, but Zoe is still a civilian."

In my periphery, I see Zoe stiffen, and it pisses me off.

Stubbing out my barely smoked cigarette, I point sharply at him. "Zoe is *mine.* She belongs to me and this club, not because of some fucked up trade with her dad, but because she is *my* girl. I may call her Princess, but make no mistake, she's the motherfucking Queen of this MC. She belongs at this table because she is part of this family. Hell, she's the Mama now, and one day, when she's ready, she will be Zoe Black. Since this is *my* turf, I say what goes, and when it comes to the Reapers, and how we are going to fucking annihilate them, Zoe will be a part of the planning process and know every fucking detail of what's happening. After that, when we win this fucking war, if she would rather not sit in on these meetings, then that's her prerogative. Does anyone here have a fucking problem with that?"

No one speaks up, and I watch a slow grin spread Dante's lips wide before he glances at Rocco.

"You were right. He makes a good fucking President."

"I fucking know." Rocco nods, looking relaxed in his wheelchair. "I knew it when the fucker was an annoying teenager."

Chuckles float around the table, and I smirk, glancing at Zoe as her shoulders relax.

"Before we continue," Dante speaks up again, and my jaw ticks with frustration that he might have another fucking problem with the way I do things. "Zoe, on behalf of the Diamond Crew, I'm truly sorry that we weren't able to keep you safe, and if there's anything we can do to help you settle back in, then please let us know."

Zoe nods next to me, her hands fisting in her lap as she trembles a little, but when she speaks, her voice is firm.

"I won't be able to settle in until every single Reaper is dead, including Gunner. And this time, I want to see his fucking corpse."

Heat flares in my chest. Pride for her strength. Anger that matches her own.

"I fucking second that." Slasher barks, stubbing out the butt of his smoke. "Gunner is the reason my brother is dead. Every fucking Reaper needs to die, but Gunner, that fucking traitor, needs to meet a slow and excruciating death."

Everyone nods, no one even considering a different outcome.

"We agree." Baz speaks up this time, relaxed back in his chair as though meetings like this are a daily fucking routine for him. Hell, they probably are. "The best way to end this war and bring peace to the Santa Cruz community is to band together. Everyone in this room has a reason to see the Reapers dead for one reason or another. Everyone wants vengeance, and the only way to achieve that is working together. We need to strategize and be smart and swift. It needs to be top priority."

"Baz is right." Dante adds. "My men are your men, Gray. I have more foot soldiers than you know. We can have men inside these walls to offer extra protection. We already have eyes on this place on the outside from all vantage points. No one is getting close without us knowing. And we have crew trained in tactical assaults and special ops. We'll fucking bring some of our UK crew over if we have to. But whatever you need, let us help."

I'm man enough to admit when we need help, so I nod, leaning back in my seat. "We appreciate that, Dante. Thank you."

"Right." Cain claps his hands together, rubbing them as he glances between everyone around the table. "Where do we start?"

Slasher speaks up then, filling everyone in on Maude's house in Watsonville and the Reapers living next door. The surveillance equipment Tido set up for them to monitor the house, and the Devil's Night events. Where it was, and who we saw there.

Dante makes a few calls, sending men to the area and to help take over surveillance of the house, plus putting some of his men to monitor the Sleep-Eazy Motel as well as Adam's parents' house.

"I'm going to put extra foot soldiers on the ground in Watsonville, and every fucking town between there and here," Dante advises. "I'll get my hackers to try to locate them online as well. I'm sure we will have some good intel in a few days."

Zoe leans forward next to me, and I glance at her frown as she eyes Dante.

"I'm sorry if this is a stupid question, but if the Reapers have been such a huge issue for so many years, why are you only now offering this level of help?"

Dante sits taller in his seat at the question, his eyes darting to Rocco, while Baz remains relaxed like it's business as usual.

"Can I answer that?" Cara asks, and Dante nods, gesturing for her to go ahead.

Zoe's eyes turn to Cara, who offers Rocco a small smile before addressing Zoe.

"When we first formed the club, it was for the sole purpose of filling the void of a local MC so the Reapers couldn't claim it. At the time, things were more personal for me and Rocco, what with my mom working with the Reapers, and them setting their sights on me. We killed a lot of Rusty's men, and suspected he was rebuilding his club and until recently, they weren't a real risk. It's only been the past couple of years that the Reapers have stepped up their attempt to try to claim this territory, wanting to wipe us out. So aside from the normal things an MC does, we were here to try to keep the community safe, while the Diamond Crew continued with their missions, focusing on people who need help, or need to be put six feet under."

When Cara finishes talking, Zoe glances at everyone around the table, before her eyes land on me.

"So my dad is what blew this war up?"

I dart forward faster than I should, hating the way she flinches back before I have a chance to steel myself.

"Zo. This is *not* your fault. The Reapers did all of this. It's obvious they sent Irina in, targeting your dad with the purpose of infiltrating us. If it wasn't your dad, then it would have been some other innocent family. Your dad. You. Your family have been tools the Reapers used, and Gunner's obsession with you is all on him. Not you." I point down the other end of the table to Dante and Baz, watching as her glassy eyes follow. "They are here to help end this. It's time for this to end. It's time to make sure no more innocent families get dragged into this."

Blinking quickly, a few tears pop from Zoe's eyes as her eyes travel to Slasher, her lower lip trembling. "But, Slayer..."

"No." Slasher leans forward, his dark eyes locking with Zoe's. "That's not your fault. That's all on Gunner."

Her head frantically darts to Rocco, and before she can say anything, he pulls himself forward in the wheelchair to get closer to the table. "The war with the Reapers started with me. Just because it's escalated doesn't mean anyone but those sick fuckers are to blame. You didn't put me in this wheelchair, Zoe. They did. Don't you dare go thinking that way."

"It's hard not to," she whispers, and Rocco nods.

"That's because you're a good person, Zoe. Too good for the likes of us."

She smiles, batting the tears from her flushed cheeks. "I wouldn't go that far."

Everyone snickers at that, and as she relaxes back in her seat, I feel that pride swelling in my chest again.

Pride for the strength she has but hasn't yet realized. Pride for the respect everyone around the table has for my princess. And pride for being their leader.

Dante's phone beeps, and he reads a message before his eyes dart up to mine.

"Two detectives are approaching the front gate."

My brows shoot up, realizing he really does have eyes on our clubhouse, and a few moments later, I hear the bell for the front gate.

I shoot Tex a message to let them in, and we take a few more minutes to reconfirm our next steps before we end the meeting.

Zoe stands on shaky legs, moving to Rocco and leaning in to talk to him, while Cara offers me a smile that somehow tells me she's just as proud of my princess as I am.

"So how'd you like your first meeting with the big king-pins?" Cain snickers as he shoulder bumps Slasher, who pushes a breath out like he's relieved.

"Intense but fucking good."

I grin and clap him on the shoulder, and fuck, I think the smile the big guy tries to hide is fucking genuine.

I imagine his brother is right by his side right now, even though we can't see him.

Dante and Baz start chatting with Slasher then, and that feeling of pride swells in my chest again, happy that they are taking the time to recognize our new VP.

Something brushes my pinky, and I glance next to me to see Zoe standing by my side, her pinky linked with mine.

I hope she feels it too. The pride. The feeling that she belongs. She's as much a part of this club as everyone else.

"The detectives are out there." I remind Zoe. "Do you want to go back up to our apartment? I can get the men to send them away."

Zoe shrugs, looking unsure. "Will it be bad if they see me?"

It's not ideal having her speak to the detectives, but they still need to question her and will keep pestering us until that happens. Better it's on our turf where we have the advantage, and I can get Zo out of here if they try to arrest her.

"I'm not sure why they are here, but seeing you will prob-ably surprise them. Whatever the reason, you don't have to talk to them even if you come out into the clubhouse with me."

She considers this for a moment, and shrugs again. "I want to stay with you, and I'd rather not go back to the apartment just yet."

Offering her a smile, I nod. "Let's go see what they want then."

Leaving church, Slasher ushers our Diamond Crew guests through the back so they can avoid the detectives, and Cara and Rocco follow us out into the main room.

It's time to see why the fuck the detectives are visiting us today.

23

Zoe

"We just want to talk to you, Zoe," Detective Nelson, Tania, repeats.

I step around Gray, still loving that he pushed me behind him the moment the detectives, now sitting at the bar, said they were here for me.

As my gaze meets Detective Nelson's, I can't help sneering at her. The way she smirks and eyes Gray like he's a piece of meat for her to peruse, has my temper flaring.

Yeah, I also still remember how she came across back when she and her partner, Steven, came to my house to talk to me and dad after mom and Leslie were killed. Maybe it's petty of me, but I feel like she should have behaved more professionally. Like, don't these people get sensitivity training? If they don't, they definitely should—

"Princess." The deep rasp pulls me out of my thoughts and I look at Gray who's angled his body so he's still half-covering me from the prying looks of the detectives. "You don't have to talk to them. We can just leave."

The last thing I want to do is talk to them, or anyone else. I'm already overwhelmed from meeting Dante and Baz, and listening to them all... plan, or what-the-hell-ever they call it.

I already know that if I say no to talking to the detectives, Gray, Cain, Mama C, Rocco—even weak as he is—and possibly even Dante and Baz will get me out of here. What I don't know is if that's the right thing to do.

Reading the indecision on my face, Gray wraps his pinky around mine. "I'm here, Princess. Whatever you want to do, I'll stay by your side."

The motion makes the icy grip around my heart thaw. Every day it lessens a bit more all thanks to Gray.

"You promise?" I whisper.

Tightening the hold on my finger, he rasps, "Pinky promise."

I don't know why something as childish and silly as a pinky promise means so much to me, but it does. There's no denying the magnitude of his words that I feel in my fucking marrow.

"Gray, I..." I cut myself off with a headshake.

This isn't the time to say those words. "I don't know what to do," I admit softly, so Gray's the only one who hears me. "Can I even talk to them? What should I say? Don't snitches get stitches?"

My insides melt when he gives me an unguarded smile, one that lights up his entire face. "Snitches get stitches?" he asks, unshed laughter wrapping itself around the words. "Were you planning on telling them club secrets, Princess?"

Shaking my head, I volley, "Of course not."

"If you're curious, how about we first find out what they want? Then we can take it from there," Gray suggests.

It sounds reasonable, and considering that I'm sure he has a lot more experience talking with the law than I do, I'll follow his lead.

"Okay," I say, turning my head to look at Steven and Tania, the detective pair I never wanted to see again. "But not here." Gesturing at the very public bar, I wonder if there's another room we can use. I haven't seen all the renovations yet, but there has to be something.

I'm not aware Cain's stayed until he clears his throat. "Maybe you have an office or a private room we can use?" he asks Gray.

"Follow me," he growls.

The detectives share a glance, and I wonder if they're worried for their safety. They're fools if they're not. With the amount of trained and skilled killers in this building they've walked straight into the lion's den.

Gray's hand moves to my lower back as he gently ushers me forward. The small touch brings so many feelings forth my breathing turns labored. It's enough to tell me he's here, and that he isn't going anywhere. It makes me feel safe, but it also serves as a reminder that even the smallest of touches make me uneasy.

I don't know how I can feel all those things at once, only that I do. Yet, I don't move away, or ask him to remove his hand. I want—*crave*—Gray's touch as much as I dread it.

Once we're all crammed into what used to be Rocco's office, we sit down around the desk. The detectives are sitting with their backs to the door, opposite the rest of us. And me, I'm positioned between Cain and Gray.

"So you want to speak to our princess," Cain says, earning a glare from Gray. "That's going to cost ya."

Detective Nelson pinches the bridge of her nose. "Good to see you again, Cain."

"No, it's not," he says, waggling his eyebrows at her. "Don't be such a sore loser, Tania. It was years ago. Get over it."

Steven laughs good-naturedly, but quickly tries to mask it as a cough when Tania turns her frosty glare on him.

As the three of them discuss an old case, one where Cain was a suspect who managed to dance around them until they gave up, I sag in my seat. The longer it takes for them to tell me why they want to talk to me, the more nervous I become.

"Why are you here?" I ask, interrupting them, not willing to wait any longer before I get some answers.

Steven clears his throat. "We wanted to see for ourselves that you're safe, Zoe."

"The fuck," Gray mumbles.

"Why?" I ask. "What's my safety to you?"

I wait with bated breath as Tania opens her briefcase and pulls some documents from it. "Have a look at these."

Curiosity drives me to take the pictures she's pushing across the table, and when I hold them in front of my face, I gasp in surprise. They're of dad in our lawyer's office, which I guess isn't so weird. But what immediately catches my attention is the date and time stamp in the top left corner.

As I flick through each picture, it shows dad there at least once a week for the month leading up to the attack that brutally ripped my mom and sister from this world.

"Why are you frowning, Zoe?" Tania asks in an annoyingly knowing tone.

This woman seriously gets on my nerves.

"Because you're showing me pictures of my dad with no context," I deadpan.

Gray takes the pictures from my hand and throws them back on the table. "If you're just here to waste our time, this meeting ends here," he thunders, pushing his chair back as he stands.

"Tania," Steven says, sounding like she's trying his patience as well. "Let's not play games."

Shrugging, she leans back in her chair and crosses one leg over the other. "I'm not playing any games," she replies. "I merely wondered why Zoe was frowning." Turning her head back to me, she cocks an eyebrow. "Maybe I should ask your dad instead. Do you know where he is?"

My body practically vibrates with anger, and my breath comes out in short, angry puffs. Red coats my vision as she casually talks about my dad like he's... like we're... like he didn't discard his entire family for a biker whore.

I'm not aware I'm out of my chair until I'm crawling across the table, headed straight for the woman across from me. "You know what I wonder?" I seethe, ignoring Gray's hand on my calf. "I wonder why you're so fucking insecure you have to play mind-games to get what you want—"

"I'm not—"

"And," I say louder, not letting her interrupt me. "I wonder why the fuck you have nothing better to do than to come harass me."

Gray lets out a string of curses while Cain laughs, like this is the best entertainment ever. "If you want to punch her, go for it," he says.

Letting go of my leg, Gray echoes the sentiment. "Want me to hold her for you, Princess?"

I don't need to look at him to know he's serious—that they both are. But that's not at all what I want. Okay, so maybe a small part of me would love nothing more than to wipe the arrogance from her face.

"Maybe another time," I say. Then I return to my seat as gracefully as possible. This time I take Gray's hand into mine, letting the touch soothe my frazzled nerves.

Fuck, I can't just go nuclear because I don't like the woman's attitude.

It's barely noticeable, but Steven discreetly shifts his chair so he's no longer sitting so close to his partner. I wonder if that's on purpose or if he just needed to move.

"We didn't come here to play games, Zoe," he says. "We really were worried about you, but we also have some questions."

Words fail me, so all I do is nod.

Steven clears his throat. "Were you present when Chris Brooks was killed?"

Gray tightens his hold on my hand when my breath hitches. "Who's Chris Brooks?" I ask, doing my best to sound aloof.

"Your sister's riding trainer," Tania says. "But you already knew that, didn't you?"

I shake my head. "No, actually. I didn't know his last name." Trying to ignore the guilt I feel for getting Chris killed, and then for only caring about my stupid letter, I meet her gaze head on. "Why do you think I was there?"

When Gray squeezes my hand again, I know I did the right thing by asking them.

"We found a note signed as Zoe and a picture of you and Leslie," Steven explains. "When our forensic team went over the scene, we also learned there were two different blood types on the floor. One matched Chris, but the other is still unknown, which means we don't have it in our database. Was it yours?"

I don't mean to look at Gray, but I'm so far out of my element here that I need some guidance.

"Where have you been for the last three months?" Tania interjects, and this time she sounds genuinely curious. "You went from being with the Cruz Kings all the time to never being around. That doesn't give the impression it was by choice."

Without thinking, I say, "It wasn't my fucking choice." My throat is thick with emotions.

Nodding, she places both her hands on the table, pushing the images of my dad out of the way. "Steven was right," she says, nodding toward her partner. "We aren't here to play games, Zoe. The reason we came was because we have things to talk about."

"What kinds of things?" Gray asks.

Steven answers, "The kind that can't leave this room."

Cain snorts and dramatically sing-songs, "da-da-da."

"First, I need to know that you're with the Kings willingly," Tania says to me, ignoring Gray's sputtering. "And that you trust them. Because if that's not the case—"

I cut her off. "I trust them," I say, willing her to hear the sincerity in my tone. The last thing I need is them thinking I'm lying. "And I'm here by choice."

She nods, and with that small motion, her entire demeanor changes. Her posture is less stiff and her eyes exude a warmth I've never seen from her.

"Then let me tell you why we're really here," she says.

I chew nervously on my bottom lip, unsure what to expect from those words. But what I'm really focusing on is the change I just saw in her. It's like she was wearing a mask I never even knew was there. It's disconcerting.

"For years Steven and I have worked on one case after the other, all of which lead to the Reapers. The cases that come across our desks aren't for the faint of heart, and most of them involve either human trafficking, drugs, violence, and, often, serious abuse of women."

A coldness spreads throughout my bones as I listen to her basically outline most of the things I witnessed when I was with them. Memories I'd hoped I'd never have to think about again stir, and my heart feels like it stops beating for a second.

"But I don't think I need to go into more detail, do I, Zoe?" she asks me, her tone brimming with concern.

Shaking my head, I manage to choke out, "No."

Steven leans forward. "For years we've known that the Cruz Kings did what they could to battle the Reapers, and to keep the community safe. But it's not enough."

I feel Gray tense next to me, but his face remains a perfect mask of neutrality as he remains quiet.

"On one case, we got too close to the truth. At least that's what we suspect," Tania says. I'm surprised to see her eyes are glassy, and there's a slight tremor in her voice. "I got a phone call from Rusty the day we asked for a warrant to search their clubhouse."

My stomach tightens, knots forming as the foreboding lacing her tone spreads through me. "W-what did he want?" I ask even though I think I have a pretty good idea.

Steven clears his throat and moves closer to Tania. The way he places his hand on top of hers isn't in the way a lover would. No, this is more like a friend trying to console her, and it seems to be working.

"He told me that if I didn't drop the case, my niece would pay the price."

I'm barely aware that Gray has moved until he slides a box of tissues across the table to the woman that's gone from frost queen to openly crying in front of us.

"Thank you," she sniffles.

While she blows her nose and dabs her eyes, I keep trying to think of ways to ask her to stop talking. I don't want to hear this story. I already know it doesn't have a happy ending. Everything the Reapers touch turns bad. They're a fucking plague, a disease that festers, leaving nothing but rot and decay in its wake.

The fear I've become used to feeling is dormant as rage burns through my veins. I'm so fucking angry that I can barely stand it.

"To cut a long story short, I didn't heed their warning and my niece was kidnapped from her high school. No matter how many resources went into looking for her, it was like she vanished into thin air." Tania takes a deep breath and rolls her shoulders back. "Until the following Devil's Night. Her body turned up then."

Bile burns my throat and tears sting my eyes. Fuck, how many nieces, sisters, and daughters did I see at the Reapers' compound without knowing it. My thoughts begin to spin out of control, but before I can get too lost, Gray wraps his pinky around mine beneath the table. His touch instantly soothes the jagged pieces of my soul.

"I...I—"

Tania shakes her head and cuts me off. "I don't want or need your sympathy, Zoe. The reason I'm telling you is so you know that I, we, know. Okay? If you were with the Reapers, we have a pretty good idea of what happened to you. What you went through."

As one, every single mark created by Gunner throbs. Some have healed completely, but a lot of them are scarred and some even still have the bumpy indents. He turned my body into a canvas of horrors, one where I'll forever be reminded of the things I had to endure.

Once I thought that the worst that could happen was being ridiculed for wearing the wrong clothes, now I wish I didn't know better. I long for the vain, shallow girl who didn't care all that much about other people.

"What does this have to do with us?" Gray asks, his voice rough.

"After the incident with Tania's niece, we began to dig deeper into the Kings," Steven explains. "And we had reason to suspect that Officer Tido is part of the inner circle."

If they're looking for confirmation, they get none.

"At first we looked into ways to stop you guys," Steven admits, and strangely enough, he sounds apologetic. "But then we realized we'd be better off helping you."

Cain begins to drum his fingers against the table. "Help them how?"

Steven sighs. "We left files out for Tido to find, and we made sure the normal PD left the Kings alone as much as possible."

"Yeah?" Gray asks, sounding like he isn't sure he believes them.

Tania nods. "We've come to ask a favor. This past Devil's Night marks the highest death count yet. The community is scared, Grayson. You have to know that."

"Do I?" he drawls, doing his best to give vague answers.

But I can see the intensity in his eyes, and I know he's absorbing every word. Likely filing it away until we're alone and he can discuss it with his brothers.

"What will it take for you to believe us?" Tania asks, reaching for her briefcase again.

My eyes widen as she places some see-through plastic bags clearly labeled evidence on the table. There's a gun in one, and bullets in another. There are more, but Steven is quick to place some paper folders on top to shield them.

"These bullets perfectly match your gun, Grayson," Tania says, picking up one of the bags and dangling it in front of us. "But the report and evidence was tainted and inadmissible because there's an error in the chain of custody."

I take a deep breath and listen to the detectives as they go on and on. They explain in great detail how they've masked the Kings' involvement in crimes, shielded them from the law as much as possible. If what they're saying is true, it's impressive.

As they systematically go through the evidence and reports they've brought, I find myself believing them. The fire in Tania seems real to me. Like when she told us about her niece.

The death of a loved one is something that chips your soul. Leaving behind a hollowness that only those who have experienced it can recognize. It's not visible or recognizable in every interaction. It requires the person to lower their guard, which Tania did. And I recognized soul-deep pain.

"I believe you," I say, interrupting whatever Steven was saying.

"You do?" Tania asks, and I kind of like how surprised she sounds.

Nodding, I lick my lips. "At least about your niece," I clarify. "But if you're telling the truth about that, I have no reason to think you're lying about the rest."

"Now that you know how important this is to us, would you like to tell us what happened to you?" Steven asks as he stretches his arms in front of him and places them with the palms up on the table.

I immediately shake my head. "No," I say vehemently. "It's none of your business."

Leaning back in his chair, he cups his chin and stares right at Gray. "Fair enough. But is there anything you can or want to tell us that might help?"

My mind keeps circling back to the same thing, and I know I have to say something. "Does Chris have any family?"

Tania's eyes haven't left me at all, and as I ask my question it feels like she's upping the intensity. "He does," she answers. "He has his sister, her husband, and their kids."

"And what... I mean..." I bite the inside of my cheek to stop my mouth from running ahead of my brain, making it harder to ask what I want to know. "Do they know what happened to him?"

Gray shifts closer so his lips are only a breath away from the shell of my ear. "You don't need to worry about that, Princess," he murmurs. "That's none of your concern."

I know he means well, and maybe he's right. But he's also extremely wrong. What happened to Chris was my fault, so I need to know.

"They know there was an attack," Tania says. "But as far as they're aware, it was a meaningless crime. A burglary gone wrong or a random attack. We didn't mention your note, your blood, and the... and any other bodily fluids we found at the place."

Oh fuck, I think I'm going to be sick. Bodily fluids is just another way of saying they found Gunner's jizz. I begin to dry heave, and tears form in my eyes. My body trembles as I'm transported back to that day in my mind's eye.

"Princess."

Fuck. No. I'm not there. I'm here with Gray.

"Princess."

Before I can answer him, Gray curses and pulls me into his lap so I'm sitting sideways with my head resting against him. He ignores my startled yelp, and hugs me close to his chest.

"You're safe," he coos. "You're here, with me. Feel my body against yours? This is real, Princess. Don't let that fancy brain of yours fool you."

The more he talks, the easier it becomes to believe him, and even coax my body into relaxing against him. I'm so focused on keeping calm that I barely register his hold on me.

"We're done here," he barks to the detectives. "Get the fuck out."

"N-no," I stammer. "Don't leave yet."

Turning my head, I look between Tania and Steven, both looking knowingly at me. I wonder how many times they've had to deal with people panicking at the news they're delivering.

"We'll stay as long as you're okay with it, Zoe," Tania says, gently.

Gray exhales audibly but doesn't argue which gives me the courage to say what I need to say. "I was there when Chris was killed," I say, surprised at how strong my voice is. "Gunner killed him in cold blood for touching me."

"He touched you?" Gray growls.

"Not like that," I hurry to clarify. "I... I hugged him and snuck the note into his pocket. But Gunner shot him for touching me, and then he... he..."

The silence spanning the room makes it abundantly clear that I don't have to spell out what came next.

"Thank you for telling us," Steven says.

At the same time, Tania asks, "Gunner used to be part of the Cruz Kings, didn't he?" Her eyes are glued to the phone in her hand, like she's reading through something. "He's also one of the guys who looked after your family, and he was perceived dead after the attack on your clubhouse."

"How did you—" I quickly stop myself from talking so I don't say something I shouldn't.

Gray clears his throat. "We thought he was dead, yes." That's all he says, and it sounds so monotone as though he's confirming something inconsequential like the weather.

"But he's alive and with the Reapers," Steven says, sounding more like he's confirming the facts than asking a question. "Is he the one who kidnapped you, Zoe?"

A humorless laugh leaves me. "No. That was my dad." For some reason I can't stop myself from talking, from wanting to set the record straight. "My dad is the reason my mom and sister died. It was part of his arrangement with the Reapers. He's with them now. With the Reapers and his new girlfriend."

The words taste sour on my tongue, and it's like I reach a new level of really understanding the fuckedupness of it all by saying it out loud.

"Gunner's their new VP and he claimed me as his Old Lady," I continue, not stopping when my voice cracks. "And my dad let it happen. He didn't even want to talk to me until it was too late."

"Too late? What do you mean?" Tania asks.

I turn in Gray's lap so I can face the detectives. "Until Devil's Night he didn't fucking care about me at all. Only his new pussy. He didn't care one bit about the things Gunner did to me, or... or..."

"Or what?" Tania prompts softly.

As my anger spikes again, I feel Gray's hands on my hips. It's subtle, but enough to remind me he's there and that he's on my side.

"I don't want to say it with you here," I murmur quietly to Gray. "You should leave."

"I'm not fucking going anywhere, Princess," he shoots back.

Nodding, I concede because I already knew as much. But it makes it harder to speak since I don't want Gray to have to hear what Gunner did to me.

"When I first arrived at the Reapers' place, they told me their new VP had claimed me. But I didn't see him for days. So I was left with Rusty and his insane sister, who's with my dad. Though I don't think it's real, I think she's playing him."

Now that I've unlocked all the shit inside me, I prattle on from the beginning and word vomit *almost* every single thing that happened.

The main thing I manage to keep to myself is the way Gunner made me come in my sleep when I was first with them. I can't see how it's going to help anyone to know, and if at all possible, I never want Gray finding out.

"It's not your fault," Steven assures me after I tell them about having to pick the way Johnny died.

Tania scoffs. "Absolutely not. You weren't his executioner, Zoe. And even if you were, it was by force." She shifts in her chair before continuing. "The same goes for Chris Brooks. That wasn't your fault either. The way you explained things I don't think Gunner would have let him live, regardless. And even if he was alive when you left, it would only be a matter of days. The Reapers never leave any loose ends. It's not part of their M.O."

Their words don't completely absolve me of the guilt I feel, but they do make me feel better about it.

"Do you understand what I'm saying, Zoe?"

At first, I flinch at Tania's question. It's harsh and sounds like I'm incapable of following the simplest logic. But when I look at her, her imploring gaze has me relaxing again.

"It's not your fault, and it's important you know and believe that. None of it was your fault. You didn't cause the deaths. You were put in an impossible situation, which was probably their intention." Tania's voice hardens toward the end. She furrows her brows and again looks down at her phone.

"I understand," I breathe.

Steven opens one of the folders on the table and skims over the contents before closing it again. "Do you have anything with Gunner's DNA on it?" he asks, suddenly.

I blanch. "His DNA?" I squeak.

"We don't need that," Tania hisses at her partner.

At the same time Gray growls, "What the hell kind of fucked up question is that?"

"To link him to the case," Steven sighs. "Look, I know it's insensitive to ask, and I'm sorry for that. But we—"

Catching on to where he's going with this, I bark out a laugh. "No, detective, I don't have his DNA."

"It's okay, Zoe, we don't need it," Tania reassures me, but I ignore her.

Steven's question has stirred something inside me, something that wants out. I don't even think as I roll the sleeves up on the shirt I'm wearing.

"But what about his teeth indents?" I ask, not paying attention to Tania's gasp or Gray's growl. "Or how about where he fucking branded me?" I twist and pull at the shirt to show them the marred skin on my shoulder. "I have a million and fucking one scars he's left behind. Is that the kind of evidence you were looking for, Steven? If not, there might be some of his fucking sperm swimming around inside my body somewhere."

I'm like a woman possessed as I show them some of what I've been hiding. Again I get the feeling of being a spectator, watching myself lash out rather than experiencing it.

Tania tilts her head to the side and stares straight at me. "Zoe, I have to ask if you've seen a doctor since you... escaped?"

I shouldn't be surprised that she's deduced as much as the reason I'm back is because I've escaped. If Tania really knows the Reapers as well as she claims, she knows there's no other way I'd be here right now.

"No," I say, looking down at the table.

"Look, I don't know how else to ask so I'm just going to come out and say it." She pauses briefly, but since I keep my eyes on the table, I don't know why. "Is there a chance you could be pregnant?"

Her words sucker punch me right in the gut, and I make a whimpering sound in the back of my throat.

Motherfucker.

I never even considered that... I mean, I have an implant, but nothing is one hundred percent effective. Gunner never wore protection... and I... I haven't had my period in months.

Could I be pregnant?

"I don't know," I sniffle. Pulling at my hair, I fidget in Gray's lap but he doesn't let me go.

When I look at Tania, she nods. "You need to see a doctor, Zoe. I'd offer to take you, but you'd probably feel more comfortable going with a girlfriend or something."

"Let me go," I demand.

As soon as Gray releases me, I throw myself to the side and onto the floor in a not so graceful heap. Like a damn cockroach, I scurry into the corner where I sit with my back against the wall. I pull my legs up, arms wrapping around my knees as I rest my forehead on the joints.

Fuck.

Pregnant.

Fuck.

Gunner's child.

Or...

Maybe...

It could be Gray's...

Fuck.

Pregnant.

The thoughts play on a loop in my mind, and I can't break myself free. I'm aware that I'm crying, but it's not until Gray crouches next to me that I realize I'm whining and making sorrowful sounds.

"It's okay, Princess. It's all going to be alright."

I snort through my tears. "No, it's not."

How can he say something like that when I might have the devil's fucking spawn growing inside me?

The thought numbs me, and as quickly as the tears sprung to life, they dissipate. I'm still crying on the inside, but outwardly there's no sign of it.

"You also need to get checked for STDs," Steven chimes in.

"Yeah, we get the fucking picture," Cain answers, and when I look at him, he's pointing a knife right at the detective. "You don't really think you need to list out all the things that could happen, do you?"

Steven shakes his head and his shoulders sag. "No, of course not," he mumbles apologetically.

Ignoring the others, Gray once again wraps his pinky around mine. "I'll fucking kill him. Slowly. Painfully," he vows in a deadly tone. "What he's done to you is..."

"Don't say it," I beg. "Don't say it out loud."

With a nod he pulls me to my feet and rests his forehead against mine. He's so close I can smell his minty breath, and feel it across my skin in small puffs.

"He'll pay, Princess. Gunner will fucking pay for everything."

It's not that I don't believe Gray, I'd be a fool not to. But there's no punishment that's big enough for what he's done. He's broken and tainted me in ways I don't know how to come back from.

Anger stirs low in my stomach, demanding I fight back, that I don't just give in like I did back when I was with the Reapers.

"Kiss me," I demand.

Gray looks like I've slapped him. "W-what?"

"You heard me," I growl. "Fucking kiss me, Gray. Reclaim me."

When he doesn't make a move, I do. I fuse my lips to his and eagerly lick at the seams of his lips.

Kissing Gray used to be an almost unholy experience. Something I could feel from the top of my head to the tip of my toes. But right now, all I feel is a big fat nothing. No fear, no excitement. No happiness, no sadness. Just pure nothing.

For some reason the nothingness feels worse than fear. Maybe it's because fear is something you can overcome. But how the fuck do you fight something that isn't there?

"No," I cry, pushing against his chest. "No. No. Fucking no."

Without giving him a chance to say anything, I turn on my heel and sprint out of the room and toward the bar, where I hope to find...

"Cara!" I almost shout as I see her leaning against the bar.

"Zoe?" she sounds puzzled. "I thought you were with—"

"You have to help me," I grind out through clenched teeth. "I need your help."

She looks behind me, and I have no doubt Gray's there.

"What do you need?" she asks on a weary sigh.

It's a good question, and I'm not quite sure of what the answer is. I just know she can help me feel less defenseless and ruined.

"Teach me to fight." I surprise myself with the words, but now as I say them, they feel oh so fucking right. "Teach me how to defend myself."

Grayson

My dick is hard as fucking stone as I watch Cara teach Zoe knife skills. As much as I try to will the fucking thing to go down, it remains stiff in my jeans, craving Zoe as much as my fucking heart does.

Leaning against the wall in the back room which is usually filled with cheap ass poker tables, I dangle my hands in front of the bulge so Zoe doesn't see. I don't want to scare her, or make her feel pressured, even though all I want to do is storm to the center of the room and fist her hair as I claim her lips.

She's not ready for that.

Yet.

Focusing my attention away from how amazing my princess looks I eye the renovations we did to this room. Knocking down the wall to make it bigger was something we should have done ages ago. Because instead of being a cluttered shitty room, it's now half-gym, half-chill. And it easily fits all of us... or most of us.

"A good way to make them suffer is slicing their skin off in pieces." Cara demonstrates on the dead pig hanging from the meat hook in the ceiling, something she had installed the first year the MC was in business. "Much like peeling an apple."

"For fuck's sake, Cara. Zoe asked you to teach her how to fight and defend herself. What the fuck does peeling skin off have to do with that?" I snap, and Cara curls her lip in a sneer, jabbing her knife in my direction.

"I told you to stay outside if you couldn't handle this, Gray."

I throw up my hands, forgetting about my hard dick for a moment. "I can fucking handle this, Cara. You didn't answer my question."

I don't miss the way Zoe bites back a smirk at Cara's huff like I'm the most annoying thing in the fucking world.

"I've taught her some fighting and self-defense techniques, which she will need to practice daily, and preferably with a partner, and now I'm showing her how to make anyone who tries to treat her the wrong way fucking regret it. They'll never expect her to torture them. Besides. It's therapeutic as fuck."

"Oh, you're a therapist now?" I hiss, storming forward, and Cara squares her shoulders, ready for a fight.

"Give me that," Zoe huffs, snatching the knife from Cara's hand, halting my advance as she presses the blade to the hanging carcass and starts to slice the flesh slowly.

Cara beams.

'*Fuck you.*' I mouth to Cara who just snickers and shoos me away with a dismissive wave of her hand.

I check my phone for the time. Dammit, it's not time for Cara to leave yet.

She needs to get back to Rocco by 4pm, but she was adamant to get in some training with Zoe today given it's been three days since Zoe asked for her help. Cara has been busy trying to juggle Rocco's physio and therapy appointments. I swear she's going to run herself into the ground if she doesn't slow down soon.

Maybe I can convince her to let us help with future appointments, after all, she did make time to come here yesterday to sit in with Zoe and Alana when the doctor came to examine my princess. Cara found a female physician so Zoe would feel more comfortable, and the initial pregnancy test came back negative. Thank fuck. The blood tests and swabs will take more time, so it will be a while before we know if

Zoe has been given a fucking STD by that fucking traitorous bastard.

Instead of returning to the side of the room, I slowly pace around the centerpiece of Zoe torturing a fucking dead pig, watching how good she is at it. The more I watch the more my dick aches with a need I can not ask my princess to sate, but I ignore the hard fucker, mesmerized by the sight of Zoe Miller getting high on the power of torturing.

I wonder how she would do with a living victim?

I stop pacing for a moment considering that.

Should I go and steal a lowlife off the streets for my princess to play with?

My heart races with the idea, but I don't think Zoe is there quite yet.

I keep pacing, the hours ticking over as Cara moves from slicing skin to dismembering, and I'm not sure how much more of this teasing I can take.

It's like I'm being edged, my eyes never willing to leave Zoe's expression, no smile but fuck there's a light in her eyes that wasn't there earlier today. It's like she's coming alive in front of me.

So I watch, and let the way her body moves push me closer and closer to needing to fist my cock.

A ding sounds in the room, and Cara sighs, her shoulders dropping a little.

"I need to get going now. Dante's men are waiting to escort me back to Rocco," she explains, moving to her phone to turn off the alarm she set.

"Thank you," Zoe rasps, her voice husky as she stabs the knife deep into what's left of the mangled flesh hanging from the hook.

Lifting a hand towel to dab at her forehead, Cara smiles back at my princess.

"Actually, thank you. I really needed this too," Cara admits, and I feel a pang in my chest, her words confirming that Rocco's care is taking a toll on her.

Knowingly, Zoe smiles, giving Cara a nod, and they say their goodbyes as I stand by, still mesmerized by my princess.

Does she feel the strength she has inside her?

I hope so.

She's always had that strength. That's what will help her get through all of this.

Now alone in the room, Zoe sighs, eyeing her masterpiece.

"Well, I guess I should clean this up."

"Not yet," I rasp, slowly approaching her as those blue eyes go wide.

Standing a few feet in front of her, I bend and tug out the knife I keep hidden in the side of my boot, flipping it open.

"What are you doing?" Zoe gasps, and I reposition the weapon in my hand, offering her the handle.

"Take this."

Her gaze darts back and forth between my eyes and the knife in my hand, confusion twisting her features. When I give it a little shake, she finally reaches out wrapping her hand around the hilt, taking it from me.

As her eyes study my blade in her hand, I shuck off my cut, laying it over the back of a chair in the corner before reaching behind my neck and pulling my shirt off.

"What's going on?" Zoe asks, this time her words have a slight tremble to them.

I lay my shirt over my cut and slowly approach her again, keeping my eyes on hers even as her blue gaze travels down over my chest and abs, coming to rest on the hard bulge in my jeans.

She takes a step back.

"Stop," I demand, but keep my tone soft.

Her eyes dart up to mine as she shakes her head.

"What are you doing?" she asks again, so I point to my knife in her hand.

"I want you to use that."

Her gaze falls to her hand, studying my knife before she glances back up, and I slowly take another step closer.

This time, she doesn't step away.

"What do you want me to use this on?" she asks, sounding unsure.

"Me."

She shakes her head quickly, but I hold up a finger to halt any words she was about to say.

"Here." I point to the healing scar on my stomach where she cut me back when I discovered she had a thing for blood play. "Open the scar back up, Princess. Make sure it never heals."

Her nostrils flare as she takes a step back, but then takes a step forward, like she's warring with the idea.

"Do it, Zo. Make me bleed. Please," I beg, needing to feel her press the knife to my skin.

She bites her lip, and I watch the rapid rise and fall of her chest as she eyes the scar.

"Please," I beg again, and she moves forward, lowering to her knees.

Fuuuck. I didn't think this through.

I hadn't considered what position she'd need to get in to do this, but fuck, when her blue gaze peers up at me through the fan of her dark lashes, I have to fight every fucking urge in me not to fist her hair and force her lips to my cock.

Thank fuck I'm still wearing my jeans.

Her eyes lower again, and she studies the scar before her gaze moves to the straining bulge in my jeans.

"You still want me?" she whispers, her eyes darting back to mine, and a growl rumbles in my chest.

"Always. But I will wait for an eternity, Princess. Ignore my dick. Focus on my scar."

At first, she doesn't ignore my dick. I think I even see her move forward a little, her gaze mere inches from it. And when her pink tongue darts out and licks her lips, my cock fucking jerks, but I remain still, determined to show her that I can control myself, even when my body so badly craves that I just let go and lose myself in her.

"Cut me, Princess," I rasp, urging her on, and she snaps out of whatever trance she was in, lifting the knife to press the sharp blade to my scar and she slowly slices it back open.

I tip my head back and moan out the satisfaction of having her do this to me, feeling the warmth of my blood ooze down my skin.

"You feel that, Princess?" I ask, my eyes dropping back to see her flushed cheeks and parted lips. "You feel how good you make me hurt?"

"Yes." Her eyes meet mine and fuck I love seeing her down there.

"See how much you own me. My body is yours, Zo. If you want to make something bleed, let it be me."

"I... I don't want to hurt you."

"You won't." I shake my head. "You will save your wrath for those that deserve it. I trust you."

Her eyes glass over before she stares at the cut she gave me, studying it. Her tongue darts out like she wants to lick the trail of blood, and as much as I fucking love the idea of that, I hope she doesn't do that.

I don't know that I'd be strong enough to hold myself back from her then.

Slowly, Zoe stands, not making a move to back away from me.

"I want you to do that to me."

"What?" My brows shoot high because surely she's not asking me to cut her.

"Cut me open too," she whispers. "I want your mark on my skin. I want you to cut me and make it bleed every day until I can no longer feel his..."

She trails off, but I know what she's saying. She's talking about the marks Gunner left on her.

I'm going to sever his fucking hands and dick, and then, I'm going to pull every fucking tooth from his head. I've seen the bite marks. His bite marks. I'm going to remove every fucking weapon he used on her, and then, I'm going to make his final hours a living hell.

I'm not going to argue with Zoe about this. If she wants me to cut her delicate flesh open to help her heal, then I'll fucking do it.

Palm up, I hold my hand out between us, and she places my knife in my grip.

"Where?" I ask and she grips the hem of my t-shirt she's wearing, pulling it high enough for me to see the underside of her black bra.

"Right here. Slice through this." She points to the bite mark scar on her stomach, left behind by Gunner, and my hand starts trembling with the need to kill.

"Are you sure?" My voice is a husky rasp, and I clear my throat hoping I don't sound like a monster.

I hate seeing his marks left behind on her, but I do like the idea of ruining them with my own. I dare say that's exactly what my princess wants.

"Yes. Please." She begs.

"You tell me to stop, and I will." I remind her, and she nods as I lower myself to my knees.

As I glance up at her, I wonder what's going through her head.

When she was in the same position, I had craved to force my cock in her mouth. I wonder if she wants to fist my hair and mash her clit against my lips.

Fuck, I'd love nothing more.

I notice her chest rising and falling quickly again, and instead of wondering if it's fear, I ask.

"Are you feeling uncomfortable right now? I'm not scaring you, am I?"

She shakes her head. "No."

I like that fucking answer.

"You're having a reaction right now. Are you sure my nearness isn't causing you distress?"

She bites her lips, her blue gaze locked on mine as she shakes her head.

"Tell me what you're feeling, Princess."

She shakes her head.

"Is it excitement?" I ignore her refusal to admit how she's feeling, and press her for an answer.

"Yes," she whispers, and I push for more.

"Do you like having me on my knees where you can look down on me?"

Her lashes flutter and her cheeks grow redder, and I chuckle.

"Zo. It's okay to feel that way. I enjoyed watching you on your knees."

"You did?"

"I did." I smirk, lifting the blade up to her flesh.

"Are you ready?"

She nods. "Yes. Please."

Her beg matches mine from a few minutes before so I start to slice her creamy flesh open.

A gasp falls from her lips as she stiffens and I freeze, my eyes darting back to hers.

"Want me to stop?"

"No. Don't stop. Never stop."

Fuck. My dick jerks from her words alone and the way it reminded me of her husky voice when we fuck.

I keep going, breaking her skin and watching her bright crimson blood leak free.

"Ohhh." She moans, but in a surprising tone, and her hands reach toward my head, but she stops, flexing her fingers like she's trying not to fist my hair.

"You can touch me, Zoe. If that's what you want. I won't touch you until you ask." I remind her, and it's like my permission pushes her over the edge.

Just as I'd thought, her fingers fist my hair, pulling painfully, but I don't fight her off. If she needs to pull every fucking strand from my head to feel better, then I'll let her do it.

I finish the cut, about two inches long to match mine and glance back up to see her head tipped back.

She's aroused. I can see it in her tense muscles, and fuck I think I can even smell it floating from her pussy mere inches in front of my face.

I want to taste her so bad. Flick my tongue over her swollen clit and make her forget any other man's touch.

A low growl rumbles in my chest, and her eyes flick back down to me.

"You're turned on," I rasp, fighting every instinct in me to give her pleasure.

"No... I..." She shakes her head but can't truly deny it.

"It's okay to be aroused by this, Zo. It's just you and me here, remember? There's no shame or guilt in what we do together or the way we feel."

"I miss what we had." She admits, and I slowly stand. "I miss wanting to kiss you. I miss loving the way you take what you want from me. I miss being consumed by you."

With each word she says, my heart races, and my need for her festers, building up inside me.

"I miss your touch." Tears burst from her eyes, and something in me snaps as I lurch forward, cupping her nape and pressing my lips to hers.

If I thought we were about to share a heated kiss that would re-ignite our relationship, then I was dead fucking wrong. Instead, my hard cock deflates like a fucking balloon when her knee hits my nuts and her hands shove me back with force.

Crumbling to the floor, sharp pain shoots through my groin up into my stomach, pulsing with sharp jabs each time it throbs as the urge to vomit hits.

"Oh my god, Gray. I'm sorry."

Zoe's voice sounds miles away as I fold in on myself, groans falling from my lips. I breathe through it, cupping my junk where I'm pretty sure my nuts have disappeared up into my fucking body and will probably never return.

"Gray. Should I get someone?"

"Noooo." I groan, feeling the throbbing start to ease and I peel my lids open, needing to see my princess.

I shouldn't have fucking done that. Why the fuck did I do that? I knew I shouldn't, yet I fucking did. Why the fuck did I think with my dick?

As I groan again, I realize it wasn't my dick that fucking speared me on. It was the ache in the center of my chest that craved to touch her and hold her close. Show her how much I love her.

"I'm sorry," I mutter and she frowns.

"No. I shouldn't have freaked. I... I..."

"Zo," I rasp, rolling onto all fours as I pant through the ebbing pain. "It was my fault. I got carried away." I tip my head back to look up at her concerned gaze. "I shouldn't have done that. I promised I wouldn't touch you until you asked me to."

"But... I felt it," she whispers, tears pooling in her eyes as she slowly lowers herself to the floor, sitting in front of me with crossed legs. "I'm sorry I'm not right in the head."

"What?" I frown, easing myself to sit in front of her. "Don't say that. This is not your fault. You're dealing with trauma, Zo. PTSD. I was the idiot who overstepped. You should have grabbed the knife and gutted me."

"There was a time I really wanted to do that to you." She grins. "But not now. Somehow I'll figure out my way back into your arms."

I hope she's right, because I ache to touch her. Not to get myself off, but to just hold her. Smell her. Taste her. Worship her.

The shrill of my phone jolts us back to reality, and I dig it out of my back pocket, my heart racing as I see the name flash across the screen.

Rusty Hunt.

"Answer it on speaker," Zoe whispers, having seen the caller too, so I lay it on the floor between us and answer it, selecting the speaker option.

"The fuck do you want?" I grit out, and the smug fuck starts chuckling.

"Is that any way to talk to a fellow President? Were you not taught the correct etiquette?"

"There's no fucking etiquette when it comes to you. What the fuck do you want?" I hiss and again he chuckles.

"Okay. Okay. Straight to business," Rusty mutters. "You have something that belongs to me."

"The fuck I do." I snap and Rusty hisses.

"You have our Zoe. We want her back."

Zoe gasps at his words, her eyes widening in fear as she starts looking around like Rusty is here.

"Oh. And there she is. I hear you little one," Rusty chuckles. "That was easier than I thought it'd be. We didn't actually know Zoe had found her way back to you, but she just gave herself away."

I growl into the speaker on my phone as Rusty chuckles.

"Have you missed us, Zoe?"

"Fuck you!" she yells, her hands fisting into her hair.

Fuck. I shouldn't have answered it on speaker. But then I told her I'd share everything that happens so she knows exactly what's going on.

No secrets.

"Now, now, Zoe. You do have such a temper," Rusty sneers, no longer finding this amusing. "I have someone here who misses you."

"Hey, Sugar."

"You fucking cunt!" I roar, fisting the phone and leaping to my feet. "I will gut you for what you've done!"

Gunner laughs manically through the line, and fuck, I can barely believe it's him. He sounds nothing like the best friend I've had by my side for so long. "Is that so? Come and fucking get me then, you pussy! I bet you can't find me!"

I see fucking red, my free hand wrapping around a chair before I throw the fucking thing at the wall and a small squeal falls from Zoe's lips.

A moment later, the doors to the room fly open as Slasher and Munroe barge in, guns raised.

"You're the coward, Eddie!" I roar again. "You fucking traitor. Why don't you grow some balls and come here?"

"I would, but I'm a little busy balls deep in a Zoe look alike."

I freeze, my gaze darting to Slasher as he lowers his weapon, realizing the threat is on the phone and not in the room.

"What did you say?" I ask, eerily calm.

"Say hi to your protector." Gunner sneers and a moment later I hear a whimper.

"Grayson..." Then she screams.

Zoe gasps and I nearly collapse to my knees at the telling guttural screams that only come from the most painful torture.

More bodies fill the room, my brothers and the Cruz Cunts, all bearing witness to the monsters on the other end of the line and the torture they are dolling out on the girl from the Sleep-Eazy Motel that resembles my princess.

Erin.

"What's your name, bitch?" Gunner's harsh voice crackles through the line as a gurgling sound meets our ears, followed by the feminine cries of Erin.

"Zoe! My name is Zoe!" she screams and with that, I fucking end the call.

"Get Loretta on the phone for me!" I bark, reaching for my shirt and shrugging it back on.

I keep my eyes on Zoe, watching as she shuts down, her head shaking frantically as if she's trying to tell herself she didn't just hear Gunner torturing an innocent girl and forcing her to use Zoe's name.

"Loretta isn't answering," Munroe calls across the room, and I turn to Slasher.

"Call Tido. Tell him to get the cops over to the Sleep-Eazy now and make sure he's first on the scene."

25

Zoe

"What was that?" I demand for the umteenth time. "Why did she say her name is Zoe?"

My imagination is good enough that I can hazard a guess, but I want to hear Gray say it. Actually, I want him to say anything. Recite the fucking microwave instructions from the pizza he had earlier. I'm not picky as long as he speaks up.

"Tell me," I say, my tone growing steely when he just continues to stare at me with a vacant look in his eyes. "You owe me the truth, Gray. Look me in the eye and tell me."

Unease prickles at my spine as I feel the Kings and Cunts behind me move around. Even though I trust them, I don't like that I can't see what they're doing. But the discomfort isn't enough to make me look away from Gray.

"Zoe, maybe we should—"

"Leave," I snarl as I interrupt Slasher. "Leave us alone."

I'm not expecting them to do as I say, so I'm surprised when feet scuff along the floor. Instead of looking, I listen intently, not relaxing until the only sound is coming from my heavy breathing.

Just as I realize I haven't heard the door close, Alana calls out, "We'll be right outside, Z." Then she closes the door behind her.

Gray stands completely still. His eyes are wild, and he keeps clenching and unclenching his hands. He opens and closes his mouth a few times, looking like he's attempting to find the words to answer me.

Back before I was at Gunner's mercy, I would have easily gone toe-to-toe with Gray. I would have jumped him or slapped him to pull him out of whatever mental block he's experiencing. But now... I lick my lips as I consider my options.

What should this version of me do?

I huff in irritation at not having the answer to something as simple as what I want to do. Then it hits me, and I quickly wrap my pinky around his. I pull at where our fingers are intertwined.

A visible shudder runs through his body as, slowly, his gaze turns sharp, focused, and he looks directly at me. "Her real name is... was Erin," he rasps.

"Okay," I say, softly.

"Fuck!" he roars, ripping his finger from mine.

I watch as he agitatedly paces the length of the room while running his fingers through his wavy hair. He keeps muttering to himself, and the only bits I pick up sound like nothing more than curses.

"Fuck!" While shouting out his frustration and anger, he kicks at everything that gets in his way.

Feeling at a loss on how to help him, I look down at my hands. That's when I see it. The blood. I don't know if it's his or mine, and it doesn't really matter.

"Gray," I call, surprised at how steady my tone is. "Get over here."

His head snaps in my direction, and when I show him my bloodied hand, he exhales audibly and rushes to my side.

"Does it hurt? Fuck, I completely forgot to—"

I roll my eyes. "Shut up for a second."

His trademark smirk makes an appearance as he cocks an eyebrow and tilts his head to the side. "I thought you wanted me to talk, Princess."

Just like that, we slip back into our old dynamic, and I let out a relieved sigh at how easy and normal it feels. So maybe that part of me hasn't changed all that much.

Again, I wrap my pinky around his and pull him down on the floor with me. I cross my legs and place my free hand on the fresh cut on my stomach. I try not to cringe as I pull my shirt up, but it stings since the blood is making it plaster to my skin.

"Show me," I whisper.

Gray doesn't need me to spell it out, and he willingly reveals my bloody handiwork on his toned stomach.

Without looking away, I unlock our pinkies and pull on his hand until it can reach my stomach. Then I run his pinky through the open wound before I do the same to him.

Every time I want to flinch away or hide from the monster I heard on the phone and the memories it stirred, Gray's dark gaze is enough to keep me in the present.

"Zo," he rasps. "What are you doing?" There's an undertone of curiosity mixed with incredulity as he asks.

"Blood to blood," I murmur. "Pinky to pinky, Gray."

His eyebrows shoot up his forehead in surprise. "That sounds like the beginning of an evil chant," he says as he shakes his head.

"Maybe it is," I quip. "So you better answer my question."

My newfound strength isn't a façade. Seeing Gray react that violently took over my own feelings, pushing them down until he became my sole focus. I hate seeing him so out of it, and if ignoring my fear helps him, then that's what I'll do.

"Erin was one of Loretta's whores," he says, and I nod for him to continue even though I'm not following. "Loretta owns the Sleep-Eazy Motel and runs a whorehouse there. While I was looking for you I found out that Adam went there, and when he did, he favored Erin. He made her say her name was Zoe."

Ignoring the way my stomach churns, I ask, "Adam? As in—"

"Yes. Him," Gray spits. "Apparently he's forgotten what it's like to have you if he thinks whores can ever compare."

I shudder at his words. "But why would Gunner—"

"She reminded me of you when I first met her," Gray admits. He sounds so defeated I wish I could make myself move to his side and hug him. "I told her to call me if she ever needed help, Princess. I fucking told her she could trust me. But that was another lie, wasn't it?"

Another? Oh fuck. Now I finally understand.

"Stop it," I snap, angered by the implication. "She wasn't me and you didn't fail me, Gray. I was the one who fucking failed you. Okay?"

He shakes his head like he doesn't believe me.

"You listen and you listen good, Grayson Black," I seethe. I'm not angry at anyone but myself. It's my fault we're here. If I'd only listened and stayed put at Dirty Diamonds, then none of this would be happening. "You told me to wait for you and not to go anywhere. I'm the one who broke my promise to you. Not the other way around. Do you understand me?"

A fire lights in his eyes as he growls, "Why the fuck do you never listen to me?"

Afraid he's going to pull away, I tighten my hold on his pinky. "I... I thought you were in danger," I admit.

He laughs scornfully. "So fucking what? Did you think I'd want you to risk your life for mine, Princess?"

His words make my temper stir in my chest. "Do you think I care what you want?" I hiss. "If there's a way to help you, you better fucking believe I'll take it. Every fucking time, Gray."

"Why?"

Now it's my turn to laugh, which I do although the answer isn't funny. "Because I fucking love you, you idiot."

I can practically see his jaw hit the floor at my admission. And while I never meant to shout the words while infused by anger, I have no regrets.

"You love me?" The shock on his face is a stark contrast to the smirking version of him from not so long ago.

"Of course I do," I choke out.

Rather than saying it back, Gray studies me. His eyes dance over every inch of my body, and he doesn't speak until they're glued to my lips. "You don't get to hear me say it until I can kiss you," he says, nodding as if to make himself clear.

His words hurt more than anything I've ever felt. Tears blur my vision as I abruptly break our interlocked pinkies and scramble to my feet.

"Fuck you," I spit. "Fuck you for holding it over my head like it's my fault." My throat is clogged by a ball of emotions and I angrily swipe the tears from my eyes.

"Sit your ass back down."

"No," I hiss.

"I swear to fucking God, Zo. If you don't sit your fine ass back down, I'm going to do something we'll both regret. So sit yourself or I'll make you."

Goosebumps spread across my body, and I struggle to breathe as the air thickens with his outburst. While I know he'd never purposefully hurt me, I also know he isn't joking. He very much means what he just said. Gray doesn't make empty threats, which means it was a warning.

Relenting, I sit back down. This time Gray forces our fingers back together, and he wraps his other hand around my wrist so I can't move.

"You're the only woman I've ever kissed, Princess. And I never want to kiss anyone that isn't you. So when I say I won't say the words back until I can kiss you, it's not to guilt trip you. It's because you'll have been my first for both of those things."

All I can manage to say is, "Oh."

"Yes, oh," Gray mocks. "Now, do you think you can fucking learn to trust me as much as you claim to love me?"

I scrunch my nose up in annoyance at his choice of words. The only reason I don't lash out again is that they're fair. Blunt as fuck, but fairer than fair. I just said I love him, so I need to do better.

"I do trust you," I say, softly. "It's..." I trail off and take a deep breath as I try to stop my brain from running a million miles an hour.

"Good," he simply says.

Then he lets go of my wrist, but we don't pull back. We keep our pinkies connected even when sitting becomes uncomfortable, and we both lie down. We don't talk, both lost in our own heads. But we're sharing so much in the silence. Instead of pulling away and each doing our own thing, we're together.

"I felt something when you kissed me," I say, out of nowhere.

"Hmm?"

Clearing my throat, I explain, "When I kissed you while the detectives were here, I felt nothing. Nothing at all, and it scared me. But when you kissed me earlier, I felt it."

He chuckles. "Is that why you introduced your knee to my goods?"

As I contemplate my literal knee jerk reaction, I decide that's not why. "No. I did that because I could, and because I trust you." The words don't have to make sense to be true. Then again, since he doesn't question it, maybe they were clear enough.

I'm half asleep when there's a knock on the door, and after Gray shouts for them to come in, Tido sticks his head through the door.

"Got an update for me?" Gray asks as he gets up and pulls me with him.

"I do, Gray. The detectives were quick to take over the scene, and they practically sent me here as soon as they arrived," he explains. I'm still not sure how I feel about the detectives. Mostly because it's weird. "Do you want Slasher here for this?"

Gray looks at me, and the concern in his eyes is easy to read. He's worried about how I'll feel being in here with three men. To help him, I offer, "I'll go find Alana."

"The fuck you will," Gray growls. "You're not leaving my side, Princess. Besides, I think you need to hear this as well."

I try to steel myself for what's undoubtedly going to be a gruesome update while Gray ushers all of us into church. But nothing could prepare me for the pictures Tido shows us on his laptop.

"This is how we found her," he says. There's no emotion in his voice as he gestures at the screen. "Her back and hair were covered in jizz, indicating it was a group thing."

I gag as I look at the young woman on the screen. Erin's eyes are sewn shut and her lips sewn together. Her cheeks are littered with cigarette burns, and her chin is like one gaping wound. All color drains from my face, and I gasp, "Gray," as I notice the mark on her forehead.

Clawing at my throat, I try to breathe, but no air reaches my lungs. I fall out of the chair, gasping for the sweet relief of oxygen that never comes.

"Princess!"

Oh God, her forehead.

An inhuman wail leaves me as I dry heave on all fours like a fucking animal.

I still remember the way it felt, and the sweet stench of burned flesh once he was done.

"Princess!"

The smell was the worst. Worse than the all-consuming pain that made screaming impossible.

"Snap the fuck out of it! Slasher, get Alana. Now."

For days I couldn't get rid of the smell, or maybe it was weeks. Even after squirting soap directly into my nostrils, I couldn't smell anything but my flesh burning.

"Gray!" I grasp onto his arms, pushing myself impossibly closer. "Don't let go," I beg as sobs make my body tremble violently in his hold.

"Shh. You're okay, Princess. You're safe. With you in my arms, this is the true definition of Nirvana."

Just like the first night I was back, it's the use of his secret cabin that breaks through my thoughts.

"Do you hear me, Princess? You're my Nirvana."

"I-I h-hear you," I stutter as I fight against the sobs. "You're my Nirvana, too."

When Slasher returns with Alana in tow, I'm softly crying into Gray's chest as I sit in his lap and his arms are holding me tight. I don't look up or answer when she says my name, I keep all my focus on breathing. Something that should come easy, but right now it's anything but.

Slasher says something to Tido, who asks, "Should I carry on?"

Even though he isn't asking me, I nod against Gray's chest. "Yeah, go on," he says, answering.

Tido talks about the brutality, and how the macabre stitches have often been thought to be when the Reapers wanted to send a message.

"In the past, they've taken the eyes or sewn them shut if the victim sees something they shouldn't," he explains. "And when it's the lips, it's been a verbal offense. Like a disrespect against Rusty or Irina, or someone who broke their code of silence."

Leaning forward I look at Tido. "B-but Erin wasn't one of theirs. So how can any of that apply to her?"

When no one answers me, the penny finally drops.

That's not Erin... that's me. And I've done both those things. I've seen things I shouldn't since I've seen their faces, and in their warped reality I've definitely been disrespectful.

As my eyes once again zone in on the brand on her forehead, I furrow my brows in confusion. That's not where mine is. My hand immediately moves to my shoulder, and I absentmindedly tap the ruined skin below my shirt while I try to figure out why it's there.

When Gray asks if there are any other marks on Erin's body, I'm almost convinced he can read my thoughts.

Tido changes to a picture of her shoulder which bears the same brand as mine. "Only this," he answers.

I shouldn't be surprised. In fact, I should have fucking expected it. Gunner's so fucking unhinged that of course he'd make a point of branding us identically.

"Why on her shoulder?" Slasher asks. The question barely leaves his lips before Alana elbows him in the stomach. "What the fuck did you do that for?" he growls.

She discreetly tips her head in my direction, but when he's too slow to pick up on hersubtle cues, I say, "Because that's where he branded me."

Alana's eyes immediately water. "Oh, Z," she cries.

I know she'd already deduced as much, but I'm also aware that suspecting and knowing isn't the same.

"Don't," I choke out. "If you cry, I'll start again."

She nods and mimes zipping her lips, then she immediately cringes as she realizes how sick that seems now.

"When you say he branded you," Tido says, pausing until he has everyone's attention. "Do you mean the same place? Or with the same—"

"Ring," I say, finishing for him. "Gunner used his beard ring." My voice holds steady even though a sliver of cold runs down my spine.

He shifts nervously. "Are you sure it's the same? I mean, could it be another one?"

I slowly get out of Gray's lap and he follows me as I walk up to Tido. Then I bare my shoulder to the cop, ignoring Alana's cry and Slasher's growl as all of them look at the completely identical brand on my shoulder.

"I'm pretty sure it's the same," I deadpan.

Once I've had enough of them staring, I pull the shirt back into place and turn to look at Tido who's tapping away on his phone.

"Is it a thumb ring?" he asks, still typing.

I shake my head. "A beard ring. A silver beard ring."

Tido asks a bunch more questions, and I answer him the best I can. I don't like talking about any of it, but it's a small price to pay if it can somehow help the PD and detectives stop the Reapers from killing more innocent women.

"Is there anything else I should know?" Gray asks.

Tido looks at him. "Yeah. The Reapers took all the other whores with them."

26

Zoe

I jerk awake and immediately roll out of bed, settling into a crouch as I reach for the knife stashed under my pillow. I blink rapidly to get used to the darkness, looking around to find the source for my rude awakening.

"What the fuck are you doing, Princess?" Gray's sleep laden tone is gruff, and by the sounds of it he's not as awake as I am.

"Someone's here," I hiss back. "Someone broke into our apartment."

His movement is nothing but a blur as he reaches for his gun, and within seconds he's in front of me, shielding me with his body.

"Where?" he whispers.

Looking around, I don't see anything out of place. "I don't know," I admit. "But I felt them. They touched me." Fear and anger make it hard to remain still.

A part of me wants to bolt, but the other demands we stand our ground and don't give as much as an inch to whoever was stupid enough to come here.

When Gray stands, I reach for him, but faster than I can make contact, he switches on the light. The bedroom is now cast in a bright light, revealing... nothing out of the ordinary.

I remain on the floor next to the bed while he systematically goes through our home, checking every nook and cranny.

As he's done every night since the call from Gunner two days ago, he returns with his arms outstretched.

"There's no one here, Princess. It was just a dream."

I vehemently shake my head. "No. I felt the touch, Gray. He... he ran his finger down my neck and across my shoulder." I shudder at the memory.

Rather than joining me on the floor, Gray pulls me back in bed. This time he isn't keeping his distance. He lies down on his side, propping his head up with his hand while reaching for my tightly braided hair.

"Is this what you felt?" he asks as a tickling sensation runs down my neck and continues to my shoulder.

Suppressing a shudder, I nod.

"A tendril has come loose," he says, calmly. "It was just your hair, Zo."

Squeezing my eyes closed I try to hide from the mortification. Every night I braid my hair as tight as possible and gather it on top of my head so I don't have to feel it down my back. The suggestion came from Rose who apparently sleeps like that because she's scared of spiders, and the long hair brushing her back while sleeping often sends her into a panic attack.

"Why don't you go shower, and I'll get us some breakfast?" Gray suggests after checking the time on his phone. "Cara will be here in just a few hours, and you just know she's going to work you hard."

After Tido left the other day, I basically blew up Cara's phone until she agreed to train with me daily. I know it's selfish and that Rocco needs her, but I can't ever be a victim again. And apart from her, I don't know who can help me.

Gray's more than capable of it, sure. But he'd take it too easy on me. He proved that much when he was against Cara showing me torture techniques. No, what I need is someone who won't shy away from bruising me, or hold me in ways that makes my heart plummet to my stomach.

"Okay," I agree. "I'm sorry for waking you again."

Before I can get off the bed, Gray takes my wrist and pulls my hand to his lips. He gently presses a kiss to my pinky. "Don't ever let me fucking hear you apologize for that again."

"Or what?" I challenge with a raised eyebrow.

"Or I'll take you over my knee and spank that fine ass of yours red," he growls, not even bothering to hide how much he likes that idea.

Arousal hits me out of nowhere, and I gasp.

"But that wouldn't be punishment for my princess, wouldn't it?" he asks with a knowing smirk. "Neither would burying my head between your legs to lick your pretty pussy."

"I... I..." Fuck, I can't think straight when he talks like that.

He's making me wet and wanton for his touch with words alone, and it's anything but fair. I'm desperate for his touch, yet I'm still fearful of it. Fuck, I haven't even allowed him to kiss me yet.

"Get out of here before either of us does something stupid." Though he's smiling, his tone is serious, and I know he's right.

I'm not ready.

Each minute around Gray makes it easier to breathe, to exist. And when I'm in his presence, I find that I don't spend time panicking, wondering who I am now. Because it doesn't matter. When we're together, we're Zoe and Gray. Zray or Groe.

I giggle to myself as I step under the warm sprays of the shower and quickly lather my body in soap. This time I don't avoid all my scars like the plague. I gently trail my fingers across the cut he made on my stomach.

It runs through one of Gunner's many bite marks, which makes it look like it's been crossed out. It's by no means gone, but I can still bask in the symbolism of Gray canceling the mark from his former club brother.

Taking a shuddering breath, I tilt my head forward and let the water cascade down my back. When I stand like this, I try to imagine the water is Gray caressing my skin. The thought of asking him to do it is growing more and more in my mind.

Maybe it's my overthinking that's ruining it. When he kissed me I felt not just something, it felt good—but in a scary way, hence the knee to the nuts reaction. But maybe I can endure more now.

Switching off the water I reach for the towel, and while I dry myself I try to muster up the courage to just run out there and throw myself at him. Or call him in here, and... yeah, no. That's not happening. The mere thought is equal parts arousing and terrifying.

I'm not completely sure what it is I'm scared of. I know he won't hurt me, just like I know he can make me feel so good I see stars. As I get dressed, I wonder again if it's only the unknown, and if so, how I can convince myself that I *do* know.

Gray and I have done so many things there can't really be any unknowns left. Can there?

My mind is so fucking jumbled I give up on trying to find the source of my fear. Instead, I eye the zip-up hoodie and decide against wearing it. Today, I'll only wear the tee and yoga pants. And if anyone notices my scars, they'll know how fucking tough I am.

Those are Mama's words, but I repeat them daily as a mantra. Just waiting until the day comes where I truly believe them.

After brushing my teeth and gathering my hair into a messy bun on top of my head, I exit the bathroom.

Gray's already dressed, and his hair is weighed down on his head from the water he's soaked it in. I know he'll shower while I train with Mama. Fuck, if it wasn't for my time with her, I don't know when he'd find the time to do it since he still refuses to leave me alone. I suppose he could do it while I'm sleeping, but I already know he wouldn't risk me waking up to find him not there.

Fuck, the lengths he goes to. It's no wonder I love him.

"What are you smiling at?" he rasps as a goofy smile splits my lips.

Sitting down I put my new trainers on. They were a gift from Mama and Rocco. Attached to the left shoe was a note that read:

KICK ASS

... and to the other...

AND DON'T CARE ABOUT THEIR NAMES!!

The notes were written in two different handwritings, so I imagine they each wrote a note. While I can't be sure, I think the shorter one was Rocco and the latter from Mama.

"Nothing," I finally answer once I've tied the laces on both shoes. "Are you ready? I'm starving."

Gray picks up the hoodie I've placed next to me on the couch. "Not wearing this today?"

I shake my head and bite the inside of my cheek. "Not today."

It's not exactly a smart decision on my part since the clubhouse isn't the warmest place. But right now the thought of being courageous is enough to keep me warm.

Gray places his hand on the small of my back and gently guides me downstairs. As we get nearer to the main room, I boldly come to a stop.

"Forgot something?" he asks, and I shake my head.

"I want to try something," I murmur. Then I take his hands and place them on my hips.

Our eyes lock on each other, darkness to light as his almost black orbs zone in on my bright blue ones.

My hands are still on top of his, and I gradually increase the pressure until my heart skips a beat and my palms become clammy.

"Princess," he rasps, licking his lips. "If you push this much further, you'll end up making me the bad guy for your impatience."

I want to point out that I'm not the only one who's being impatient, only... I'm not sure that's true. Gray hasn't once given me reason to think he wouldn't wait forever. He's right, it's totally me that's eager to get over this stage.

"Just one more minute," I say, my tone barely above a whisper. Clearing my throat, I try to explain the way I feel.

"I don't want to rush us. But Gray, I'm scared that it'll never get better if I do nothing. Does that make sense?"

He ponders the words for a couple of minutes—which feels like an eternity in the ensuing silence. "Yeah," he finally answers.

Stretching to my tiptoes I move my lips until they're almost touching his. Almost. I hold myself still, loving the way his breath fans across my sensitive skin.

A door slams in the distance, and a chair sounds like it's being toppled over. As soon as the noises register, I shrink in on myself, no longer feeling strong or adventurous.

"I'll fucking kill them," Gray growls as he pulls me to his side.

Without another word he wraps his arm around my middle, pretending not to notice the way I tense as we walk into the main room.

"Zoe!" Rose squeals.

"Now that's perfect timing," Beth grins, pointing at the takeout bags on the table.

Alana sits at the end of the table, smiling widely when she catches me looking. "Kept the seat warm for you," she smirks as she moves to the one to the right.

Gray chuckles in my ear and gently nudges me toward the group of women. Most of them I've only seen briefly if at all in the couple of weeks I've been back, but I've still missed them. Not like Alana, more as a unit I've grown to love.

"What are you all doing up?" I ask since it's rare they're able to function this early.

"Our almighty Prez texted Alana that you were coming down for breakfast today, so we decided to celebrate," Izzy sing-songs.

I furrow my brows in confusion. "This isn't the first time I'm here for breakfast," I muse.

"Why are you trying to take our reason to celebrate away from us?" Rose pouts. "Let us celebrate with empty calories and a sugar coma if we want to."

I laugh.

The Cunts eagerly open the bags and begin to pull an obscene amount of containers out. Seriously, it looks like they've ordered everything from the menu. There are pancakes, French toast, scrambled eggs, fried eggs, bacon for days, hash browns, doughnuts, pies... you name a breakfast food, and it's here.

"Did someone say mimosas?" Tex asks as he joins us.

"No one said that," I laugh.

Shooting me a wink, he says, "Well, you should have."

Once he's dished out drinks to everyone, he takes one for himself, and like the Cunts, he empties his in one go while I slowly sip at mine.

While we eat, Gray hangs out at the bar with Tex. Slasher, Tido, and Munroe are quick to join them. Though the Kings send envious glances in our direction, no one says anything.

At least not until Tio enters the room.

"What's this?" he asks, grinning widely. "I can fucking smell all the goodness all the way upstairs." He eagerly rubs his hands together and tries to get Rose and Izzy to scoot over and make room for him.

"Excuse you," Alana says, raising her voice as she throws a scrunched up paperback at his head where it bounces off to land on the floor. "This is our fucking food. Order your own if you're too lazy to cook."

Her eyes flash with a malice she's reserved especially for him since he voted for her punishment for helping to free me to either be a public lashing or branding. I shudder at the memory.

Sick fuck.

"What?" he growls, clearly not liking her tone.

"You heard me," she says, flipping him off with a shit-eating grin on her lips. "Get lost, Tio. This is *our* food."

He narrows his eyes at her. "Listen up. You're a fucking Cunt and I'm a King. So show some fucking respect."

Quick as lightning, Alana's out of her chair. She cocks her hip and tosses her hair over her shoulder. "What did you say?" she seethes.

Their standoff garners the attention of the other Kings, and I can feel them moving closer.

"Tio," Slasher growls, moving in front of Alana, who quickly pushes him out of the way.

"No," she hisses. "I know you mean well, baby. But this isn't your fight."

I swallow thickly as sweat trickles down my back. My hands shake, and all I can see is his cocksure grin the day he said "aye" when Rocco read out the sick and sadistic punishments Mama—Cara had concocted. But she's not the Mama anymore. Her rules mean jack shit.

Without thinking, I shoot out of my chair and round on Tio. "Back off," I warn, jabbing my finger into his chest.

"Zo—"

Shaking my head, I will Gray to stay out of it. Alana's right. This isn't a battle our men need to fight for us. It's *mine*—and only motherfucking *mine* because I'm the Mama and these are *my* Cunts.

"If you have a problem with Alana, or any of my Cunts, you're welcome to submit a complaint via email to whogive saflyingfuck@fuckoff.fuckyou," I seethe.

Tio looks like he can't believe I just said that, and if I'm honest, I can't quite believe it myself. "Prez," he calls.

"What?" Gray barks.

"You might want to control your fucking woman," Tio says, taking a step closer to me. "She might not know all our rules yet, but she should know—"

"Know what?" I say, interrupting his tirade. "The Mama has full control of the Cunts. That much I know. And since Rocco declared me the Mama, which, no one has fucking challenged, Alana is under my protection. Unless my Cunts paid for this meal with money from your wallet, I don't really fucking care for your entitled outburst."

I place my hands on my hips as I glare daggers at Tio, refusing to bow down.

"Rose," I call without looking away. "As the former Mama's right hand tell me this. Are there any rules about the Cunts not being allowed their own money?"

Her feminine giggle sounds wrong with how thick the tension is. "No."

"Munroe," I call, still not averting my gaze or moving.

"Yes, Mama," he replies and I swear I can hear the grin in his voice.

"Are there any such rules in place?"

He guffaws. "Absolutely fucking not."

I nod, satisfied I've asked the right people. It might have been more natural to ask Gray, but since he's the Prez, I refuse to drag him into a ridiculous squabble like this. There's also the minor fact that I'm not sure he would answer honestly and not bend the rules for me.

"Mama," Tex calls. "If I may say something..." He trails off, obviously waiting for my answer.

"Of course," I say, turning my head and giving him a smile.

He points to the over the top stocked and fancy bar. "The Cruz Cunts paid for a good chunk of the renovations. As you may have noticed, everything is brand new and of the highest quality. Even with our insurance and extra jobs, all of this is better than we could have hoped for because of them."

"Thank you for telling me," I say. Then I turn back to Tio. "Tell me, Tio. Do you have a brand new mattress? Are you well-fed? Do you get pussy when you want it?"

He swallows. "Yes, Mama."

"Good," I say, giving him another icy stare. "If I ever find you harassing my Cunts like that again, I'll be voting for *you* to be lashed or branded. Fuck, I might just anyway."

Only when he slinks away, do I look at Gray. Nervous about what I'm going to see written on his face. But I shouldn't have worried. The man looking back at me does so with pride in his eyes and a smirk on his lips.

"A bit over the top for my taste, but not half bad," Munroe says. "You'll do well here, Zoe."

As though Munroe's seal of approval was the missing factor, we sit back down and continue our meal, while the Kings gather around the bar again.

Looking toward the door I make a mental note that I need to ask Gray to leave Tio alone. If he goes to him and makes any demands, he'll undermine my status as Mama. And while I might not have wanted it when Rocco made it so, it's mine now and I'm not giving it up.

I'm so deep in thought I barely notice Gray coming to my side. "Cara's here," he says.

I get up and go to follow him, but Alana's hand on my elbow halts me. "Zoe... Mama," she says, correcting herself. "Thank you."

"Don't thank me," I say, returning her watery smile. "I meant what I said." I turn and look at every single Cunt at the table. "You're mine now. So if you ever have a problem, I want you to come to me. I don't care if it's about period cramps or a complaint against a King. Even if said King is the Prez himself. You tell me. Understood?"

They all say "Yes, Mama" in unison.

I'll be fucking damned if I allow the past to repeat itself. I don't want the Cunts to feel like they have to hide if one of the Kings scares them. They need to tell me so I can let Gray know.

With a sigh, I greet Cara who's waiting in our usual training room. Huh, she must have used the back entrance since I didn't see her come in.

As I watch her, I decide that today's the day. I'm going to ask her what's been on my mind for so long. How the fuck didn't she know her Cunts were scared of Gunner?

27

Grayson

Pride has me standing taller today after witnessing the strength of Zoe yesterday standing up for her Cruz Cunts. Even though Rocco forced her into the role after he banished Cara, she's taken the duty by both hands and fucking made it her own.

I wouldn't have cared if she didn't want to continue with the responsibility. All I cared was that she was here safe, but fuck, each day that passes she gets stronger and stronger, fighting demons we can't even see, but know taunt her every waking and sleeping moment.

I used to think strength was a physical thing. Muscle. Toughness. Who could beat who down faster with their fists.

Zoe has shown me just how fucking superficial that thought process was.

In the dictionary next to the word strength should be the name, Zoe Miller.

Ever since yesterday when Zoe reconfirmed her position as the Mama, the Cruz Cunts have been buzzing around on some sort of fucking high. It's good to see them happy, and even though Tio stepped over the line yesterday, the Cruz Cunts' good mood had them seeking the poor guy out and showing him again how they care for him.

It's the first time since taking on the role of Prez that things have felt relatively normal.

Light.

Almost like we aren't at war with another club.

Unfortunately Zoe's scars, which she is showing freely now, are a reminder to us all that things are very much not normal. And they won't be until the Reapers are gone.

Until Gunner has been executed, Kings' style.

His betrayal sits like lead in the pit of my stomach. I should have fucking known. I should have fucking questioned his behavior. I should never have been so fucking blind.

If only I had paid more attention to his attitude toward the decisions Rocco was making. The way he wanted Zoe to be traded in return for our money with the Reapers. Hell, if we had done that, then he would have left sooner and taken his place as the Reapers VP, torturing Zoe earlier.

It was always about her.

Why the fuck didn't I see that until it was too late?

One thing is for sure. I'll never be blindsided again.

The gate bell rings, and Tex checks the screen, advising me that Baz is here.

Dante had sent a message earlier today saying he was sending someone with an intel update, but I naturally thought it would be Cain. Not Baz.

When the clubhouse door opens, and the sharply dressed dark-haired Aussie strides in, a hush falls over the room.

I snicker. "You look too fucking fancy to be dressed like that here." I gesture to his suit that probably cost more than everything in this fucking room.

He cocks a dark brow. "You want me to take off my jacket and shirt and show you what I have underneath, Black? I bet you I fit in better than you."

Chuckling, I nod, moving in his direction. "Probably." We meet in the middle, shaking hands. "Where shall we do this?"

Baz shrugs. "If this information is confidential, then let's go to your office. If not, here's fine."

I turn, examining the room and the people in it. A lot of my club brothers are here, and the Cruz Cunts are sitting with Zoe across the room talking about how much cash they are raking in with their fans' website. There's nothing to indicate that we have a mole anymore. In fact, since Gunner and Rhiannon left, we haven't had any issues suggesting we have a rat.

"Here is fine." I gesture to the table next to us, and Baz sits, laying out his laptop and a folder.

Gesturing to Tex with my fingers, he gives me a nod, grabbing the bottle of Jack and two glasses, as I take a seat with Baz before Tex comes over, pouring us each a drink. Baz nods a thanks, and I swear Tex has fucking stars in his eyes as he smiles warmly back at the Mafia man in our clubhouse before he hurries back over to the bar.

"Your men aren't very fucking scary," Baz mutters as he flips open the laptop, a slight smirk tugging at his lips and I chuckle.

"Not when you're around, apparently. You look too fucking pretty."

Baz smirks wider, nodding like he's in fucking agreement. "Sometimes it's hard being this hot."

I scoff, and he shrugs, still smirking.

Angling the laptop in my direction, he starts showing me things that would normally be right over my head, but I quickly learn how they have been tracking phones, digital footprints left from social media, emails and apps, and how they have narrowed down the Reapers' whereabouts to five different locations between Santa Cruz and Watsonville.

As Baz talks, I call Slasher, Munroe, Stretch and Doug over to listen in as well. He opens the folder, laying out photos of the houses, some of the Reapers, and one of Gunner and Rusty as they laugh about something.

Low growls sound around me as my club brothers see the photo of Gunner.

He fucking betrayed us all.

We all want a piece of him, and I'm determined to make sure we get that. Gunner won't get a quick death if I have anything to do with it.

"With this information, you can arrange a timed attack on all locations at once with the help of the Diamond Crew," Baz suggests, sitting back in his chair to take a swig of his

JD. "They are still watching all locations, so if they move somewhere else, we'll know."

"Which house is Gunner in?" I ask, and Baz stares at me for a moment, his eyes dark and analyzing. "I just wanna know, man. I'm not going to go half cocked and hit his location. I believe in your strategies."

Giving me a sharp nod, Baz breaks our eye lock, but eyes the men around us. He's not sure one of them won't go off half cocked, though.

"Leave us," I snap, and without argument, my club brothers move away, giving Baz and I the space we need. "They're gone. Now tell me."

Taking another slow swig of the amber liquid in his glass, Baz takes his sweet fucking time before responding.

"I trust that you won't go off half cocked, but your men all crave vengeance on Gunner, especially your VP."

"With fucking reason," I hiss and he nods.

"I'm not saying that he doesn't have a good fucking reason. But Dante needs this to go as smoothly as possible. Minimal casualties and a war won. He especially doesn't want another President shot down. This community is scared, and even though you are outlaws, they rely on your protection."

"I'm aware of our fucking duty," I snap, and he grins.

"You're just as fucking mouthy as you were when you were a teenager."

I roll my eyes. "Are you going to tell me which house Gunner is in or fucking not?"

"The outcome is on you. Don't forget that," he rasps, and then points to one of the crosses on the map that pinpoints the Reapers safe houses. "He's shacked up with Rusty Hunt and his sister. We've had one sighting of Brian Miller at that location, too."

Fuck. We really have them.

It's not lost on me that perhaps we should have asked for more assistance from the Diamond Crew long before this war escalated. They have associates and crew that have skills that simply can't be found in an MC.

I can't think like that though. The past is the past. It can't be changed.

But the future. Well, we are about to write it in our favor.

"Thanks for this," I mutter, eyeing the map and the address that currently houses our biggest enemy.

"Happy to help. Scum like the Reapers need to be dealt with. Cops' hands are tied with fucking red tape, but us," he grins almost sinisterly, and I get a glimpse of his wicked nature, "we were put on this earth to be the nightmare for the nightmares."

He stands then, closing his laptop and pushing the file closer to me.

"Are you sticking around for the final showdown?" I ask and he bobs his head.

"Wouldn't fucking miss it. Reach out when you want to strategize a plan of attack."

We shake hands again, and as Baz leaves, I turn to see all eyes on the Mafia man as he walks back out the clubhouse door.

"Close your mouths." I grumble toward the Cruz Cunts, who all look to be drooling over the dark and sinister man. Even my fucking princess.

The Cunts giggle, turning back to each other and whispering excitedly, while my brothers sit on bar stools with fucking dreamy eyes.

"What the fuck is wrong with you?" I snap at them, and they all shake their heads like I've pulled them out of a trance. "Fucking hell. Are you all hard for Barrett fucking Marx?"

When Stretch glances down at his crotch to check if his dick is hard, I roll my eyes and turn to the Cunts.

"Can we get some Cunt action over here to satisfy these fuckers?"

Rose grins, bouncing up from her chair and skipping over as Izzy and Cilla follow.

Approaching Alana and Beth who are still sitting at the table, I realize we are running short of available cunt.

"Slasher." I bark, turning back to look at my VP. "Just reconfirming Alana's is no longer free game?"

"Anyone tries to touch her and I'll gut them." He snaps, making me smirk.

Possessive bastard.

I know how he feels.

Turning my eyes to Beth, I stare at her silently for a long moment, watching her shrink back in her chair.

"Gray, do you have to be so intimidating to my girls?" Zoe snaps, and I eye my princess briefly, biting back a smirk.

I fucking love it when she challenges me in front of everyone. It shows her courage, but also, it makes my dick hard, eager to remind her who's boss behind closed doors. She's not ready for that yet, but she knows what challenging me means. I'll keep each account stored in my brain for a raincheck.

"When they aren't standing up to their duties, then yes," I remark, ignoring her death glare as I turn back to Beth.

"Why are you still sitting here instead of entertaining the men?" I ask her, and her lips thin like she's willing them not to speak.

"Maybe she's on her period," Zoe snaps, like the mention of her monthly bleed will make me uncomfortable.

It doesn't.

"She still has a mouth." I point out and I don't miss the way Zoe's mouth drops open in disgust.

This is fun. Stirring her.

I pull out a chair and sit down next to Beth, leaning my forearms on my thighs as I shift close to her.

"I asked you a question. And for the record, there's no wrong answer, but I do expect one."

Beth's worried eyes dart to Alana and Zoe before landing back on me, and she leans in closer.

"I know we aren't meant to get feelings for the men. I know I'm here to help look after them, and the girls and show support, and offer myself, which I never minded... until..."

"Until?" I cock a brow and she glances across the room to the bar. Not to where some of the men sit, but behind it, to where a certain prospect is hooking up the TV.

I chuckle. "You have a thing for Titch?"

Her cheeks go red, and she shakes her head even as her words contradict the action. "Yes, but I know it's wrong and I know he hasn't even been patched in yet, so I shouldn't be—"

"Titch!" I yell over the sound of laughter coming from the Cruz Cunts entertaining the men at the bar, and Beth flinches back.

"It's not his fault." Beth cries but I ignore her, watching Titch step down off the ladder and stroll over to us.

"Prez?" he asks, looking a little nervous, his eyes darting to Beth. He doesn't have to say anything. I can see how much he cares for her.

I feel kind of shit that we haven't made time to patch him in yet. He deserved it months ago, but I've been too fucking consumed with needing to find Zoe and figure out how to lead the club with Rocco standing down that it honestly slipped my mind.

"She your girl?" I ask, and even though his eyes look concerned, he puffs his chest out and nods.

"If she'll have me."

I grin. "Well, she won't have anyone else, so have at it."

Beth gasps, and Alana giggles as Titch rounds the table and offers Beth his hand. She takes it and he lifts her in his arms, her legs wrapping around his waist as they start kissing.

Naturally, my eyes fall to Zoe, and this time her glare is gone and her cheeks are flushed as she grins at me.

"We have a shortage of available Cunts." I point at her. "I think Mama Z needs to do some recruiting."

Once again, her grin falls and her mouth drops open in exasperation, and I chuckle as I stand, striding off to study the files Baz left me.

I need to start planning.

As laughter and even some sounds of fucking fill the air, I zone everything out and jot down a few different ideas to discuss with Slasher.

Zoe comes to join me a little later, asking questions about the intel I have and I tell her everything.

No secrets.

Slasher and Munroe join us after they've had their fix, and we toss around some ideas, strategizing long into the night.

By the time we go up to bed, I'm exhausted, but my brain is too fucking preoccupied with our different options to end this war.

I lay in bed with Zoe until she falls asleep, and then retreat to the chair in the corner, not wanting to disturb her with my tossing and turning.

It's not until Zoe rolls over in bed some time later, the sheet getting kicked off like the thin layer is annoying her, that I finally get distracted.

Her legs part revealing the triangle of fabric that covers her mound, and I'm instantly drawn to the idea of crawling on the bed and kissing the fabric until she comes in her sleep.

It's something we've both enjoyed in the past, but everything is different now. I have no doubt that I could make her slick with need, so much so that if she did wake up, all she'd want to do is sate the thirst. It's exactly how I used to make her pliable for me.

Now though, not asking her permission seems wrong. Fuck, it was probably wrong in the first place, and if she didn't love it so much, I wouldn't have continued doing it, but now, I need to know it's what she wants before I touch her that way.

My dick is throbbing from just the thoughts running through my head, and instinctively, I lean to the side where there is a pile of her dirty clothes bundled, and rifle through the items until I find a pair of her panties.

I have my cock out of my sweatpants and in my fist so fucking fast as I press the fabric to my nose and take in her scent.

Biting back a moan, I pump my hard length, slow at first to really play with the pleasure coursing through me, and then faster as I chase the high. I don't let myself go though, stopping before my climax hits, and releasing my cock, teasing myself.

Fuck, I want to bury myself inside her. I just want to reclaim her. Replace all the bad things done to her with new memories. I want to be all over her.

Wrapping my hand around my cock again, I start pumping it slowly, restarting the process.

Zoe shifts on the bed and it's too dark for me to see her face in the shadow of her body, but I imagine her blue gaze on me, watching everything I do.

The thought sends a rush of blood to my dick, so I stop again, not yet ready to reach my release, desperate for this to last longer.

Pressing her panties to my nose again, I inhale deeply before darting my tongue out to swipe over the crotch. I moan and tip my head back, my fist gripping my cock again, as I start thrusting up into my own palm.

"Fuck yes, Zoe. You smell so fucking good," I whisper, but then a whimper meets my ears, and my eyes snap open and I still my hand, my gaze darting to the bed.

"Are you awake, Princess?"

She doesn't move or make a sound, and even though I should be embarrassed about nearly getting busted wanking in the fucking corner as I sniff and taste her panties, all I feel is disappointed.

I miss sharing my depravity with her.

With my eyes still on her, I jerk my dick again, not taking my eyes off her.

I don't fist my cock as tight this time, not ready to edge myself too far as I wonder what Zoe would do if she found me like this.

Would she scream, and grab that knife she keeps nearby, lunging to stab me?

Would she cry bloody murder, and retreat into herself, too traumatized by the idea of any sort of sexual act?

Or would she be curious? Maybe want to watch? Maybe want to fuck me?

No.

She's not there yet.

Disappointment swarms me. Not because she doesn't want me like that, but because I miss the girl that challenged me. Who matched my passion. Who fed my cravings.

I let go of my cock, wishing it would deflate already, no longer in the mood to chase this high.

"Don't stop."

The faint words meet me through the dark room, and my eyes lock on Zoe as she slowly sits up.

"Princess, I—"

"Keep going. Please."

There's a beg in her tone that I can't deny, and my hand finds my throbbing dick, resuming.

"You want to watch me, Princess?" I ask, feeling heat travel through my veins at having her eyes on me.

"Yes."

"Turn the lamp on." I urge, slowly sliding my hand up and down my length.

Doing as I asked, Zoe leans over to the bedside table and flicks the lamp on, illuminating the space we share.

As she leans back against the headboard, I take in her flushed cheeks and her plump lips as they part, her blue eyes darting from my face, to my cock.

"It feels so good," I tell her, gripping my dick tighter.

"It does?" she asks, eyeing the tip of my dick where pre-cum beads.

"It really does," I rasp, going a little faster and thrusting my hips.

Zoe shifts on the bed, squeezing her legs together. A whimper escapes her again, and she bites her lip as she squirms.

"Do you like my cock, Princess?" I stop thrusting and use my thumb to swirl the pre-cum over my straining tip, gliding it over the rim. "I imagine you when I do this. Touching me. Licking me." I lean over and spit on my cock, rubbing my saliva over it and start pumping again, loving the wet sound it makes. "I imagine sinking it inside your tight cunt, just the way you like."

She whimpers again, her hand moving to press between her legs, but then she darts her hand away.

"It's okay to touch yourself if it makes you feel good, Zo." I start pumping faster. "This feels so fucking good."

Her chest rises and falls quickly as she watches, her lips still parted, her tongue darting out every now and then before she bites her lip.

"What's in your other hand?" she asks, gesturing her head to me, and a slow grin spreads my lips wide.

"These." I hold up her panties, letting them dangle from my finger. "I like to smell your cunt while I jerk off." I press the fabric to my nose and inhale deeply again. "Fucking delectable." I moan and thrust harder, knowing I won't edge myself this time. With her eyes on me, I want to crash over the edge.

The moment she parts her legs a little and slides her hand between them again, I fucking nearly lose my load, but I force it back, wanting to help her get over the line.

"You know what else I like to do with your panties?" I ask her, and she shakes her head, a frown creasing her brow. "I like to lick the crotch, and suck what you leave behind off the fabric."

My admission is fucking dirty. Filthy. I'd never admit doing that to anyone else. Only her.

Her hand moves faster as she rubs over her panty clad mound, and I show her what I do with her panties by pressing the dirty crotch into my mouth and sucking on them.

Her eyes flare with excitement and her fingers work faster and even though her frown deepens, I'm too far gone to pull back now.

With need controlling me, my fist pumps and my dick pistons into my grip as I suck on her panties and intense pleasure starts pulsing through me. I jerk my cock so fucking fast it must be a new record, and I explode with ecstasy as cum starts shooting from my dick, flying up to hit my chin, my chest, and over my sweatpants in a load so full it's proof of how long it's been since I let myself release.

As I start to come down, I hear a frustrated growl fly from my princess, and I watch her thump her fists on the mattress next to her hips.

"Zo?" I pant. "I'm sorry. I should have waited for you to come first."

She sneers at me. "You would have been waiting forever then."

"What?" I pant, using her panties to start wiping up my jizz. "What do you mean?"

Her shoulders slump, and a sob escapes her. "I can't... I can't make it feel good when I touch myself."

My heart sinks.

Fuck.

My princess.

Standing, I tuck my dick back in my sweatpants and approach the bed.

"I'm sorry. I should never have done that in here while you're trying to... recover."

She shakes her head. "I liked what you were doing though. I felt something again. Deep inside me. I felt it and I wanted to... But when I touched myself, the urge went away. It just vanished."

Shifting closer, I reach out and cup her cheek, loving the way she leans into my touch instead of flinching from it. "You just need time, Zo. Don't pressure yourself. It'll happen eventually."

A tear pops from her eye and she nods, more to satisfy me than anything, and I hate that.

I don't want her telling me things she thinks I want to hear, but I don't say anything in this moment.

This isn't about me. It's about her, and whatever I can do to help her, I fucking will.

28

Zoe

Life isn't fucking fair.

Watching Gray work his cock was the most erotic thing I've ever seen. He was so lost in the sensation, and I'm envious of the pleasure I knew he felt.

I felt it too while watching him. Waking up to that sight had my need for him skyrocketing, and all the memories of our times together made me breathless. But the second I touched my clit, it disappeared. Vanishing into the night, leaving me feeling bereft.

"I'm sorry," Gray rasps again as he sits down next to me on the bed.

I huff in frustration. "I don't want you to be sorry," I say. "What I want is to feel like that. I want the ecstasy running through my veins. The pleasure that's downright unbearable and definitely addictive."

The truth is that what I want is both complicated and extremely easy. I want Gray, body and soul. I want what we had back, and I want to get lost in each other's bodies. But right now I'm so fucking horny and frustrated that I'd settle for just getting a release.

Yeah, my mind really is a fucked up place.

"What can I do to help?" he asks, almost begging, like I'm withholding a secret.

"I don't know," I breathe because I don't know the answer.

Taking his hand, I slowly move it to my knee. When his touch doesn't make me panic, I grow a little bolder and slide it up my thigh. So slowly it's... the moment he hits my mid-thigh, my body locks down and my breathing intensifies.

I squeeze my eyes shut and breathe through the panic building in my chest. But no matter how much I try to push it back down, I'm not ready for Gray's touch.

While my eyes are closed, he shifts on the mattress. It dips as he moves, and I move forward so he can sit himself behind me. His legs are spread wide, so he's not caging me in.

"Let me try something," he murmurs, reaching for my hands that are balled into fists. "I promise I won't touch anything but your hands."

Gradually, I relax and let him put his hands on top of mine. His touch is light, barely there, which makes it easy to endure.

"Spread your legs," he rasps.

"I won't let you touch me," I snap as I press my thighs firmer together. "I-I can't bear it."

The pain following that admission is enough to make my eyes misty. Fuck, how I wish I wasn't this terrified in my own skin.

"Do you trust me?" Gray asks.

"Yes," I answer immediately, since I don't need to think about the answer.

His head is resting on my shoulder so I feel the nod. "Then spread your legs, Princess."

I slowly do as he says, leaning back ever so slightly and using him to keep my balance as I open my thighs.

"Move your hand to your thigh," he commands.

My core tightens in anticipation, and I lick my lips as I mimic what I tried to do with his hand earlier. I place my own on my thigh and slowly slide upward with his hand on top of mine. I hesitate as we reach the edge of my panties, but with a sharp intake of air, I move my fingers to my core.

Gray's fingers are perfectly splayed on top of mine, so when I press my index finger to my pulsating clit, it's like we're both touching me.

"Oh," I gasp, my head falling back against him as pleasure makes me breathless.

He nips at the shell of my ear. "Does it feel good, Princess?"

"Yes," I whimper, adding more pressure.

I'm so relieved that I can still feel pleasure that I come to a stop, not moving at all. Misreading the situation, Gray removes his face from my shoulder and tries to move his hand away from mine.

"No," I rush out. "What are you doing?"

His voice is coated in concern as he asks, "Are you sure you're okay?"

"I didn't think about... *it* at all," I admit.

"So, why did you stop?"

Sighing, I say, "I guess I was thinking about *it*. But only in the sense that I'm glad I can still feel good. I wasn't... it wasn't... don't ruin this by making me talk about that." I can't keep the annoyance I feel from my tone at the last part.

I love how concerned and observant Gray is. But this is about letting go, and I can't do that if he's going to analyze every movement or sound I make.

When his hand is back on mine, I roll my clit again, moaning at how amazing it feels. The worry and fear that's been weighing me down morphs into pleasure, giving me a single-minded goal. I want to come.

"Talk to me," I say, my tone sultry with need.

Gray licks down the length of my neck and blows on the wet trail. My nipples tighten into hard peaks and my pussy throbs. I'm so caught in the web of erotica he's spinning that I don't worry or shy away from the unexpected touch of his tongue.

"I bet you're soaking wet," he rasps. "And it's killing me that it's going to waste. I want to lick the cum from your cunt so badly."

Moaning, I slip our hands between the panties. Then I slide our index fingers through my folds, and he's right. I'm fucking drenched.

"More," I beg.

His hard cock is pressing into my back, and I'm tempted to reach for it—him. To wrap my hand around it, and...

"Oh, God," I cry as he adds pressure from his finger onto mine, and I feel my needy nub swell. "Again."

He does it again. Even without touching my pussy directly, he manages to dominate the experience, and before long, I'm panting and writhing, ready to fall over the edge.

"That's it, Princess," he groans. "Our fingers are making you come. This is us, Zo. You and me. Together."

"Yes," I pant.

"I can feel your wetness," he rasps. "I bet your tight little cunt is glistening. Fuck. I can fucking feel it pulsating."

Whether it's true or not, I don't know. But I secretly hope it is. I want him to know how good this feels which is all thanks to him.

"Gray!" I cry out, my pleasure erupting as we barrel down on my sensitive clit, rubbing it faster and harder together. "Oh. Fuck. I... I... more."

He rubs his whisker-littered cheek along the crook of my neck, and I swear the roughness makes my orgasm even more intense.

I know it must be torture that he can't touch me directly, kiss me, or even nip at my skin as he's done so many times in the past. How he manages to control himself, I'll never know. But I love him even more for it.

"Holy shit," I breathe when my orgasm subsides.

"Feel better now?" he asks.

Unable to form words, I merely nod while I wait for my breathing to return to normal. Our hands are still beneath the panties, resting on my mound.

As I think about how much I wish I could do something for him, namely help him with the hardness that's poking into my back, I get an idea. Though he can't see my face, I grin as I slide our fingers through my folds, coating them in my arousal.

"Princess, what—"

"Shh," I say. I half turn in his arms so I can look at him. "Close your eyes and open your mouth."

He does what I say without questioning it, and the instant he parts his lips, I put my finger on his tongue. I slowly move it all around the organ, making sure he gets every drop of cum coating my finger.

"Fuck," he groans, tightening his hands that are now resting at his sides. "So good."

His reaction makes me feel brazen and wanted, so I move two fingers to my core, scooping up as much of my juices as possible before I feed it to him again.

He relishes every drop, groaning like a man that's wandered the desert for days and finally gets to satiate his thirst with cold water.

I pointedly look down at the hard-to-miss bulge between his legs and lick my lips. "Can I have a taste as well?" I ask, breathily.

Gray gives me a wicked grin that has my pussy fluttering. "You want to taste my pre-cum, Princess?"

"Yes," I squeak, slightly embarrassed by my need to have his taste in my mouth. "But I don't want to... you know."

His smile vanishes. "I would never make you do that," he gruffly says.

"I know that," I explain, feeling bad I made him have to clarify that. "I was saying it more to myself."

When he doesn't ease up, I know I just ruined the damn mood by running my mouth. And though I want to apologize, I don't. He doesn't want to hear it, even if I mean it and think I should.

After moving to his side of the bed, Gray reaches for his phone. "Do you want to go back to sleep or get up?"

"What time is it?" I ask since I thought it was the middle of the night. Then again, it's been a long night, and giving me my first orgasm in over three months—since the beginning of my time with Gunner—probably took longer than it felt like at the moment. "Doesn't matter. I don't want to go back to sleep."

Instead of giving him time to answer, I slink out of bed and have a quick shower. Then I get dressed in one of his tees and a pair of my yoga pants. Ma-Cara isn't coming today, but she's made me promise I'll run laps in the room we use for training, even on the days I'm by myself.

No matter how much I loathe running, I don't think it's the worst idea right now. My thoughts are all over the fucking place, and I can't get the look on Gray's face out of my head. He looked like I'd fucking slapped him when I implied that I didn't want to suck him off, and maybe, in some way, I did with my words.

I didn't mean for it to sound like I thought he'd make me, but just because that's not how I intended it, doesn't mean that's not how he heard it. Fuck, I really made a mess of what was such a huge step.

When I exit the bathroom, Gray's sitting on the couch, waiting for me. Before he can get up, I sit down on the coffee table and reach for his hand. As soon as our pinkies are locked together, I look into his dark eyes, where it looks like a storm is brewing.

"I know you'd never do anything that I didn't want," I say, rushing out the words before he can stop me. "But a part of me was salivating at the thought of sucking you off. Even if my head and heart aren't ready, my body still wants things. That's why I said what I said."

He looks taken aback, like he wasn't expecting my unguarded honesty. "Okay..."

"I need you to know that it was about me and not you, Gray," I say, leaning closer to him until his scent invades my nostrils.

He shudders. "Do you promise I didn't make you feel like you had to?"

I tighten my hold on his pinky. "Pinky promise," I vow.

Time ceases to exist as we sit there and stare at each other. I don't know if he's looking for any sign that I might be lying, but I'm not. What I told him is the complete truth, and I need him to know that—which is why I made a pinky promise.

Once he's satisfied that there's nothing more to it, he lifts my pinky to his mouth and presses a kiss to it. Then he gets up, taking me with him, and we wordlessly walk downstairs.

He never leaves me alone, instead he sits in the corner of the room while I run laps until it hurts to breathe and I wish an excruciating death on Cara for making me do something as vile as running.

Despite my complaints, I can't deny that it makes my head feel clearer, and though it isn't much, I can see a daily difference. I lasted thirty seconds longer today than the day before. To some it's nothing. To me, it's akin to winning gold at the Olympics.

As I take the cold water Gray's offering me and gulp it down like I'm on the verge of dying of thirst, Alana comes stumbling in.

"Mama Z," she whoops, throwing her hands up in the air. "Mama's in the house, yo."

I burst out laughing. "Drunk are we?" I ask even though I can smell the liquor wafting off of her.

"Shh," she slurs, holding her finger up to her lips. "Don't say it so loud. Slasher didn't want me to get drunk."

My eyes draw to the hulking silhouette behind her. "I think it's too late for that." I smile. "He's right behind you."

She almost falls when she spins around. "Where have you been?" she says, pointing a finger accusingly at him. "You left me alone with a bottle of tequila and told me not to get drunk. This is all your fault."

He moves closer and lifts her off the ground. "That's not what I said," he corrects. "I said not to get *too* drunk. And since you can still walk, I count that as a win."

Before long they're engaged in a pretty heavy makeout session, and when Slasher moves them against the wall it's clear they're about to take it further. My attempts at looking away are all in vain, and my eyes stay glued on the way he grinds his crotch against hers.

"Do you like what you see?" Gray rasps. When I nod, he moves his hands to my hips and pulls me back against him. "Remember watching Alana get fucked at our Fourth of July party?" I nod again. "It made you so fucking wet and desperate for me."

"Gray," I whimper.

"With the way you're squeezing your thighs together I'd say nothing has changed. You're just as horny and filthy as before. Your wants haven't changed."

I know what he's doing. He's showing me the ways I'm the same, focusing on those rather than the changes.

"You're hard," I say, arching my back and pushing my ass firmer against his cock. "I like how it feels."

Gray chuckles. "You like feeling my hard cock against your ass, Princess?"

"Yes," I moan.

We both know nothing more than this will happen right now, but it feels like enough. Like we've crossed another line neither of us want between us.

Like the perv I am, I keep watching until Slasher grunts and Alana cries out in ecstasy. Then he lets her down, and she wobbles a little in her heels.

"Did you like the show?" she giggles, completely unbothered that I can't stop gawking.

I consider lying, but I don't want to do that. "Kinda," I admit.

She takes my hand and pulls me into a hug. "You can always watch me," she purrs. "I like knowing people are looking."

I sigh wistfully because I used to like that as well. The thrill of knowing people could see, at least. Hopefully, I'll get my voracious appetite back one day.

"Right, I'm stealing Mama Z," Alana declares. "I need a shower and I need her to wash my back."

"The hell you are," Gray growls. "I'm not fucking leaving Zoe's side. So unless you're extending that invitation to me, it's not happening."

Slasher lets out his own growl. "You're not going any-fucking-where near Alana showering."

Alana links her arm with mine and sighs theatrically. "Fine. In that case I'm taking her to the common room. But you two need to keep your distance. We need some fucking girl time."

I can't stop laughing as she waves them off and drags me to the main room, only stumbling a few times. I consider telling her she's only wearing one shoe, but then decide against it. She's wearing the shoes I gave her, so I know she'd panic and want to find the other one right away.

The main room is almost empty, sans Tex and Tio at the bar. I smile and greet them both. Despite our clash the other day, Tio says hi, though he does leave quickly. I know the Cunts made sure he knows they're not upset with him, and honestly, neither am I. If he continues acting weird I have to make sure he knows that.

"I don't think there's any tequila left," Tex chuckles. "So I hope you're not here for more."

Alana sticks her tongue out at him. "What about the fancy bottle you don't think we know you're keeping hidden?" Tex stiffens and glares daggers at her until she starts laughing. "Relax, Tex. I wouldn't dream of touching your private stash. But I wouldn't say no to some coffee."

With the renovations Tex has made it even clearer that only those he approves of are welcome behind the bar, so he prefers to bring us stuff and keep his bar tidy.

Once we sit with two steaming cups of Joe, he leaves the pot with us and heads to bed. Gray and Slasher move into his office, leaving the door open. I know it's so they can both keep an eye on us. Which I find that I don't mind at all.

"So," Alana says.

"So?" I ask before taking a sip of the delicious smelling coffee.

Alana makes herself comfortable in the chair as she looks at me over the rim of her cup. "Have you taken a ride on Gray's dick yet?"

I'm so shocked by her question I swallow wrong and end up coughing and sputtering until coffee comes out of my nostrils. "W-what?" I gasp.

Rolling her eyes, Alana says, "Don't pretend you didn't hear me, Z. I asked if you've taken a ride on his disco stick. Played hide the sausage. Knocked boots. Bumped uglies—"

"Okay, okay, I get it," I laugh. "Stop making up disgusting euphemisms."

"If you don't answer the question I'll continue," she challenges, and I have no doubt she's serious.

I wring my hands together in front of me. "No, not yet. But I want to."

"So what's holding you back?"

With a sigh, I say, "If I knew, I'd have ridden his disco stick already."

That sends us into a fit of laughter, which feels both freeing and good. We laugh until we both have tears in our eyes, and my stomach hurts.

"Every time he touches me, I feel... off," I say, trying to explain now that the hilarity has subsided. "It's like I'm both pulling and pushing at the same time. I want him to touch me, but I can't stand it when he does."

Explaining it to someone who hasn't been there to see it is hard. With Gray it's easier because he sees the honest effort I put into it. But as I explain it to Alana it almost sounds like excuses.

Alana nods slowly as though she's pondering my words. "Is it everywhere you can't stand his touch?"

"No. It's like..." Trailing off, I swirl my hand in the air as I try to find the right words to describe it. "It's more the intent. I think. Like when I know it's leading somewhere or if he takes me by surprise like when he kissed me and I kneed him in the balls."

Her eyes widen, and she giggles into her hand. It's only then I remember no one else knows about that, so I quickly fill her in.

"RIP balls," she exclaims once I've told her what happened. "But hey, good on you for standing up for yourself. Did it make you feel better?"

"No," I whine. "Terrible. That's how it fucking felt. I don't want to hurt Gray. I want to love him and…" I abruptly stop speaking when I'm dangerously close to sounding like a fucking Hallmark sap.

"You want what you had back. Orgasms and all," Alana says, successfully defusing the cheese with her bluntness.

"Orgasms and all," I agree. "If I ever get there." The last part sounds wistful which I suppose is appropriate.

"You will," Alana says. There's so much conviction in her tone I almost feel it.

"Oh?"

"Yep," she says, popping the P before taking another sip of her coffee. "You've come so far in such a short amount of time, Z. In the beginning you could barely stand having anyone that wasn't me or Gray around, and now you're training with Cara, putting Tio in his place, claiming your rightful title, and you stayed to watch me and Slasher dry hump like teenagers."

When she puts it like that it sounds a lot more impressive than it's felt to me. But as she lists out the things I've done, I have to admit it isn't half bad.

"You even sat in that meeting with Baz and Dante who you've never met before. And talk about scary dudes. Those two could probably bleed the state dry in a single night if they really wanted to."

I have to admit that my friend isn't making me sound half-bad. If someone told me they'd done all those things within a month, I'd be fucking impressed. Maybe I just need to give myself time and stop trying to force the issue.

"Okay," I agree. "I get it."

Alana pretends to pick a piece of something off her bare shoulder before inspecting her cuticles.

"Fine," I laugh. "You smart, me dumb. Happy now?"

She flashes her teeth at me in an innocent smile. "Very. Thank you for saying it out loud, Mama Z."

I flip her off and finish the remainder of my coffee before refilling our cups. As I slowly drink it I remember that I never got to ask Cara why she didn't know about the Cunts being scared of Gunner. I had every intention to, but she worked me so hard I could barely remember my name after our session.

"Alana?"

"Hmm?" she hums.

"I want to ask you something and you have to promise you'll be straight with me," I demand.

She quirks an eyebrow. "When am I not?"

Fair point.

I take a deep breath. "Why didn't you or any of the Cunts ever tell Cara that you were scared of Gunner?"

"So we're jumping straight in with no lube," she smarts. "I think that's mostly my fault. Back before Rocco and Cara formed the Cruz Kings, they were part of Dante's Crew. Me and Rose were there. So we know how Cara doted on Gray and Gunner."

What the hell?

"I mean they were very close. Gunner's the one who designed the Kings' logo together with Cara. So I guess both me and Rose always wondered if she somehow knew and turned a blind eye to the entire thing."

While Alana sounds so matter-of-fact like we're discussing the weather, my heart bleeds for her—for all the Cunts.

"Do you still think that?" I ask, gently.

Shaking her head, Alana says, "I don't think I ever really believed it. It was more a... fear. Like you being scared of Gray's touch even if you claim to know he won't hurt you."

Well, with that comparison there's no way I don't understand where they came from.

Alana yawns and stretches. "I think I'm about to crash," she says.

When she makes to move out of the chair, I quickly take her hand. "Just one more question." I grimace at the harshness of my voice and add, "Please."

"One," Alana clarifies, holding her index finger up for good measure. "Then I need to get some beauty sleep."

I don't know why I'm nervous to ask my next question. Maybe it's because I don't know how she'll react. "If Rose was Cara's second in command, why did she ask you to help set me free back when I ran?" I ask.

It's a question that's been plaguing my mind since Cara was banished, but I haven't had the opportunity or courage to ask until now. I mean the Rose part doesn't matter. But the part with Alana does because she ran a big risk, and I feel like it was an unfair ask of Cara. And in the end, it got Alana punished in a demeaning and cruel way.

"Oh," Alana gasps. "That's an easy one. Because I was the one who told her she should do it."

"You what?" I almost screech.

"I'd told her many times that you didn't belong here. Even before the... err... gunpoint incident. But after that, I started harassing her almost hourly about it until she gave in."

My jaw practically hits the table with how slack it's gotten. All this time I thought it was Cara's idea, even admired her for facing her consequences with so much dignity. At the same time I felt it was unfair of her to drag Alana into it.

But now I know she was covering for Alana, and that paints Cara in a very different light.

"Don't look at me like that," Alana spits defensively. "I know it's my fault she was banished. She took her punishment from her fucking husband of all people and lost her found family all because of me."

Something else clicks in my head. "That's why you never fought Rocco on you getting punished, isn't it?"

She shrugs. "Yes, and no. I mean technically he was operating inside club rules. But you're right, even if he wasn't, I'd gladly take my punishment because I deserved it."

"No more," I hiss. "I want that fucking rule book destroyed. And then I'll make a new one where we actually fucking listen to people instead of this bullshit."

Alana laughs. "As the Mama you can do almost whatever you want."

That reminds me... "I need a second-in-command," I say. "Will you be it?"

Her eyebrows shoot up her forehead in surprise, and she lets out a surprised gasp. "Really?"

I playfully roll my eyes. "Of course. Who else would I pick?"

With a squeal, she darts to my side and pulls me in for a bone-crushing hug. "I'll be the best fucking second, Z. I'll do you proud," she vows. "Thank you."

As I'm about to tell her there's no one else I'd trust to have my back, Slasher and Gray emerge from the office. They mumble something I can't hear, and then Slasher literally takes Alana from my arms and throws her over his shoulder.

"Time for bed," he says, slapping her ass loudly. "Say goodnight, Candy."

She chirps, "Goodnight, Candy," and laughs when he slaps her ass again.

As soon as they're gone, Gray joins me at the table. He shifts nervously in his seat like something's bothering him.

"What is it?" I ask, immediately imagining the worst. "Is everything okay?"

He sighs and runs a hand down his face. "Slasher asked me something about you, and I don't know the answer. But I don't really want to ask."

"You can ask me anything," I gulp.

"You know we have to fight the Reapers, right?"

I nod.

"And you know guns will be involved, right?"

Oh... shit, yeah. I didn't think about that because the truth is that it doesn't matter to me anymore. But Gray doesn't know that... yet.

"I know," I say, my voice cracks so I clear it before carrying on. "But they don't bother me anymore."

The fact is that guns haven't bothered me or made me uneasy since Gunner shot Chris. How could something like a bullet scare me when living was so much worse than death could ever be?

Gray tilts his head to the side and scrutinizes me. "Are you sure?"

"I'm sure," I say. When he doesn't look convinced I close my eyes and count to ten.

Then I tell him what happened right after Gunner shot Chris. I don't spare any details, the word picture I paint is as gruesome as it was to live through it.

"That was the first time he raped me," I sob into my hands, letting myself feel the despair, fear, shock, loneliness, and helplessness I felt when it happened. "He had done other stuff, but never done that."

He doesn't say anything, but I don't need to see him to know I have his full attention.

"H-he threw me down on the floor and fucking raped me right there. With Chris' body on my left, and the picture of me and Leslie on the right."

I pause and shakily take a deep breath.

"Before that he'd... he'd... fuck. I thought I was dreaming about you, Gray. But it wasn't a dream, and it wasn't you." I scream the last part as I'm hit with the betrayal I felt when Gunner brought it up like he'd done me a favor by making a mockery of mine and Gray's intimate moments. "He said he'd done it for my benefit. To get me ready and b-because h-he wanted me to—"

Gray picks up the now empty coffee pot and hurls it at the wall. The cups Alana and I used are quick to follow, and every item breaks into a million pieces.

The rage marring his features and the feral growls falling steadily from his mouth should scare me, but they don't. Instead, they awaken a feeling I'd almost forgotten I was capable of feeling. Pure, unadulterated, all-consuming love for this man.

I've told him I loved him, and I meant it. I've felt it in my core. But this... as he loses his shit because of what happened to me, the feeling intensifies, morphing into liquid fire that thrums through my veins.

"Gray," I gasp.

At hearing his name, he snaps his head to me, his eyes seeing only me through what I imagine being a red haze of anger.

"I love you," I croak.

His eyes turn to slits as he stalks closer to me, and it doesn't once occur that I should recoil or feel scared. The monster in front of me is my monster, and I know he's paying close attention to my body language and words.

I cup his face when he's in front of me, and without looking away I press my lips to his. It's only a peck, yet it's enough to make the air around us spark.

"And I love you," he growls, staying true to his word. "My princess. Zo. Zoe. You're every-fucking-thing to me."

The words cause a tension I wasn't even aware of to unfurl inside me. It's silly, really. I knew he loved me. It was tangible between us in every touch and look we've shared. Yet there's no denying how great it feels to hear it.

"We'll make him pay, Princess. I swear it."

"We?" I question, not sure I heard him right.

With how protective Gray is, I never thought he'd include me in a plan for revenge as it means I have to get close to Gunner. And if I'm honest, despite what I've said to Cara, I wasn't sure I would really be able to do it.

But as I look at Gray, I know I can with him at my side.

"Yes," he rasps. "Together. That's the only way. I can never give you back what he took from you, but I can give you revenge."

Apparently threats of violence against my abuser is my kind of love language, because my heart jumps in joy.

Grayson

Titch stands at the end of the room, his cheeks red and his lips pulled into a smile as I stand from my chair in church.

"This is a long time coming," I rasp, approaching him holding our Cruz Kings' skull head patch. "Take your cut off."

Thumps on the table sound through the room as my club brothers' fists pound the table, and my eyes dart to Zoe to check that she is doing alright.

It goes against all typical club rules to have her in church with us, but I'm *the* King now, and I'll be fucked if I don't have my princess by my side. My brothers don't seem concerned with having Zoe here, thank fuck, and although she still seems a little unsure of what she's meant to be doing, she sits tall with her chin raised showing the same poise she used to carry before any MC got their claws into her.

"Rory Titchwell, do you swear your alleg—"

"Yes." He cuts me off, his green eyes wide with excitement. "I swear my allegiance to our President, Grayson Black, and the Cruz Kings MC and its members, both patch, and pussy. I swear to uphold the club values with honor and protect each member with my life."

I chuckle. "You had that memorized?"

He nods. "I memorized it the first week I was here and recited it in my head every day since."

Clapping him on the shoulder, I hand him the new skull head and top and bottom rocker patches. "Welcome to the family, brother."

Taking the patches, he lurches forward, pulling me in for a back slapping hug, and I can't fucking fight the smile that lights up my face. Titch's enthusiasm fills me with pride.

He came to us for help last year after killing his abusive grandma and he's shown nothing but loyalty and dedication to our cause. I don't doubt that one day, he will be sitting in my seat, leading future and current members.

One by one, the men stand from their seats, coming to the end of the table to congratulate their new club brother, while I return to the end of the table to my princess.

Her blue gaze tracks my movements, an analyzing stare falling to my cut.

"What's going through your head, Princess?"

Her gaze travels to the end of the room before sliding back to mine as I take my seat next to her, and she tilts her head, staring at the front of my cut again.

"Why is your President badge crooked?"

"Badge?" I bite back my smirk at her incorrect terminology, and she frowns.

"That." She points to my President patch.

"You mean my patch?"

"Oh." Her blue eyes dart up to mine. "It's called a patch? Not a badge?"

Smirking, I nod and drop my eyes to it and peel back the corner. "It's crooked because it's stuck on with double-sided tape. It's not stitched into place yet."

Confusion furrows her brows, and she reaches out peeling back the corner to see for herself. "But you've been Prez for a while, right?" Her gaze darts up to meet mine again. "Why haven't you stitched it on properly?"

Slowly reaching up, I take her hand from the chest of my cut, stroking my thumb over the back as I rest our hands on my thigh.

"Typically, the Cruz Cunts are the ones to stitch it on," I tell her. "And since you are the only woman I want touching my cut, I used double-sided tape until..." I trail off and she nods.

"Until I came back to you?"

"Yes," I growl, hating that we were apart for so fucking long.

"I've been back for a while. Why haven't you asked me to do it?"

Lifting her hand to my lips, I press a kiss to her warm skin before I respond.

"There have been more important things to worry about. But when you're ready, you can stitch my patch on. If you'd like to."

She stands abruptly. "Is this meeting over?"

Turning to look at the guys, I nod, clearing my throat. "Time to celebrate our new member," I call over the noise before slamming the gavel on the table, and my club brothers hoot, ushering Titch out of the room.

"The meeting is over." I advise Zoe who tugs me up from my seat.

"Take your cut off."

My brows lift even as I smirk, but Zoe stands with determination written across her expression, holding her hand out for my leather.

Once I shrug my cut off, Zoe takes it and storms out of church, on a mission, and I can't help but fucking grin from ear to ear.

I knew it was worth waiting for her to do it. Looking after me is part of her role, and mine is to make sure no one ever hurts her again.

The clubhouse is already filled with chatter and laughter by the time I follow Zoe out. The Cruz Cunts, having been notified beforehand, have set up some food and music for the celebration, and Tex has drinks lined up on the bar as the men start drinking them down.

"She's on a mission." Slasher chuckles next to me as we both watch Zoe talking with Alana, holding my cut.

"She sure is."

"You guys fucked yet?" he asks, and I snap my head toward him and hiss.

"How the fuck is it any of your business?"

Holding his hands up in a calming gesture, Slasher takes a step back. "Chill, man. I'm just trying to be a VP. Be an ear to chew off or a shoulder to lean on."

My shoulders drop. "Shit. Sorry, man." I shake my head. "Things are just so…" I glance back at Zoe as she sits down and rummages through a sewing kit Alana placed on the table. "Tense."

"She talks to Alana a bit." Slasher turns back to look at the two women in question. "Alana doesn't tell me everything, but she shares her concerns for Zoe. When she was drunk a couple of nights ago, Alana mentioned that Zoe's struggling to get her brain to let you touch her even when she craves it so much." He turns back to me. "That must be tough."

"You have no idea." I practically whisper watching Zoe thread a needle with ease before she sits back in her seat and starts to stitch my patch in place.

"Hang in there, brother." He claps me on the shoulder. "I'm sure she will find a way over time."

I nod, pretty sure of that fact too.

I don't even care that she's not ready for me to touch her yet. I care that she cares that she can't go that far. I can see how much she wants to. How much she aches for my hands to make her forget, but the trauma she's been through isn't something that just disappears overnight. She's already come so far in a short space of time. I'll wait an eternity if I have to. Just as long as she's happy.

Fuck. If the me from six months ago could hear my thoughts now, he'd try to punch me, I'm sure. But fuck him. He was a coward, not willing to let anyone close enough, and why?

Fear of losing them?

Maybe, but I can't live out the rest of my days having not really felt what love is like.

Do I fucking deserve that sort of love? Probably not. But if Zoe is willing to give it to me, then I'll happily be a greedy fucker and take it in whatever form she can give it.

While the celebrations turn rowdy, Slasher and I sip on light fucking beer, not willing to risk intoxication in case we get any unwanted visitors. The men and Cunts clearly needed this sort of event to let loose, and after Zoe saunters over to me, handing me my cut with my patch stitched in place, Alana starts feeding her a couple of drinks too.

Taking a seat in the corner, we sit out of the way watching the antics stretch through the night, my eyes mainly on my princess as I see the strain fall from her shoulders and a hint of happiness light her mood.

Alana is good with her. Offering her a new drink for every two she has, but also making sure Zoe eats at the same time.

It's clear the two girls have a strong connection, and I'm not even surprised when the Cunts clear the tables out of the way to make more room to dance, and Alana manages to get Zoe up to move to the music as well.

My eyes follow every place Alana touches my princess, and not once does she flinch from the contact. Not even when their dancing turns more sultry. None of the other Cunts get as close to Zoe, even when the Cunts huddle close and start fucking grinding on each other, tempting my club brothers with dark promises.

My eyes remain on Zoe though, the way she sways her hips, her hands in the air and her head tipped back like the temptress she is.

Hands slide over the curve of her hips then and I stiffen waiting for my princess to freak out. But she doesn't. She keeps swaying and giggling to whatever Alana says as she steps around her and from behind, presses herself up close to Zoe's back.

"Is it bad that I really want to watch this movie?" Slasher asks, eyeing his girl as she grinds up against my girl's ass.

Chuckling, I take a swig of my beer as I study my princess feeling so comfortable dancing up close to another woman.

"It would be one hell of a movie." I agree but then turn to look at my VP. "Not that I'd let you watch."

Smirking, Slasher raises a brow. "What if Zoe doesn't want you to watch either? Maybe she's more into Alana than you."

Fucker.

The beer I just swigged nearly bursts from my lips as I laugh at his words. "Nah man. I'm pretty sure Zoe isn't a carpet muncher."

Slasher scoffs. "Pretty sure isn't sure, brother."

My grin drops. He's right. What if Zoe would rather have Alana?

Even as I think it, I know I'm being fucking ridiculous, the possessive asshole in me ready to beat my chest like a caveman to get her attention.

Even so, she does seem to enjoy Alana's hands on her.

Every so often, Zoe's eyes will meet mine across the space, filled with desire I know she wants to sate, but isn't yet sure how to.

When our new club brother lifts Beth into his arms and lays her on a table, I know this party is about to turn into a fucking orgy, and I wonder if I should get Zoe out of here before that happens.

I don't know all the horror she was exposed to while with the Reapers, but I have no doubt there were orgies there too, and I get the feeling they aren't so thoughtful of the women they use for sex. Will watching an all-out orgy trigger Zo?

She does like to watch though, and she didn't shy away from watching Alana and Slasher a few days ago.

Maybe it's just Alana she likes watching.

Fuck. No. Stop thinking that way.

"It's a pity Zoe isn't into sex right now," Slasher mutters, without warning continuing the conversation I've spaced out on. "I wouldn't mind watching her and Alana together."

Even though a growl of disapproval rumbles in my chest, the thought makes my dick hard.

I'm not into Alana, but fuck if it wouldn't be hot watching Zoe experience pleasure from a chick.

Slasher chuckles. "Bro, my eyes would be glued to Alana, mostly. Don't fucking kill me for liking the idea of it."

"Mostly," I grumble, and Slasher chuckles.

"You're such a possessive prick."

"Don't you fucking forget it. And if the girls wanna explore each other, I'll be the only man in the fucking room."

Slasher growls this time, and I chuckle. "Who's a possessive prick now?"

"Fuck off," he mutters, and we both smirk, continuing to watch the two girls dance while everyone else falls into an orgy.

A good half an hour goes by with the sounds of fucking blending with the music, and Alana and Zoe stay attached, hands held as they round the group, watching like it's their live entertainment.

I can tell Zoe is aroused, not just by the strain of her nipples under my t-shirt, or the way she presses her thighs together on occasion, but it's the heat in her eyes every time she glances at me. The way her cheeks are flushed and her plump lips part as she dances pressed close to Alana while watching me.

My dick is as hard as fuck, and I'm happy when my club brothers start taking the party and the Cunts to their rooms, leaving only Tex, Slasher, Alana and Zoe behind.

As if on cue, the music slows, and fuck the girls move closer, dancing against each other right in front of the table Slasher and I are at.

"Tex. That will be all," I call, and he chuckles, muttering a goodnight as he hangs up his apron behind the bar and leaves the main room.

"You two sure do like dancing together," Slasher smirks, taking another swig of his beer, and Alana shoots him a wicked grin, filled with sin and dirty thoughts.

Fuck.

"You like her hands on you, Princess?"

My words don't shock Zoe, her lips spreading into a smile as she nods.

"They are soft, and small."

"The opposite of a man's." I acknowledge the obvious and when she nods, I push for more. "So her hands and the press of her body against yours doesn't bring forth bad memories?"

Zoe frowns for a moment, and a look of regret crosses her features.

"It's okay, Zo. It makes sense."

Her lips part to say something, but it's Alana who speaks.

"You like the way I touch you, Mama?" Her voice is husky with lust as she presses close behind Zoe again and glides her hands over Zoe's hips and up to rest under the swell of her tits.

"Yes." Zoe breathes and Alana presses her nose into the column of Zoe's neck.

"Fuck," Slasher mutters quietly next to me, and for a fucking moment, I forgot he was here.

"Can I touch your aching tits, Mama?" Alana asks before nipping at Zoe's ear, and my princess lets her lids flutter shut, nodding.

"Yes."

Alana's eyes dart to mine, a silent question behind them.

"Brother," I mutter to Slasher, not taking my eyes off the two girls before us. "I don't mean to be a prick, but..."

Slasher growls. "You want me to leave?"

"I won't touch her, but fuck, if Zoe wants her touch, then I can't let you watch that."

Painfully, I drag my eyes from the women and lock eyes with my club brother. My VP.

He glares at me. "Touch my Cunt, and there will be blood, Prez."

"I fucking know. And I would never. There's only one woman I ever want to touch, and right now, she can only get satisfaction from your woman."

I can't hide the pain in my words, and Slasher must pick up on it, nodding before he claps my shoulder. "I won't watch, but if you think I'm not going to listen, then you're fucking delusional."

His smirk is sinister, and a laugh escapes me as the fucker drags himself from his seat and moves toward the girls.

Zoe's half lidded gaze watches on, her chest rising and falling with the arousal coursing through her veins, and while Alana's hands remain close to the underside of Zoe's tits straining against the fabric of my tee, Slasher fists Alana's hair and drags her head back for a searing kiss.

Not once does Zoe watch or even flinch with Slasher so close to her, her gaze remaining on me as she presses her thighs together.

When Slasher is done marking his territory, he strides out of the room, but I know he isn't far, probably just around the corner, dick in hand, ready to listen.

"Gray?" My name rolling off Zoe's tongue is a question, so I gesture my hand with a wave in the air.

"You heard her, Alana. She gave you permission to touch her tits."

Zoe doesn't even have a chance to rebut as Alana's hands immediately glide up over each swell and cup her tits before flicking her thumbs over the straining peaks through the fabric.

Crying out in response, Zoe's thighs press together, her eyes remaining locked on me.

"You like that, Princess? Feeling your friend's hands on you?"

"Yes," she pants, and Alana glides her tongue up Zoe's neck.

Fuuuuck. Zoe arches her neck to the side to give Alana better access and my hand is undoing my fucking jeans to free my dick in an instant.

"Would you like me to take your t-shirt off, Mama?" Alana asks and Zoe nods, her eyes meeting mine again.

I see the moment she realizes my cock is out, and even as Alana keeps her focus on Zoe, lifting the fabric up over her head, Zoe turns possessive.

"Alana, don't look at Gray or his cock, or we are going to have a problem."

Snickering, Alana nods, dropping the tee to the floor. "As you wish."

Alana's words are light and understanding of our possessive nature, and she steps around to stand in front of Zoe, positioning her side on so I still get a good view.

"You want her to touch your bare tits, Princess? Maybe even lick them?" I ask, and Zoe nods, dragging her attention from where I'm fisting my cock, to her friend in front of her.

Slowly, Alana reaches out with both hands, cupping the swell of Zoe's full tits before flicking her thumbs over the nipples again. Zoe reacts by arching into her friend's touch, her blue gaze locked on Alana's face as she draws closer, hovering her lips before one of Zoe's pebbled nipples.

The two girls stare at each other as Alana closes the distance and lashes her tongue out over Zoe's straining peak, and like lightning, Zoe's hand fists in Alana's hair, dragging her closer.

"Fuck, Princess," I rasp, pumping my cock almost painfully. "You want more from Alana?"

"Yes," Zoe pants, probably not even realizing how her hips arch forward, seeking something.

"You want her hand between your legs? On your sweet cunt?" I ask and again, Zoe nods, while Alana switches to Zoe's other tit. "You want her to make you come?"

"Yes," Zoe cries, and Alana releases Zoe's nipple with a pop, blowing over the peak until it's straining.

"You want to touch me too, Mama?" Alana asks, gaining Zoe's attention again. "Or would you like me to just touch you?"

Seeking blue eyes turn to me, and I smirk while still running my hand up and down my length. "It's your decision, Zo. If you want to touch her, then touch her."

Biting her lower lip, Zoe's gaze returns to Alana, dropping to the bikini top Alana is wearing.

"I want to touch you, too."

Grinning, Alana nods, standing tall to reach behind her and tug on the string holding the scrap of fabric over her tits. When they bounce free, Zoe doesn't even bother checking to see if I'm looking at Alana, her focus solely on the tits of her friend.

With a tremble to her hand, Zoe lifts it, reaching out to gently touch Alana's exposed breasts, and the moment they make contact, Zoe steps closer.

"They're so soft," she whispers, and Alana giggles.

"Much like yours."

Nodding, Zoe studies her friend's tits, palming them and rolling her nipples, and the next thing I know, she leans down and sucks one into her mouth.

Fuck.

I squeeze the base of my dick, trying to hold back my fucking orgasm.

Talk about arriving to the party too fucking soon.

Jesus. If Zoe only knew what she does to me.

Things escalate from there, my words no longer needed to help urge Zoe on, her own desires taking over.

The girls press together, tits against tits, panties against panties as Alana presses her lips into the crook of Zoe's neck, and they start grinding their mounds together.

Fuck.

I think I was wrong.

I don't know if I can handle this.

I want to be in Alana's place right now.

I want to be the one feeling the heat of Zoe's mound grinding against my dick.

"I need..." Zoe cries out, and Alana pulls back, gliding her hand between their bodies.

"Is this what you need?"

The moment Alana's hand rubs over Zoe's apex, she cries out, thrusting forward, desperate for release.

Knowing how to give Zoe what she needs, Alana rounds Zoe, pressing up behind her again, not once looking at me as she directs her eyes down the front of Zoe's body and speaks directly in her ear.

"Look at your King, Mama."

Zoe's eyes flutter open, connecting with mine as I pump my dick again.

"Look at how much he desires you. Look at how much he craves to touch you the way you ache for." Alana slides one hand around to Zoe's tits on the far side, while gliding her other hand to press between Zoe's legs.

Zoe moans, her eyes staying on me and my cock as Alana starts gently rubbing Zoe's panty clad clit.

"Do you like his cock, Mama?" Alana asks in her ear and Zoe whimpers.

"Yes."

"Do you like how much it stretches you when he sinks inside you?"

"Yes," Zoe cries out, starting to gyrate her hips.

"Do you like it when he fills you with his cum, owning your cunt?"

"Yes." Zoe bucks, and I know she's close.

Which is a good fucking thing, because I'm ready to blow.

"Spread your legs wider," Alana demands. "Fuck my hand, Zoe. Fuck it like it's Gray's face."

Something in Zoe snaps, her own hand pressing over Alana's like she's worried she'll pull away before she reaches her high, and with her legs spread further, she grinds on their hands in a desperate frenzy.

"Gray," she cries out as her legs wobble, fighting to keep her upright.

Alana notices too, tugging Zoe back into the chair, parting her thighs to drag Zoe's wider.

Fucking hell. I'm not going to last. To watch Zoe unravel is something else.

"Gray," she cries again as she removes her hand from Alana's and grips the arm of the chair. "Come here."

I'm fucking out of my seat like lightning, my dick in hand, nearly fucking tripping with my jeans tumbling to my fucking ankles.

"I'm here," I rasp, noticing Alana's nose still pressed into Zoe's neck, not betraying her friend to look at me. "What do you need, Princess?"

"I need..." she pants, her hips thrusting even as Alana's hand mashes her panty clad clit with fervor, and I can see the wet patch soaking Zoe's crotch.

"Tell me, Zo. What do you need?"

"Cum in my mouth," she cries, her desperate eyes locked on mine with a plea.

She doesn't have to ask me twice.

"I'm ready to come now," I rasp, barely able to hold back.

"Yes," she cries. "Please."

Shifting as close as I can between the girls' legs, I make sure not to touch Alana as I press my hips forward, my dick hovering at Zoe's parted lips as the wave of ecstasy detonates through me.

With my hand working faster than it ever has, I drag out the orgasm until I feel the first rope of cum shoot from my tip, stilling as my white seed lands on Zoe's tongue and fills her mouth.

Her own cries meet my ears, her body jerking even as she swallows my cum, and her scream pierces the air as she shatters in Alana's arms.

I step back, not wanting to be that close to Alana, and reach for my jeans, pulling them back up.

Panting breaths fill the space, not just mine and Zoe's, but I'm pretty sure I can hear Slasher's out in the hall.

"Let's get you covered up," Alana suggests, her eyes still not meeting mine as she remains loyal to her word.

She shifts Zoe to stand, and as my princess comes down out of her orgasm haze, her cheeks turn red in embarrassment.

"But I didn't make you..." She trails off, turning to look at her friend.

"Mama, I didn't do that to get myself off. I did that for you. Besides," she shrugs, pulling my t-shirt over Zoe's head, "Slasher is waiting for me, and I'm going to ride his face until he's nearly drowning. He will get me off nice and good."

A burst of laughter flies from Zoe's lips, and she slaps her hand over her mouth, trying to ward it off.

I can't help but fucking smirk.

Covering her bare chest with her arm, most likely out of respect for Zoe's wishes, Alana bids us a goodnight and hurries to the hallway, where I hear her squeal and a moment later the deep rasp of Slasher's voice as they reunite.

"I... was that... okay?" Zoe asks, her worried gaze darting to me.

Reaching out slowly, I cup her cheek, my dark eyes locking with hers so she can see my honesty.

"I want whatever you want, Zo. If you needed Alana to be the one to bring you pleasure tonight, then that's what I want too. But..." This time I trail off, and her brows shoot high.

"But?"

"You're still mine, right? You still love me and aren't into chicks now, right?"

Zoe's face drops in shock, and then she starts giggling.

"Oh my god. Is Grayson Black insecure?"

I growl, stepping closer to her. "When it comes to you. Yes, I fucking am."

Her giggles fall away, and her expression softens as she leans into my hand still cupping her cheek.

"Gray, I love you. Thank you for letting Alana do that for me, and for staying and watching. I really like you watching me."

I can't help it. I fucking grin from ear to ear. "I fucking love watching you, Princess. I'll never get enough of watching you come undone."

Pressing her hand over mine at her face, her gaze darts to my lips, her pink tongue peeking out to glide over her lower lip.

"Do you want me to kiss you?" I ask, fucking aching to feel my lips on hers again. She pecked me the other day, and I've ached for that small gesture ever since.

"Yes. Just a small one," she whispers and my lip tugs up at one corner.

"How about you control the kiss? You lead and I'll follow."

Sucking in an audible breath, Zoe nods, rising on her toes to close the distance.

The moment our lips touch, I fucking feel like I'm home. It takes everything in me to fight the urge to grasp her shoulders and drag her closer to deepen the kiss.

I'm expecting a peck, but this time, Zoe starts slowly nibbling on my lips, sending me fucking crazy, but fuck it's nice. There are no tongues involved. They start trapped in our mouths, but as her lips part against mine a fraction, my chest warms with the notion that this is yet another step forward.

After a moment, Zoe pulls back, biting her lip even as her gaze meets mine through the fan of her lashes.

"Come on. Let's get you up to bed. It's been a long day."

Nodding, Zoe lets me lead her from the room where I take her to our bed, and she lets me cuddle her to sleep.

30

Zoe

"Come on, Mama Z. You can do better than that," Cara taunts as she kicks me again.

"That doesn't count," I hiss. Straightening my spine, I wipe the sweat from my forehead and glare daggers at her. "I said I needed a minute."

Cara scoffs. "You wanted me to teach you how to fight, correct? Well, you can't fucking ask for timeouts." Propping her hands on her hips, she looks at me like I'm being stupid. "Did you ever ask Irina for a break? Or what about Rusty? No, I know. When Gunner was just about to rape and mark you, you just asked for a break. Right?"

"That's enough, Cara," Gray roars angrily. "Show some fucking respect."

I blow a few errant tendrils away, but the stubborn fuckers are sticking to my clammy forehead. Needing time to absorb Cara's words, I take the time to stick them back into the messy bun I'm sporting.

"She's right," I sigh, not happy to admit it. "I can't just ask for a timeout." Then I tilt my head to the side and peer up at Cara, trying to appear innocent. "Did you ever ask Rusty and your mom for a break?"

Cara squares her shoulders and gives me a look that resembles reluctant respect. Well, I'm not the one who went dirty first. She fucking did. And if she can dish it out, she can take it.

"Touché," she says. "I'm not trying to be a bitch, Zoe. But you have to stick it out. No one is going to cut you any slack just because you twist an ankle or need water. Fucking hell, woman. I don't even know why I have to tell you that when you already know what they're capable of."

Running my hand over my thigh where her kick landed, I wince. Cara's kicks are no fucking joke, and now it hurts to even rest my weight on that leg.

"I know," I sigh.

Still unwilling to afford me time to put my head on straight, Cara snaps her fingers in my face. "Focus," she hisses. "I've fucking told you I'm a kickboxer. So what does that tell you?"

Her words from previous lessons come back to me. "To get up close because you have an advantage if I keep my distance."

"Exactly," she beams. "But I believe my exact words were that I would break your fucking bones if you keep hesitating."

I grumble something and flip her off. Then I step back to the X she drew on the mat to indicate my starting position. Okay, so I need to find a way to bait her kick, and then use it to move closer to her until she's forced to use her arms.

As Gray counts down from ten, I keep repeating that plan to myself. Though I know it's what I need to do, so far I've kept trying to avoid her lethal legs because... well, because it fucking hurts and I don't relish being hurt. But I have to get over that. Because it's always going to hurt.

"One," Gray says, and I immediately snap into focus.

I circle Cara twice, testing the way my leg feels. God, I hate the superior smile on her lips. But then I realize something I haven't fully understood until now. That's her downfall. She's so fucking sure she's better than me, she can already taste the win. She'd never expect me to be able to pull one over her.

Moving closer, I limp a little, favoring my uninjured leg, which I know she'll notice. When I'm within reach of her, she takes half a step back, changing her weight to the opposite leg. It feels like time's slowing down, and this time I see the shift in her balance, and the way she draws up her leg before it comes toward me.

I shift to the side so her heel only grazes my thigh instead of hitting it with full impact. Then I grip her ankle and twist it, unbalancing her as I keep my hold on it.

She hisses, her eyes turning dark as I refuse to let go, no matter how much she tries to break free. I secure her ankle against my side, using my hand to keep it flush against me so she doesn't have any wiggle room.

Then I slowly move closer, forcing her to adjust by jumping around on one leg. Instead of coming straight for her, I drag it out and begin to circle her again. I don't know if my plan is good, but I imagine it must be a strain, and if I can tire her out before she can retaliate, well that's fucking good for me—and my poor, aching body.

I don't notice more people have joined us until I hear Rose shout, "My money's on Cara."

"No way," Alana laughs. "This is all Z's show."

I recognize Munroe's deep voice. "C versus Z. Am I the only one who's fucking hard right now?" The next thing I hear is an "Ow" and I can't help smiling as I imagine Gray punching him.

He isn't wrong, though. It is a turn on.

I'm not wet, but my body is highly attuned to every friction from my clothing, and I'm fucking high on the fact that I've made progress against someone as impressive and skilled as Cara.

"Not bad, Mama Z," she cackles. "Not bad at all."

I know it's not fucking bad, I don't need her to tell me that. Stiffening my spine, I curl my upper lip. A rebuttal on my tongue, begging for me to take her down a peg or two. But before I can say anything, I see it. The fleeting look in her eyes tells me that I have her, which means she's trying to unnerve me so I lose it.

"What's the matter? Cat got your tongue?"

I almost lose it when she says that. My mind wanting to transport me back to the Reapers' house when I last heard those words. But I shake my head and grit my teeth, refusing to let her throw me off.

"Careful, Zoe." Cara grins. "I think my foot is touching one of your scars."

This time, there's no stopping myself. With a scream, I let go of her foot and lunge forward. I manage to take her to the floor, but that's where my upper hand ends. Cara swiftly spins us around so she's on top, and then she proceeds to place her knees on my arms so I can't move.

"Fuck you," I spit. "How the fuck can you use that against me? I thought you were my friend." Betrayal tastes like fucking poison on my tongue, and I'm so engulfed in my rage I imagine what it would be like to really hurt her—like she just did to me by using my trauma against me.

"Relax, Zoe," Cara coos, her soft tone at odds with her sharp knees. "Breathe."

Because I'm still a brat at my core, I shake my head and hold my breath, which makes her laugh. This time, it isn't a cackle, it's a genuine laugh.

"Why are you training?" she asks.

The question takes me off-guard and I inhale sharply. "Because I want to fucking make all of them hurt, like they did to me," I volley. "Should I add you to that list?"

Cara cocks her head to the side like she's listening to someone else, but all I can hear is the blood whooshing in my ears. "And do you think they're going to fight fair?" she asks. "Are you still that little girl who believes in knights in shining armor and enemies who stop when it becomes too much?"

She doesn't say it in a way that's unkind, but more like she's trying to figure me out. And as I really look at her, the penny finally drops. Cara isn't trying to be cruel, she's trying to prepare me for when I come head-to-head with Gunner and Irina. Probably Rusty, too. But he's more akin to a thorn in my side, whereas with the other two, it's deeply personal.

"Because if you don't think they'll say or do anything to rattle you, you've learned nothing." Cara leans down and trails a finger over one of my many scars. "Especially since we both know you'll never face them without Gray being near. I know Gunner, and he'll love throwing the shit he's done in Gray's face. You know that, right?"

Well, fuck... I hadn't considered that at all. Which just goes to show how seriously Cara takes our practice. She's lived through this, so I need to listen to her and keep my fucking cool.

"I get it," I huff, and I really do. "Let's go again."

"Are you sure?" she asks.

Instead of nodding my acquiescence, I buck underneath her. The movement surprises her enough that she slides to the side, making it easy for me to roll us around so I'm on top.

"Give me your best shot." I stand up and get back into position. "Or kick," I amend, winking at her.

Gray counts down again and while he does, I'm momentarily distracted. I know it isn't easy for him to watch Cara hurt me, yet he can collect himself to stay out of it. If he can do that while watching me getting kicked, then I can block Cara's hurtful words out.

"One," he shouts, startling me as I realize I didn't spend the time coming up with a plan.

Maybe that's for the best, though. Cara's way more experienced than I am, so I suppose I need to turn that around. If I plan, she has time to do it as well. But if I just...

I let loose a war-cry as I run at her with no plan on what to do. I see her leg zooming toward me, but instead of dodging or blocking it, I twist so the heel of her foot lands against my shoulder. The momentum shocks me, it's harder than before. But I don't let it stop me.

With a new sense of urgency, I close the distance between us and just before I crash into her, I drop to my knees and roll between her spread legs. Then I push myself halfway up and kick at the back of her knee, sending her stumbling.

Cara lets out a surprised gasp, spinning around to face me. But I'm ahead of her, and the moment she turns, I slide between her legs again, keeping myself behind her.

I manage to get in one more kick before she rounds on me, and tangles her fingers in my hair. She forces my neck back at an uncomfortable angle. Then she traps my legs with hers, closing her thighs around mine while resting on her knees.

"Impressive for a little girl," she sneers. "But now you're in the perfect position for me to use your mouth."

The implication of what she means hangs heavy between us, and I wonder how far she's willing to take it. Is she going to literally rub her crotch against my mouth? I doubt it... no, I don't. Cara is shameless, fierce, and she isn't going to stop until she's done everything she can.

"I'll fucking bite you," I warn. "Try me."

She laughs and stands up. The shift in her position means I can relax my neck, but only for a second. Until she forces me to bend it as she pulls on my hair from above.

"I can't wait to be inside you again," she grits out through clenched teeth.

As I look up, I see the disgust written all over her face. Not at me, but at what she just said. I can't say I'm enjoying hearing it, but it's needed. I can't keep being scared of the past if I want to take control of my present and future.

"Never again," I vow. "You'll never fucking touch me again. And if you do, I want you to know that I'll still never belong to you. You can force me, but that's all it'll ever be. Force. While I might fear you, I can never respect or love you. You're fucking pathetic." As I speak, I pretend I'm looking into the face of evil—Gunner.

The biggest difference from now and then is that if he gets me a second time around, I'll have something worth fighting for. Now I know Gray isn't dead, and I'll fight fucking tooth and nail to get back to him.

Even as I think that, I know that's not strictly true. Because if Gunner gets his hands on me again, it'll mean Gray is really dead. That's the only way he'll allow it to happen. And if Gray's dead, I'll fucking follow.

I've already lived in a world where I thought Gray was gone, and all I can say is, never a-fucking-gain.

Letting my thoughts consume me comes at a price, and I cry out when Cara pulls harder on my hair, angling my head against her thigh. I do the only thing I can think of. I fucking bite into the flesh through her yoga pants. She hisses in pain but doesn't let go.

Not wanting to admit defeat, I knock my head against her inner thigh, throwing as much of my weight into it as I can. She wavers, and I use the distraction to headbutt her pubic bone.

"You bitch," she shouts, and I'm pretty sure she's done acting, which is okay by me. She's landed enough solid kicks and punches that I don't feel bad for her.

As I prepare to repeat the motion, she lets go of my hair and jumps back. I surge to my feet, placing my feet wide apart as I anticipate she's going to kick me. And she does, but just like earlier, I capture her foot.

This time I don't try to wear her out because I'm fucking exhausted. Instead, I twist it, forcing her to move to relieve the pressure. When she stumbles, I let go of her foot and quickly jump onto her back. I wrap my arms around her throat, adding pressure like she's taught me to do.

Then I place my lips against her ear, and whisper, "Maybe I'll turn the tables this time. You were so interested in my ass, weren't you? Is that because you secretly wanted someone to play with yours?"

I'm not expecting the laughter that follows, but Cara's entire body is shaking. "Y-you'll what?" she hiccups.

Although it's not funny at all, I can't stop myself from joining in. Call it trauma laugh or whatever. I don't give a shit. To me, it's a victory in itself that we can laugh at a time like this.

Despite the laughter, I don't let go of Cara's neck. Loosen my hold, absolutely. But I refuse to let go until she tells me what we both—the entire room—already know.

"Fine," Cara sighs dramatically as though she can read my thoughts. Then she uses her free hand to tap the mattress three times, and it's the sweetest sound. "I give up. You won, Zoe."

As soon as she's said it, I let go and help her up. I pull her into a hug. "Thank you for all your help," I whisper. "And for not holding back."

"Yeah?" she whispers back. "I didn't take it too far?"

Pulling back, I meet her gaze head on. "You abso-fuck-ing-lutely took it too far. But it was needed. So thank you."

I sense that Cara isn't great at this gratitude thing when she waves me off and scoffs, "Gray would kill me if I didn't prepare you. So thank him."

All thoughts dissipate as I whirl around and see Gray standing only a foot away. His eyes shine with pride. He appears relaxed with his arms hanging at his sides, but I know he's anything but. Having seen and heard all of that can't have been easy.

But I did it. I fucking won against the fiercest woman I know.

I run toward him, and instead of stopping, I throw myself into his arms. Still high on the victory, I climb his body like a tree and wrap my thighs around his hips at the same time as his arms close around my back.

"I did it," I breathe.

Without waiting for him to say anything, I slam my lips to his in an almost brutal kiss. I nip at his lips, and when he opens up for me, I delve my tongue into his mouth. I moan as I feel him growing hard between us, and for the first time since I've been back, I feel like throwing caution to the wind and giving in to what we both want.

"Fuck," Gray groans, breaking our kiss. "I've missed that."

I giggle. "Fuck is right." For good measure, I slide my core along his rigid shaft.

"Keep teasing me, Princess. And I'll toss you over my shoulder and carry you upstairs right fucking now," he growls.

I'm tempted to push him, but decide against it. I kiss my way from the corner of his mouth, across his cheek and down his neck instead. "I've missed this, too," I murmur against his skin.

He lets out a rumbling noise which is the only warning I get, before he moves one hand to my throat. He doesn't add pressure, only holds it there. "Kiss me again," he demands.

I fuse our lips together again, stroking his tongue with mine. This is the feeling I've longed for. The one that has my toes curling and every hair on my body standing at attention. I can feel Gray everywhere, and I fucking love it.

Before I can decide if we should take it further or not, we're interrupted by Slasher. "Prez, got something you want to see."

"What?" Gray barks, annoyance coating his tone as he pulls back for the second time. "What can possibly be more important than kissing my woman?"

I pat his chest and wiggle until he sets me down on my feet. "Don't bite the head off your VP," I grin, trying to make light of it. But if I'm honest, I'm annoyed at the interruption as well.

"Sorry, man," Slasher says, looking it as well. "But Tido just called and... fuck. You have to see this."

Gray takes my hand and I follow him to the door where Slasher's waiting with a tablet in his hand. When we reach him, he presses play on what looks to be a live news stream.

"We're downtown in front of the body that was only discovered ten minutes ago," the news reporter says. "The young woman who's been brutally murdered is covered in burn marks and what looks to be stab wounds. But the most horrific thing is the way her lips are sewn together, and the brand that matches the logo of the notorious motorcycle gang that calls themselves the Reapers."

While she talks, there's a picture edited onto the live stream featuring the woman in question.

"The young woman is believed to be a former prostitute, and she's not unknown to the police who confirmed she went missing after the murder at Sleep-Eazy Motel."

She stops talking and turns her head, listening to someone behind her. The words aren't clear enough for me to hear.

"We've just been informed that the blonde hair is a wig and that the woman's own hair was removed."

Fuck... the hair... I didn't even notice it. I absentmindedly run my hands through my own hair as I look at hers, which matches perfectly in the color and length.

Slasher cuts the stream off and points at a message on his phone from Tido.

> **Tido:** You know I can't go into details yet. But tell Grayson there was a handwritten note stuffed into her mouth. The Reapers are going to kill a woman every hour until Zoe gives herself back to them.

I know I should probably feel guilty for being the reason countless women are going to lose their lives, yet all I feel is anger. How fucking dare they do this.

"I'm not doing it," I say abruptly. "Don't make me. Please don't make me—"

Slasher's the first one to speak. "What the fuck? Why would you even say that? You're one of us, Zoe. And we protect what's ours."

Gray moves behind me and wraps his arms around my waist. He doesn't say anything, but he doesn't need to. All I need is his touch and knowing he's got me.

"What are we going to do?" I whisper, feeling sick that my first thought was about my own safety. "Can we help the women?"

"We're not going to do a fucking thing," Tio says, proving that even though he isn't close, he's still heard us. "You're our Mama and we'll fucking protect you to the end."

As one the Kings and Cunts voice their agreement, assuring me that I'm not going anywhere.

The hours pass in slow motion.

Five hours, five bodies...

Ten hours, ten bodies...

Fifteen hours, fifteen bodies...

We're all holed up in the main room, but for once it's void of any chatter. Everyone stares at the clock on the wall, waiting with bated breath for the next body to turn up.

I haven't slept a wink, and I don't think any of us have. We just sit here, not even bothering to indulge in alcohol or eat or anything. We just exist, keeping our eyes glued to the big screen Slasher and Munroe hooked the tablet up to so we can all follow the live news.

"It's almost been twenty-four hours," the news reporter says.

Alana leans closer and clutches my hand in hers as we both sit on our men's laps. "It'll be okay," she says for the millionth time. "They're just fishing. Trying to scare you."

"It's working," I admit, licking my dry lips.

Though I mostly feel numb, the gruesomeness of it all has reawakened my fear. The thrill I felt for finally making real progress with Cara only lasted until the first body showed up. And the one that followed felt like nails in my coffin.

Gray squeezes my hips, silently giving me his strength.

"Oh, wait," the woman on the screen gasps. "She's alive. I mean... it's not a body this time. The woman is alive."

I don't know why that sounds worse, but it does. And my gut feeling is proven to be right when the camera shows a woman with her eyes sewn shut. She's wearing the same kind of wig they've all been sporting, and blood seeps from multiple stab wounds.

"Zoe," she screams, flailing her arms around, hitting police and medical professionals alike when they try to get closer to her. "Zoe Miller!"

The reporter frowns and I feel like she's looking straight at me. "I think the woman's name is Zoe Miller—"

"I have a message for Zoe," the woman screams, repeating it over and over. "Give up now, Zoe. You won't like what else we have in store for you."

The reporter cries out, tears brimming in her big, doe-like eyes. "This is Betsy K and I'm fucking done." She makes a strangled noise and we all watch as she tears the earpiece out and throws it at someone, maybe her cameraman. "This is so fucking sick. I need to go home. My family. My—" a sob cuts her off, but I know exactly what she feels.

This is all too fucking much and the Reapers have just proven they don't care what it takes.

They won't stop until they have me back.

31

Grayson

I've never wanted to go against all the planning we've done and just let loose to the rage inside me more in my life. Those fucking sick fucks are using other women to flush Zoe out. Innocent bystanders that have nothing to do with our war, yet they have been dragged into it and lost their lives in such brutal tragedy for it.

It's only natural that Zoe feels responsible for it. She knows it's not her fault, but the kind heart that beats inside her chest is wracked with guilt that these women are paying the price for her defiance against the Reapers.

Against Gunner.

Fuck. Having my hands wrapped around his throat can't come soon enough.

To make matters worse, after a day of doing exactly what they said and delivering up woman after woman every hour in different public locations around Santa Cruz for the news teams to report on, the community is fucking terrified. People have stopped leaving their homes. Businesses have closed their doors with notes stuck to the window that they will reopen soon, but no one knows when soon is.

With more new intel coming in from the Diamond Crew daily, we start planning our attack. We have to be smart about it, making sure all bases are covered, so no one gets away.

Most of the planning happens in church. Zoe sits by my side watching and absorbing, offering thoughts every so often, while my brothers take her suggestions and make her feel like one of them.

A part of me still fucking hates that she has to be exposed to all of this planning and intel, but I refuse to keep anything from her. The more she knows, the better she can use that knowledge or protect herself should something happen.

"What are you scheming?" I ask Zoe as she lowers herself to my lap in the main clubroom.

"I don't know what you mean." She pokes her tongue out and curls up on my lap and fuck I suddenly don't care what her and the Cruz Cunts have been whispering about over the last few days. It's probably another strike or some pranks to liven up the dull mood that has swept through the club.

"Turn on the news," Slasher calls, storming into the main clubhouse room, and all eyes dart to the TV over the top of the bar as Tex turns it on and it flicks to life.

An audible gasp sounds from the Cunts as they merge together in a group, holding on to each other as we all prepare for the worst.

"I'd hoped it was over," Zoe whispers as she shifts on my lap, eyes darting to the TV as the sound fills the room.

"The Reapers have struck again, after a long delay which had the community wondering if they had finally been caught, but as you can see behind me, the Santa Cruz Police Department have taped off the Pier, where it seems another body has been strung up on display."

Behind the reporter is an array of police vehicles and barriers put in place to stop anyone from entering the pier and my heart fucking sinks with wonder of who the new victim might be.

According to Loretta, all the women that the Reapers took from the Sleep-Eazy have turned up dead, all bar the last one who had a message for my princess. So who the fuck is their latest victim?

"According to our sources, the latest victim is a male who suffered a very brutal end before being hung by the neck from a light post toward the end of the pier. Police have not revealed who this man is yet, and we all wait with bated breath for confirmation on who it is." The reporter clears her throat before stepping closer to the camera so it's only her face that fills the screen. "My network would like me to apologize for my outburst when the last victim was found. The only thing I will apologize for is that there will be no apology. I am a local Santa Cruz woman. I have lived in this community since the day I was born, and to see this level of heinous atrocity targeting our locals is utterly heartbreaking and quite frankly, stomach turning. I will not pretend that this doesn't affect me right to my core."

She waves in front of the camera then, and the live feed cuts out, going straight to the newsroom where they start speculating on who the latest victim could be.

Zoe remains staring at the screen, her body stiff, her spine rigid.

"Zo," I rasp, leaning into her ear which seems to snap her out of her trance.

"Call Tido. I need to know who it is."

I was already intending on doing that after I made sure she's doing okay, but there is a layer of steel to her voice. A hardness I'm not used to hearing from her, so I don't coddle her. I don't argue. I take out my phone and call Tido.

"Ma, I'm busy working," he says down the line, and I snicker, knowing he must be around his colleagues if he just called me Ma.

"Who was it?" I ask, watching Zoe's blue gaze lock on mine as she turns to face me on my lap.

"I'll call our accountant about your request tomorrow," Tido snaps, and I still.

"Are you sure?" I ask him, dropping my gaze from Zoe. I don't want her to see the answer in my eyes.

Fuck.

"Yes," Tido snaps. "Got to go, Ma. I'll be home late."

The call ends and I take in a ragged breath as I try to figure out the best way to tell my princess.

"Gray?" she whispers, knowing the news isn't good. "Just tell me."

When my gaze darts back up to hers, I notice Slasher, Munroe, and Alana standing behind her, waiting to hear who it was too. I don't look at them though. I keep my eyes glued to my princess and clear my throat.

"Zo. I'm sorry. It was your dad."

A gasp flies from Alana before she can stop it, and in my peripheral, I see Slasher pull her into his side to offer her comfort, but I don't take my eyes off Zoe.

She's calm.

Too calm.

"Zo?"

"They killed my dad and strung him up on the pier?" she asks in a monotone voice.

"Yes," I say quietly.

"They killed him because I haven't handed myself in to them?" she asks, but it's rhetorical.

"You can't think like that." I counter, not wanting her to carry that burden.

Slowly, Zoe stands from my lap, keeping her gaze locked with mine. "Good. I'm glad he's dead. My only regret is that I wasn't the one to end his life."

She turns then, and moves across the space to leave the room, all eyes on her before she turns back.

"Ask Tido to send the photos through. I want to see his dead body for myself."

With those final words, she steps out of the room, and all eyes flick to me.

Fuck.

"Slasher, ask Tido to send everything through when he can." I stand and follow my princess, not willing to leave her alone for even a minute.

I find her in the back room, slipping the gloves on that she's been using with her training, and she starts pounding the bag swinging from the meat hook in the ceiling.

"You want to talk about it?" I ask, but she grunts.

"Not particularly."

I nod to myself, knowing she just needs to process this in her own way, so I approach the bag and shove it toward her. She reacts quickly, kicking out just like Cara taught her to fight off the attack.

And that's where we stay for the next few hours.

By the time Slasher comes to find us, the daylight has fallen to darkness beyond the frosted glass windows that sit high along one wall, the room now lit with white fluorescent light that does nothing to help the paleness of Zoe's face.

She needs to eat. She needs to rest. Yet she refuses to do either.

"Prez." Slasher holds up his phone, and Zoe stops punching the bag, darting her head toward our VP.

"Give me that," she demands, and Slasher looks to me for guidance as Zoe uses her teeth to release the bind of the first glove.

I give him a nod, and he approaches her. Holding out his phone as she tugs one glove free and works on the other.

They drop to the floor forgotten as she snatches the phone from Slasher, her breaths ragged from working herself so hard for the last few hours.

Moving up behind her, I peer over her shoulder to see the gruesome images of her dad's corpse.

Using her fingers over the screen, Zoe zooms in on one image, not to see the way her father's intestines are hanging free of his torn open gut, and not to see the way his eyes are sewn shut just like the other victims, but to see the words carved into her dad's chest, all bloody and scabbed.

Irina + Brian 4 eva!

The phone tumbles from Zoe's grasp, clattering to the floor before her hands fist in her hair and a guttural scream rips from her lungs.

"Leave us," I snap at Slasher, who nods and retrieves his phone before exiting quickly.

Another howling scream lurches from Zoe's lungs as she bends at the waist, tugging her hair so forcefully that I fear she'll rip it from her scalp.

"Zo!" I reach for her wrists, trying to control her, but she spins, her blue eyes nearly black with the rage swimming in them.

"I want her fucking head cut from her body!"

"Yes," I nod. "You will get that."

"I want to stab a blade into her gut and watch her fucking insides fall out!" she bellows, her face contorting with so much rage I'm not sure if I'll ever help her find her way back.

"Yes, Princess. I will make sure you are the one to do that," I promise her and she leaps at me, her dainty hands fisting in the front of my shirt as she seethes in my face.

"I want to hold her heart in my hand and feel it take it's last fucking beat before I dice it into little pieces."

Jesus. Her words.

She's like Cain's prodigy.

"Whatever you want, Zoe. It's yours."

A sob escapes her then, the blackness in her eyes dissipating as she shows me her pain.

"I need you," she whispers and I grip her hips, walking her backward until her back meets the wall.

"You have me. Always."

Leaning into her, my heart flips in my chest as she arches her back, pressing her tits against my chest.

"Make me feel good," she whispers. "Just like this. Right here." She hovers her lips over mine. "Make me feel good."

I close the distance, not able to hold back, and the moment my lips slant over hers, she parts for me letting my tongue in.

Fuck.

A frenzy takes over the moment our tongues dance.

My body melts into hers, my dick already hard and pressing into her. Lifting her thigh to wrap her leg around my hip, she moans into my mouth as I gently grind my jean clad cock into the apex of her thighs.

"More," she pants, one of her hands reaching around to claw into my ass, forcing me forward as she rolls her hips.

"Fuck, Zo," I rasp against her lips. "Is this really okay?"

"Yes." She nips at my lips, mashing her fabric covered mound against me. "Just like this."

I get what she's saying. The barrier of our clothing is giving her the security she needs as well as the friction she craves, so I give her what she wants.

Lips on lips, hands roaming and gripping and clawing, we press into each other, gyrating, mashing, humping.

I've never wanted my clothes to vanish so much, yet at the same time, I fucking love the tease of it, feeling the rub of her cunt through the barrier of our clothes as she chases her climax.

I'm fucking starved for her. Starved to feel myself sink inside her. Starved for her to consume me.

"Grind on my cock, Princess." I thrust forward as she tips her head back against the wall, her lids closing as she lets go. "You're so fucking beautiful."

"Gray," she cries, her fingers now digging into my shoulders as she dry humps the bulge of my cock. "I'm going to..."

She trails off as she holds her breath, her hips working faster to grind her cunt against me, and then a cry rips free as she plummets into her orgasm.

The friction, her cries, the way her sweet scent wraps around me has me following, and my whole fucking body jerks as I come in pulsing hot spurts into my fucking jeans.

"Fuck, Zo," I pant into her neck, feeling her body relax as she winds her arms around my neck.

"I love the way you love me," she whispers.

Pulling back, I take in her rosy cheeks and swollen lips as her pants turn into regular breaths.

"Thank you for trusting me." My eyes lock with hers, and I still see so much pain swimming in her blue pools.

"Do you have your knife?" she asks and my brows shoot up.

"Always."

"Can you give me a new scar today?" Her voice is soft and small, almost like she's unsure if it's okay to ask such a thing, so I remind her that she doesn't have to hide anything from me.

"Of course. Where?" I grin, and her lips spread wide in return.

"Through the brand on my shoulder blade."

Fuck. Gunner's fucking brand.

I've wanted to cut the fucking thing off her body, but I'll never subject her to that.

"Let's do it." I nod, and she beams as I release my hold on her thigh and step back from her body.

Ignoring the sticky patch in my jeans, I lead Zoe to a chair and sit her down before taking out my knife. She peels her top off, exposing her creamy skin, and I step behind her as she combs her ponytail out of the way.

Like every time I see the brand on her back, I nearly fucking lose it.

This isn't about me though. It's about my princess, so I step up close and hover the blade near her skin.

"Ready, Princess?"

She nods. "Do it."

Pressing the sharp edge to her flesh, I glide it down over the brand and watch the crimson of her blood seep from the cut.

Zoe moans like it gives her relief, and I wonder if it's as much relief as I get from watching me claim back that part of her skin.

It's mine.

She's mine.

And I'm fucking proud to be hers.

"I know you have it all planned out, and I love the plan," Zoe says, looking at me with a wistful look in her eye. "But can't we do it now?"

"You already know everything we have planned, Princess. The only thing not set in stone is the timeline. But I can move it up to the morning, after everyone has had a bit of sleep and I've had time to update Cain and Dante." Reaching over her shoulder, Zoe runs her fingers over the cut before eyeing the blood on her fingertips with a satisfied grin tugging her plump lips. "But first, we need a shower."

32

Zoe

Of course, Gray let me shower first, which is perfect for what I have planned, and the second Gray closes the bathroom door, I push the blankets off and get dressed as quickly as I can. Then I pick his phone up from the bedside table, checking if the pin I saw him use the other day still works. It does.

I quickly put the phone on silent and shove it into the pocket of my hoodie. Before I leave, I pause at the door.

"I'm sorry," I whisper to the empty room. "But I can't wait until the morning. I can't give them time to attack first, so it has to be this way. Please forgive me."

Not wanting to give myself time to change my mind, I hurry out of our apartment and rush downstairs where Alana, Rose, and Izzy are already waiting.

"For the record," Alana says, crossing her arms over her chest. "I don't agree with this."

The other two Cunts don't look much happier with my decision.

"It doesn't matter," I say, scrolling through Gray's phone. "Contact Cain and tell him to come now."

I know I'm asking a lot, and I don't feel good about it. But I prefer the guilt to being a sitting duck, allowing others to have control of my fate. Never again.

Never. A-fucking-gain.

As soon as I find the number I need in Gray's phone, I press it, waiting with bated breath as it rings twice.

"What now?" he barks as a way of greeting me.

"I hear you're looking for me, Rusty," I say, forcing my voice not to crack. "I don't want anyone else to die."

He chuckles. "Well, I'll be fucking damned. Zoe Miller as I live and breathe. Too bad you didn't come to your senses before your old man paid the price."

If he wants the words to make me feel bad, he's way off the mark. My dad is the one who created this mess, and he gave up on me before I did him. Of course, I still feel bad, just not enough to be reduced to a blubbering mess.

But Rusty doesn't know that, so I play into it and lower my voice. "Please don't," I beg. "I-I'm ready now. Tell me what to do."

As soon as he's given me the instructions I need, I end the call and turn to Alana.

"It's time."

Grayson

"The fuck have you done?!"

My yell makes Zoe flinch as my brothers' heavy feet pound the clubhouse floor, hurrying to see what all the drama is about. Meanwhile, the Cunts are really fucking quiet, watching on behind me.

"I had to do it this way, Gray."

I shake my head, pointing in her face. "No, you fucking didn't. We had a plan, Zoe. You didn't have to make the call early. I said we'd do it tomorrow."

"Tomorrow could be too late." She throws her hands up in exasperation, like I'm the one being fucking unreasonable. "What if they attack first? Tonight? We can't sit and wait any longer. We need to get it done now."

"That's not your fucking decision," I snap feeling my rage heat my fucking cheeks.

The moment I stepped out of the bathroom and noticed *my* princess and *my* fucking phone missing I knew something was up. I barely managed to get dressed fast enough to go in search of her, and when I found her, well... let's just say, she doesn't have a good fucking poker face. Not with me anyway.

"Well, it's done now. I made the call without you. We need to go." She shrugs like her taking matters into her own hands is no fucking big deal and tries to step past me, but I bare my teeth in a hiss, gripping her arm and dragging her nose to nose. "If you think for one fucking minute that I'm just going to let you go off and meet him alone, then you are fucking delusional."

She scoffs, ripping her arm from my grip and poking me in the chest with a sharp jab of her finger. "And if you think that's what I want, you're delusional. I never said I was going off to meet him alone, we stick together, remember? I just made the call early instead of waiting for tomorrow. The rest of the plan can still go ahead. It just has to happen now."

Our chests rise and fall quickly as we stare each other down, but it's Slasher's words that break the bubble of rage we're in.

"Prez, Cain is pulling in the gate."

I shoot a look to my VP, confused, and he gives me a shrug, looking just as fucking confused. It's in that moment that the Cunts start moving behind me, and a quick glance over my shoulder shows them cautiously walking toward the clubhouse doors carrying bags.

"Princess!" I snap, returning my glare to her with a really bad fucking feeling that Cain's presence has something to do with her. "Why the fuck is Cain here?"

"To take the Cunts to Dirty Diamonds, of course. Just like we planned, it's just a little earlier."

A low growl reverberates in my chest as the clubhouse door swings open, and Cain's voice sounds too fucking cheery for the current mood.

"Where are my sexy little Cunts?"

"Not your Cunts." Slasher barks in Cain's direction.

"Ouch," Cain says way too loudly. "Someone's a grump today."

Ignoring the snickering Cunts, my glare shoots to Zoe again, and the fucking brat simply lifts a brow.

"Trust me for once, Gray."

Trust her? Fucking trust her? Is she mad?

"You deceived me, Princess. You deliberately went behind my back. I've been honest with you about every fucking thing. I've taken you into the sacred space of church, which is un-fucking-heard of. I've kept you in the loop about our plans for the Reapers. I haven't fucking kept a single thing from you, yet you go behind my back and make the call to Rusty early." I hold my phone up flashing her the call log, but all she does is fucking roll her eyes.

My hand is around her throat in an instant, and I charge forward, forcing her to walk backward until her back thumps against the wall, her blue eyes wide with shock.

"Gray," she gasps, but I sneer in her face.

"This fucking situation isn't a fucking eye rolling situation, Princess. Have you forgotten what they did to you!"

"No, I haven't forgotten!" she screams in my face, tears springing to her eyes. "I'll never be able to forget!"

The whole room falls quiet as Zoe and I face off, our emotions running molten, and I'd fuck her right here right now if we had time because as angry as she makes me, my fucking cock is hard and hasn't got the memo that this isn't foreplay. But now isn't the time.

"I will burn this whole fucking world for you, Zo," I rasp, quieter now, and I feel her swallow thickly under the palm of my hand still tight around her throat.

"I know you will."

"Then why do you keep insisting on taking matters into your own hands?"

Her lower lip trembles, and she swallows again, so I loosen my hold on her throat, but I don't release her.

"I need to do this." She whispers, "I need them to see that they haven't broken me."

Fuck.

FUCK.

I understand that, which means now I have to fucking accept it.

"Cain," I bark, not taking my eyes off my princess. "Take them."

"Of course." He fucking sing-songs. "Come on, ladies. Your chariot awaits."

Murmurs from the Cunts saying goodbye to my club brothers fill the room as I stay in an eye lock with my princess.

As they leave and I hear the doors of whatever car or van Cain drove here to cart them all in, I take in a deep breath, hoping for fucking calm so I can clear my head and focus on what needs to be done.

"Are you sure Rusty believes you're coming alone?"

She nods at my question as we continue to stare into each other's eyes for a long beat.

Then I release her throat, taking a step back and turning to see my club brothers waiting quietly for my orders.

"The plan has changed. We leave now, get Zoe into position, and make sure we are close enough to protect her without being seen," I tell my men before addressing Slasher. "Call Dante. Tell him to get his men in place now. The plan moves forward tonight."

Slasher nods as my men hurry to arm themselves, and I turn back to my princess, gripping her chin roughly and tilting her head back.

"If you fucking die, I hope you know I'll be right fucking behind you, Zoe. If you're not in this world, then I'm not either."

Her blue eyes pool with tears as a sob escapes, but I swallow it, claiming her lips as I remind her with my demanding tongue that we are a fucking team. We either walk this earth side by side, or leave it together.

34

Zoe

The clearing is lit up only by the pale shine from the moon high above, and it feels like I'm standing in the middle of a natural, cold spotlight.

I fold my arms tighter around my middle as I wait with bated breath.

Waiting.

Waiting.

Fuck, this is harder than I thought it would be. Every second feels like an hour, and each minute feels like days. But it has to be done. Too many women have suffered at the hands of the Reapers and their gruesome reign.

Not thinking about Erin and the poor women who were slaughtered to send a message to me and the Kings, I might have been the latest on their victim list. But the list is long, too long. To me, the highlights of names are all those I love, strong women who helped shape me.

Cara, Leslie, and my mom.

I chant their names over and over in my mind. It's almost compulsory as I find myself unable to stop. It's like my mind is digging them into its crevices, hiding them in a safe place where they can never be forgotten.

Suddenly, and seemingly out of nowhere, my mom's letter comes to the forefront of my mind. One part especially stands out from the rest.

You're strong, baby. You're going to be a force to be reckoned with once you find your footing.

Fuck, I hope she was right. Everyone wants to think of themselves as strong, and I'm no exception. But tonight, I have to be. The lives of the Cunts, the future of the Kings. Fuck, my own future with Gray depends on it.

The more I think about it, the heavier my breathing becomes. I clench my fists at my sides, trying to control the warring emotions tearing at my insides. There are too many to count, let alone name. I'm feeling every single emotion known to man, but I refuse to let them rule me.

I can't decide if it's the chill in the air or anticipation that makes a shiver run down my spine.

Both.

Neither.

It doesn't matter.

All that matters is that today, we end this fucking thing.

Today I take my life back, preferably by ending at least one other. Two would be preferable.

Gunner and Irina.

Sighing, I gnaw on my bottom lip, keeping my eyes peeled on the clearing I'm standing in. Any minute now, Rusty will be here, and with any luck, he's brought his fucking vile VP and bitch of a sister with him.

Fuck, I never knew I could look forward to seeing someone dying. Then again, I also never thought I'd be held captive, raped, abused, and whatever else to name all the things they did to me.

Turns out Karma isn't the biggest, baddest bitch around. Because thanks to Cara's training, when I get my hands on Irina, she'll wish it was Karma and not me coming for her.

I fight the urge to look behind me, feeling Gray's eyes bore into me. He's angry, and I get it. I broke the plan and went solo. While the plan was always for me to lure Rusty here by calling him and pretending to hand myself over, I wasn't meant to make the call without Gray at my side.

That part of the plan was unspoken, but it was the only part that didn't need to be verbalized. With the way we've been clinging together, it was a fair assumption. One that I was all too aware of. That's why I waited until he was in the bathroom before I went downstairs.

I decidedly and willingly abused his trust. I own that, and I regret nothing. It was the way it had to be done.

The wind kicks up, and if it wasn't for the black hood on my hoodie pulled over my head, the strands would whip wildly around my face. Though I long to tie my hair, I resist the urge and let it fly free.

My head is down turned, hopefully shadowed enough that the darkness clouds my features. It's vital to the next part of the plan. It's not merely the plan the Kings came up with. No, that one is good, but it lacked something. But with the help of my Cunts, I dare say it's close to perfection.

Yet another thing Gray doesn't know about. But he will soon enough.

I think back on the unhappy look on the Cruz Cunts faces when I called Rusty early. I know they're onboard with the plan, hell they begged for it, even contacted Cain to get his help. So that's not what they were disagreeing with. If we'd had more time, I would have asked, but I couldn't risk waiting any longer, so I didn't. Though I'm pretty sure the Cunts were mostly conflicted because I snuck away from Gray to call Rusty instead of doing it with him.

The Cruz Cunts might be mine to command, love, and protect. But their respect for their Prez runs deep. And I think that's part of why I'm proud to be their Mama. I want Gray to be surrounded by people he can trust. And as for me, I don't want blind obedience.

Even if I don't listen to them, I want them to challenge me and speak up when they feel it's needed. That's the only way we won't end up with a similar situation on our hands. One where a member turns on the rest and terrorizes the women he's meant to protect.

I turn my head from side to side, looking at the barren landscape on either side of me. This is the place where the Devil's Night Brawl took place, so it's almost biblical to be back here with an ambush waiting at my back.

Gray and Slasher weren't surprised when Rusty chose this place, and I guess I shouldn't have been either. He's a scavenger, after all, and I guess this is his metaphorical den. A place filled with decomposing horrors.

Fuck, we should burn it to the ground. Erase every trace of the Reapers as a favor to the future owners, so they can restore the land, bringing it back to a thing of beauty.

The sound of approaching footsteps pulls me from my inner musings, and I slowly cock my head to the side they're coming from. If I'm not mistaken, there are only four sets, each hitting the ground in perfect synchrony.

I silently send a thank you to Cara for thinking of everything. Part of her training was to cast the room in darkness and blindfold me, then moving around, demanding I pinpointed her exact location only through listening. Occasionally, she'd bring more people in, making me sort through the sounds and know—not guess—how many people were circling me.

"Sugar, you're a sight for sore eyes." Even without the use of the disgusting pet name, I'd recognize Gunner's throaty rasp anywhere. "My dick's been missing you. Are you ready to bleed on it?"

Standing completely still, I fight the urge to recoil from his words. I don't reply or give any visible sign I'm even listening. On the outside, I'm completely still, but on the inside, I'm a mess. All of a sudden, I'm thinking of things I didn't even consider until now.

Like, what if Cain changed his mind? Shit... yes, what if he decided to take the Cunts back to Dirty Diamonds as Gray had originally planned, instead of doing what the Cunts asked for? Or what if the Cunts aren't here yet? What if something—anything—went wrong?

Since I arrived with the Kings, I know they're all waiting at my back, hiding in the shadows. But the Cunts... that's all up in the air. Since the Kings don't know what we planned, the women needed to wait on the other side and only move closer once Rusty showed up.

"Aww, there she is," Irina coos. "I've missed you, Zoe. You and me are going to have so much fun being roommates. I might even ask Gunner if you can sleep in my bed every now and then since your dad isn't around to keep it warm anymore."

I clench my fists so tight at my sides that my nails break the skin, warm blood pebbling to the surface.

Fuck, I no longer feel so good about this. What the hell were we thinking? No, I can't doubt them now. Gray confirmed Dante's men saw Cain pick them up.

I inhale sharply, reminding myself I need to stay calm. Cain would have found a way to alert me or Gray if something went wrong. I have to believe that.

The clearing becomes dark as clouds momentarily cover the rays of the moon, and I use the nature given opportunity to reach into the pocket on my hoodie and tap the phone I've hidden.

"Irina," I say.

Only, it's not in my voice. Thanks to the app suggested by Cain, it's distorted much in the same way the Reapers did to me when they chased me on Devil's Night.

Leaves rustle and branches crack on the ground as a group of women join us. My voice echoes from each of their directions. Every one of them is dressed like me; wearing black sneakers, black yoga pants, and a black hoodie with the hood pulled over their face, only showing off the blonde strands peeking out at the sides.

"What is this?" Rusty growls, spinning around as the women form a circle around them.

I chew on the inside of my cheek to stop myself from smiling. Fuck, the Cunts are perfect.

"One, two," I sing-song. "We've come for you."

Gunner's and Irina's heads dart from side-to-side, then all three of them spin around. It's like a deadly version of finding Waldo, except it's Zoe they want—me.

"Three, four," I continue in the eerie tone provided by the app. "Are you ready for more?"

Again they turn, craning their necks to get a good look at us. But all of us are keeping our distance, making it harder to see our downcast faces.

"Five, six." This time I step to the left, and each of the Cunts do the same, making it seem like the circle we've created is spinning. "Find the right one in the mix."

I take another step to the left.

"Seven, eight. You don't want to be late."

"You've fucking known her for years. Which one is she?" Rusty barks, and I'm surprised at the voice that answers.

"I don't fucking know," Adam snaps. "Maybe that one." I peek up in time to see him pointing at one of the Cunts. "Or that one." He points at another.

Irina hisses, "Gunner, you're the one who's obsessed with the bitch. Find her and kill the others so we can get out of here."

"Nine, ten," I continue, interrupting their squabbling. "Never leave revenge up to the men."

I force a laugh that sounds like a cackle as it reverberates through the clearing, which makes Irina flinch. Huh, I guess she doesn't like it when the tables are turned.

When Rose and Izzy showed what they'd come up with, I was in awe. It never would have occurred to me to draw inspiration from the iconic nursery rhyme from the Nightmare on Elm Street movies.

"What do you want us to do, Prez?" Adam asks, sounding unsure. Whether it's of the situation or what his next move should be, I don't know. And frankly, I don't care.

I allow myself to feel satisfaction at seeing him—all of them—look less cocksure. It's about fucking time they learn they're not the predators. Tonight, they're the prey.

"Fucking shoot them all," Rusty growls.

"No," Gunner bellows. "Don't fucking hurt her. Only I get to do that."

Irina sighs. "Fine. Then you shoot each of the bitches in the foot or something. Surely you'll recognize her scream."

35

Grayson

What the fuck has Zoe done now? I can barely believe my eyes at the large group of women all dressed the same, with blonde hair flowing out the sides of the hoods. And the distorted voice coming from all directions, speakers we can't see projecting the voice that sends a fucking chill up my spine.

She's fucking brilliant.

Her ass is going to be glowing fucking red from my hand when this is over. She made her own plans as Reaper bait, her quiet whispers with the Cruz Cunts, who must be the ones dressed like her, over the past few days slamming to the forefront of my mind.

Shit, had she already set this up with Cain beforehand? Did he know about her plan to include the women in this trap all along?

I'll fucking kick his ass for keeping it from me if he did.

My princess planned this fucking well, something I'm undecided about sharing with her. She deserves to hear it, but it may have to wait until I'm not so fucking angry.

I'm impressed. But also, fucking pissed. Hence why her ass is going to fucking glow.

As the women circling Rusty, Irina, Gunner, and Adam in the clearing keep moving slowly, loud distorted cackles make our prey shift nervously as they try to figure out what to do.

"What do we do?" Munroe asks at my side, but Slasher answers for me.

"We protect all the women."

It's a complication even though it's a brilliant one.

My princess is giving those sick fuckers a taste of their own medicine, and I don't take my eyes off the Reapers in the middle, watching their faces morph with concern.

I especially watch Gunner as Irina suggests shooting the women.

Seeing him here now is giving me tunnel vision.

I want to hurt him. Torture him. Be his worst fucking nightmare for the betrayal to the club. The betrayal to me. And more than anything, for what he did to Zoe.

"Move in. Be careful of the women," I snap the moment Gunner pulls his gun free and aims at one of them.

With my heart nearly lurching from my throat with fear that my princess will get hurt, as one, me and my brothers storm from the shadows, guns raised, voices yelling to distract Gunner.

It doesn't work.

The loud crack of his gun pierces the air, one of the women is hit in the back of her leg before she screams and tumbles to the ground.

Everything happens quickly then.

Chaos erupts.

With our women in the way, we can't shoot freely, and by the time we reach the panicking Zoe look-alikes, Gunner has shot another two rounds.

As I break through the barrier of women, I aim and shoot Rusty in the knee, watching him cry out in pain as he crashes to the ground before I turn to yell over my shoulder.

"You need to get out of here!"

More gunfire sounds, my eyes darting to Adam as he joins Gunner, shooting at the women, one jerking as a bullet slams into her hip, throwing her forward.

Her scream is loud, and I hold my fucking breath, hoping like fuck it's not my princess.

"No!" Slasher bellows as the hood comes off the woman and the wig falls free.

Alana.

Shit.

With a murderous roar, Slasher charges Adam, gun raised, with round after round hitting Adam where he stands as Slasher fills him with lead.

A bullet whizzes past my head before my eyes meet Rusty's where he trembles in the bloodstained dirt, his gun raised to me.

I don't hesitate. I squeeze the trigger of the heavy metal in my hand and watch his face contort in more pain as my bullet peels through the flesh on his arm and his gun tumbles to the dirt.

"You're mine now." I rasp, kicking his gun away and lurching forward to fist his hair, reefing his head back. "The Reapers are over."

Rusty hisses in my face, but I ignore the hate he's about to spew, pressing the barrel of my gun to his upper arm that's unharmed, and pull the trigger, making sure he's too injured to fight.

His bellow is met with an animalistic female growl as someone leaps on my back.

"Leave him alone!" Irina screeches, her fists hitting the side of my head as she swings wildly.

I reach back, trying to grab her, but she's like a monkey on my back, clinging to me.

"Get off him!" Zoe's scream meets my ears before I'm pulled backward, nearly falling as Irina is torn off me. "No one fucking touches what's mine. Least of all you, you psychotic bitch."

Spinning, I watch as my princess unleashes her monster, fists pummeling, leg kicking out to knock Irina to the dirt before a second kick to Irina's head knocks her out cold.

"Fuck," Stretch mutters, skidding to a stop next to Zoe, his gun trained on Irina. "I was coming to help, but it looks like you had that under control, Mama Z."

Zoe's only reaction to Stretch's words is giving a shrug before her eyes dart around frantically.

I follow her gaze, seeing women on the ground bleeding, while others attend to them. Adam's body is only feet away, lifeless eyes open and blood seeping from a hole in his head, courtesy of Slasher. Irina is still out cold, and Rusty Hunt, the Reapers' President, is panting in pain, with only one leg uninjured.

He's not going anywhere.

"Where is he?" Zoe whispers next to me, and I do another fucking scan of the clearing we're in.

"Where's Gunner?" I call out, my men surrounding us.

Everyone falls still, glancing around in confusion, but the way my brothers look around cluelessly, it's clear there's no sign of him.

FUCK!

He's not fucking here. How the fuck did he get away?

"Roll call!" I bellow, hearing my brothers make themselves known, my shoulders relaxing when they are all accounted for. That's a good sign. No casualties.

"Cunts, your turn!" Zoe's voice is strong as she demands the attention of the women.

Sobs fill the air as each Cunt confirms their presence, and I count them off on my fingers making sure they are all here, but we are one short.

Zoe's terrified blue gaze darts to me, coming to the same conclusion.

"Shit. Izzy," she whispers before turning to the group. "Izzy!"

A piercing scream floats to us from the treeline then, and all eyes shoot in that direction to see the dark figure of Gunner dragging Izzy away from us.

"No!" Zoe screams, before she starts bolting in that direction.

Fuck.

I take chase, turning to Stretch and Tex over my shoulder.

"Get Rusty and Irina in the truck and make sure they are secure!"

I don't look back to see if they heard me. There's no fucking time with how fast Zoe is running toward fucking danger.

I hear the heavy boots of some of my brothers behind me as I reach Zoe's side, running with her even though I really want to drag her in the other direction.

She needs this just as much as the rest of us.

Right as we lurch through the treeline, bullets spray in our direction, and I grab Zoe's wrist, dragging her to the ground behind a fallen tree stump.

My men follow, skidding in the dirt with us, ducking in case more bullets come our way.

"Where the fuck is he?" Slasher hisses, appearing on Zoe's other side.

"I can't see where the shots came from." Munroe pants from behind us.

Izzy's scream echoes through the trees, closer this time, followed by Gunner's voice.

"You're the reason people keep dying, Sugar!"

Zoe stiffens at the sound of his voice and the words that I'm sure she's already using to blame herself with.

Slowly, I move to peer up over the log, not able to see where the motherfucker is.

"Here's another to add to your count, Sugar!" Gunner bellows and this time, the sound of his voice shows me where he stands up on the ridge with Izzy, right before her cries turn to gargles as he slashes his blade across her throat.

"No!" Zoe screams, leaping up as I do and together, we tear over the log, racing toward Izzy's crumpled body.

Gunfire sounds around us as my brothers shoot in the direction Gunner was, but it's no use. He's no longer there.

Reaching Izzy, I remain standing, my gun trained in the direction Gunner went as Zoe falls to the ground, trying desperately to stop the rushing blood coming from Izzy's neck, but it's too late. She's already gone.

"Doug, Munroe, Tio, search up on the ridge for Gunner. If you find him, make sure he can't run or use his hands, but keep him alive," I order, and they nod, charging ahead up over the ridge as Slasher remains with me and Zoe.

"Izzy. No. I'm so sorry," Zoe whimpers, pressing her hands to the large gash severing Izzy's carotid artery as it empties.

I don't do anything but stand guard, my gun at the ready in case that sick fucker is playing with us.

I wouldn't put it past him.

"Gray," Doug pants, coming back to the ridge. "He got away in a van. It must have been what they came here in."

"Are you sure?" I snap as Munroe and Tio appear next to Doug.

"Yeah. He was halfway down the track leading in the other direction by the time we got there. Saw the taillights." Doug advises and my gut twists.

We were so fucking close.

How did that fucker get away?

Fuuuuck!

Lowering my gun, I drag a rough hand through my hair, dropping my gaze to my princess.

"I'll call Dante. See if his men have eyes on Gunner," Slasher advises as he tucks his gun away and pulls out his phone.

"Get an update on their operation while you're at it. I want to make sure this is the fucking end." I hiss, knowing it's still not over until Gunner is dead.

Dante and his crew were lying in wait at all the safehouses, and the moment I saw Rusty, Irina, Gunner and Adam step into the clearing, I sent a text to Dante to give the okay to breach the houses and kill the occupants. The Reaper occupants.

This was all meant to end here tonight. I can't fucking believe Gunner got away.

"Got it, Prez." Slasher agrees and I nod to myself, watching my princess jerk with sobs.

"Zo," I say, reaching down to squeeze her shoulder. "There's nothing you can do."

Her sobs cut off abruptly and her blue eyes dart to mine, swimming with fury as her top lip curls.

"You're wrong. There's something I can do, and it's all going to start with that slut faced bitch who brainwashed my dad."

Irina.

I don't argue with her. There's not a single thing I can say to stop her wrath. All I can do is join her and be there for her when she comes out on the other side, no matter what version that may be.

36

Zoe

A fresh wave of unrelenting guilt slams into me the second I step foot into Dirty Diamonds, where the Diamonds are already busy treating the injured Cunts.

Most of my girls lost their wig in the chaos. They're dirty and bloody. Yet every single one of them sits straight with their shoulders rolled back, and a satisfied glint in their eyes. Even Alana and the others who took a bullet. Okay, so my friend's expression is mostly marred by her hissing in pain as she writhes on the table, but I still see it in the depths of her eyes.

"Did we get them?" Cilla asks.

Like a deer caught in the proverbial headlights, I freeze. I scan all of them until I've memorized their individual injuries.

"We got Rusty and Irina, who are with Cain as we speak, getting acquainted with their new home down in the basement. And Adam is dead," I confirm. My throat clogs with the ball of emotions resting there. "But we... we..."

Fuck.

The words won't come. Knowing I'm about to remove their pride by announcing the death of one of their own is fucking brutal.

"Where's Izzy?" Rose asks, and when her shrewd gaze finds mine, I get the feeling she's trying to help me along. Like she's picked up on a tell I'm not aware of.

"Gunner took Izzy," I explain, trying to keep my emotions in check. "And he killed her."

A tear falls down my cheek as I think about the beautiful soul who paid with her life for my continued freedom.

The room grows quiet, no one making a sound. Heartbreak is palpable in the air, and I feel like another piece of my organ is chipped away.

"I'm so sorry," I say, my voice wavering. "I should never have asked you to be there."

Rose shakes her head. "No. Apology not fucking accepted, Mama Z. We wanted to be there. This is on Gunner. Not you."

The others join in, echoing Rose's sentiment.

"Izzy knew the risk," Cilla says, quietly. "We all did. But we wanted to be there."

"Search Izzy's pocket," Alana grinds out through clenched teeth.

My brows furrow. "Why?" I ask, feeling confused. "What's in her pocket?"

Before she can answer me, rushed footsteps approach. "The hell were you thinking?" Slasher snaps. At first I think he's talking to me, but then he forcefully makes his way to Alana. "Why the fuck didn't you tell me what you were up to? You could have died."

Alana rolls her eyes, but reaches up and cups his face. "Do you really think this is the best time to scold me? I've been shot, you know." Her voice slurs a bit and I wonder if it's because of any pain relief they might have given her.

A familiar pair of arms wrap around my middle, and I know it's Gray pulling me back until I'm flush against him. "I want an answer to that question, too," he commands. "What the fuck were you all thinking? Do you know how hard you made it when we couldn't just shoot them with you in the way?"

I hadn't thought about that ahead of time, but yeah, now I see how that didn't help the situation.

"Well, well, well," Cain drawls as he lazily saunters into the room. "All the Kings, Cunts, and even a princess under my roof again. You guys know you're always welcome, right? You don't have to get shot to stop by."

His over the top commentary is entirely welcome, and I feel myself relax a little. The combination of his weirdness and being in Gray's arms works its magic, and I lean back against Gray, tilting my head to the side when he begins kissing up my neck.

"You okay, Princess?" he asks, and not for the first time. He asked at least a thousand times during our drive here, and the answer always remained the same as it is now.

"I'm fine," I confirm. Then I clarify. "Physically."

"Good," he rasps, licking up my neck before biting my earlobe. "Because I'm fucking furious with you." His tone becomes darker, sending shivers up my spine.

I gasp when he lets go of me, but before I can fully process what he's doing, he takes my hand in his iron grip and forces me to follow as he walks out of there.

"Gray," I gasp, trying to rip my hand out of his as I scramble to keep up with him.

"No," he replies. "You lied to me for days, Princess. You risked the lives of your Cunts and your own. One is unacceptable to me as Prez, and the other as the man who's spent all this time loving and protecting you."

Faster than I can react, he comes to a stop and pushes me against the wall of the dark hallway. Gray places his arms on either side of my face, caging me in.

"Why did you do it?" he asks, his tone deceptively smooth, a stark contrast to the anger brewing in his dark eyes. "Why did you fucking lie to me? Why didn't you just come to me about moving the plan up? Why didn't you tell me about involving the Cunts?"

Indignation and guilt rises to the surface. "I never fucking lied," I volley. "But I never told you because you would have said no. You wouldn't have moved the plan up to right away, and you wouldn't have let the Cunts get involved like they did."

"That's because it's fucking dangerous. We, the men, are trying to protect you all." He gestures behind him where the Kings move about helping the injured Cunts.

"I know that." I shrug. "But it's done now, Gray."

The smile he gives me is all teeth. "Has my respect for your boundaries given you the illusion you can just fucking push me around?" he asks as his hand moves to my throat, wrapping around it and squeezing like he used to. And even though it should send my anxiety through the roof, there's something comforting about it. "Do you see me as a pet you can just play with? Is that it, Princess?"

I ball my hands into fists and punch his shoulder. "Let me go," I demand, my breathing ragged. "Let go of me right fucking now, Gray."

"No," he smirks. That one word paired with his obnoxious expression is all it takes to obliterate all traces of the man who's been tip-toeing around me, always careful not to spook me or set my anxiety off. "I don't think I will. Apparently, you need a fucking reminder of who I am."

His lips descend on mine in a bruising kiss. Our teeth clash, and he bites my lip until the taste of blood fills my mouth. The kiss is brutal, hurried, and so fucking perfect. Returning the fervor, I stroke his tongue with mine, and it doesn't take long before I'm panting into his mouth.

With one hand still clasped around my throat, Gray moves the other to my hip, squeezing the bone until I whimper. Then he trails searing fingers down my thigh to my knee, lifting my leg and moving it around his hip.

"Are you going to lie to me again and tell me you don't like this?" he asks.

I consider doing just that. The denial of how good and familiar it feels, but I don't. "No," I say, breathily. "I won't lie to you."

Desperate to feel him closer, I stop fighting him, and eagerly let him move me however he wants. And when he rolls his hips so his cock grazes my core, I throw my arms around his neck and moan.

"Yes, Gray. Yes."

This is what I need. Him to take over, so I don't have to think. For him to just make me feel.

"I told myself I'd make your ass so red the only white part left will be my handprint," he rasps. His words make my blood run cold, but it's quickly morphing into pleasure when he grinds his hardness against me again. "But I'll wait. This isn't the time for that."

Even though I'm not sure I'd be able to handle a spanking, I'm still disappointed at the prospect of not getting one.

"What if I want you to?" I ask.

He chuckles. "That's even more reason to wait, Princess. You've been a bad girl."

The goading words aren't what's catching my attention. It's the way he looks at me, like he's imagining losing me. He closes his eyes as a shudder runs through his body.

"Don't fight me right now, Princess." It's almost a plea.

"I won't," I say, cupping his face between both my hands. "Take what you want from me. I promise I want it too."

As though my words are the key to the shackles he's used to bind his volatile nature, he growls menacingly. Then he claims my lips again, flexing his hand around my throat while using the other to roughly push my yoga pants down.

I let out a mixture of a moan and gasp when he savagely cups my weeping cunt. Despite all the time that's passed, my body comes alive at his touch. I gyrate my hips, seeking a friction and fullness only he can give me.

"Say it," he demands. His fingers graze my pussy lips, but he doesn't do more than that. "I want to hear you ask me for it."

My eyes fall closed, my breathing rapid. "Touch me, Gray."

"Look at me and ask for my fingers in your cunt, Princess."

As I open my eyes and peer up at him through my lashes, I want to give him what he's asking for. What he needs. But when I open my mouth, the words get stuck in my throat. "I-I... please... I want..." I stutter, acting like a Victorian virgin on her wedding night rather than someone who's been fucked in every imaginable way by this man.

Gray's expression softens. "Repeat after me. I want your fingers in my cunt."

"I want your fingers in my cunt," I say, echoing him.

"Please finger fuck me."

Again, I repeat the words. "Finger fuck me, Gray. Please."

He growls. "So fucking pliable when you want to be. How can I deny you when you beg so sweetly?"

Instead of dragging it out, he parts my folds with his fingers, easing two into me. Despite wanting—craving—this, my cunt squeezes around his fingers, and my breath saws out of me. I keep my eyes open, needing to remind myself that this is Gray and that I want it as much as he does.

"You okay?" he asks, worry making his eyebrows draw together, creating a crevice between them.

"I... I..." I pant through the onslaught of emotions. "Give me a minute."

Gray halts his movement, his fingers only half inside of me. Then he slams his lips to mine, and the taste of him makes it easier to focus on him—us.

His tongue skillfully wrestles mine into submission, and we lick at each other. My hands tangle in the messy waves of his hair, pulling on the roots until he growls into my mouth.

When I'm so lost in the sensation of our kiss, he pushes his fingers all the way inside me. "Fuck," I moan, almost biting his tongue.

Gray pulls back. "Fuck's right, Princess. First, I'm going to make you come on my hand, then on my cock. And you're going to take it, aren't you?"

I nod, beyond words, as he curls his fingers deep inside me, teasingly grazing that sweet spot deep inside me. Throwing my head back against the wall, I moan into the empty hallway. His dominating words and rough handling like a form of foreplay with a direct line to my cunt that's aching for him.

"Y-yes," I cry out, both in answer to his question and the way he's working me, playing my body like it's an instrument he's spent years learning to master.

He picks up the pace, pistoning his fingers in and out of me, grinding the heel of his hand against my aching clit.

My legs begin to shake, and my orgasm is so close I can practically taste it. Yet, it refuses to claim me.

"I can't," I huff in frustration. "I'm too fucking broken." The last part comes out as a sob.

Gray tightens his hold on my throat and rips his lips from mine. "Broken or not, Princess," he growls. "You're mine. Your body is fucking mine. And if I want you to come, you have no choice but to obey. Isn't that right?"

"I can't," I repeat when my body still isn't getting the memo.

He lets go of me and jerks his pants open with rough movements, pushing them all the way down until they're pooling at his feet. The next thing to go is his shirt. Then he unzips my hoodie and throws it over his shoulder.

"We're not leaving this hallway until you come, Princess. And I have all fucking day."

I blink in confusion until I remember it's early in the morning. Despite the falseness of his words, I know he means them. He'll stay between my legs until I come, shirking his duties as Prez, until he's conquered this obstacle.

Reaching out, I wrap my hand around his hard shaft, tugging until he shifts closer. "Then show me what you can do with that magnificent cock," I purr. "Make my body remember its master."

The answering growl ripped from his throat can only be described as feral. "Oh, I fucking will."

He lowers to his knees and I think he's going to eat me out, but instead he lifts each leg and gently removes my shoes so he can get rid of my pants altogether. Then he lifts me up, bracing me against the wall.

"Tell me to fuck you," he says, his tone filled with gravel.

I brace my hands on his shoulders and look right into his eyes. "Fuck me, Gray," I pant.

He rubs his head against my wet opening, slicking the tip before he eases inside me. We don't look away as my body slowly lets him in, and I let him see everything I feel play out like a movie on my face. The anticipation, surprise, apprehension, and my complete need for him.

We're both panting by the time he finally bottoms out, and I angle my hips. Being like this with Gray is like riding a bike. My body remembers the smallest adjustments needed to make it better.

"Oh, God," I moan when he slowly pulls almost all the way out before slamming back into me. "Yes. Just like that." My inner walls flutter around him, attempting to get him farther inside.

"Princess," Gray groans. "So fucking good."

He picks up the pace, thrusting into me like we're rushing to the finish line, and it's exactly what I need. With no time to think, my body is primed for release and it feels like mere minutes passing before my pussy clamps down on him.

"Yes. Yes. That's it. Gray. Yes," I chant, repeating the words over and over as a violent orgasm tears through me, making tears pool in my eyes. "Fuck. I... I... Gray—"

Gray silences me with his lips, swallowing my moans, greedily drinking down my pleasure as I come on his cock.

Tears form in my eyes, falling down my cheeks. Relief that we can still have sex, that I'm not broken beyond repair, makes the moment even more poignant.

"See," Gray rasps, tilting his head to the side. "You're not broken. You're simply mine, and your body just needs to be reminded of that."

I half laugh and half sob because saying something like that is so like him. He's not wrong. But it's so uniquely him to simplify things that way. Just like it's typical for me to overthink it.

"I love you so much," I say. "It's you and me to the end." As if to punctuate the words, I tighten my cunt around him.

With a growl, he slams into me over and over, seeking his own release. "To the fucking end and beyond," he groans as he shoots hot spurts of cum into me.

He rests his forehead against mine, closing his eyes, and I do the same, wanting to savor this moment. I don't even care that we don't have a modicum of privacy since anyone could walk by. Though Cain's smart enough to make sure no one disturbs us.

Gray sets me down once our breathing is back under control. "I'm still furious with you," he says, giving me a crooked smile as he pulls his pants back up and fastens them.

"Of course you are," I mutter, rolling my eyes as I reach for my panties.

"Nuh-uh," he grins. "I'll keep those. You haven't earned the right to wear them."

Pinching the bridge of my nose, I let out an exasperated sigh. "Seriously?"

He nods. "Absolutely."

I flip him off and quickly put my yoga pants back on before shoving my feet into the shoes. Then I zip my hoodie back up and comb my fingers through my hair.

"Fine," I say, smirking. "They're not mine, anyway. I ran out of clean ones and borrowed a pair of Alana's." So much for promising not to lie to him again, because that's so not true.

He laughs and takes my hand. "I know that's not true, Princess. Do you really think I haven't memorized what all your panties look like?"

With no good comeback or a believable story to back up my ridiculous lie, I just shrug and follow him back to where we left the others.

When we enter, Slasher's still at Alana's side. Her eyes are unfocused and she's giggling, pointing above her. "But look," she insists. "It's the dust bunny monster."

Slasher sighs and runs his hand down his face. "You're right," he relents. When he spots us, he glares at me. "You're fucking lucky Alana is your second."

"What's that supposed to mean?" I ask, baffled.

"Before the doc took care of her, she told me the Cunts pressed you into including them in your idea. That's the only reason I'm not holding you responsible for *my* Cunt being shot."

I feel Gray tense next to me, but I squeeze his hand. "That's fair," I say, because it is. I'm supposed to be responsible for them, and our plan backfired.

Maybe backfired is too strong a word since it worked. It just didn't play out how we'd imagined. But then again... perhaps it did. Rose went to great lengths to talk about the danger and the chances of someone dying.

I was the one who kept repeating things would be okay. Not because I believed the plan to be infallible, but what other choice did I have? I'm not as strong or seasoned as some of them. So I did what I thought was best.

"Zoe, you need to see this," Cilla calls out. Turning, I walk over to her, taking the small piece of paper she holds out to me. "Before we left to be your clones, Alana made us all write a note in case we didn't make it. We each carried it in our pocket, and this is Izzy's."

My throat tightens as I unfold the small piece of paper and read.

If I don't make it through tonight, I want everyone to know I died free. I'm not a strong fighter, but I'm devoted to my found family. The choice was mine. Don't make my death mean nothing by blaming each other.

All hail Mama Z.

Izzy

"Oh my God," I choke out. Tears fall from my eyes again, dripping onto the paper. I look at Alana, but she's too busy swatting away something only she can see, still giggling to herself. "Is she okay?" I ask Slasher.

"High as a fucking kite, but she'll be fine," he confirms.

I look at everyone else, taking in their expressions. They range from somber to relieved, and everything in between.

"I have a question," Munroe says. "How the fuck did the Cunts get out of Dirty Diamonds after Cain took them?"

"They obviously snuck out," Stretch answers.

"What? You think they got past Cain's watchful eye?" Munroe questions. "Even if they did, then how did they get to the clearing?"

Cain chooses that exact moment to whistle while innocently looking up at the ceiling. "I see what you mean, Alana," he says. "The bunnies are out of control."

"Fucking," she sniggers. "Fucking like dust bunnies."

He nods. "That's what I always say. We should—"

"Cain," Gray growls, clearly not entertained by the evasion and crazy talk. "Just fucking tell us already."

Leaning back against the wall, Cain props one leg up. "You see, it all started with a call from the lovely Alana—"

"She fucking what?" Slasher barks. His outburst causes Alana to pinch her brows together.

"You're disturbing the cloud," she says, pointing above her head.

Slasher shakes his head. "Never mind. Carry on."

Nodding, Cain continues. "She told me about the plan and asked if I'd help. Being an equal opportunist, I of course said I'd obey by our Princess' ruling."

"My princess. Mine. Not fucking yours," Gray growls like that's what matters. "Continue."

If I leave the story up to Cain, we'll never get any-fucking-where. He's easily distracted and has a penchant for hiding the story between details that don't matter. So I clear my throat.

"Since Cain was already meant to pick up the Cunts, he agreed to drop them off at the clearing, before hitting the Reapers' safehouses with the rest of his... crew."

Even though no one has asked, there's so much tension in the air I have to clarify something else. Coming clean might not mean a thing to anyone else, but it does to me.

"They wanted to be there and to do their part," I say, gesturing toward the Cunts. "Every single one of them volunteered. There was no vote or demands."

The last part is mostly disclosed for my benefit, because even if they asked for it, I still feel guilty for letting them.

Gray nods slowly. "And you didn't tell us because—"

"Because we knew you'd stop us," Rose says, interrupting him. "We wanted it. Even if Zoe had said no, we would have found a way. This is our war as much as it's yours. And it's our Mama that was threatened."

"Just for the record," Tio says from somewhere in the back, "I think their plan was brilliant."

"You can't be serious," Doug interjects. "They could have blown the entire thing."

"They fucking distracted us," Sully adds.

Slasher stands abruptly. "It was fucking reckless. But it was a great plan. And they're right, we wouldn't have allowed it if we'd known. That's our mistake to fucking own."

I'm surprised he's the one who's defending the plan since Alana got hurt the worst. Well... of the survivors.

"What's done is done," Gray says, sounding exhausted. "So I'll make a fucking promise as your Prez. From here on out, if the Cunts want to be included, we won't discard that decision. But in return, I want you to fucking swear that you won't pull a stunt like this again."

Even though no one looks at me, I take a step forward. "I promise we won't go behind your backs again. And I'm sorry."

The Kings all nod and grunt like that's good enough for them. I know Gray's still pissed, and he has every right to be. But that's between me and him, not the club. And even if I apologize, which I can't bring myself to do, I still abused his trust. Something like that needs actions and not placating words to mend.

"If we're done with pointing fingers, can we please talk about the prisoners?" Cain asks, smacking his lips together.

"Are they kept separate?" Gray asks, and Cain nods.

"Oh, yes. I've personally made sure that they're... actually, why don't you just follow me?"

Since everyone is exhausted and in desperate need of sleep—hell, getting laid and maybe drinking and snorting shit to unwind—it's quickly decided that the rest will stay while Gray and I follow Cain.

The crazy fucker takes us down to the basement, but it's nothing like what I saw the last time I was here when Gray tortured the Reaper.

"Did you redecorate again?" Gray asks, dryly.

Cain's head bobs eagerly. "On Wednesdays we don't crucify people," he says, like that's an explanation.

"What the hell?" I gasp as he turns the lights on, revealing more of the basement than I saw the last time.

The huge concrete room is cleverly divided into sections. Yes, one is what I've already seen, but there's also a part completely covered in mirrors, and one that's...

"Why are the makeshift walls painted pink?" I ask in disbelief.

Cain winks. "You won't believe how it can drive people crazy to look at a color that is uncomfortable. So when I keep them awake and it's all they see... it yields some interesting results."

I don't fucking doubt it. Not in the slightest.

"I'll show you all of it another day," Gray says, probably more to make sure Cain doesn't go off topic.

Cain leads us to the furthest part, where two glass boxes are placed. They're small, but big enough to fit a person if they're crouched.

"Oh," I exclaim, smiling as I realize that's exactly what's happening. "They're in there?"

Bowing, Cain sweeps his hand out. "Welcome to the black and white room. Well, boxes. Well... you know what I mean."

And I do, since one box is completely black and the other white.

"We can see in," Cain explains. "But they can't see us or hear us."

"Soundproof glass," Gray mutters.

"Yes," Cain confirms. Then he pulls his phone out of his pocket and opens an app. "But there's a microphone in each box, so we can still hear them. And a speaker, so I've been talking to Rusty."

Cain taps away on his phone and suddenly the sound of nails on a chalkboard sounds, which prompts Rusty to groan. "No more."

"And Irina?" I ask, folding my arms over my chest. "What have you done to her?"

Gray answers. "If he knows what's good for him, he hasn't touched her. Irina is yours, Princess."

The sick words shouldn't fill me with joy, but they do. "Really?" I ask excitedly.

"Really," he chuckles. "Though I have a few suggestions."

I'm not opposed to suggestions because apart from Cara's training, I don't know shit about it. But there are a few things I absolutely want the crazy bitch to suffer.

Holding my hand out, I demand, "I need a knife."

Gray doesn't even hesitate in giving me his, and as soon as I'm clutching it, I look at Cain. "How do I get in there?" I ask, pointing at the box that definitely won't fit two people.

He chuckles. "Wait there for a second."

I take Gray's hand, using my body to tell him that I want him close. This might be my mission, but we're a team. When I say 'I', it should automatically involve him.

"Here," Cain says, returning with three pairs of glasses. "They're night vision glasses. Before opening one of the surfaces of the box, I'll black the room out so she can't see anything."

"She'll feel the shift in the air," Gray points out.

Cain shrugs. "She will. But she's handcuffed to her chair. A special request from our princess."

I beam. "Let's do it."

We put the glasses on, and Cain does everything he described. Then he moves out of the way, making sure to stay in the background as Gray and I move closer to Irina.

"Irina," I sing-song, using my own voice this time. "I'm so glad to finally catch up with you."

"Fuck you, Zoe!"

I cluck at her. "Where are your manners? We're talking Mama to Mama so you should show some respect."

She bares her teeth and lets out a string of curses.

I try my best to keep my emotions locked down, but the longer I look at her, the more impossible it becomes. This is the woman who's responsible for destroying my family, for my captivity. She played mind games with me that in some ways were a lot worse than Gunner's abuse. And she killed my dad. Even if he didn't die by her hand, it was by her actions.

As much as I've tried to disown my dad in my head and heart, it's not that simple. I've known him—or thought I knew him—my entire life. Once upon a time, he was my hero, the one to check for monsters under the bed.

For all the bad he's done, and the list is long, he didn't deserve to die like that. Or maybe he did, but I didn't allow it.

Clutching the knife in my hand, I angrily cut Irina's shirt from her body, making sure her torso is bare to me.

"You wrote 4 eva," I said. "So let's make it so."

Then I dig the end of the knife into her skin, slicing until she's literally bleeding the message that's forever etched into my dad's flesh.

Irina + Brian 4 eva!

Disappointment clings to me, making the experience bittersweet when Irina barely inhales sharply. But not a sound falls from her lips, much to my dismay.

"You're going to be tough to break," I say, admiring my sloppy handiwork. "But I won't disappoint you, Irina. I'm more than up for the challenge."

I barely recognize my tone. It doesn't sound like me at all. And if I'm being completely honest, this doesn't feel like me. Yet it's something I need to see through. Not just for myself. But also for my mom, dad, Leslie, Slayer, Izzy, Sasha, and all the other people Irina has helped hurt.

37

Grayson

I jerk awake, my lids snapping open and frantically darting around my room.

Something's not right.

Turning my head on the pillow, I glance over to see Zoe's still sound asleep next to me, her deep breaths of slumber meeting my ears.

Why did I just wake up?

I strain my ears trying to hear beyond the bedroom, but everything sounds so quiet.

Did a noise wake me up?

Slowly sitting up, being careful not to disturb Zoe, I check my phone to see there aren't any notifications informing of a breach or any movement picked up on the motion sensors.

Blowing out a breath I didn't realize I was holding, I relax my tense shoulders, accepting that perhaps a dream snapped me from sleep so quickly.

Fuck. I think I'm losing my shit.

Running a hand down my face, I slide my phone back onto the nightstand and reach for the lamp, flicking it on... Only no light illuminates the space.

Frowning, I flick the lamp switch off and on again a few times before I ease out of bed and move to the wall switch by the door, flicking it on.

Nothing.

Shit.

I stand still for a minute, listening again, and realize the reason it is so quiet is because I can't hear the hum of the fridge.

The power is out.

"Gray?" Zoe's husky voice floats from the bed, and I move over to her quickly.

"Princess, I'm sure it's nothing, so don't panic, but the power is out. I need to do a sweep of the building."

Zoe bolts upright, and from the little light filtering in through the window from the moon, I can see how wide her eyes are as she looks around the space.

"Are we in danger?" she whisper-yells and I chuckle.

"What about don't panic, don't you understand, Princess?"

Even in the dull light, I see the glare she shoots me.

"Instead of being a prick, how about you answer my question?"

Sighing, I slip my hand through the long strands of her hair and cup her nape.

"Sorry, Zo. But I wouldn't be joking around if I thought we were in any danger. The cameras and motion sensors haven't picked up any activity, and the alarm system hasn't gone off."

"The power is out. Wouldn't they stop working?"

She has a point, but I shake my head. "We were assured the backup batteries would kick in as soon as general power cuts." I lean in and press my lips to her forehead. "Put some pants on. If I'm doing a sweep, then so are you."

Nodding, Zoe shifts on the bed, and I release her, moving out of her way and go to my side of the bed to grab my phone. Bringing up Slasher's number, I hit call.

"Prez?" he rasps, voice husky from sleep.

"The power is out. Get a couple of our brothers up to do a sweep outside and check that Sully and Titch are doing okay at the gate. I'm taking Zoe with me to do a sweep inside."

"Got it. I'll get Tex up. He can help us check inside, too."

I grunt my agreement and end the call, picking up my gun and moving to Zoe's side now that she's wearing pants.

"Let's go," I mutter, linking my fingers with hers and raising my gun. "Get the door," I whisper, and Zoe reaches out to turn the handle.

We step out into the main room of my apartment, my gun darting in all directions as our eyes scan the dark space for anything out of place. We quickly see that there's no threat in here, so we venture out of the apartment.

It takes us about fifteen minutes to check every room and hiding space before the lights flicker back on and we all breathe a sigh of relief.

I'm paranoid as fuck knowing Gunner is still out there, but I don't think he'd be so stupid as to take on the entire club on his own.

"Sully and Titch are okay at the gate." Slasher announces as he approaches me and Zoe as we enter the main clubroom. "They said it's been quiet, and the power went off out on the street as well. It wasn't just us."

"Oh, thank God." Zoe slaps her hand to her chest, clearly relieved we all overreacted.

Chuckling, I pull her to my side and press my lips to her hair, inhaling her clean and sweet scent. Just that action alone gives movement to my dick.

"I'd better get back to Alana." Slasher steps aside, ready to leave the room, but Zoe stops him.

"How is she?"

A frown pulls in his dark brows before his gaze meets hers. "She's in a bit of pain, but she'll be okay."

"Well, let me know if you want me to help." Zoe insists. "She nursed me back to health. The least I can do is return the favor."

"Will do." This time Slasher grins, and even though he's tired, I see an edge of lightness in his eyes that hasn't been there much since his twin died.

Alana makes him happy.

I speak to the other guys for a few minutes before going back to our apartment. I should probably have moved into the apartment assigned for the President and let Slasher move into the one I occupy, but things have been too chaotic to even think about shit like that.

Soon, though.

Soon, this war will be over once and for all, and we can all focus on moving forward with our lives.

It's actually a daunting fucking thought.

All I've really known is this war with the Reapers. Even though the situation is completely fucked, it's the Reaper war that brought my princess to me. I can't imagine I'd have her by my side any other way.

Locking ourselves back into our apartment, Zoe leads me to the couch instead of the bedroom and tugs me down next to her as she snuggles into my chest.

"You know, we could do this in bed." I remind her and she nods against my t-shirt.

"I know. I'm just really awake now." She pushes up off me, her blue gaze locking with mine. "I don't think I can go back to sleep just yet."

A slow smirk spreads my lips wide. "Whatever will we do?"

A blush creeps up Zoe's neck, flaring over her cheeks. "I kind of liked what we did in the hallway at Dirty Diamonds a couple of days ago."

"Kind of?" I snap, my brows hitching high.

"You know what I mean." She slaps my shoulder, shooting me a glare.

Chuckling, I nod, gripping her hips and dragging her to straddle my lap on the couch. "I do know what you mean," I rasp, tugging her closer until we are nose to nose. "You want me to make you feel good, Princess?"

When she nods, pressing her lips to mine, I don't kiss her back.

"Maybe you don't deserve to feel good. Maybe I'm still punishing you for lying to me about what you and the Cunts had schemed up." I point out, and a whimper escapes her parted lips as she grinds her center to the hard bulge of my cock through our clothes.

"You've already punished me," she whines, fisting my hair and dragging my lips to hers.

Fuck.

She feels so good, her scent egging my dick on, desperate to have her again.

It felt so fucking good to bury my cock deep inside her at Dirty Diamonds two days ago. I'd wanted to reclaim her that way for so long, but with everything she'd been through, for a time there, I didn't think she'd ever be able to accept me back inside her body.

Thank fuck she did. I'll never admit to her how much I ached for it. I don't ever want to make her feel bad for needing to take time and process things the way she needed to.

Besides, she knew how much I wanted her. Still want her. I don't need to point that out.

As much as I'd like to punish her now and torture her by withholding orgasms, I'm not fucking strong enough.

I can't fucking help it. I want to make her feel good all the fucking time.

"Clothes off," I demand after breaking our kiss.

Zoe doesn't hesitate, shifting off my lap and quickly stripping her clothes off.

I do the same, not taking my eyes off her creamy skin for a moment, drinking in the sight of her and doing my fucking best to ignore all the permanent marks Gunner put on her.

Your time is coming, motherfucker.

Zoe's blue pools drink me in, her gaze hungry as she licks her lips, zoning in on my stiff cock, so I grip the base and angle it in her direction.

"You want this?"

"Yes." She nods, stepping closer, and I stretch out on the seat of the couch, laying down.

"You can have my cock once you've ridden my face."

Her brows shoot up, but she doesn't hesitate, moving to straddle my head with her eyes locked on mine.

I shake my head. "Face the other way, Princess. I want to see your ass while you suffocate me."

"You have a weird obsession with my ass." She jokes, turning the other way and straddling me.

My sight is filled with the creamy flesh of her ass and back, and again, I ignore the marks marring her flesh. My hands grip her hips, guiding her down and the moment I feel her folds part and the silky flesh of her cunt press over my lips and nose, I dart my tongue out and start lapping at her.

I can't really give her much guidance with the way she smothers me so fucking good, but she doesn't need it, her body remembering mine and how we belong together like this.

She starts rolling her hips, her moans meeting my ears as she does what I asked of her and rides my face.

Using my hands, I part her ass cheeks wider, my gaze trying to focus on her puckered hole, but I'm too fucking close to it, and she wastes no time pressing the tight opening to the tip of my nose as her greedy cunt chases relief.

I focus on the muscles coiling in her back, and the way she moves over me, and the strange sensation of fingers hitting my chin every so often as she circles her clit.

That's it, baby. Smother me. Take what you need.

Zoe leans forward over me as she picks up her pace, and my cock jerks as dainty fingers wrap around its girth before her tight grip starts pumping me.

Fuck yes.

She's perfect.

Every so often, Zoe shifts enough for me to suck in a breath, but it's not enough to stop the lightheadedness from hitting.

I want her to come before I pass out or die. I need her to know she can chase her orgasm and still reach it, something that she's been struggling with a lot.

I start fucking my tongue into her cunt, her juices slick against my tongue, hitting the back of my throat.

It's at this point that my princess loses control.

She fucks my face with forceful grinds, trying to force my tongue deeper and deeper as she speeds up her rhythm around my cock.

"Gray!" She cries out, mashing her drenched folds over my mouth, and as she stiffens, her moans filling the room as the walls of her cunt start squeezing my tongue, her grip on my cock clamps tighter than a vise as she pumps me.

Her hair flies in my vision as she throws her head back, reaching the peak of her climax before she starts coming down, and she suddenly lurches forward, finally allowing me to take in much needed air.

My cock is ready to explode and the feel of her lips wrapping around it has my hips surging up to sink deeper toward her throat.

"Fuck, Princess," I rasp. "Your mouth feels so good."

Zoe hums around my cock, right before she starts sucking.

Her mouth is like a fucking suction cup, and any thoughts of me fucking her mouth fall away as the sucking sensation increases.

I buck, not able to fight the way my body reacts to the feeling, and my nuts tighten, reminding me that this will be fast.

Zoe gives the term, suck a dick, a whole new fucking meaning, not sucking it like a lollipop, but like a fucking vacuum, trying to extract every last drop of cum from my balls.

My whole body convulses under her as I erupt violently, the suction not breaking as my cock jerks and pulses with each rope of cum that shoots from the tip.

"Fuuuuck, Princess," I yell, the sound higher pitched than I'd like for my alpha male image.

Finally, Zoe releases my dick with a pop, and the fucking thing slaps to my abs, making me jump from how fucking sensitive my knob is.

"Mmm," she moans. "That was a good drink."

A deep rumble of laughter bursts from my lips, and even though I feel shaky as fuck, I manage to grip her hips, still hovering near my head, and lift her as I sit up, turning her to face me in another straddle.

"Any fucking time you're thirsty, you can drink me if you do it like that."

She beams. "I'll take that as a compliment."

"You fucking should." I lean in and press my lips to hers, and she melts into me, wrapping her arms around my neck as we kiss slowly, tasting each other on our tongues.

We stay like that for a long time, kissing and nipping at each other's lips before we finally break, our foreheads pressing together.

"How are you feeling?" I ask. "You know, with what happened in the clearing. We haven't really taken the time to talk about it."

Easing back, Zoe's eyes drop to where our chests meld together. "I know I shouldn't have gone behind your back, but I really wanted to fuck with their heads. I really needed that."

When her eyes dart up to lock with mine, I nod.

"I get it, Zo. And I know you'll never go behind my back like that again, but that's not what I'm talking about. I want to know how you're doing after coming face to face with them again. It can't have been easy seeing Gunner again."

A shiver of disgust ripples through her, and I squeeze her tighter, reminding her that she's safe. I'm here.

"It was... hard. But necessary." Her eyes brim with tears and she swallows thickly, like she's trying to dislodge a lump in her throat. "I needed to face them, though. I needed them to see they didn't break me."

Reaching up, I swipe away a tear that escapes her eye before cupping her cheek.

"You're a warrior Zoe Miller. Your mom and Leslie would be so proud."

"Shit," she sobs, as more tears spring free. "I really miss them."

"I know," I whisper, pulling her in to hug her close.

Running my hand up and down her back, I try to keep her warm as we sit, a tangle of limbs, naked in the living room. I let her cry it out, her sobs relatively quiet as she mourns her family.

What I wouldn't give to turn back time and decline Brian Miller's offer to help us with our books. Of course, it wasn't just me who announced a 'yay' at church to bring him on as an associate, but fuck, even one 'no' and he wouldn't have penetrated our ranks.

I wouldn't have Zoe then, but I also wouldn't have found out what it's really like to love and be loved. I would never have known what I was missing.

The past is the past though, and she is mine as much as I am hers, and fuck, that's a future I can look forward to.

The war is nearly over. All Reapers, bar Rusty, Gunner and Irina are dead, thanks to the coordinated help of Dante and the Diamond Crew. Two of them are being held captive in Cain's dungeons, while the other is in the wind. For now.

When Zoe's sobs dry up, I shift with her in my lap and push myself to stand.

She lets out a squeal.

"What are you doing?"

"Relax, Princess. I'm going to grab us a couple of waters and then take us to bed."

"Oh." She relaxes, locking her feet behind my back as I ignore our strewn clothes on the floor and walk into the kitchen.

Her lips come to my ear, nibbling on the lobe, which makes me squirm and we both laugh as I stumble to the fridge and tug it open.

"Behave, Princess." I slap her bare ass.

"Never." She rasps against my ear, and again I chuckle, reaching in to grab a couple of water bottles before stepping back and closing the fridge door.

Then I freeze.

No.

My eyes widen, fury churning inside my chest as my eyes lock on a photo stuck on the fridge door.

"Gray?" Zoe asks, her voice questioning against my ear, but I can't fucking speak.

I shake my head, willing my brain to be playing fucking tricks on me, and I blink my eyes closed, only to find the picture still there when I open them.

"Gray. What's wrong?" Zoe shifts against me, moving to get down, but I grip her tighter.

"No." I snap, desperately not wanting her to see the picture. Especially after what we just shared together.

My breathing quickens the longer I stare at it, my blood turning to lava, ready for my monster to erupt.

"Gray!" Zoe slaps at my shoulder, managing to squirm free, her concerned gaze studying my face as she stands in front of me.

I don't look at her, though. I can't fucking move. My eyes are forced to see the thing I never wanted to see.

"What's going o—"

Her words cut off as she looks over her shoulder, her eyes obviously locking on to the same thing I'm seeing.

A sob lurches from her parted lips, and she slaps her hand over her mouth, muffling the "no's" that tumble from her.

She spins, barely making it to the sink behind us as she starts to heave, her stomach protesting and trying to empty.

Killing him won't be enough.

Death is too fucking kind for my old best friend and club brother.

Snapping my hand out, I tug the picture from the fridge, taking one last glance at it.

My beautiful princess, wrists tied to the head of a bed, her face contorted in pain as what looks like a scream is falling from her lips, tears streaming from her eyes. Her tits are pressed to the mattress, biting fingers digging into the delicate flesh there with trails of blood coming from them. The fingers belonging to Gunner, who is buried deep inside her, his eyes wild as he fucks her from behind in a way that I know must have been excruciating.

Zoe's heaving fades away as ringing fills my ears and red swarms my vision.

It's like I float out of my body as my monster takes over, unleashing hell on anything that gets in its way.

I hear the crash of the dining table, watching it flip with force and smash into the wall. Picture frames get torn from the wall, a chair sails across the space, shattering into the wide screen TV. Havoc erupts.

"Gray!" voices yell, but I can't make them out. All I see are obstacles in my fucking way, stopping me from getting to Gunner.

"Gray!"

Hands come from all directions, digging into my limbs before I'm dragged to the floor.

"NO!" I bellow, fighting against the restraints, but more come, so many more, and I can't fucking fight them. "LET ME GO!"

A sharp slap stings my cheek, snapping my head to the side, and I blink to see the fury of my warrior princess seething at me.

"Snap the fuck out of it!" she screams, straddling me as my senses slam me back to reality.

I heave, my breaths almost hurting as strong arms wrap around me from behind, and I realize someone is under me where we lay on the floor. I can't move my feet, and I notice my wrists are being restrained as well.

The red haze of my rage filters away, and my eyes dart everywhere, trying to take stock of what's going on.

Sully has one of my wrists pinned to the floor, and Slasher has the other. Straining to the side, glancing past Zoe, I see Stretch forcing all of his weight down on one of my ankles, while Tex is at the other.

"Who the fuck is under me?" I snap.

"Fucking me." Munroe's voice meets my ears. "You crazy bastard."

All the guys smirk then, but not Zoe. Her expression is hard as she stares at me.

"Zo."

She shakes her head. "Don't you see? This is what he wants. To push you over the edge. To distract us with this shit." She holds up her hand, a screwed-up picture in her fist.

I must have dropped it.

My mind goes back to what happened, and then my eyes widen, traveling over Zoe's body as I remember her being naked only minutes ago.

Thank fuck she's wearing one of my tees big enough to be a dress on her.

"Don't let him win, Gray." She hisses through clenched teeth, leaning in closer. "The past is the past. We can't change what happened. Now we focus on the future and that means making sure they are all gone. He is gone. Okay?"

I nod, knowing she is right.

"I'm sorry. I don't..." I trail off, feeling like shit for letting my rage consume me.

"No." She presses her free hand to my face, right where she slapped me. "None of us need to be sorry. They are the ones that need to be sorry, and the only way for them to atone is to suffer at our hands before we end their lives."

"Here fucking here." Sully agrees, releasing my wrist, and the others follow, freeing me.

Zoe climbs off me, and Munroe unwinds his arms before I roll off the big guy, feeling fucking ashamed.

It's then that I realize I'm fucking stark naked.

"You're lucky we love you." Munroe chuckles, obviously reading my expression, and Tex agrees.

"I don't think I've ever been that up close and personal with your nuts before, Prez."

Zoe giggles, but it's Slasher who reminds us that we have a situation.

"Where did the picture come from?"

Glancing at Zoe as I find my pants and slip them on, I gesture my head to the kitchen.

"It was on the fridge."

"It wasn't there earlier," Zoe murmurs, squeezing her fist tighter around the picture.

Slasher's dark gaze meets mine. "Nothing was detected on the cameras. Do you think we have another mole?"

I shrug. "I'd like to think we don't, but then how the fuck did it get on my fridge?"

We all fall silent, and I wonder if the others are thinking what I'm thinking.

Fuck! If we have another fucking rat amongst our ranks, I will burn them alive!

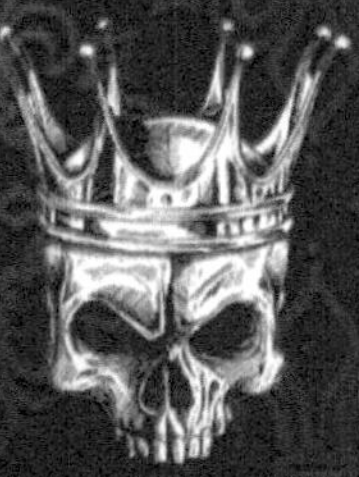

Zoe

Hands hold me down and I'm unable to move. I can't even open my mouth to scream for help. Not that it'll help, it never does.

Breathe, Zoe.

I keep telling myself to breathe, but I'm incapable of anything but shallow breaths as an unknown weight holds me down, pinning me to the body behind me.

Breathe, Zoe. Just breathe.

My eyes fly open, and at first I'm confused about where I am. Then I notice the fucking mess Gray made of the apartment. Shattered glass and splintered wood swept into one of the corners, but the broken furniture and other stuff still litter the floor.

Gray...

Yes, we fell asleep on the couch. It's his breath tickling my skin and his arms wrapped tightly around me.

I crane my head and look at him over my shoulder. He looks so peaceful in his sleep. His long, dark eyelashes caress his cheekbones, and there's no trace of the toll the war with the Reapers—with Gunner—is taking on him. No unbidden creases or divots in his skin. It's completely smooth.

"I can feel you watching me," he says, the remnants of sleep adding gravel to his tone.

Okay, so I guess he's awake.

"I like watching you," I answer easily. "Did you know the furrow between your brows is gone when you're asleep?"

He slowly opens his eyes and props his head up on his hand. "How the fuck would I know that?"

Grinning, I turn to my back and move my finger to the place I'm talking about. "If you don't stop frowning so much, you'll get wrinkles ahead of time."

"So?" He smirks. "I already have my eye candy. I don't need my looks anymore."

"Is that so?" I challenge, biting down on my lip to stop a goofy smile from spreading. "What if I only want you for your looks?"

He tilts his hips, pressing his hard cock against my naked thigh. "Princess," he rasps. "As long as I have a working cock, you're not going anywhere. You're too addicted."

I burst out laughing. This is one of the many reasons I love Gray. To the others he might be a hotheaded badass, and he is. But to me, he's so much more than that. When we're alone and he doesn't have to worry about anyone else, I get to see sides of him that I doubt anyone else ever has.

Like last night when he wanted to talk about how I was doing. Pillow talk rather than dirty talk. Who would have thought it?

"I love you," I say, looking into his dark eyes as I sweep an errant wavy lock from his forehead. "Promise me we'll always find time for this."

The look he gives me is all I need to know that he doesn't need me to clarify. He already knows what I mean.

"I promise," he solemnly vows. "But not now, Princess." He reaches for his phone. "It's already noon, and after last night... well, this morning..." He trails off.

Sighing, I snuggle closer, looping my arm around his waist and up his back. "I know. Just give me five more minutes of us. Then I promise I'll get up and face the day."

Gray cups my cheek in his hand before moving so he can capture my lips. "Five minutes," he growls. "And not a minute more."

I giggle into his mouth. "Start counting," I murmur.

The kiss isn't sweet or playful for long. It only takes a moment before Gray's dominance rears its beautiful head. He nips, sucks, and greedily licks every inch of my mouth, leaving me breathless for more.

I reach for his cock that's so hard and hot it feels like it's searing into my thigh. "Princess," he groans as I wrap my hand around his length. "We have to get—"

"Shh!" I don't let him stop me.

After seeing that picture last night, I need this. I want him to reclaim me in every way possible. I want us to create so many amazing memories that the bad ones don't stand a fucking chance.

I wrap my leg around his waist and, with his help, twist us around so he's lying on his back and I'm straddling his thighs.

"Let me have this first," I beg, moving up his body until my pussy is seated on his cock. I swirl and gyrate my hips, rubbing my cunt over his length so the tip hits my clit just perfectly. "Please."

Gray grips my hips, halting my movement. "Are you sure?" he rasps, licking his lips. "Is this really what you want after last night, Princess?"

"Yes," I whine, annoyed he's stopping.

He lets out a shuddering breath. "Is it because you feel you need to prove something? Because—"

"No," I hiss. "Yes. You said you own my body, so prove it. Don't let him taint it with the past."

My words light a fire in his eyes, and he growls. "Oh, he's tainted it alright. But that changes nothing. Your body is mine, Princess. And I'll fucking prove it."

I get the sense that the words are more for himself than they're for me. Like he's reminding himself of the fact that I belong to him. Body and soul. Everything I am is Gray's and no one else's.

Gray starts urging me to move again, and I immediately rotate my hips. I grind on him until we're both breathless and my breath comes out in fast puffs.

"I'm so close," I moan. "Come with me."

He growls my name, gripping my hips harder and moving me faster. I bend down and fuse my lips to his. I don't stop moving as we kiss passionately, and as a result, my sensitive nipples graze the coarse hair on his chest.

"Fuck," I moan. "I need... Gray."

"I've got you," he rasps.

He moves his hand between us, rubbing two fingers between my folds. Before I can demand he fingers me, he moves them and roughly spreads my ass cheeks. I feel one of the digits press against my tight opening, and I try to relax and let him in. But it's not easy when every part of me is coiled tight, ready to detonate.

"Relax, Princess," he growls just as he penetrates my ass.

"Gray," I almost scream.

I nip his bottom lip one last time before I sit up, tilt my hips and pick up my pace. His cock twitches beneath me, and I unashamedly grind harder down on it while he stretches my ass by adding a second finger.

"You're so fucking tight here," he rasps.

As I look down at him, I feel the need to say something I hadn't thought of before. "You're the only one who's ever had my ass," I admit. "That's all yours, Gray."

The growl coming from him is almost feral, and his eyes darken until they're almost black. "Only me?" he asks, like he needs the confirmation.

I nod. "Only you."

He bucks his hips, adding to the growing pressure building between my legs. Then he lets go of one of my ass cheeks and wraps his hand around my throat where it belongs.

It only takes moments before I scream out his name as a powerful, all-consuming orgasm tears through me. My ass clenches around his fingers, and I grind harder, faster.

The moment his cock swells and jerks, I move back and wrap my hand around the base, pointing the head toward my stomach and tits.

"Paint my skin," I purr as he erupts, shooting his cum onto my skin.

"Fuck. Princess," he groans. Then he surges up, pressing his lips to mine. "You're so fucking perfect."

When he lies back down, I capture his gaze and lick my lips while rubbing his cum into my skin. "I want to wear you all day," I say.

He arches an eyebrow. "Really?"

I grin at his shocked expression and jump off the couch before he can stop me. Then I hurry to the bedroom, wanting to get dressed as quickly as possible. I know I should probably shower, but I don't want to wash the remnants of our shared pleasure away.

Gray joins me, and I feel him looking at me while we go through the domestic routine of getting dressed. We even brush our teeth together, and while he runs wet hands through his messy waves, I collect mine in two braids that hang down my back.

While we go through the motions of getting ready, it hits me how normal it feels. With everything we've been through together, normalcy isn't something I thought about when thinking about our relationship. But now... I don't know how to phrase it.

Perfection. Utopia.

No... Nirvana.

"Gray?" I ask when he's tying the laces on his boots.

"Hmm?"

I swallow audibly and wipe my clammy hands on my jeans. I don't know why I'm so nervous to ask. "What happens once we win the war?"

"What do you mean?" he asks, and when he looks up, that crease between his eyebrows is back.

I hold my arms out wide. "You're the Prez now, so I understand you have obligations. But what if..." Shit, I don't know how to ask what's on my mind.

Gray gets to his feet and slowly joins me where I'm leaning against the wall. He wraps his hand around my throat, a gesture I've come to love. Where it once made me feel threatened and like I didn't have any control, it now makes me feel powerful and wanted. Loved, even.

"Just spit it out already, Princess," he rasps encouragingly.

"Can we ever go back to Nirvana?" I ask softly.

He studies my face, scrutinizing every millimeter. "Of course we can, Princess. Maybe not right away. But I promise we'll make it back there one day."

That's all I need for now. A promise that we'll go back to a place where there's no one else around for miles.

During my time with the Reapers, I thought a lot about Nirvana. In hindsight, I think that's where things changed for both of us. It's where I proved to Gray he could trust me when I took care of him and didn't run after he passed out. And... it's where he gave me some of my control back when he ate me out at gunpoint.

But more importantly, it's where he showed me his heart when he gave me back my mom's letter.

"I'd like that," I sigh wistfully as I open the door. "Maybe in the summer."

Gray takes my hand and lifts it up to his lips so he can kiss it. "Definitely."

We don't say anything else as we make our way downstairs. I don't know about him, but I'm already planning our next trip to Nirvana. Maybe we should make a tradition of going there for a few days leading up to the Fourth of July and then come back here to celebrate with our shared family.

"Morning." Munroe yawns as he joins us.

"Hi Munroe," I laugh.

"Fuck, I'm getting too old for late night shit," he grumbles. "Especially when there's no pussy involved."

"Christ," Gray says, rolling his eyes. "Didn't you find a Cunt to fuck afterward?"

Munroe shakes his head. "No time, man. Slasher changed the guard schedule and had everyone doubling up so no one walks alone. And he wanted us to change every two hours."

Gray nods thoughtfully.

"I'm not complaining." Munroe is quick to add, probably misreading Gray's silence.

"Hey," I interject, even though I should probably stay out of it. "Want me to send one of the Cunts to your room?"

I mentally start going through the list of available girls. Fuck, Gray's right. With the way couple fever is hitting the ranks, and the loss of Sasha, Izzy, and even the traitor Rhiannon, I do need to recruit more to keep the Kings satisfied without exhausting the Cunts.

Munroe winks at me. "That's a nice offer, Mama. I might take you up on it later." As we round the corner and are greeted by Stretch, Slasher, and Doug, all filing in through the backdoor, Slasher looks like he's on the brink of exhaustion, and the other two don't look much better.

"Any news?" Gray asks, looking between them.

"None," Slasher says.

"We've talked with Tido but there's been no local reporting of the blackout, so it's doubtful he'll find anything useful at the station," Doug says.

While they catch up, I forge ahead and open the door into the main room. I immediately head toward the bar, needing to get some coffee going. But I only manage two steps before I see it.

I let out a startled scream.

Feet pound on the floor, and it only takes seconds before I'm pushed behind Gray.

"What?"

"Did you see him?"

"What's going on?"

Question after question is fired at me, but all I can do is point at the stuffed unicorn hanging from the rafter with a rope around its neck.

"A fucking plushie got you screaming the roof down?" Doug grumbles.

"W-when... w-what..." I can barely utter a word as my eyes stay glued on the teddy.

Not seeing the immediate danger, Gray turns and faces me, bending so we're eye-to-eye. "Talk to me, Princess," he urges, cupping my cheek. "What scared you?"

I point at the unicorn.

"Don't tell me our mighty Mama Z is scared of stuffed shit," Munroe laughs good-naturedly.

Shaking my head, I try again. "L-Leslie," I stutter, and I see the moment Gray understands.

He curses under his breath. "That was your sister's?"

I nod. "G-Gunner took it. H-he gave it to me when I was with the R-Reapers." I swallow and ball my hands into fists. Then I resolutely step forward until I can reach it and look at the bottom. Sure enough, it has the initials LM stitched into the bottom of one of its hooves. "Look."

Holding it toward Gray, I show him, but I'm not sure he needs to see it. Now that he knows, I'm sure he recognized it from when I kept it in our room after taking it from my old house and bringing it here.

"Fuck," he spits, running a hand down his face. Proving that he understood my rambling perfectly, he looks between his brothers. "That was Leslie's unicorn. Zoe took it from their house and brought it here, but Gunner took it before faking his fucking death."

Slasher seems to be the first one who understands the significance of this. "How?" he asks.

Munroe is the next one to pick up on it. "How the fuck is that possible?" he growls menacingly. "I triple fucking checked this room this morning. It wasn't here then."

"I was in here for a drink two hours ago and it wasn't here then," Doug says.

Stretch's the one who says what I don't even want to think. "Prez, do we have another mole?"

Gray kicks one of the chairs and whirls on his brother. "If we do, I'll personally fucking make sure they live to regret it."

"What are your orders?" Slasher asks calmly.

When Gray doesn't immediately answer, I say, "We have to get rid of Rusty and Irina before Gunner, or whoever is behind this, gets to them."

"They're safe with the Diamond Crew," Stretch says, sounding like they don't matter.

I can't say I blame him, since I don't know if he's ever had any personal interaction with them. But I have, so I know firsthand just how fucking lethal the siblings are.

"And we're supposed to be safe here," I volley. "I'm not willing to take the chance. Right now Gunner's alone, or at the most, working with a mole or two. I refuse to let him get his group back together."

"She's right," Munroe says. "This isn't a time to leave anything up to chance."

"Of course she's right," Gray barks, still looking at the unicorn. "We'll leave right fucking now. Wake everyone up. I want fucking double the people on every post. Tell Tex his eyes need to stay glued to security. If he needs to piss, someone needs to hand him a fucking bottle."

The drive to Dirty Diamonds is done in half the time. Gray flies down the roads on his bike, barely stopping for pedestrians and red lights. I spend the time clinging to him while trying not to scream for fear of startling him.

"You fucking lunatic," I spit as I jump off the bike and rip the helmet off. "I almost thought we were going to die on the road."

Gray pats the handle and elegantly swings his legs over the bike. "What a way to go," he smirks.

Even though I like that his murderous mood is gone, even if it's just for a brief moment, I slam the helmet into his stomach. "I didn't fucking live through hell just to splatter on the pavement," I seethe.

He scowls. "Don't even fucking joke about that, Princess."

"Who's joking?" I deadpan as I open the door to the club.

We weave through the hallways to the elevator and take it downstairs where Cain's waiting for us.

"How do you want to do this?" he asks without preamble, practically oozing giddiness. When we don't answer him right away, he continues. "Because I have a few ideas."

"Let's hear them," I say, taking Gray's hand.

My thumb rubs a circle on the back of Gray's hand as Cain explains his idea. "Remember the mirrors?" he asks, and we nod. "They're not normal mirrors. But more like the fun house variety. I've always wanted to test them for a hunt, but never had the chance."

The way he pouts would be comical under different circumstances. Boohoo. Poor little psycho.

"I like that," I say, perking up at the idea of seeing Irina run for her fucking life like she made me do. "A lot."

"Do you agree with the Princess' decree, King Gray?" Cain asks, bowing deeply as he addresses Gray.

I giggle while Gray rolls his eyes. "As long as it doesn't take all day," he barks. "We have to get back as soon as possible."

While we walk over to the section with the mirrors, Cain assures us it won't take long. "It can be anything from minutes to hours. It all depends on you, really." He stops in front of a chest of drawers and rummages through the top one. "How good is your aim, Princess?"

I smirk at Gray, pointedly looking at his shoulder. "I'd say it's impeccable," I say.

Gray absentmindedly rubs his shoulder where I shot him back in another lifetime. Before I really got to know him. "She can definitely handle herself with a gun," he says, winking at me.

Cain quickly hands me a gun. I spin it around on my finger and test the weight. I don't know enough about firearms to know what model or brand it is, but I like the feel of it.

"And I also kept this in case you want to use it," Cain says as he pulls a blonde wig from the second drawer.

A dark smile splits my lips in two as an idea hits me. "Ooh," I coo. "Yes. Irina should wear this."

Gray's menacing smile is downright sinful. "Fuck yeah, she should. Cain?"

"Yeah?"

"Do you have a mask for Rusty and Irina? The siblings don't have to know they're facing each other."

I clap my hands together in excitement. "Yes."

At the same time, Cain slaps Gray on the back. "Always knew you had an inner me, Gray." He sounds proud, like this is a moment he's been waiting for. "Come to think about it, they don't need to talk, do they?"

I shake my head. "It might be better if they can't."

While Cain forces the Miss Piggy mask on Rusty, Gray follows me over to Irina's box where I put the wig on her, and then slap the duct tape Gray hands me over her mouth before placing the Kermit mask on her face. I ignore all her muffled screams.

"There we go, Irina," I say once I'm done. "If you ask me, you look prettier this way."

I barely get the words out before Gray hauls me into his arms. "You look so fucking hot right now, Princess," he rasps. "Have I told you how much I love you?"

Even though it isn't the time, I melt and wind my arms around his neck so I can pull him down for a scorching and completely inappropriate kiss.

"If it's half as much as I love you, I'll consider myself a very lucky woman," I pant against his lips.

Chuckling, Gray steps back. "Oh, trust me, Princess. I love you more than you could ever love me. You fucking saved me and you don't even know it."

His words sink beneath my skin and wrap themselves around my heart where I want to store them until I'm old and gray.

"We can debate who loves who the most later," I quip. "For now, I think Irina deserves a chance at winning her freedom."

The crazy bitch stops trying to scream and becomes completely still, clearly listening intently.

Gray picks up on my thoughts right away. "Here's the deal, Irina," he says, crouching down in front of her. "If you escape me in the house of mirrors, you're free. You'll never see either of us again. But you have to do it with your mask on. If you remove it, you're dead. Nod if you understand."

She eagerly nods.

"And because we're not complete savages, unlike you," I say, unable to resist the taunt. "You get a weapon. A knife."

We didn't discuss the rules of the game upfront, but fuck if I don't love this development. While I'm sane enough to know it's grotesque and beyond cruel, it fits the people we made them up for to a T.

"Sit tight," Gray says. "If you move or make a sound, you don't get the weapon."

Taking my hand, he drags me over to Cain and Rusty, where we repeat the rules. The only change is that Gray tells him it'll be me Rusty's facing, which is perfect with the blonde wig.

While Cain gets Rusty ready, I peek over at Irina. The clothes she's wearing are similar enough to mine that I can help fuck with Rusty. I quickly unbraid my hair and run my fingers through it to muss it up.

I can feel both Cain's and Gray's eyes on me, but they're smart enough not to say anything with Rusty within hearing range.

As Cain hauls Rusty over to the mirrors, me and Gray take our own masks from the drawers. We both pick black masquerade masks that cover half our face.

"Are you ready, Princess?" Gray rasps.

"Yes," I breathe, turning to join Cain at the mirrors. When Gray doesn't move, I look at him over my shoulder. "Do you need more time?"

He chuckles. "This won't be the first time I kill, Princess. So no, I don't need more time. But are you sure you want to do this?"

My heart swells at his concern. "I have to," I say, moving back to his side. "I can't leave their deaths up to anyone else. Gunner fooled us once. I won't make that mistake again. And this is the bitch who annihilated my family for no other reason than to get some money. Trust me, I need this."

"Then let's do it," he says.

When we're back at Irina's box, which we left open since she's cuffed to the chair that's bolted to the floor, Cain's right there, jingling the key right in front of her. He doesn't hesitate in setting her free, but before she can move, Gray roughly pulls her over to the mirrors.

I'm only half surprised that she doesn't fight him at all. I guess my threat about her not getting a weapon really stuck.

The siblings are now standing on opposite sides of the mirrors, unable to see each other. Their breathing is hard, and Rusty struggles to stand after Gray shot him, but he still refuses to falter. I guess he really wants to get out of here alive.

"Let the games begin," Cain eagerly shouts.

Gray rolls his eyes. "Did you forget about the knives?"

"Of course not," Cain says, sounding offended at the accusation. He pulls two pocket knives from his pocket and throws them at first Rusty then Irina. "Now can we begin?"

"Yes," Gray and I say in unison.

We keep our distance while the siblings feel around for their knives. Irina gets hers first since she can move around easily, whereas Rusty doesn't have that luxury.

As soon as they both clutch their respective knives, ominous music blares from speakers we can't see. It sounds like a dark version of biblical chanting. It's like it's taken straight out of a horror movie, and it's making the small hairs at the back of my neck stand at attention.

I squeeze Gray's hand one last time, then I pull my mask into place and walk closer to Rusty so he can see my reflection in the mirror.

"Rusty," I call out. "Come and play."

He lunges toward the mirror.

"Rusty."

I keep repeating his name as I lure him closer and closer to the end of the row. I know he can't see me clearly through the small peepholes in his mask, but it's enough to see my long, blonde hair sway with every move I make.

Though I can't see it, I know Gray's doing something similar on the other side, getting Irina closer to me. I wish I could be the one fucking with her, but then the plan would need to be changed. Well, I say plan... it's more like an idea we've all built on without talking much about it.

Rusty lunges again, and this time, I step to the side. Fuck, he'd gotten closer than I'd realized. He grunts as he falls to his knees, and instead of getting up, he crawls closer.

I hear movement behind me and turn in time to see Gray heading toward me, Irina not far behind. In a swift movement, Gray bends and quickly swaps his mask for Rusty's, and as Irina comes closer, I do the same, careful to avoid her knife.

It's a good thing that the masks give you tunnel vision, nearly making it impossible to see anything but what's right in front of you.

Then we back off, satisfied when the siblings come face-to-face. Or rather, Rusty comes face-to-knees with his sister.

While we silently watch, I move in front of Gray and move his arms around my middle. My throat burns with emotions that are threatening to spill over. I'm so close to my moment of vengeance I can taste it on the air.

Irina takes one step, then another, and that's when she bumps into Rusty, who's still crawling—or pulling himself... I'm not quite sure how to describe it.

Her head whips in all directions, but when she doesn't see anything, she takes a step back. Her knife is poised, ready to strike. Only there's no one to aim for. She finally tilts her head down, and when she sees who she presumes to be Gray on the ground, she makes some gleeful noises behind the tape and kicks.

Rusty grunts and rolls to the side. He easily captures her foot, wrenching it to the side, unbalancing her. Irina falls to the ground, panting as she kicks out again, but Rusty skillfully avoids her attacks and throws himself on top of her.

I gasp when Irina's knife sinks into his shoulder, and despite the tape, there's no doubt the howl he lets out is from the pain. Clenching his fist, he slams it into her face once, twice. He doesn't stop until she lets go of the knife still embedded in his shoulder.

Then he pulls the blade free, wasting no time in driving it into her abdomen over and over. The squelching sounds are disgusting, and I do my best to ignore them. But I can't stop watching. Knowing that the sick fuckers are fighting for their life is more satisfying than I ever imagined.

Irina bucks her hips, but Rusty isn't budging. He keeps stabbing her like he's in a frenzy. He doesn't even aim anymore, he's haphazardly driving the knife into her body everywhere he can reach.

Her pitiful noises are faltering, becoming less and less powerful. And it only takes seconds before she doesn't make a single sound.

"I think she's dead," Gray whispers into my ear. I nod to show I agree. "Come on."

He unfolds his arms and places his hand on the small of my back as he leads me over to a panting Rusty who's finally stopped swinging his knife around.

"Congratulations," Gray says, coldly. "You won."

Quickly, he kicks the knife out of Rusty's hand, making sure to get them both away from the rival Prez before bending down to rip the mask and tape away.

Rusty stares up at him with wide eyes. "I really won?" he asks, like he's not quite believing what he heard.

He really fucking shouldn't.

I almost move back, not wanting Rusty to see me yet. But his eyes aren't on his surroundings. He's looking directly at Gray.

Gray nods. "You did. You won."

I'm not sure why Rusty isn't realizing something is off. If he'd just killed me, there's no way Gray would be this calm and collected.

"I won," Rusty repeats. "I really fucking won."

Rusty rolls off the body and onto his back, which also just seems fucking stupid to me. Never show your soft side or underbelly to your enemy. Isn't that like rule number one? If not, it totally should be.

While Rusty catches his breath, Gray removes the mask and wig from Irina. "Have a look at your victim."

The Reaper Prez rolls to his side. One minute he's smiling triumphantly, and the next, his expression morphs into one of pure horror.

"No!" he bellows. "Fuck. Irina. No."

There's nothing fun about the situation, but I still manage to force a laugh. "Your own flesh and blood, Rusty," I scold as I move closer.

"What did you do, you crazy fucking cunt?" he screams at me, anguish clear on his face.

I shake my head at him. "I didn't do anything. That right there," I point at Irina's mangled body. "That was all you, Rusty. You shouldn't have fucked with me and my family."

Since I'm not in the mood to listen to him, I pull the gun from the back of my jeans and flick off the safety. The only sound to be heard is the click as I pull the trigger, ending his miserable existence.

"I hope you fucking burn in hell," I seethe as I look into his unseeing eyes.

39

Grayson

As soon as we open our apartment door the next morning, we hear screaming. My gun is tugged from my jeans and in my palm in a fucking instant as Zoe and I run downstairs to see what the ruckus is about.

"Who did it?!"

The screech is from one of the Cunts, and as we follow the sound and burst into their shared room, we see Rose seething at anyone and everyone looking like a madwoman.

"Oh no," Zoe whispers, taking in Rose's hair. Or lack thereof, especially on one side of her head.

"Who fucking cut my hair?! Why would you do this?!"

Zoe's frantic eyes meet mine, and she doesn't even have to say the words for me to know what she's thinking.

The rat is still messing with us.

"Rose. Calm down and tell me what happened." Zoe approaches her with cautious confidence.

"Someone cut my fucking hair! That's what happened!" Rose holds something up in front of her face, and I realize it's a handheld mirror.

"We didn't cut your hair, Rose. Why would we?" Beth speaks on behalf of the other Cunts and Rose screeches again, throwing the hand mirror with force against the wall where it shatters.

"Why did you do that?" Cilla asks, looking mortified. "That's seven years of bad luck."

"Bad luck? Bad fucking luck!" Rose screams. "Who will want to fuck me looking like this?!"

I study each person in the room, now over full with my club brothers joining us to see what all the fuss was about. Everyone looks just as shocked as the next person.

Who the fuck would have done this?

We had a small celebration last night after I let Zoe announce to everyone that Rusty and Irina are now dead. There were cheers and fists thumping chests as a wave of relief washed over the room. Given Gunner is still on the loose, having a full-blown celebration was off limits. That will have to wait until we know he is dead too, so my brothers had a three drink limit with the Cunts only having two drinks, ensuring everyone was alert enough to react.

So why didn't Rose wake up when whoever it was cut her fucking hair?

And why didn't any of the other Cunts wake up?

"We will fix your hair." Zoe suggests, her eyes darting to me again before moving to Slasher. "Alana is good with this stuff. Do you think she's well enough today to help Rose with her hair?"

Slasher nods. "Of course. I'll get her."

"Church," I snap, gaining Slasher's attention as he walks past to leave the room. "Anyone who isn't on watch duty right now needs to meet me in church in five minutes."

"On it," he mutters as he leaves and I approach Rose, who has fallen silent now, tears spilling from her eyes.

"Look at me," I demand when her eyes remain on the floor at our feet.

Slowly, she looks up, batting the tears away, even as her lower lip trembles.

I glance at her hair, one half cut in short chunks while the other half is a long-tangled mess.

Rose has been around from the beginning. She's been loyal and has proven to be a valued member of our found family. Hell, she even lost some digits because of this fucking Reaper war.

"I actually like it short," I say, glancing from one side to the other. "If anyone can pull off a short haircut, it's you, Rose."

"Y-you think?"

I nod. "Absolutely. Whoever did this thought they were tainting you, when, in actual fact, they just made you more beautiful."

The low growl of Zoe at my side meets my ears, and I bite the inside of my cheek, trying to hold back my smirk at her possessiveness.

"Prez is right." Munroe chimes in, stepping to Rose's side and reaching out to run his fingers through the short strands. "It's hot."

The moment Rose's shoulders drop in relief, I turn my eyes to my princess and raise a knowing brow.

She rolls her eyes at me.

"I'm here." Alana's voice is raspy as Slasher carries her into the room cradled to his chest. "Let's get you tidied up."

Munroe steps back, shooting Rose a wink, while the other Cunts rally around her and start the process of balancing out her new fucking hairstyle.

I spin on my heel, snatching up Zoe's hand, and pull her from the room with my brothers following.

No one speaks as we head to the back of the clubhouse and enter our sacred space.

Taking seats, my brothers light up cigarettes and some pour double shots of whiskey, despite the fact it's not even nine in the morning, while Zoe and I take our thrones at the head of the table.

"I want to move the Cunts," I announce, and everyone falls still, except for Zoe at my side, who leans forward to shoot me a 'what the fuck' expression. "Slasher, contact Cain and see if he can take the women on until this is over."

"You want to split us up?" Zoe snaps, and I eye her, hoping she's not about to rip me a new one in front of my brothers.

"I want the Cunts safe. It will also help to illuminate and narrow down other... possibilities."

"You mean a rat?" Stretch asks and I nod, not wanting to say those words out loud. Not again.

"How long are you thinking?" Munroe asks, ashing his cigarette before he takes another drag and I sit back in my seat.

"As long as it takes to catch Gunner and end this. You can still visit the Cunts. I'll get Zoe to draw up a schedule."

The men nod, but Zoe's eyes are still piercing the side of my head. Reluctantly, I glance at her.

With a hitched brow, she looks at me, unimpressed. "I hope you don't think I'm going to Dirty Diamonds, too?"

"Well—"

"I'm not going." She cuts me off, her blue eyes filled with anger. "You know I'm not the mole, and I'm sure as shit not going to go and hide because someone is trying to play mind games with us. I won't let fear rule me."

Smirking, I reach for the pack of cigarettes on the table and tap one out, pinching it between my fingers as I glance back at her.

"I was going to say I'm not letting you out of my sight, so you'll be staying with me." I shrug, and my brothers chuckle as I close my lips over the smoke and light it up.

Zoe's expression falls to a whole new level of unimpressed before she rolls her eyes.

"It's good to see we're on the same page then," she huffs, flopping backward in the seat with her arms crossed over her chest.

Exhaling the smoke to join the haze passively floating above our heads, I refocus on my brothers.

"Slasher, I want you to stay with the women at Dirty Diamonds. Take Titch too." I announce before taking another deep drag. "I want them protected by our men. Zoe and I will come to help get the Cunts settled and I'll have a chat with Dante and Cain. I'm sure they can assign some of their men too, but they're our Cunts. So we protect them." My words turn sharp as I try to speak while holding the smoke in my lungs, and when I stop speaking, I release it.

"And the rest of us?" Tex asks from further down the table.

"Everyone else is to remain here. The war isn't over yet, but it will be soon."

"Has Dante's crew found any new information on Gunner, yet?" Munroe asks, and I shake my head.

I spent some time on the phone with Dante last night. His men have scoured the streets of Santa Cruz and Watsonville and everything in between, and there have been no sightings of Gunner. CCTV and facial rec haven't picked him up either, and there's been no visitors to the Reapers' safehouses.

He's a fucking ghost.

"No new intel yet, but they won't stop until we have him."

Everyone nods, most likely knowing there'd be nothing new to tell since they know I'd share it with them as soon as I get it.

"Okay. Slasher, pull Titch from his watch at the gate and tell him to pack a bag." My eyes move to Sully. "Sul, you can take Titch's watch for now."

"Yep." He nods in agreement, and I glance around the table.

"Tex, Munroe and Stretch. Go tell the Cunts they are going on a little vacation and help them pack."

When they nod, I lift the gavel and slam it on the table surface with a bang.

My brothers stand and leave, but Slasher hangs back.

"Any thoughts on who might be our mole?"

I shake my head. "Nope. If it's a Cunt, I'm hoping you and Titch notice any strange behavior. I'll watch the men. Let's see what the next twenty-four hours bring."

Standing, Slasher claps me on the shoulder and exits church, leaving me alone with my princess.

"Get your panties off and get your ass on this fucking table, now."

A gasp flies from Zoe's lips, but I don't even look at her, taking one last drag of my cigarette as I wait for her to comply.

When I hear her move next to me, I can't hide my fucking smirk.

"Am I about to get pleasure or punishment?" she asks, sliding onto the table in front of me as our eyes lock.

I butt out the smoke in the ashtray next to her on the table. "Both."

Her brow hitches as she rests back on her hands. "Why am I getting punished?"

"Because, Princess," I rasp, gripping her knees and parting her legs to reveal the silk of her cunt peeking out from under the fabric of her dress. "You thought I would send you away? You should know better than that after everything that's happened."

I ignore her eye roll, which she seems to be doing a lot today, and I push the fabric back to her hips, revealing her already wet folds.

I lick my lips.

"You realize your punishments are something I enjoy, right?" she asks, and I smirk up at her as she watches me scoot forward in my chair.

"Be careful what you say, Princess. You might find yourself eating your words."

Leaning in, I dart my tongue out and flick her clit, gripping her thighs and spreading them wider when she jerks from the touch.

"Gray," she moans, shifting back to her elbows and tipping her head back.

I lap at her, swirling my tongue around her clit and then diving it deep between her folds. Her hips rise up to meet my mouth, and I add two fingers, slipping them in deep.

My hard cock jerks in my jeans, wanting to be the object sinking into her heat. But there will be time for that later. Right now, I just want to make her feel good, and maybe remind her of something.

Rising out of my chair, I stand between her legs, watching her head tip up and her lazy lids flutter open before her blue pools lock on to me.

"What are yo—"

I press my hand to the top of her mound with my fingers still buried in her cunt and I start massaging her upper wall.

"You got a little snarky earlier when I called Rose beautiful," I say, watching her confusion turn into a glare, all while continuing to knead the inside of her cunt.

"I won't apologize for that," she pants, and I press harder onto her mound.

She cries out.

"I need you to know something, Princess." I move my fingers faster inside her and her cries turn to mewling. "Rose and all the Cunts are family. You already know that. So even if she looked absolutely hideous, there was no way I would tell her that." I pick up the pace, mashing her upper wall as my hand presses down harder again on her mound, making sure I hit just the right spot. "But mark my fucking words, when I say it to you," she writhes under me as I assault her pussy, part of her trying to get away while the other part of her wants nothing more than to chase the brutal climax she's about to be hit with, "you'd better believe I mean every fucking word."

"Yes!" she cries. "Okay. Please." She begs, my fingers now working inside her so fast that I fear they may cramp up at any second.

"Come for me," I growl, and she explodes in a shower of spray that has me mashing harder and harder until the waves turn into a trickle.

"Fuck," she whimpers, falling lax on the tabletop, her legs flopping open, her cunt deep in color and swollen as it shines with the cum she squirted everywhere.

"Fucking prefect," I mutter, shifting my hand to my jeans to undo them and release my dick, only the sight of something stuck to the underside of the gavel draws my attention.

Reaching up past Zoe's head, I lift the gavel that must have gotten knocked over by Zoe's writhing and turn it over.

"Gray?" Zoe pants, but I don't answer her, my blood heating with the familiar sense of anger that only comes from seeing Gunner rape my princess.

"What is it?" Zoe rasps, struggling to sit up.

Holding the gavel out of the way, I lock eyes with her.

"I know you'll insist on seeing it, but I'm not showing you. All you need to know is someone has stuck another picture of you and Gunner onto my gavel."

They fucking cut it to the size of the bottom of the gavel, and I didn't even notice it when I slammed it down before. It's only small, like half the size of a polaroid, but I don't need fucking glasses to see what he's doing to my princess.

Her cheeks flush red with her own anger brewing, but she doesn't fight me on it.

"Is it as bad as the one on the fridge?"

"Yes." I nod. The picture of Gunner pressing something to Zoe's shoulder blade as he fucks her from behind and she screams in unimaginable pain is something I'll never be able to unsee.

Zoe lived it. She doesn't need to see it.

I study her expression, her brow furrowing, causing a crease between them, her eyes darting to my chest, but I can tell she's not looking at anything in particular.

She's thinking. Or perhaps remembering.

"Can you at least tell me what the picture is of?" she asks, her big blue eyes darting up through the fan of her dark lashes. "I get why you don't want me to see it, and honestly, I don't know that I want the visual. The last one..." she shakes her head, letting her forehead fall to my chest. "I can't get the image of the last one out of my head."

"I know," I rasp, cupping her face and angling her head back so I can see into her eyes. "It's one thing to be there and experience it. I'm sure those memories will haunt you for a long time."

She nods. "Yes. They will. But seeing how I looked, how he looked," she chokes a little before clearing her throat. "At least when he did it from behind, I didn't have to look at him."

Fuck.

I want to rage and unleash my beast again, but what the fuck will that help? It'll probably just make my princess clam up and stop sharing the things she needs to get off her chest. And as much as I want to let the violence brewing in me take over, more than that, I want her to never stop sharing her darkest secrets. Her fears. And her desires.

"Zoe, I…"

Now I'm lost for fucking words. What the fuck do I say to make this right?

There's nothing I can say.

"Just tell me what the picture is of. My memories will fill in the blanks. I just need to know at least that part."

Brushing back some of her blonde strands that must have got messed up while I made her come, I swallow thickly, preparing to reveal the vulgarness of the image left here to taunt us.

"It's of the time he branded your shoulder," I rasp, nearly fucking choking on the words.

A shudder ripples through her, sending a smattering of goosebumps up her neck.

"I'm so sorry, Zo."

Her trembling hand comes up to cup my jaw as she forces a smile even though her eyes are brimming with unshed tears.

"You don't need to be sorry, Gray. I'm where I belong now, and everything that happened before this moment with… others is nothing but the past. The future is ours now, and I can't wait to spend it with you."

"Fuck." I choke out, closing the distance and sealing my lips to hers.

How someone can be knocked down time after time, be subjected to some of the most heinous acts imaginable, and still have hope is a fucking miracle.

Then again, Zoe Miller has never been normal or typical. She's always been a force to be reckoned with.

Whoever is trying to fuck with us should know that much about Zoe already. There's a possibility one of the Cruz Cunts is doing Gunner's bidding again, which is why sending them to stay with Cain is the best plan. If they aren't here, then the taunts will stop, and I'll know it's one of them.

But if the taunts keep coming, I know then that one of my men is just as traitorous as Gunner, and they will fucking regret that when I'm burning their flesh from their body.

40

Gray and I are the last to arrive at Dirty Diamonds, and the others have already pushed tables together. They're so busy sliding bottles around the table and hitting the alcohol that they barely notice us.

On one side of the makeshift long table sits Slasher, Alana, and most of the Cruz Cunts—those who don't fit sit on the other side along with Cain, Cara, Rocco, and Titch.

At first glance, they look fine, but it only takes a minute for me to notice the tension brewing between them. It's almost as palpable as the cloud of smoke forming above their heads from the chain smoking.

Rose's wearing a cap that hides her new hairdo, and both Rocco and Cara look shellshocked—a far cry from the hardened people I first met.

My eyes glance to Cain, and I'm oddly relieved he's leaning his chair back against the wall so it only rests on two legs, while trying to stack potato chips on his nose. It makes some of my own tension bleed away, so I don't look away until Alana makes them all look our way.

"There you are," she says. Her smile doesn't reach her eyes and her tone isn't as upbeat as usual.

"What's going on?" I ask, following Gray over to the two empty seats at the head of the table.

I don't even hesitate before I sit down, even though I know it should be Slasher sitting on Gray's right, and Alana should be at mine. Fucking traditions.

Too busy scowling at each other, no one speaks.

Cara fidgets in her seat, and for some reason, that makes me uneasy. There's something about her hardness that's become a constant, so seeing her this... nervous rubs off on me.

"Cara?" I ask when no one volunteers any information.

Gray squeezes my knee under the table. The small touch sends zings throughout my body, making me sit taller and roll my shoulders back.

"Fine," Alana snaps, glaring at every single King at the table, including Slasher and Gray. The former is harder since she's perched on his lap, but she still manages. "If no one will say what's on their mind, I fucking will."

Gray swirls his hand in the air, silently telling her to go on.

"The fuckers at this table—"

"Hey!" Cain interjects.

Alana pinches the bridge of her nose. "All the men except Cain," she clarifies while penetrating him with her deadly glare. "Seem to think the Cunts can't be trusted."

"We never said that," Titch says, throwing his arms up in the air.

"Really?" Rose seethes. "Then why the fuck did you ask for our phones?"

At the accusation, he shrinks in his chair, looking between Gray and Slasher. "It just seemed like a good idea," he explains.

"A fair request given the circumstances," Rocco says.

"Oh, really?" Beth volleys. "And why is that? Why are you all too scared to say what's on your mind? Fucking pussies."

"Beth!" Cara snaps. "Calm your fucking tits and show some respect."

I'm surprised as fuck when Cilla lets out a humorless cackle. "Respect is earned, Cara. You can't fucking demand it. And if I'm honest, you have no right asking that from us."

The former Mama looks like she's been slapped, which causes Rocco to hurl his glass toward Cilla, who easily moves out of the line of fire so the glass splinters against the wall behind her.

"Enough!" Gray bellows, making me jump in my seat. "What the fuck has gotten into all of you?"

His question is met with silence.

I can feel anger and sadness rolling off him in thick waves, matching my own feelings perfectly. Or maybe I'm just projecting. But seeing our family at each other's throats like this is beyond fucked up. And the fact that Cain hasn't made an inappropriate comment just seals the seriousness of the situation.

"Slasher," Gray barks. "Tell me what happened."

A part of me wants to speak up and make someone else do it. Asking Slasher isn't fair, it's like making him choose between Alana and Gray. But I know this isn't my call and one of those times where I have to let Gray do his Prez thing.

"Titch and I discussed the probability of the rat being one of the Cunts—"

"Oh my God," Alana screeches. "You were in on it? You really think it's me?"

Shaking his head, Slasher growls, "Of course not. But you know I can't give you preferential treatment. Besides, what if someone had hacked into your phone without you knowing? We couldn't leave any phone unchecked."

Though the reasoning sounds fair to me, I also have enough self-awareness to know just how pissed I'd be if Gray had done that to me. Not that I have a phone to check, but that's beside the fucking point.

Gray leans across the table and jabs a finger in Alana's direction. "One more fucking outburst, and we'll continue the meeting without you." Straightening, he looks between everyone at the table, me included. "That goes for every single fucking person here. Understood?"

We all murmur our agreement, and he squeezes my thigh when I do. I think he's thanking me for playing along. Or maybe it's a reminder that it really does include me, which it totally should. Now it's up to me not to put him in the position of having to make me leave.

"Continue," he says, looking at Slasher.

Slasher clears his throat. "When we asked for the phones, the Cunts wanted to know why. So Titch told them."

Gray exhales audibly and pins Titch with a dark look. "What exactly did you tell them?"

Titch doesn't look happy to answer the question. "I fucked up, Prez," he admits. "I told them we needed to make sure they hadn't turned on us. But I didn't mean it like that. I mean, I did, but I also didn't."

"For fuck's sake," Gray growls. He closes his eyes for a moment, and when he reopens them, there's a fucking war brewing in the dark depths. "I know it's a testy subject for everyone. But after what Rhiannon did, can you blame us for being cautious?"

Though the question is clearly aimed at the women at the table, he doesn't look at anyone in particular.

"Yes," Rose shouts, slapping her mangled hand on the surface of the table. "Because the reason we're in this fucked up situation is because of a King and not a Cunt."

Gray darts to his feet so abruptly his chair falls over. "I lost my fucking princess because of a Cunt," he roars. "So don't fucking give me that shit, Rose. Not now. Not fucking ever."

Despite the scene playing out in front of me, I can't stop looking at Cara and Rocco. They're unnaturally quiet. Still, almost. His arm is around her shoulders and she looks like breathing physically hurts her. There's definitely something going on there.

"And who took her?" Alana challenges. "A former King. Let's not fucking lose sight of the bigger picture. I won't defend Rhiannon's treacherous ass because she stole from me, too. She took my best fucking friend. But fair's fair. So let's place the blame where it rightfully belongs. It. Was. A. Fucking. King."

Gray rakes his hands through his hair, making it look wilder than usual. "I know," he sighs. "Okay? I fucking know it's all because of our former brother. The Kings aren't innocent in this. Rocco and I failed at protecting the club, and—"

The scraping across the floor from Cara's chair halts Gray from continuing. The former Mama stands, and the expression on her face makes it clear that she's shaken to her core.

"If you want someone to blame, place the blame at my feet," she croaks. "I failed at protecting my girls. I thought I was good for the club." Her laugh is filled with self-deprecation. "But it turns out they didn't trust me enough to tell me about Gunner. That's on me and not them. I failed the Cunts and the club. I should have seen the signs."

Now I know why her expression called to me. It's the same guilt I'm trying my best not to allow to swallow me whole. But it's hard. The death of Sasha, Izzy, Slayer, and so many more weigh heavily on me.

It might not have been my hand that ended their lives, but it was the actions of my dad that led us all here. I know his sins aren't mine, but the consequences are. I refuse to let it be any other way. I'm not him, and I will help us all survive this.

Taking Gray's hand, I tug on it, urging him to sit back down. Tempers are high, but I know in my heart that the only way to get through this is together.

Once Gray is sitting down again, I lean in and sweetly kiss his cheek. Then I stand up, waiting with bated breath until everyone looks at me.

"A lot of shit has happened," I say, willing my voice not to waver. "Pretending there hasn't been betrayal from all angles isn't possible. But we need to stick together. I personally trust everyone in this room."

I look at every single person at the table, needing them to see my sincerity.

"Rocco and Gray brought me into your lives to right my dad's wrong after he stole your money, and I still think that something needs to be done—"

Rose scoffs. "No one fucking cares about the money."

I give her a tight smile. "I wasn't talking about the money."

"Oh," she mumbles, looking ashamed to have interrupted me.

"When Baz and Dante came to the clubhouse, I found out it was my dad's fucking actions that escalated the war with the Reapers. Or reopened it..." I trail off, not sure how to best word it. Then I shake my head. "Semantics doesn't matter. The point is that my dad was the reason for the loss, heartache, and brutality we've all been through. And I'm so fucking sorry for that."

I pause and take Gray's hand, needing his touch to draw strength from.

"And it's Gunner's obsession with me that propelled the shitshow along. Rose," I look at her. "It's because of me you lost your fingers and hair." Then I look at Alana. "You were shot because of me."

They both open their mouths, undoubtedly to contradict me, but I hold my hand up to stop them.

"Slasher, you lost your twin because of me." Despite not wanting to, I look at Rocco. "And you lost your place as Prez and the ability to walk because of me."

Closing my eyes, I inhale deeply before looking at Cara. "Yet the only person here I will apologize to is Cara. Because despite everything I just said, she's the only person who suffered consequences I controlled. The rest of you might have lost something because of me, but it wasn't my doing. Cara losing her place in the club was because I couldn't cope. So that's my fault—"

"The hell it is," Gray growls. "Cara set you free because I lost sight of my humanity. So that's on me."

I shake my head and give him a sad smile. "You're not understanding my point, Gray. What I'm trying to say is that out of everything we're all angry and heartbroken about, there's only one situation we were in control of. It doesn't matter how it came about, it's still the reality."

"She's right," Titch says.

Rose, Beth, and Cilla are next to voice their agreement.

Cara smiles and dips her head respectfully. "You were born to lead, Zoe. Continue being unapologetically you and the club will be fine. All hail Mama fucking Z."

As one, they all reach for their glass or bottle and raise it. Then they repeat Cara's words. "All hail Mama fucking Z."

Tears distort my vision, but for once, they're not born of hurt, anger, sadness, or any other negative emotion. I'm touched and overwhelmed by the love and support I feel wrap around me like a blanket.

Wanting to offer Cara some sort of comfort, I say, "You know you'll always have a place with us, right?"

She leans closer to Rocco and whispers something I can't hear in his ear. The eyes of the former Prez dart to the new one, Gray, and then he nods slowly.

"We're leaving," Cara announces as she steeples her fingers together in front of her.

"Say fucking what now?" Cain sputters. Damn, I'd almost forgotten he's here. That's how quiet he's been. "But you can't leave."

"Dante's arranged for a private recovery facility for Rocco," Cara explains. "And Baz has generously offered to let us use his private jet to get there. We're leaving tonight. But we could probably delay it if you need—"

"No!" Gray and I practically shout at the same time.

Forgetting all about their previous ire directed at Cara, the Cunts sniffle.

"Well, fuck," Slasher murmurs.

"The hell," Titch mutters at the same time.

"We know the timing is horrible," Cara continues. "But... we both need this."

As I look at her small hand in her husband's large one, I feel a warmth spreading through me. Even though he banished her, they're here, and they're leaving together.

I selfishly want Cara to stay, but I'm selfless enough to want this for them. They've given their all to the club, and now it's time they focus on themselves.

Leaving Gray's side, I get up and walk over to Cara. I crouch next to her and take her hand. "Thank you for everything you've done for me," I whisper. "You've shown me what it means to be a Mama and taught me how to reach my inner strength. I can't thank you enough."

Her eyes glisten. "Promise me you'll take good care of them, Zoe. All of them. Don't grow complacent like we did. Have Gray's back and help him even when he doesn't think he needs it."

"I promise," I say, my voice thick with emotions as I fully realize this is goodbye.

"Zoe." I tilt my head so I can look at Rocco, who's holding his hand out to me. "I've never apologized for my role in what happened to you. I should never have held you responsible for your dad's sins."

Cocking my eyebrow, I say, "No. You shouldn't have." Then I allow a smile to spread. "But I don't accept your apology, Rocco. It's not needed. Because the path you chose gave me more things than I can count. Love, a family... hell, a fucking purpose. So for that, I should thank you."

He laughs. "But let me guess, you're not going to?"

I grin. "I will when you walk back through the clubhouse door."

Both he and Cara burst into laughter, but he doesn't look away from me. And I feel like a mutual understanding of respect and duty passes between us. Or maybe that's just me.

"Were you even going to say goodbye?" Gray asks as he joins us, slapping Rocco's shoulder.

"Honestly," Cara says. "No. You know I hate goodbyes. And it's not forever. We'll be back one day."

Gray nods and mumbles something that sounds like him, almost wishing he didn't know.

Since the cat's out of the bag now, everyone at the table says their goodbye, and expresses sadness that not all the Kings are here. But in the end, that's life, isn't it? Not everything gets wrapped up in a happy ending with a pretty bow on top.

When it's time, Gray's the one who pushes Rocco's wheelchair out, taking him to the back entrance where Dante and Baz are waiting.

Cara and I trail behind. I'm so caught up in wondering if I should ask her about this and that, but in the end I don't ask a single question about the club or the life as a Mama. I just walk next to her, trying to feel like this isn't the end of an era.

"You and Rocco," I say. It might not be my business, but I'm dying to know what's going on there.

"I'm his wife," she says, simply, deciphering where I was going with those three words. "And he's my husband. Until death do us part, Zoe. Since death hasn't come for either of us yet, those vows remain."

"Good for you," I say, meaning it. "I'd hate to think about what it would mean for all of us if we had to pick a side."

Cara laughs. "Not likely. I knew what it might cost me when I went behind Rocco's back and set you free. I could have talked to him, but I didn't. So it was me who sealed my fate." She looks almost wistful for a moment. "Not that I regret it. Setting you free was the right thing to do. But in hindsight, I should have demanded he did it instead of making it a club matter. Keep that in mind if Gray ever does something similar."

I can't contain my snort at the idea. "If something similar ever happens, I'll interfere long before it gets that drastic."

It's not a dig at Cara as much as it's a promise to myself. Not that I can ever imagine a similar situation arising. But if it does, I won't sit by and twiddle my thumbs while the Kings torment an innocent woman.

Cara pulls me in for a hug that I immediately return. "Take good care of yourself, Mama Z."

"You too, Mama C," I say, loving the sound of it even if it isn't her title anymore.

"And for God's sake, send us fucking postcards," Cain says from behind us. His voice startles me since I hadn't noticed him following.

Rocco chuckles. "I'll personally send you one that says 'I'm glad you aren't here.'"

Those are the last words said before Dante and Baz help Rocco into the waiting SUV. Cara climbs into the back with her husband while the other two take the front. The windows are dark, so I don't know if they're waving, but I am.

Gray pulls me to his side, and we remain outside like that until the car disappears, nothing more than a black speck in the distance. Then we slowly make our way back inside.

As soon as we're back in the bar area, Titch's groan floats through the air. "Not this again."

Rose giggles. "Why not?"

He rolls his eyes. "Fuck. You're like the annoying little sister I'm happy I never had."

"That you know of," Cilla chirps, which earns her a playful glare from Titch.

I'm glad the mood has changed and that the Kings and Cunts are no longer at each other's throats. It's... wait...

Coming to a crashing halt, I snap my head in Titch's direction. "What did you just say?" I ask, anxiety unfurling in my stomach. "Repeat it."

"Princess?"

Ignoring Gray's question and probing eyes, I wait for Titch to answer me.

"Umm, I said that Rose was like the annoying little sister I never wanted. Why?"

"That's it," I mutter mostly to myself.

"What's it?" Gray asks, spinning me around so I'm facing him. "What the hell are you mumbling about?"

My breath saws out of me as I remember a phase Leslie went through in another life. "Leslie was always doing things to annoy me when we were younger," I explain. Or try to. "One of her favorite things was hiding inside my closet whenever I had friends over. She'd stay there for hours listening to us until we went to sleep, then sneak out and eat all of our candy or steal our nail polish while we slept. Sometimes we had no idea she'd been there, and other times, she'd leave a sticky note calling me a sucker. We had no idea she'd been there the whole time."

"So?" Slasher asks. "Slayer and I used to do that to each other all the time."

"What if that's how it's happening?" I ask, scrambling to make them see the dots I've already connected. "What if we don't have a mole? What if it's Gunner, and he's already inside the clubhouse?"

41

Zoe

The room falls quiet, but it's only the calm before the storm.

"The blackout," Gray growls. "Doing the entire neighborhood was to throw us off his scent."

"It explains how he could get to me," Rose says, pointing to her hair that's hidden under the cap.

Alana's gaze finds mine. "The pictures and unicorn," she whispers.

I nod, everything falling into place as they list every single incident.

"What do we do?" Titch asks.

At the same time as Slasher demands, "What are your orders, Prez?"

"We need to call the others and warn them," Cilla murmurs.

"No," I shout, startling all of them. "We can't."

Rose immediately agrees. "If he's inside the clubhouse, we can't call them. He could overhear. But we can text—"

Shaking my head, I say, "We can't risk texting them, either. Without knowing exactly where Gunner's hiding, how can we know he isn't in a place where he can read the texts?"

"Fuck!" Gray roars. "You're right."

His hand is shaking with anger as he wraps it around my upper arm, dragging me out of the room while shouting over his shoulder. "Stay here. Don't fucking split up. We're going back."

"But Zoe—"

I interrupt Alana. "I'm not fucking hiding here. I won't believe he's dead unless I see it for myself this time."

She says something else, but I don't hear it as Gray drags me back to the bike. I hurry to put my helmet on and take my seat behind him.

"Should we say goodbye to Cain?" I ask just before he starts the engine.

"No," he answers. "Since he didn't follow us back inside after Rocco and Cara left, I guess he needs a minute. Slasher can catch him up."

The bike roars to life and I cling to him as he breaks his previous record of insane driving, getting us back to the clubhouse in no time at all.

Despite being in a rush, he takes his time parking it perfectly. That's where his patience ends. As soon as Gray's off the bike, he rips my helmet off and claims my lips in a bruising kiss.

"You're mine," he growls angrily. "Say it."

"I'm yours."

"That's fucking right. And I protect what's mine. You'll never be at his mercy again, Princess. I fucking swear it."

Pulling back, I take his hand and lock our pinkies together. "Pinky promise?"

The grin he gives me is more teeth than anything, but I get it. That's how I feel as well. There's nothing to smile about. Not when we're about to reclaim our fucking home and commit pesticide.

"I fucking pinky promise."

Gray pulls me in for another toe-curling kiss. I can taste the desperation and anger on his tongue, and I whimper as I suck it into my mouth, swallowing it. I know that's not how it works, but I can't help but feel like the small act might lessen his burden, even if it's just a little.

"One more thing," he whispers against my lips. "It's you and me to the end. But when we walk through those doors,

I'm your fucking Prez. You don't have to like it as long as you follow my orders."

I fully understand what he's trying so hard not to say. "I know," I murmur.

The truth is that even though Gray hasn't left my side apart from reluctantly letting me go to the bathroom by myself, we both know that's no way to live. I haven't pushed him on it since I've needed the security from his constant presence as much as he's needed to have eyes on me at all times.

Despite that, he can't protect and lead his club while also constantly worrying about me. So for this, for what comes next, I need to cooperate. There's another reason as well, one I won't tell him. If Gunner's behavior has taught me anything, it's how deep his obsession runs.

I'm pretty sure he won't show himself as long as I'm surrounded by the Kings, least of all Gray. So if we're ever to hope to smoke him out, I'll have to be the bait. Again. And just like last time, I'm not telling Gray the full truth—or at least, what I suspect to be that. If I do, there's no way he'll do what he must.

All those thoughts run through my head in the short time it takes to walk through the doors. The Kings that stayed behind all look in our direction when Gray violently slams them open.

Everyone, bar the ones on guard duty and the two left at Dirty Diamonds, are gathered in the main room. Their eyes are bloodshot and they look like they're in desperate need of several hours of sleep.

"Sup?" Munroe asks, his gaze flicking between us. The second he notices the anger on Gray's face, he pulls himself up so he's standing straight. "What's happening?"

"We have a fucking rat problem," Gray sneers.

I arch a brow when Tex casually reaches for the rifle he hides under the bar. "Do tell," he says as he swings it over his shoulder.

Knowing this is for Gray to explain, I suck my lips between my teeth to stop myself from blurting out what he still hasn't said. I don't know if he isn't noticing the suspicious looks his brothers are sending each other, but I wish he'd just hurry the fuck up and set the record straight.

"Gunner's in the building," Gray growls, like he heard my thoughts. "I don't fucking know where. But it's safe to assume he can hear everything we're saying."

Now that we're here, my bravado is beginning to falter. I can't let that stop him from doing what he has to do, though. So I roll my shoulders back and straighten my spine in an attempt to look unfazed.

"Fuck no," Munroe roars. He reaches for his gun. "This ain't a place for rats."

As one, they all let loose a string of curses, while readying themselves for the battle that's in the air.

Gray turns to me. "Where do you want to be?"

For a moment, I consider telling him it doesn't matter since I know Gunner will come to me. But I keep the words inside, trusting Gray will stay close.

"Here," I say, gesturing at the room. "It's as good a place as any."

His brows shoot up his forehead. "Are you sure? What about the apartment?"

I shake my head. "It doesn't really matter. He's already proven he can move around freely. Besides, if he really has eyes on us, I'd rather not waste time trying to find the perfect hiding place. Especially not in a place that used to be his home."

"My brave princess," Gray rasps. "I'll be back as soon as I can."

He pulls me in and places a chaste kiss on my cheek, but that's not what's surprising me. It's his hand as it slips under my shirt and I feel the cold touch of metal against my skin.

"Don't do anything stupid," he says. Then he turns toward his brothers. "Gunner isn't the only one who knows this place like the back of his fucking hand. We'll split into two groups." He keeps talking as they file out of the room, but the farther away they get, the harder it becomes to hear them.

Panic grips me, making my blood run cold when the door swings closed. It's like a realization of dread knowing I'm all alone. Except... I'm not. I might not know where Gunner is, but I can feel his fucking eyes on me.

Or maybe I can't... it's possible that's only in my head. Knowing that does nothing to ease the growing tension in my stomach.

Without thinking, I walk behind Tex's new, precious bar and pour myself a drink. I don't even look at the label on the bottle, or the color of the liquid in the glass I empty in one. The burn that follows is just what I need, as it gives me something else to focus on.

As I pour myself a second drink, I feel the air shift. Goose-bumps spread across my skin, and every hair on my body stands at attention.

He's here.

I know he is.

"We're finally alone, Sugar," he croons.

His voice is the stuff of nightmares. But instead of conjuring up images of the horrific stuff he's done to me, my mind shuts down. I become numb.

It doesn't feel like me when I lift my hand, moving the glass to my mouth before emptying it. And it definitely doesn't feel like me when I spin around and come face-to-face with a haggard-looking Gunner.

His hair is plastered to his scalp instead of in its usual bun. The beard he kept sleek and well-groomed, while with the Reapers, is wild and unkempt. As I take him in, I notice the dried blood on his green hoodie and the holes in his jeans that are anything but fashionable. He looks like he's been on the run for months rather than days.

"Got nothing to say?" he asks, winking like we're old friends who are destined for a catch up.

Despite all the things I've imagined myself screaming at him, no words come to mind. No accusation or insult. It's almost like a black vortex has swallowed up all my thoughts or feelings, making it impossible for me to access them.

Gunner throws his arms out to the side. "I don't think I've ever suffered this much for a hole before. So if I were you, I'd make sure our reunion is extra sweet. I'm beginning to think it's not worth keeping you around."

I whimper and take a step back when he stalks closer. The bar is still between us, but it won't be for long. I've stupidly trapped myself back here.

Why the fuck didn't I tell Gray about my suspicion? No, I can't think like that. It was the right thing to do. I've already had this conversation with myself, and I can't second-guess it just because...

I startle when Gunner leaps on top of the bar, and it only takes seconds for him to reach me. When I open my mouth to scream, he wraps his hand around my hair, and slams my head into the bar.

"None of that, Sugar. I'm not ready for them to come running to your rescue just yet." His breath is foul and I gag as it washes over me. "Then again, they might not come back," he chuckles.

Finally finding my voice, I croak, "What did you do?"

Gunner pulls me up by the hair and pushes me around. His hands move to my waist as he brings our crotches so close together I can feel his hardness. "Who, me? Oh, nothing big. Just a few booby-traps. That's all."

When he sinks his teeth into my shoulder, I'm finally freed from the mental haze that kept me inactive. I scream bloody murder and jam my knee into his junk.

Gunner falters back, his hands protectively covering his disgusting dick. "You b-bitch," he cries.

I don't pay attention to his words. Instead, I use my hand to reach for a bottle, and as soon as I have one in my hand, I swing it down on his head.

Wasting no time, I push him aside and dart around the bar. But I don't even make it three steps, before he stops me with a hand fisted into my shirt.

"You're only making the game more fun, Sugar," he drawls, sounding crazed.

"Let me go," I seethe, using all my weight to try to move forward to break his hold. But his pathetic appearance is misleading. He's way stronger than he looks.

With an evil laugh, he moves his hand to the nape of my neck, adding pressure until I cry out.

"On your knees, Sugar," he grins.

"No!" I scream.

Gunner reaches behind him and shows me the gun now clutched in his hand. "I said, on your fucking knees."

I gulp. "N-no," I repeat, shaking my head.

After Gray forced me to suck him off at gunpoint, I promised myself I'd never go to my knees at gunpoint again, and it's a promise I intend to fucking uphold. If I'm to die, I'll do so on my feet with my shoulders square.

Blood seeps from Gunner's head where I hit him, but he isn't bothered by it. Doesn't even wipe it away. He just stands there, grinning with blood flowing freely down his face.

"I hoped you'd say no," he says, pitching his voice low like he's telling me a secret. "It's no fun if you don't fight."

"W-why do you need me to fight?" I sputter.

He clucks his tongue like he's disappointed in me for asking. "If you do it freely, I won't have taken it from *him.*"

I don't know if it's his attempt at reverse psychology. Something tells me he's being completely truthful.

"Why is it so important to take me from Gray—" Before I can finish the question, Gunner backhands me so hard I stagger to the side, barely able to stay upright.

"Don't say his fucking name," Gunner hisses, no longer sounding like he's enjoying himself.

And even though I feel lightheaded and he split my lip, I force a grin. "Whose name? Grayson's?"

When he lunges for me, I'm prepared. I sidestep him, twisting to the side like Cara taught me and kick him square in the chest.

For a moment, he looks at me like he can't quite believe I did that, and I use it to my advantage. Reaching into my pocket, I take out the knife Gray shoved in there before leaving with his brothers.

I kick him again, this time in the thigh. Then I spin closer and rake the blade across his arm. Well, I aimed for his stomach, but he blocked it.

As his surprise wears off, it's replaced with excitement. He rolls on the balls of his feet and holds his arms out wide.

"Come at me all you want, Sugar. We both know how this is ending. With your cunt dripping blood onto my cock."

Angered by his words, I let out a war cry of sorts and jump at him again. But he's prepared for me to act, and this time he wraps his arms around my back and holds me flush against him. For a second I'm unsure of what to do, but I don't have time to think about it as he headbutts me.

Pain flares to life, making it feel like my skull is on fire as black spots dance at the edge of my vision.

"No," I scream, refusing to pass out. "No."

I try to recall Cara's words of wisdom. She said something about... no, she told me to... fuck. Why can't I remember?

Before I know what's happening, my air is forced out of me and I find myself sprawled on the floor, looking up at the ceiling.

The knife that was in my hand is now pressed against my throat.

"Scream for me, Sugar," Gunner cackles. "Call out for *him*. If you make him come in here, I promise to let you go."

A tear falls from my eyes. "I w-won't," I choke out. "I won't help you kill him."

Using the last of my strength, I lift my head, effectively pressing my throat harder against the knife to show him I don't care about my own life.

Gunner's eyes sparkle with untold horrors and menace. "You think I'm going to kill you that quickly, Sugar? Guess again."

He digs the knife into my skin, making me hiss out as I feel it slice through my skin. Only, it's not in a way one would do with the intention to kill. It's like a paper cut and nothing more.

"Let's have some fun first," he growls.

I stiffen as he removes the knife long enough to rip my shirt off. He does it so quickly and effortlessly there's no way for me to attack or as much as flail my arms.

Once I'm lying under him in nothing but my bra and jeans, he hums while using the knife to slice through the straps and the small bow holding the cups together.

"Fuck, I've missed those titties," he groans when my chest is completely bare to him.

Where the hell is the numbness when I want it? I know what's coming. I can see it in the depth of his evil eyes. He's going to use me, rape me. Probably repeatedly.

I can't go through that again.

Not when Gray has just... to say he's fixed me sounds ugly, yet that's the only word that comes to mind. Fix. I was fixed.

"There it is," Gunner taunts. Then he leans down and licks the tears trailing down my cheeks. "The despair and fear I've been dreaming about. Go for it, Princess. Seal his fate by screaming for *him.*"

Fuck.

I can't do that either.

What the fuck do I do?

42

Grayson

"She doesn't have to scream for me. I'm already fucking here."

I revel in the way Gunner stiffens at feeling the press of my gun to the back of his head. It's a rush of power I wasn't expecting, but one I fucking embrace.

"Now, now, brother. You don't want to get your whore all messy with my blood, do you?"

I scoff, hearing the heavy steps of my men file in behind me before seeing Munroe, Sully, Tex, and Stretch fan out around us, guns pointed at Gunner.

"Don't fucking call me brother. You lost that right when you betrayed us." I jab the nozzle of my gun hard into his thick hair. "Now fucking stand up."

"Okay. Okay." He slowly starts to rise off Zoe, and I take a moment to check her over, seeing that she's half naked with a shallow cut on her neck and a bruise forming on her forehead.

Quickly shucking off my cut and tugging off my shirt, I toss it over to Zoe. "Put this on, Princess."

With his hands raised, Gunner takes stock of the situation he's in, his eyes darting to every gun trained on him. Still, the fucker glances at Zoe like he's imagining what she's hiding under my shirt.

Yeah, he has nowhere to fucking run.

"Hands behind your head," I snap as I slip my arms back through my cut, and he nods, not looking at me, instead looking down at Zoe as she scurries backward across the floor to get clear of him.

Then he fucking shoots her a wink.

With a hard crack, I hit him over the side of his head with the butt of my gun, sending him tumbling forward, crashing to his knees.

Every ounce of anger that has been brewing over his betrayal boils to the surface, and I toss my gun behind me before using my fists to start pummeling him as I let myself embrace the rage.

I punch, kick, shove, and knee my former best friend, not stopping when he no longer tries to shield himself from the blows. He knows fighting back is futile. He's already made peace with the fact death is coming for him. Unluckily for him, I won't make it come easily.

By the time I stop my assault, he's lying in a pool of his own blood, his face swelling with bruises already forming.

I spit on his crumpled form as he heaves for air.

"Tell me why!" I roar. "Why the fuck would you betray us?! Betray me!" I lower to my haunches and grab a fistful of his hair, dragging his head back so I can look at his beaten face. "Why the fuck would you trade the Kings for the fucking Reapers?"

A low, maniacal laugh rattles from his chest, and the fucker even has the audacity to smirk.

"That's easy," he rasps, trying to pry one lid open enough to see me. "Everything was always about you." He coughs. "I was part of the Diamond Crew before you. I practically grew up with them, but then you came along, and everyone just fucking *loved you.*" He rolls to his back, forcing his lid to open further to see me looming over him. "Hell, even Rocco declared you VP even though you hadn't been around for long. You always got the good stuff, while I was always forgotten about, stuck in your fucking shadow."

I jerk back a little, absorbing his words.

This is all about jealousy?

"Why didn't you speak up?" I snap. "Talk with me or Rocco. We would have fucking listened."

Tugging his head back forcefully, my grip releases on his hair and he flops his head back to the floor as he scoffs.

"Rocco never heard me. He always fucking dismissed me, and you," he glares up at me, curling his top lip to reveal blood coated teeth, "you always took what I wanted. Including Zoe."

I shake my head. "Don't use Zoe as an excuse. This obviously started before her."

Gunner laughs, but there's no humor to it.

"Tell me when?" I snap. "When did you decide to betray our club and stand with our enemy?"

His smirk fucking pisses me off. I want to fucking cut his lips from his face.

"Tell me!" I roar.

"Irina approached me first. I knew who she was, and she was gagging for my dick, so I gave it to her. A cunt is a cunt, after all."

"You sick bastard." Zoe hisses, and he flashes his blood coated teeth in her direction.

"Don't fucking look at her!" I yell, kicking him in the gut, the air flying from his lungs as he starts wheezing. "What happened with Irina?"

"She saw my potential," he pants, struggling for air. "She knew I was made to rule instead of just being a foot soldier, so she made a proposal to come and speak with Rusty." He coughs, and I fucking hate having to let him hack his way through it to hear more of what happened.

"Hurry the fuck up and spit it out already."

He glares at my impatience, but fucking does as I say.

"I met with Rusty, and we struck a deal. I'd help him infiltrate the Kings, and in return, he'd make me VP. Of course, things changed when Irina manipulated Brian to help." He glances over at Zoe again. "The moment I laid eyes on you, Sugar, I knew I had to make you part of the deal too."

Snarling, I reach down and fist the front of Gunner's shirt, lifting him a little so we are nose to fucking nose.

"Don't fucking talk to her," I grit out.

Again, he chuckles, manically this time. "What's wrong, brother? Scared she enjoyed the way I fucked her better than the way you do?"

My fist rears back before I feel his cheekbone shatter under my knuckles, blood spraying across my face and the floor.

Still, the manic laughter continues.

I shove him back, hearing the back of his head crack on the hardwood floor, cutting off his laughing.

"So you really are the one responsible for my mom's and sister's deaths?" Zoe asks, moving forward to loom over him.

"Your mom's death, yes. Leslie's? No. That bullet was meant for Gray." Gunner sneers at me like it's my fault his aim was off. "Leslie was meant to be kept alive. We had so many plans for her. Do you know how much money we could have got selling a virgin minor?"

Zoe's crazed scream rips through the clubhouse as she launches herself at Gunner, but I reach her before she makes contact, circling my arms around her middle, holding her back for now.

When she kills him, I want her to be clearheaded and not consumed by unbridled rage. She will want to remember that moment.

"Princess," I rasp into her hair near her ear. "Not yet. Soon. I promise."

Slowly, she stops fighting, her flailing arms and legs going lax as she heaves in much needed oxygen, and I set her feet back on the floor before releasing my hold on her.

My heart races at hearing Gunner's confession. I knew he was obsessed with Zoe after finding the pictures and videos in his apartment, but I never knew the other stuff.

"You're fucking pathetic," I hiss, standing over him again and darting my gaze back to Zoe. "You alright, Princess?"

She's standing by Munroe's side now, her hands trembling even as she nods and juts up her chin. "I'll be even better when he's dead."

I give her a sharp nod, knowing this isn't over until Gunner is no longer breathing.

"Munroe, call Slasher. Tell him and Titch to get the Cunts back here. We have an execution ceremony to perform."

Munroe nods, pulling out his phone while still keeping his gun raised on Gunner and making the call.

I pat Gunner down, checking him for weapons and finding the knife he keeps in his boot, just like me.

"Why didn't you try to use this?" I ask, eyeing him and he slowly shrugs one shoulder like it brings him pain just to do that one small action. "In fact, why are you here at all? You had to know you'd get caught."

A slow smirk spreads his bloody lips and beard wide. "It took you long enough. I've been right under your nose this whole fucking time."

"The blackout?" I ask, and he chuckles. "It was all too easy."

I feel the air shift beside me, and glance up to see Zoe standing beside me. Her brows are tugging inward as anger contorts her expression, and I do a quick check of her hands to make sure she's not holding a gun.

I mean, I'd get it if she just wanted to shoot him dead. She has every right, and frankly, I think that's what Gunner wants. But the club needs this execution. Everyone needs this closure and we all need reminding of what happens to members that betray us.

"Did you watch Gray fuck me while you were hiding under our noses?" Zoe asks Gunner, her tone sharp and hateful.

Gunner's eyes widen and his nostrils flare, which just eggs Zoe on.

"You did, didn't you?" she scoffs. "Did you see how good he made me feel? How he owned my body. Every single fucking inch."

"Shut up." Gunner hisses through gritted teeth, and I fucking grin, crossing my arms over my chest as I watch his inner torment come to life.

"Did you see how easily his dick slid into me? No fucking lube needed. I was so wet for him. Unlike with you." She sneers that last sentence. "You had to slick your own rotten dick because you never once made me wet. Never once did I want you. Never once did you make me feel good."

Gunner's lip twitches at each word Zoe throws at him, but then he chuckles.

"Oh, I did fucking make you feel good, Sugar. Don't you remember?"

I stiffen at the same time Zoe snarls and I dart my eyes to her.

What the fuck is he talking about?

"Uh-oh, Sugar. Haven't you told him? The way you writhed under me while you slept, your legs spread wide as I tongue fucked you. Do you remember how hard you came on my tongue?"

"Shut the fuck up!" Zoe screams, her face red with fury as she balls her fists like she'd love nothing more than to punch the fuck out of him.

"You always did like it when Gray came to you in your sleep. Naturally, your body still thought it was him, but it was my tongue that licked and drank you those nights when you first came to the Reapers. Your cum tastes so sweet, Sugar."

My whole fucking body is vibrating with rage as his words sink in.

He assaulted her in her sleep, and she had no fucking idea. Her subconscious would have thought it was me because I'd done that to her so many times, and she'd fucking loved it.

Now he's taken that from us too.

I'm about to leap forward, ready to strangle the life from him, but Zoe beats me to it, producing a knife that I didn't see her holding before, and she plunges it into his shoulder with a scream.

"I HATE YOU!" she screams, stabbing him again. "I FUCKING HATE YOU!"

I'm trying to decide if I should stop her or just let her have at him, but I don't need to do anything because Zoe stops, her lungs heaving audibly as she forces herself to stay in control.

"Stretch!" she barks, and my club brother hurries forward, eyes pinned to her as he awaits her words. "Tie his hands behind his back and get him in a chair."

I fucking smirk.

She really is a ruler.

Their queen, but always my princess.

Stretch follows Zoe's orders as she stands with the knife still gripped in her hand at her side, Gunner's blood dripping to the floor.

"Zo," I rasp, stepping in front of her so she'll stop looking at Gunner, and I cup her cheek.

"I'm okay," she whispers, answering a question I never asked, her eyes glassy as they connect with mine.

"You're the strongest person I've ever met." I admit, loving the way she tilts her head into my palm, accepting the small bit of comfort I'm offering.

"I'm only strong because of the support you give me in the moments when I'm not."

Fuck. I've never heard truer words. She's that for me, too. She makes me want to be a better man.

I pull her to my chest, and we stand wrapped in each other's arms while Stretch gets Gunner tied and onto a chair, and shortly after, Slasher, Titch and the Cruz Cunts start walking back through the clubhouse doors.

Everyone is silent as they take in our captive, the Cunts taking a wide berth while my brothers glare at him, ready to claim their piece of his punishment.

"Princess," I rasp quietly against Zoe's ear, gaining her attention. "I have to enforce our club punishment, followed by the execution. I haven't had a chance to fill you in on what happens, but if you want to leave, no one will mind."

Easing back to look into my eyes, Zoe shakes her head. "I was forced to be the judge and hand out a sentence when I was with the Reapers. I've already seen an execution and I may not know what's about to happen, but I'm here for it, Gray. I won't leave this room until he's dead."

Warmth rushes through my chest. There's no doubt Zoe Miller was put on this earth for me. I may have had a hand in corrupting her soul, but she owns that corruption like it's always been rushing through her veins.

"Then let's finish this."

With a sharp nod, Zoe rolls her shoulders back and we separate to stand side by side, facing our club and the traitor.

"Eddie Gunn, you swore an oath to this club of which you've broken through acts of deceit, betrayal, and treason. Do you have anything to say?"

All eyes are on Gunner as he sits slumped in the chair, his face swollen from my beating, but even behind his bushy beard, we can all see his fucking smirk.

"Just get on with it," he rasps, the words nothing but fuel for the anger everyone in this room has toward him.

"Cut his clothes free," I order, and it's Munroe and Sully that step forward, shredding every bit of fabric from his body, not bothering to be careful not to nick him before pulling him up to stand.

No one shies away from staring at his pathetic naked state. The humiliation of it is part of the process, and even though Gunner's expression doesn't show an ounce of shame, the way his toes curl on the timber floor is a dead giveaway that his bravery is nothing but a façade.

I glance to Slasher, who is a ball of fury to my right and give his shoulder a nudge with mine.

"You wanna do this next part?"

His eyes dart to mine, wide with what can only be excitement, and he nods.

"That's okay?"

"Yes. After what he took from you, it's yours if you want it."

Nodding again, Slasher watches as I point my thumb over my shoulder.

"Mini blow torch is over there."

He disappears from my line of sight, and I turn back to my club.

"Eddie Gunn, for the acts you have committed against this club, we strip you of your membership."

Slasher steps into the center, and Sully spins Gunner so his back is to the rest of us, showing us his large Cruz Kings' skull head tattoo, and the jagged cross that's been struck through it, most likely with a knife.

With a click, Slasher ignites the mini blow torch and doesn't waste a second, hovering the blue flame over Gunner's flesh as he starts to burn off the ink only loyal members of the Cruz Kings have the right to wear.

The smell of burnt flesh engulfs the space as Gunner releases a howl of pain, and I realize having this ceremony inside was a bad fucking idea. Tex is on it though, quietly darting around to open windows and doors before turning the overhead fans on to help move the stench out faster.

Risking a glance at Zoe, I see her still standing tall with her shoulders back as she watches on, not shying away from the brutality of what Slasher is doing while Sully and Stretch keep Gunner on his feet to endure his punishment.

I turn my eyes to the Cunts next, noticing them standing just as tall as their Mama as they too watch on, and even though this is a pretty fucking sick ceremony we have to perform, I'm fucking proud of my members and how they have rallied to watch out for each other and not complained when the hard shit has to happen, like burning our club skull head off our traitor's back.

Slasher finishes up, glaring at Gunner as Sully and Stretch shift him around to face everyone again. Then he spits in our former club member's face.

"Watch your back when you get to hell. Slayer is waiting for you."

Tears start then from a couple of the Cunts at the reminder that Gunner is responsible for Slayer's death, plus so many more.

"Eddie Gunn," I snarl, eager to get this over with so everyone here can start to move on, "With your membership now stripped, as one, we will send you to hell."

Reaching into my boot, I pull my knife free, snapping it open and holding it up.

"Cunts and Kings, take your pound of flesh."

After Sully and Stretch sit Gunner back on the chair, Munroe is the first to take my knife, approaching Gunner and seething down at him from his tall height. "Fuck you," he hisses in Gunner's face before plunging the blade deep into his abdomen.

Gunner chokes out as Munroe twists the blade before pulling it free, holding it up for the next Cunt or King, before spitting in Gunner's face.

Rose is next, pushing through Titch and Tio to get to the front of the line, eager to have her turn.

"You sick son of a bitch," she slashes the knife across his face, opening the skin from his temple, over the tip of his nose and corner of his lip before reaching his jaw. "I hope there is a hell for those in hell. A place worse than anyone can ever imagine, and I hope you get subjected to all the most heinous acts imaginable." She stabs the knife into his abdomen, a few inches from the gash Munroe made.

Following Munroe and Slasher's lead, she spits in his face, ignoring his gasps of pain before spinning and placing the knife in Tio's hand.

One by one, Cunts and Kings step forward to snarl their thoughts to Gunner, stabbing him as Stretch and Sully keep him upright on the chair, who get their turn too, when Doug and Tio trade places with them.

Slasher helps Alana move forward, her gunshot injury still affecting her ability to walk properly, and Slasher takes the knife from Cilla, pressing it into Alana's palm.

"This is for having a part in the rape of Sasha and her murder." Alana bares her teeth, looking more violent than I've ever seen her, and then she slams the blade right into Gunner's dick, pinning it to the chair under him.

On instinct I cover my fucking junk, while most of my club brothers do the same, some strangled coughs sounding around the room. Gunner's cry is high pitched, terror washing over his expression at the realization of what has just been done.

"And this is for Izzy," Alana hisses, being greedy with the knife since we are only meant to stab once, but who the fuck am I to deny our dead Cunts their revenge as well?

She jerks the knife free, plunging it into his gut, and this time Gunner makes no noise as he passes out.

"Get the smelling salts," I bark, and Tex appears with them, running them under Gunner's nose until he starts rousing.

"You doing okay, Princess?" I ask, not taking my eyes off Gunner as he gets pulled from unconsciousness and, for a moment, fear flits across his expression.

Yeah, fucker, you're still in living hell.

"I'm good," Zoe responds with a strong tone before her fingers brush with mine and I link our hands together.

"He's back," Tex sing-songs and some of the men chuckle, while Alana moves back in.

"You pussy. Can't even take torture like a man." She stabs him again. "That one's for me." Then she spits in his face and Rose comes forward to help Alana into a nearby chair while Slasher stares at the knife in his hand.

Then he pulls another one free.

"As twins, we always used to do everything together." Slasher slowly peers up, his dark hair hanging in a long mess as he makes eye contact with Gunner. "We used to eat together, sleep in the same room, fuck in the same room, share the same women." His hands wrap around the hilt of each knife as he leans in. "And just because he's dead, doesn't mean he's not here right fucking now, to take his pound of flesh, too."

Slasher plunges both knives into each side of Gunner's ribs at the same time, probably puncturing his lungs if Gunner's short, rapid gasps are anything to go by.

Knowing there's not much time before he bleeds out, I lift Zoe's hand in mine, bringing it to my lips to press a kiss there, and her gaze shifts to mine.

"Still have that knife from before?" I ask, and she nods, pulling it from the back pocket of her jeans and flicking it open. "Will you do the kill shot with me?"

Her brows shoot high.

"Is that allowed?" she whispers, and I smirk.

"I make the rules, and I want you by my side through everything."

Slowly, her plump lips tip up and she nods, so I hold out my hand to Slasher.

"Knife," I bark, and the hilt meets my open palm as I turn back to face everyone.

"I, Grayson Black, President of the Cruz Kings MC, sentence Eddie Gunn to death for his sins against us."

Together, Zoe and I step forward, mine in my left hand and Zoe's in her right. I stare at the man who used to be my best friend, knowing that was a fucking lie too.

"One, two," I count, "three."

In unison, Zoe and I plunge our knives into the center of Gunner's chest, breaking through bone and piercing the beating organ that's been fighting to keep him alive with a pop.

My eyes lock with Zoe's, both of us breathing deeply from the emotion of this act, and like we had planned it, but actually hadn't even said a word to each other, we both twist the blades embedded in his chest just for good measure as finally, we all get the peace we've been seeking, and Gunner never takes another breath again.

Even though his heart has stopped, when I drop my hand away, Zoe's remains. Tilting my head to get a better look at her face, I see so much rage wash over her, a growl like sound reverberating from her chest as she curls her top lip and bares her teeth.

"This is for my mom." She chokes out, her hand pulling the knife free before she lets loose a feral scream and plunges it into his right eye. "And this is for Leslie!" She screeches, tugging the knife free and burying it in his left eye.

A loud sob bursts past her lips, and I risk placing my hand on her shoulder, unsure if she's here with us right now, or lost in her head.

She doesn't flinch at my touch, instead standing taller, her chest heaving as she pulls the blade free again.

"And this is for the man my dad used to be before you had Irina brainwash him."

Closing both of her fists around the hilt, she shoves the sharp tip up under his blood-soaked bush beard, right through his throat.

Fuck.

I didn't expect her to do that, but I'm fucking glad she did if it helps her to get some semblance of fucking closure over all of this.

Slowly, Zoe turns to face everyone, her eyes glassy with tears, but her chin high and her shoulders back.

"It's over. The Cruz Kings can now reign in peace."

I've never felt fucking prouder.

Reaching down, I link my fingers with hers, gaining her attention as her blue stormy gaze locks with mine.

"I fucking love you, Zo."

Her lips spread wide in one of the sincerest smiles I've seen her give me. "I fucking love you too, Gray."

EPILOGUE 1

Zoe

January 1st

*D*ear diary...

I'm not sure I like the idea of writing to an inanimate object. Maybe I'll pretend I'm writing to my-self—future me.

Hi future me. This is... us... me... you, but a past version. If you/I read this years from now, and have forgot-ten why this seemed important, I suppose that's a good thing. But at the same time, I want to remember the why.

With all the downtime I have now, since I don't con-stantly need to look over my shoulder, I've had time to reflect on the past. Especially my time with the Reapers. And while the obvious things are the worst, there's one thing in particular I can't shake.

Not knowing something as simple and trivial as the date... ugh. That's something I never want to experience again. It's hard to explain why it's so significant to me. Fuck, I'm not even sure I fully understand it.

But here I am—still dwelling on it. So I'm trying something new.

My New Year's resolution is to commemorate some-thing from every day. And what better place is there to start than at the beginning?

It's almost seven in the morning, and the New Year celebrations have only just died down. I'm not going to lie, I'm tired as fuck, beyond buzzed—not to mention freshly fucked.

Gray's asleep. You'll know what I mean when I say he's in stage three of five when it comes to snoring.

It's good, though. Because there's something about the quietness—minus the snoring—that makes it easier to think.

The time that's passed since we won the war against the Reapers has gone by in a blur of activity and emotions.

After Gunner took his last breath, it felt like an invisible order swept through the room. All the Kings jumped into solving mode, hauling Gunner's ass out of there. Slasher and Munroe disappeared for a few hours, and when they returned, it was without the body. So it's safe to assume they disposed of it.

By the way, future me, don't ask questions about that. We don't need to know!!

Together with the Cunts, I cleaned the main room until my fingers ached and bleach covered every inch of the room. We opened every fucking window and door, burned incense, and sprayed perfume.

But despite the Kings' insistence that they couldn't smell the sickly sweet, vomit inducing stench from Gunner's burned flesh anymore, we could. We, as in me and the Cunts. I still don't believe the Kings couldn't smell it because it was everywhere.

Seriously, I had to put a thin sheen of toothpaste on my upper lip so as to not smell it.

So, we once again went to Dirty Diamonds, where we stayed for five days. During that time, Gray revealed they'd put Izzy on ice so we could give her a proper sendoff.

I'll admit, I still don't know why she was iced since they just disposed of her body the usual way. But whatever. The goodbye ceremony was nice—as nice as saying goodbye to a friend can be.

On the fifth day, Gray had enough. He wanted to go home, and I think everyone agreed. Dirty Diamonds is like a prime destination for partying, but it's not a—our—home.

Who knew the Kings and Cunts could get their fill of booze, drugs, and pussy/dick? I didn't. Not until we left.

Anyway, back at the clubhouse, the Cunts all entered nesting mode. At least that's what I dubbed it. If I'm being completely honest, I did as well.

With so much time spent being scared and looking over our shoulder, letting go was hard. But it became easier with new projects to focus on.

Even though the war was over, the aftermath had only just started. There was only so much Tido could do to shield the Kings from the law. So Slasher and Gray reached out to the detectives, who helped us as much as they were able to.

The biggest thing for me was one I hadn't seen coming. Tania was the one who reminded me I'd been neglecting to pick up my monthly allowance check, and, well, I wasn't at Harvard, which meant no tuition money was deducted from my trust.

She and Steven talked to my family's lawyer and somehow convinced him I'd been a key witness and had needed to lay low, which is why I'd been out of touch. It was sweet, even if I suspect it was wholly unnecessary. In the end, I left with a check to cover all the months I hadn't been able to pick one up.

My first thought was to funnel the money into the club, but Gray wouldn't hear of it. So instead, I spent a good amount on Christmas presents for the community. Specifically, large donations to some businesses the Reapers had targeted, and, of course, the kids' burn unit. The same one we visited on the Fourth of July.

After experiencing my first Kings' Christmas, I can now officially say I've seen it all. While I expected another blowout, it was oddly domestic.

I'm pretty sure it was the Cunts' doing. Because after I'd told them how my family celebrated Christmas, my amazing girls took it upon themselves to recreate the magic. And when I came downstairs on Christmas morning, they were waiting.

Each of them wore a red dress and black pumps. They'd all braided their hair, some into one big one, others into two smaller ones. Except for Rose, who proudly displayed her short bob, refusing to hide behind a wig. The red Christmas hat was the icing on the cake, and I burst into tears when they showed me the presents under the tree.

The Cunts later told me they'd tried to convince the Kings to dress up in suits, which they'd all promptly refused. However, they did wear the Christmas hats the Cunts imposed as part of the day's dress code. Doug even wore a fake Santa beard and kept asking the Cunts to sit on his lap.

We had dinner delivered from one of the local restaurants, a full-on Christmas meal with all the trimmings. For dessert, the Cunts baked cookies.

Pro tip: never, ever, ever, ever eat any cookies Rose makes. Seriously, I still can't believe I didn't chip a tooth. And honestly, how can anyone think a pinch of salt means a handful? I think I love her more for messing it up, though.

I'm sure there are more things I can't remember right now. But all there really is to say is that I'm happy. I'm so fucking happy I could burst. I've found my place in the world. I no longer dream of Ivy League halls or materialistic shit.

I've found my purpose, my place, and most importantly; my tribe.

Goodnight future me.

Love, Zoe

"Are you sure this is what you want to do?" Gray rasps, pulling me to his side as we stand outside the morgue. "No one will blame you if you want to—"

"I'm sure," I sigh, cutting him off. "This is the end for him and me. He chose his path just like I'm choosing mine. And I don't want him to have a place in my future."

It's been a few days since I started writing to my future self, and so far I've kept my promise to myself by writing daily. I haven't read anything I've written, so for all I know it's a whole lot of nothing that might not even make sense.

But that hardly matters as long as it serves its purpose, which it does. It's almost like a cleansing of the soul, and it makes it easier for me to deal when things become hard or when difficult decisions need to be made. Like the reason we're here now.

When the Santa Cruz PD finally released my dad's body to his family, namely me, I didn't know what to do. At first, I wanted nothing to do with him. The wound of his betrayal was still too fresh. But now, thanks to countless conversations with Gray, and so many journal entries I'm losing count, I finally know what I want to do.

"I'm sure," I repeat, probably mostly to myself. Then I push the pull door, making us both laugh.

Inside, we're greeted by an elderly man, Joel, I think his name is. "Ahh, Mr. and Mrs. Black," he says, shaking both our hands.

The first time he made the assumption, Gray elbowed me when I tried to correct the man, so now I just let it go.

Though we haven't talked about marriage, I know it's something Gray wants. He made it clear when he told Dante why I was allowed at the meeting they had back when we were still at war with the Reapers.

It's something I try not to think too much about because I'm not ready yet. My hesitance doesn't come from doubts or anything like that. Gray's mine, that'll never change. But I'm only eighteen and not in a rush. Now that I've gotten a second, third, and probably even fourth chance at life, I want to live it to the fullest.

"Have you decided what you want to do with your dad's body?"

Joel's question pulls me out of my thoughts, and I nod. "I want him buried in the unknown cemetery," I say.

"I see. And you're sure about this decision?" Joel asks.

Gray squeezes my hand. "She's sure. Can it be arranged or not?" he asks, his tone leaving no room for discussion.

"Of course, of course," Joel mutters. "But are you—"

I sigh. "I'm absolutely certain. He wasn't my dad at the end. He was a stranger who didn't care until it was too late."

Joel nods and mutters to himself. I don't pay much attention, annoyed at being questioned like that. I mean, I get it. It's not a decision I'm taking lightly. But I've already had to convince myself that this was okay, so I don't want to have to convince anyone else as well.

The thing is that, yes, Brian Miller was my biological dad. He raised me, and for years he was the picture perfect parent. But there's no way I can forgive, let alone forget, what he did. His actions and choices are the reason mom and Leslie were killed. The reason I was tortured and raped.

Maybe he really grew a conscience in the end. Hell, maybe he had a plan all along... I'll never know. But in the end, it doesn't fucking matter. There's no redemption for the shit he did, and I don't want a place to visit him. I want him gone from my life, simple as.

I said the same thing to our family lawyer when he told me that part of my inheritance from dad was a letter. Unlike the one my mom left me, I never even saw the envelope my dad's last words were wrapped in. I asked for it to be destroyed, and as far as I know, the words are gone. Maybe I'll regret it one day, but I doubt it.

Everyone thinks they have reasons that justify the actions they take in life, and I'm sure my dad is no different. But that doesn't mean he gets to poison my present and future with it.

We spend hours going over the necessary paperwork, and I'm quick to sign on every dotted line presented to me.

"Do you want to say goodbye to him?" Joel asks, his green eyes boring into mine.

I shake my head. "No," I say, handing him my credit card. "We're done."

As soon as we're finished, we leave, and I don't look back over my shoulder. I get straight on Gray's bike, and after a quick stop at a florist, he takes me to the cemetery so I can visit mom and Leslie.

"Come here," I say, patting the cold dirt next to where I'm sitting.

"Are you sure?" Gray asks.

I roll my eyes. "Yes," I simply answer.

When he joins me, I take his hand, and introduce him to mom first.

"Hey mom. So, I don't know how it works up there. Can you guys really look down and see us scrambling on earth? If you can, well, then you already know everything that's happened. And if you can't... well, let's just say some things are better left unsaid."

Gray chuckles.

"I want to introduce you to Grayson Black. I know you already know him, kinda. But I want you to see who he is to me, okay?"

A yelp slips past my lips as Gray suddenly pulls me into his lap, wrapping his arms around me. "Can't make a good impression if I let you sit on the ground, can I?" he whispers directly into my ear.

"You see what I mean?" I ask, continuing to talk to my dead mom. "That's his version of being a gentleman, mom. But don't think he's only like this to suck up to you because he's not. He even holds doors for me, and he once gave me the last food he had instead of eating it himself."

I close my eyes, letting memories of all the things Gray's done for me play out like a movie behind my lids.

"He's the love of my life," I whisper, too choked up to speak at a normal volume.

"Is that so? Am I really the love of your life, Mrs. Black?" Grayson rasps, and when I turn my head, I see him playfully waggle his eyebrows.

"I take that back," I laugh. "He's the bane of my existence."

We stay at the cemetery until the cold has made my cheeks numb, and the tears I've shed both from laughter and hurt have long since dried.

"Fine," I mock scoff when another gust of wind hits me. "Is this your way of saying it's time for us to leave, huh, Leslie? You were always such a little shit."

Gray playfully pokes me in the side, making me squeal with laughter. "Behave."

"Okay," I relent between bouts of laughter. "Look, I love you, Leslie. And I'm adopting your entire stuffed unicorn collection. I'll give them a nice home near nature. Some could even say it'll be their Nirvana."

When Gray groans that he doesn't want unicorns eyeing his junk while he's balls deep inside me, I decide it really is time to go. I don't know if I believe my mom and sister can hear us, but on the off chance they can, I don't want them to hear anything else.

"I love you guys," I say. "And I promise I'll be back soon."

On the ride back to the clubhouse, I try to let go of the conflicting emotions brewing inside me. Ever since Gunner disclosed the Reapers' plans for Leslie, I've been fighting the way it made me feel. Because knowing what they had in store for her made me glad she died instead of having to live through that horror. But that's followed by torment over being glad my sister died.

It's a catch fucking 22.

Opening the door to our home, we're immediately greeted by deep grunts, groans, and moans that cause my core to clench.

"Fuck's sake," Gray grumbles. "Can't even leave them alone for a few hours."

I giggle. "Are you complaining?"

"Yes," he rasps. "You're seeing way too many cocks that aren't mine. It's not right."

Spinning around, I jump into his arms. "But I only touch yours," I purr, wrapping my arms and legs around him. "My pussy only gets wet for yours." I angle my hips so his hardening cock is perfectly nestled against my heat.

"You fucking better," he growls.

We stumble through the door, Gray carrying me while also trying to rip my leather jacket off. I imagine it looks anything but graceful, but I don't care.

"I want you," I whimper, barely paying attention to the gyrating bodies dancing in my peripheral. "Fuck me, Gray."

"Here? Or do you want me to take you upstairs?"

Since the Reapers took me, I haven't wanted to participate in the orgies, so I get why he's asking. But right now, I don't care about the others.

"Here," I confirm.

A moan slips free as my gaze trails over Slasher and Alana as they go at it on the bar. Slasher's on his back, and Alana is bouncing on his cock while Rose's being railed by Doug right next to them.

Fuck me, the cacophony of their pleasure has me so wet I can barely stand it.

"Gray," I whimper when he's taking too long to touch me.

"Patience, Princess," he rasps.

Despite his words, he removes my clothes so quickly it feels like one fluent motion before I'm standing in front of him in nothing but my bra and thong.

I reach for his pants, and while he removes his shirt and cut, I unbuckle his belt and rip the button free so I can push his pants and boxers down. His impressive cock juts out from his body, pre-cum glistening at the tip.

Licking my lips, I drop to my haunches and lick the tip.

"Fuck. Zo—" His words turn into a guttural groan when I swallow his length, taking him down my throat while my tongue snakes around the shaft.

Gray moves his hand to the back of my head, keeping me in place until I can't breathe. I hiss around his length and dig my nails into his thighs.

When he lets me pull back, I wait for flashbacks of the things Gunner did to hit me, but they never do. Enveloped in Gray's touch, smell, and taste, my mind knows it's safe. The thought makes me bolder, and I stop holding back, giving him everything I have.

While I lick, suck, and let him fuck my mouth, I move a hand between my legs, rolling my clit until I'm ready to come.

"Don't you fucking dare come until I'm inside you," Gray groans, throwing his head back as I create suction around his dick. "I want to feel your cunt squeeze my cock."

Albeit reluctantly, I remove my hand and stand up. "Then fuck me, Gray," I purr. "Because I want to come. Now."

His eyes darken with lust as I issue my command, and fuck if it isn't the sexiest thing ever to know he loves it when I tell him exactly what I want.

"Whatever my princess commands," he groans.

Gray moves us further into the main room, and just as I think he's about to push me against the wall, he surprises me by spinning us around so I'm facing the room.

"Do you trust me?"

"Of course," I answer with no hesitation.

After quickly ridding me of my underwear, he moves his hands to my shoulders, adding pressure until I bend. I barely have time to get used to the position before he positions the head of his cock against my folds, slamming all the way into me.

"Gray," I cry out when his fingers dig into my shoulders to keep me in place.

"I got you, Princess," he rasps. "I'll always catch you."

His thrusts are hard, punishing almost, and I fucking love it.

Despite the naked bodies in front of me, I don't pay them any attention. I'm too full and desperate for more to focus on anything but Gray's cock inside me.

"Do you want Alana to join us?" he asks, so suddenly I lose my train of thought.

"W-what?" I stutter. Surely I didn't hear him right.

"She could eat you out while I fuck you," he suggests.

"Where the fuck is this coming from?" I hiss. "Do you want her face that close to your cock? Because if you do—"

"Of course not," he scoffs. "But you liked her hands on your body, and I don't want to deprive you."

Closing my eyes, I pray for the strength to deal with the neanderthal that should be fucking me until I can barely stand instead of discussing adding another person to our tryst.

"I don't fucking want Alana or anyone else to join us," I spit. Then I take a deep breath and soften my tone. "What we did was a one off, and not something I'm secretly wanting to repeat."

While I talk, Gray begins to fuck me again. This time with long, agonizingly slow strokes.

"It was never really about her, anyway. It was like... she was helping me—us. She was your stand-in, Gray. I wanted you. Your hands, your tongue, and your glorious cock. But..." Trailing off, I swallow thickly.

"Are you sure?" he rasps.

There's something in his tone that finally makes me realize what inspired the question in the first place. He isn't asking for himself, but for me. It's his way of telling me that he'll give me anything I want.

"I've never been surer about anything in my life," I whimper. "You and me, Gray. To the end."

As though he was waiting for my words, he picks up his pace. Slamming into me so hard, I cry out from the pleasure-filled pain of being fucked ruthlessly in this position.

"To. The. End," he groans, punctuating every word with a savage thrust.

My legs begin to shake, and I'm beyond words as his cock continues to hit that magical spot inside me. My stomach tightens, the release so close I can feel the inevitable detonation building, taking me higher and higher.

"Come with me," I moan. "Fill me with your cum. Gray, I want... I need... Gray!"

A groan builds in his chest as my cunt squeezes him when my orgasm washes over me. I forget about everything and everyone that isn't us.

Gray slams into me one last time, and while my cunt squeezes around him, milking the cum from his cock, he slides his hands into my hair and pulls me back against him. I turn my head around just in time for his lips to slam against mine.

"You're mine, Mrs. Black," he groans into my mouth.

"You've never asked," I pant.

With a chuckle, he says, "I don't ask for what I already own."

EPILOGUE 2

Grayson

One week later.

Watching my princess sleep over the last six or so weeks has become something I enjoy daily. I often wake before her and sit in the chair just watching, taking in her sleeping form in my bed. Our bed.

She's safe now. It's still a hard notion to get used to, given the fight mode we've been in for so fucking long.

We have no more enemies. We've cleaned shop thanks to the help of Dante and his crew, and now we get to exist without having to look over our shoulders everywhere we go. For the first time in years, we celebrated Christmas and welcomed the New Year without the threat of looming danger.

Zoe stirs in the bed, kicking off the sheets the same way she often does in the morning before her body starts to wake. It's a fucking tease given her naked state.

We don't bother with clothes in bed anymore. There's just something about the skin-on-skin contact while we sleep that eases our tortured souls. I fucking love waking up with her tit in my hand and my dick digging into the valley of her ass.

Instead of taking my cock and slipping it inside her heat while she sleeps, I drag myself over to the chair and watch her, wishing I could shake this fucking urge I have to take her in her sleep, just like I used to.

Gunner fucking took that from us. He knew how much I loved doing that to Zo. He fucking knew how much she loved me doing it to her, too. He couldn't fucking stand it, so he took it. He took her when she was unconscious. Unaware. In a state of sleep where she was free of the nightmare just for a brief moment. He took her and used her body against her to work an orgasm from her, and then he threw it in our faces.

Gunner's words fucking torment me. I'm glad Zoe never told me, obviously knowing how much it would gut me.

Now, I fight my fucking obsessive urge to reclaim that part back while she sleeps, wanting her to feel me in sleep and wake, knowing it was fucking real. It was me.

Shifting on the bed again, Zoe's legs part further as her knee lifts and flops to the side, opening her to expose her pink lips and the sweet hole that grips my cock so fucking good.

Christ.

Raking my hand through my hair, I find myself standing and moving to the end of the bed, my eyes locked on her natural beauty splayed out for me like a fucking feast.

I want her.

I swallow thickly, my hand absentmindedly rubbing over my straining cock before I lick my lips.

Reclaim her.

Take what's yours.

Remind her who she belongs to.

Fuck.

Just one taste.

My eyes dart up to her face as I carefully lower my upper body on the mattress between her legs, hovering close to her parted folds, and I inhale deeply.

Fucking sweet.

My chest starts rising and falling as I fight my most primal urge to bury my head between her legs and sink my tongue deep into her cunt.

I shouldn't. Not without talking to her first. Should I?

Fuuuck.

I hate that I'm hesitating. I hate that something we once shared could potentially send her spiraling into panic if I try to do it again.

But what if it doesn't?

I feel my whole fucking body start to vibrate with the need to eat her and bring her to the brink while she's unconscious.

I never used to ask before. I just took, and she fucking loved it. What if that's what I'm meant to do now? Just take and remind her that she's mine, and I will always worship her, even in sleep.

Teasing myself further, I lean closer, the tip of my nose practically brushing her clit, and I inhale again.

"You want this, Princess?" I whisper, addressing her even though I'm pretty fucking sure I'm just trying to convince myself that it's okay and I'm not about to violate her.

Then, I flick my tongue out and glide it gently through her folds.

That one act is all it takes for me to throw out any notion that she'll hate this.

I'll make her feel good. Just like I used to.

Like a man starved, I shift closer, using my tongue and then lips to kiss her folds, giving her clit some attention too as I feel the bud start to swell under my lips.

The moment she moans in her sleep, I fucking nearly lose it, my dick jerking against the mattress, desperate for release.

"That's it, Princess. Take what you need," I whisper between tongue flicks and lip nibbles.

Shifting, Zoe moans again, her hips doing a little lift like they are chasing something, and it's that moment I add more pressure.

I can feel her slickness seeping from her entrance, and I bring my hand up between me and the mattress and press the tip to her.

"Are you ready for me to fill you?" I ask her a little louder than before, but she doesn't respond, still trapped in sleep as her body starts to writhe with arousal.

Slowly, I ease my digit into her tight heat, feeling her cunt grip my finger and practically suck it in as it pulses with need, trapping me inside her.

I'm totally fucking consumed by this act now, and I need to see it through, hoping like hell that the moment she wakes, she won't fucking freak out.

Her hips lift, her hand shifting to slide to her mound, and she starts rubbing her clit.

Fuck, that's hot.

Looking up over her writhing body from the valley of her apex is fucking intoxicating. Her back arches, her tits straining while her fingers move quickly over her greedy bud.

Adding another digit, I fill Zoe more, stretching her tight opening before I curl my fingers up, focusing on the upper wall just inside her cunt.

"Gray."

My moaned name fills the space, right before she stiffens, and her lids snap open.

I don't stop.

Instead, I step up my onslaught.

Using my free hand, I palm her ass, holding her to me as I bury my nose against her fingers, still pressed to her clit, and sink my tongue into her slick heat as far as it can go to join my fingers.

My eyes remain locked on hers, watching an array of emotions flick across her expression.

First fear. Then confusion. And finally, acceptance.

I fucking devour her, reminding her how things are meant to be between us. Reminding her that I'll always worship her. Reminding her that she's still safe.

I'm not gentle now, my tongue a force to be reckoned with as it dives in, glides through, flicks over, doing all the things it already knows Zoe loves.

"Gray. Yes," Zoe cries out, gyrating under me before her back arches off the bed and she screams out her release while she gushes over my face.

Something worth drowning in.

"Fuck... Gray," she pants, shoving at my head as I continue to lick her clean. "Get up here."

Chuckling as I pull back from between her legs, I crawl up her body as she hooks her legs around my waist and tugs my hips forward, the head of my cock finding her entrance.

"I need you inside me." She writhes, accepting my straining cock as it sinks in.

"You're not mad?" I grit out, trying not to come to the party too early. She feels so fucking good.

"No." She shakes her head. "Thank you."

Her lips claim mine in a searing kiss, tongues clashing as I start moving inside her.

My hand palms the swell of her breast between us, and she breaks the kiss when my thumb grazes her nipple.

"You feel so good," she breathes, one hand fisted in my hair while the nails of her other hand dig into my hip.

"I didn't want to scare you," I rasp, biting her earlobe, "but I needed to claim that back."

Moaning, Zoe shifts under me, urging me to the side so I follow her lead, letting her roll us so I'm on my back with her straddling me.

"It's yours, Gray," she growls, her blue gaze fierce as she raises her eyes to look at me.

"Fuck, Zo. You're so fucking beautiful."

I can't stop my hands from wandering as I stare up at her sheer beauty, her blonde hair tumbling over her shoulder on one side while I cup both tits this time.

"You're so deep," she moans, grinding her cunt on me. "I want to swallow you whole."

A primal growl escapes me, loving how consumed she is by this act.

"Take it all," I choke out, feeling her clamp around me.

Her fingers dart to her clit, mashing it as she throws her head back, taking everything I give, and everything she needs.

Before I know what's happening, she convulses around my cock, squeezing it to the point of no return, and my own climax bursts free as we ride it out together and I fill her full of my cum.

I spent way too long in bed with my princess today, and it's hard to think of anything else but forcing her to go to sleep so I can wake her with my tongue again. But duty calls.

"Are you sure you want to share Nirvana with Slasher and Alana?" Zoe asks quietly as we come down the stairs, and when she glances over her shoulder at me, she catches me watching her ass as she walks.

I shoot her a wink.

"Focus, Gray."

"Yeah, I'm sure." I give in and drag my eyes from the round globes of her ass, giving it a little slap as we reach the bottom of the staircase, and veer left to head toward church. "I thought about what you said. About trust and building a stronger relationship with my VP to create a club that's more than rules and how we can make more money." I reach out and pull her to me, spinning her so we are nose to nose. "You're right, Mrs. Black. The Cruz Kings is more than a club. It's a family. Our family."

Zoe's lips spread wide, her dainty hands coming up to cup either side of my jaw. "Yes. They are our family."

She closes the distance, her soft lips pressing to mine, and I growl with want as I hook my arm around her back and tug her flush with me, deepening the kiss.

"Get a room," Slasher chuckles as he brushes by us in the hallway, and I sigh into Zoe's mouth, wishing we were back upstairs in bed again.

"Come on," Zoe giggles, breaking the kiss and pulling back to take my hand. "It's time for church."

Church doesn't have such a serious vibe since we obliterated the Reapers. Mostly, we've been focused on ways to bring back a sense of safety and security to the Santa Cruz community.

We assisted Loretta and Gertie in the cleanup of the Sleep-Eazy after the Reapers trashed it when they killed Erin and kidnapped Loretta's whores. The two women will never admit it, but I know it's taken a toll that their women were taken without them noticing. Fucking serves them right and maybe now they'll keep a better eye and not go to the back to get high for hours. Probably not, though.

Maude's house has been returned to normal in Watsonville, and with any cash we recovered in the Reapers' safe houses, we donated to the hospital's ER. What the staff did for us that day we took Rocco in, practically dead, and what the doc did by coming to us with information about the Reapers living next door to his mom, well, how could we not repay them by giving what we can?

We could have kept the cash for ourselves, especially since we haven't been able to recover what the Reapers stole from us, but we've accepted that the money is gone. It just doesn't mean what it did in the beginning. As far as we're concerned, it's tainted, and if we were ever to get it back, I'm pretty fucking sure my club brothers would happily have us donate that, too.

"What's on today's agenda?" I ask Slasher, who leaves the cigarette he's smoking hanging from his lips with smoke billowing up into the room as he reads the sheet of paper.

"New prospects, honorary tattoos, and this week's run."

I nod, all eyes on me as I address the group.

"As most of you know, we are getting daily walk ups for guys wanting to join us. I don't want to get too big too quickly, so I'm thinking three prospects for now."

"Sounds good, Prez." Munroe nods as Slasher passes a stack of papers to Tex, who's sitting next to him.

"Here's the list of candidates," Slasher rasps, before blowing out the nicotine cloud he was holding in his lungs. "Have a read through and bring us two preferences by church next week. We start the official process with the voted chosen prospects at the start of February."

Fists thump on the table in agreement, and I can't help but smirk at Titch, who still can't wipe his fucking grin off his face every time he gets to sit in on church now.

"There's another thing we should discuss," I say, lighting up another cigarette. "This is something I want everyone's input on, so the vote needs to be unanimous."

I pause and inhale deeply, letting smoke fill my lungs before I blow it into the air. A part of me didn't even want to hear about it when Slasher mentioned it. But as the days passed, I realized he had a point, and as Prez, it's my duty to find out if it's an issue, even if I don't think it should be.

"Gunner was a big part of designing the club patch we have, and—"

"With all due respect, Prez," Doug says, interrupting me. "I, for one, don't wanna hear it. That patch is *ours* and not Gunner's. There's nothing to discuss."

"Second that," Munroe agrees.

I never get to finish the question before they all make it clear that there's no issue with the club patch, and that it's ours.

"To the matter of honorary tattoos," I say, leaning back in my seat and taking Zoe's hand in mine, resting them on my thigh.

She's so fucking quiet in these meetings that I wonder if she even likes coming to them. I could probably tell her she doesn't have to come anymore if she doesn't want to, but I'm a possessive fucker. I want her by my side every fucking minute of the day.

"I would like to put forward a vote to offer the Cunts honorary Cruz Kings tattoos in recognition for their dedication and the sacrifices they made by fighting the Reaper war with us."

Zoe sits taller next to me, and I bite back a smirk.

I didn't tell her we were going to be considering this.

"Yays?" I ask, and one by one, my club brothers say "Yay," before thumping their fist over their heart.

"Yays have it," I declare before turning to Zoe. "Mrs. Black. Can you please present that offer to the Cunts? We will arrange to have them done next week."

"Yes." She rolls her eyes at my use of Mrs. Black before nodding, looking excited. "Of course."

Shooting her a wink, I turn back to the table, discussing this week's run up to San Francisco, allocating men before I slam the gavel to close church.

"Be ready to leave in five," I tell Slasher, who nods before following my club brothers out of the room.

"I didn't know you were going to do that." Zoe smiles, tugging me up to stand from my chair.

"What? The ink?"

"Yeah." She nods, her blue pools wide with something that is damn fucking close to happiness. "You have no idea what that gesture will do for the women."

"The offer is open to you too, Princess."

Her mouth drops open.

"What? You never thought of getting ink?"

She shakes her head. "No, that's not it. I just never thought I deserved something like that. It kind of makes me feel like I really am part of this family."

Frowning, I drag her to my chest. "How could you even question that?"

She shrugs. "I'm still trying to get used to the fact that I have a family when I thought I'd lost everything only a couple of months back. Sometimes I think it just catches me off guard that we made it out the other side in one piece."

Pressing my lips to her forehead, I shake my head. "Time to embrace it, Zo. And just so you know, when the burn scar on your shoulder blade has healed another couple of years, I'll sit with you when you get my face inked over it."

Laughing, she pushes me back and slaps my shoulder. "If I get your face tattooed on my body, it will be on my ass so I can sit on your face all the time."

Throwing my head back with a roar of laughter, I let Zoe tug me out of church, leading me to the main clubhouse doors where Slasher and Alana are waiting for us.

"Can you tell us where we are going yet?" Alana asks, looking like a ball of excited energy.

"No," I tell her as Zoe rolls her eyes.

"How many times do I have to tell you? It's not a surprise if we tell you." Zoe beams before taking her friend's hand in hers and dragging her through the doors.

"Are you gonna at least tell me where we are going?" Slasher asks, and I shake my head. "I swear if you're trying to use my girl for another fucking threesome that I have to hear and not fucking participate in, I'll fucking resign and take her with me."

Throwing my head back, I laugh at my broody VP, shaking my head and slapping him on his shoulder.

"Just get your girl on your bike and follow me."

Separating Zoe and Alana, we get them on the backs of our bikes before riding out of the gate and leaving the clubhouse for the rest of the day.

Riding up the highway sure fucking feels good with Zoe behind me again. She holds on tight, her arms wrapped around me as Slasher follows behind with Alana.

Just under an hour later, we slow our rides as we come to the track that leads to Nirvana.

I feel unusually nervous about this, even though it was my idea that we show this place to Slasher and Alana. Until Zoe came along, I'd never wanted to share my sacred space with anyone. Not even Rocco and Gunner.

Now though, Slasher and Alana have become the closest family can get without being a couple, in my opinion. Slasher, my brother, and Alana, the sister I never had.

I know Zoe feels the same way.

Pulling up outside my cabin, I cut the engine, hearing Slasher's fall quiet a moment later, and we pull off our helmets before dismounting the bikes.

"What is this place?" Alana asks, and Zoe is so full of excited energy that I'm surprised she doesn't start jumping around.

"Yeah, so this is mine," I say, feeling so fucking awkward, my hand rubbing at the back of my neck.

"Yours?" Slasher asks, and I nod before Zoe can no longer contain herself.

"You have to see this place. It's so cute. Well, I mean it will be as soon as I get my hands on some decent decor and restyle the inside, but it's so charming and..."

Zoe's voice filters away as she hooks elbows with Alana and leads her up the porch steps.

"Cute? Decor?" Slasher smirks.

"Shut the fuck up," I grin back.

"How long have you had this place?" Slasher asks, watching Zoe unlock the door and disappear inside with Alana.

"A few years." I shrug before pinning him with a look. "No one knows about it."

"I fucking know no one knows about it. Why is that?" he asks, but his words hold no mirth.

"I just needed a *me* space, and then somehow Zoe ended up here with me." I shrug, taking in the rustic cabin. "And now, you and your girl know about it, too."

"Why are you telling me?" he asks, and I can tell he's genuinely confused.

"I don't want to keep secrets from my second. For now, it's only us four that know about this place, and you're more than welcome to come here to have some space from the club when you need it. Maybe sometime down the track I'll share this place with others, but for now, I need it to be my Nirvana."

Slasher nods, like he understands exactly what I'm talking about.

"Come on. Let's get inside before Zoe redesigns the whole place in her head."

EPILOGUE 3

Zoe

Six months later.

"You're really not going to tell him?" Rose asks, cackling when I shake my head.

"No." I smile. "This is for me to know, and him to find out if he ever fucking asks instead of acting like it's a done deal."

Alana shakes her head, smiling widely. "You know we won't tell him."

I already know my Cunts can be trusted. That's why I allowed them to come with me when I got the tattoo last week while Gray was on a run for the club.

The first tattoo I ever got was the skull head. After I told the Cunts about the Kings wanting them to have honorary tats, they could only wait two days before they all wanted to go get it done. When we went I wasn't sure I wanted it, but while watching them, I decided to have the skull cover one of the many scars Gunner left behind.

I've heard about the addiction of tattoos before, but until I had my first one, I don't think I ever believed the hype. But I was back the week after, taking Gray with me that time. And I got a black, gothic looking unicorn tattooed on my wrist.

A constant reminder of Leslie, without it being too cutesy. I mean, it's still pretty, obviously. I'm still me, and I still love pretty things.

"And he still hasn't noticed it?" Rose probes, pointing to the spot behind my ear I've successfully managed to keep hidden from Gray.

I strategically arrange my hair to cover the top of my ear. "It's not like we play hide the saltine, so why would he ever look behind my ear?"

"And if they did, that's definitely not where she'd hide it," Alana screeches with laughter.

Pulling a face, I answer, "Absolutely fucking not."

"Well, if we're not going to talk about where to hide the saltine, should we get a move on?" Rose asks, impatient as ever.

I clutch the rule book Cara made harder against my chest. "We might as well get it over with," I answer.

As we're entering a new sense of normalcy and everyday life, I want to get rid of this cursed thing once and for all. I know I've mentioned it before, but it wasn't the right time. Now, though, it definitely is.

Especially with the changes Gray has already propelled into reality. Like the Cunts, and me, getting honorary logo tattoos, which is just one of the many changes he and Slasher have brought about.

It might not sound like a big deal, but it's changed the atmosphere in the club. The Cunts have embraced the honor, in their own way treating it like them being a vital part of the club, which they undoubtedly are.

Now, they share their riches from their fans' website freely. There's no more divide in the money. Hell, last month they even decided to hire a cleaner and brought the proposal to Gray without me knowing. Of course, he insisted on vetting the cleaners, but once Cain suggested a company, it was a done deal.

Two of the women from the company have been spending more and more time here at the club, and I even saw one of them come out of the storage room with her hair and clothes in disarray a few days ago.

Gray's reminded me that I need to recruit more Cunts, which is something I'm reluctant to do. As I've explained,

I'm not opposed to having more women around. But just as he's picky with the Kings and has prospects, I need a similar system. Being a Cunt is an honor, and I won't sully the status by just accepting anyone who'll spread their legs for the Kings.

"What do you guys think about Sweet Butts?" I ask Alana and Rose, momentarily forgetting they aren't privy to my thoughts. "I mean for new women who hang around steadily, but that we aren't ready to make Cunts?"

Rose's eyes dart from me to Alana, and she looks reluctant to answer. "That's your decision, Mama Z," she says.

I roll my eyes. "But now I'm asking you, Rose. I want your opinion, regardless of the fucking hierarchy."

Alana nods. "It should be a decision we all make together, and not just Zoe or me."

"I like that idea," Rose says, barely able to contain her happiness at being asked. "I think the others will, too. But we should—"

"We're definitely going to ask them," I say, cutting her off. "One thing at a time, though. Let's restore justice and get rid of the old rule book first."

Everyone is already waiting in the main room, thanks to Cilla who I asked to gather all the Kings and Cunts.

"What's up?" Titch asks, eyeing me curiously.

Taking a deep breath, I steel myself while trying to remember the words I've rehearsed. "Cara's rulebook," I say, holding it up for everyone to see. "Is outdated and downright fucking toxic."

"Hear, hear," Alana yells as she takes a seat next to Slasher.

"As the new Mama, I hereby declare it null and void."

The Cunts all clap and whoop enthusiastically.

"So what about punishments?" Munroe asks.

Turning my head, I glare at him. "I'll decide the punishments for my girls," I hiss. "On a case-by-case basis."

My eyes lock on Gray as he takes a drag of the cigarette between his lips. "That won't work, Princess," he drawls. "If you want to throw out the old rules, you have to put new ones into place."

I nod, knowing there's no way to get around that.

"Okay," I relent. "I'll come up with new ones that match the severity of the crime. But the Kings shouldn't be allowed to vote on a Cunt's punishment."

"Agreed." I'm surprised when Tio agrees with me. "Keep that shit between yourselves."

"Aye," Slasher says. "Unless it's big shit that involves the club, I see no need for the Kings to have a say. And even then, it should be between our Prez and Mama."

I nod again because I can get behind that.

"All those in favor?" Gray calls, and he's met with ayes from all the Kings and Cunts.

"Perfect," I beam, making a big show of throwing Cara's old rule book in the trash. "But before we can completely close that chapter, there's an old wrong that needs to be righted."

Slasher and Gray chuckle like they already know where I'm going with this.

"Alana's punishment was fucking brutal," I seethe, remembering what it felt like to force the Cunts to slap one of their own, all so Rocco wouldn't make the Kings slap her instead.

"So what now? You want Alana to slap us?" Slasher asks. His knowing smile convinces me that Alana has clued him in on what she wanted, which is more than fair since I told Gray as well.

"Exactly," I say. As my gaze darts between all the Kings, I try not to laugh at their varying expressions of surprise and disbelief.

"You can't be serious," Munroe scoffs.

"No," Tio almost shouts, crossing his arms over his chest. "Not fucking happening."

Stretch grins. "What's the matter, Tio? Scared she'll hurt you? Look at her, man."

Now that Stretch has turned it into an ego thing, no one else complains. Albeit grudgingly, the Kings all stand.

"Let's get it over with," Tex chuckles.

Alana stands slowly, swinging her arms to the side like she's warming up. Then she rubs her hands together with a wicked grin on her lips.

She walks over to Tio first. Raising her hand, she swings it toward his cheek, but when it's almost touching his skin, she slows her movement and barely taps him. Then she throws her arms around his neck and hugs him.

"Thanks for protecting us," she says.

Tio looks at Slasher, probably wondering if he's allowed to hug her back. But when Slasher nods, he doesn't hesitate. "Sorry for the votes," Tio mumbles, barely loud enough for me to hear.

Alana doesn't even pretend she's going to slap the other Kings, instead, she goes straight in for the hug and thanks them. When she reaches Gray, she looks at me, not moving until I give her a nod.

I don't hear what she whispers to him, but whatever it is has him smiling like the damn Cheshire cat. Fuckers. They're not meant to have secrets from me. Alana and me from Gray, sure. But not the other way around. Nuh-uh.

"Okay, that's enough," I say when I feel like their embrace has gone on for longer than what's needed.

Gray just grins wider, and Alana has the audacity to wink at me. I swear, the next time I'm making her a drink, I'll make it a virgin. Serves her right.

"I love seeing you jealous, Mrs. Black," Gray rasps when he moves behind me, resting his head on my shoulder.

Letting out a puff of air, I crane my neck so I can look at him. "You still haven't asked."

"You've already said you're mine."

I feign a sigh. "Then I guess you'll never hear my answer."

Gray spins me around so quickly I almost trip over my feet. "You know what your answer would be?" he asks, excitement making his eyes shine brighter than usual.

"Of course," I say with a shrug.

"Do I get a hint?"

I shoot him a devilish smirk. "Sure... my answer is three letters—"

His face lights up, and I almost feel bad. *Almost.*

"The real question is whether it's yay or nay," I sing-song as I move out of his hold.

Before he can recover from that, I dance out of the room.

"You're going to fucking pay for that," he growls, and I don't need to look to know he's hot on my heels.

I laugh as I bounce up the stairs, only making it halfway up before he wraps his arms around me.

"Gotcha, Mrs. Black," he rasps. "You're going to pay for that."

One year later.

I groan as I wake up to a shadow looming over me, shielding me from the delicious rays of the unrelenting July sun.

"It's time," Gray rasps, smirking down at me.

Narrowing my eyes, I look at him from behind my sunglasses. "What? Already? But the Fourth of July isn't until tomorrow," I huff. Or is it today? Ugh, after falling asleep in the sun, I'm not sure if it's even the same day.

With a chuckle, he sits down next to me on the blanket I've splayed across the ground. "Turn around," he commands, and I do as he says, turning to my stomach while still trying to make sense of the dates.

We've been at Nirvana for three days. Three days of uninterrupted us time.

Since we showed the place to Alana and Slasher, we've made a few changes to the cabin. Nothing big, as it was already perfect in its simplicity. But it needed a woman's touch—my touch, which it now has in abundance.

That's not strictly true. I haven't stuffed the cabin with frills and useless ornaments, just enough to make it feel more homey. Like the picture of me and Leslie that we got back from the detectives once the case was finally completely shut. That picture now hangs in a gold frame above the couch.

All the floors are covered by carpets due to how cold it gets during winter, and we now have a fully functioning kitchen. Not that it wasn't working before, but it's nicer now. While I'm not big on cooking or domestic chores in general, I love it when we're alone.

We've expanded the bedroom and bathroom, and by we, I mean Gray. Ever the control freak, he has slaved with his bare hands to make this the perfect getaway location for the two of us.

I squeal in surprise when something cold lands on my back. "What the fuck?"

Gray laughs, a carefree sound I've heard more and more often since the war with the Reapers ended. "It's time to rub more lotion on your back." I moan as his large hands begin to rub the lotion into my skin. "You know how serious I am about your health," he says as he pays extra attention to my ass cheeks.

Since there's no one else around for miles, I don't bother with a bikini here, so I'm already completely naked.

"I don't think I'm going to get sunburned *there*," I grin when his finger slides into the crevice of my ass.

"Now you definitely won't," he rasps.

My eyes flutter closed. I part my legs more and lift my hips to make room for his hand as he slides it underneath me and to my front, parting my folds.

"Already so fucking wet for me," he says approvingly. "Were you dreaming about me?"

I don't mean to stroke his ego by telling him the truth, but when he slides two fingers into my cunt, there's no playing it cool. "Always," I moan.

He groans his approval while working his fingers into me with quick pumps. My stomach tightens, and I'm right on the precipice when he suddenly removes his fingers and asks, "Do you ever regret it?"

"Regret what?" I snap, annoyed he stopped me from coming.

"Not going to Harvard," he clarifies.

I'm getting fucking whiplash from the change in his mood. Instead of being playful, he's now wistful.

"No," I answer. "That was a plan from before I met you. From before I found my true calling."

He nods. "But you're not sure about us?"

My jaw becomes slack. "Where the hell is this coming from, Gray? We live together. We're building a life together. Which part of that makes you think I'm unsure?"

When he looks away, I have my answer.

"Gray?"

There's something about being here at Nirvana that transforms my hardened biker into a normal guy. One with insecurities and doubts just like everyone else. Though it's not as sexy as his rough sides, it's endearing and so fucking lovable. Seriously, those are the times I know we're in this until the end. Because those are the sides of him that no one but me ever gets to see.

"Why haven't you said yes?"

Ah, so that's what this is about.

Shaking my head, I move my sunglasses up my forehead and look into his eyes. "You've never asked, Gray. You call me Mrs. Black and assume it's a done deal. But I want you to get on your knees and—"

"Hey." He holds his hands up in surrender. "I was on my knees for hours yesterday, eating you out."

My cheeks burn at the memory.

"But you still didn't ask," I point out. "Eating me out and asking me to marry you isn't the same thing. If you want my answer, you have to ask first."

My hand moves to my ear, covering the tattoo with my answer if he ever asks. The answer isn't for me, it's for him. So he knows that I'm already irrevocably his in every way possible. All he has to do is ask.

With an animalistic growl, he palms my hips and pulls them upward until my ass is in the air. I don't have time to make myself comfortable before there's a loud smack followed by a stinging sensation spreading across my ass cheek.

"W-wha—"

Smack.

The next one comes just as fast, and now both cheeks sting.

I whimper, the sound caused both by pain and pleasure. My pussy gushes, loving the rough way he treats me.

Gray gently moves his hand across both my ass cheeks, lulling me into a false sense of security.

Smack.

I moan.

"This is what you do to me," he rasps. "You drive me so fucking crazy, Princess. You make me both ache and feel content. That's how you feel right now, isn't it?"

When I'm not quick enough to answer him, he slaps my ass again.

"Yes," I cry out. "Stop torturing me and fuck me already."

Being his usual stubborn, dominant self, Gray doesn't give me what I want. Instead, he positions himself perfectly behind me, rubbing his cock between my burning ass cheeks. I huff and move until I'm perched on all fours.

Then I take matters into my own hands, shamelessly rubbing myself along his hard length. I moan at how good it feels.

"You like that, Princess?" he rasps. "You like rubbing all over me like a bitch in fucking heat?"

I'm so needy for him that I don't even care that he just compared me to a canine. "Yes," I breathe.

Gray grips my neck and pulls me up so my back is flush against his chest. His other hand snakes around to my front, pinching and rolling my nipple between his fingers.

"Are you going to give me what I want?"

I shake my head. "You have to ask." A part of me almost hopes he never does. I love our push and pull. It's what we do best. Drive each other so fucking insane the only way to solve things is with explosive, mind-blowing sex.

But on a deeper level, I want him to ask so I can show him the answer tattooed behind my ear. Even after all this time, he still hasn't noticed it. I did have it made small for that exact purpose. Because I love knowing he could have had his answer sooner if he'd just relented and asked. Or looked behind my ear.

A moan tumbles from my lips when Gray positions his cock between my thighs. He fucks into the gap, the tip of his cock perfectly hitting my sensitive bundle of nerves on every thrust.

"Stop playing around," I gasp. "I want you inside me."

Gray ruts against me, and as I come, I arch my back and cry out his name. "That's it, Princess," he rasps, moving his hand from my neck to my throat, perfectly placing it on top of the necklace tattooed into my skin. "Scream my name."

"G-Gray," I moan.

He chuckles and pinches my nipple harder. "I said scream for me, Princess."

When he tightens his grip on my throat, I give him what he wants. I scream his name as I come from the merciless grinding he's administering between my legs. Black spots dance at the edge of my vision, but as always when I'm with Gray, I know I'm safe, loved, and treasured. So it's easy to let go of what little control I have.

As my orgasm ebbs, Gray quickly slides into me, filling me with his hard, throbbing cock. "Are you ready to be Mrs. Black?" He lets out a groan as I tighten my cunt around him. "Fuck."

"Was that your version of proposing?" I quip, tilting my hips to perfectly meet him every time he pumps into me.

Gray lets go of my nipple and throat, and quickly spins us around so he's on his back and I'm straddling him. I grin before I turn so I'm facing away from him. Then I take him back inside me, and work myself up and down until we're both moaning in perfect symphony.

"Fuck. I love watching your ass bounce up and down when you fuck me," he praises. He moves his hands to the soft globes, squeezing them until I let out a gasp. "Keep going, Princess."

He parts the flesh, and I know he's watching the space where he disappears into me. My cunt squeezes him again, and I can barely keep up the movement as another orgasm builds inside me.

"Gray," I pant.

The only answer I get is a groan as I feel his finger prod against my tight opening. "Let me in, Princess."

Though I'm trying to relax, it's almost impossible when my entire body is coiled tight in anticipation of the release waiting just around the corner.

Gray pushes harder against my back entrance, and I'm screaming, delirious with pleasure as he finds his way inside first with one finger, then two.

"I'm so... I'm so... Gray!" My words turn nonsensical as it takes everything in me to keep moving.

"I know you're close," Gray rasps, his fingers pistoning into my ass. "Come for me, Mrs. Black."

His words are my undoing, and instead of giving him a snarky reply, I chant his name over and over as I come so hard, he needs to steady me so I don't fall off his cock.

I feel like I black out from sheer pleasure, and maybe I do, because when my vision comes back, he's changed our position without me noticing it. Where he was behind me before, I'm now looking up at him as he now hovers above me. His cock is still hard, twitching inside me.

"If I ask."

Thrust.

"You."

Thrust.

"Better."

Thrust.

"Say."

Thrust.

"Yes."

I don't get a chance to answer before he bends down and claims my lips with his. His tongue delves into my mouth, and it feels like he's sucking the air from my lungs and into his as he kisses me with a passion that could start a forest fire.

His breathing speeds up and his cock jerks and pulsates deep in my pussy, his hot cum painting my insides with hot strokes.

Gray moves to the side, his spent dick still inside me. I'm not ready for him to pull out, so I roll with him and hoist my leg up and around his waist, keeping us together.

"I love you, Gray."

His eyes flutter open. "And I fucking love you, Zo. Now tell me you'll be Mrs. Bl—"

With a grin, I place my finger against his lips and stop him from finishing that sentence. "That's still not a question."

EPILOGUE 4

Grayson

A couple of years later.

Whistles and hoots fill the air as Zoe blows the candles out, making sure to get each of the twenty-one burning wicks in one breath. I can't fucking wipe the smile from my face as I watch her straighten and gasp for air, her lips spreading into a wide smile right before Alana launches forward, shaking a bottle of champagne and spraying it over us.

"Alana!" Zoe screeches through her laughter right as more alcohol starts spraying from all directions, drenching not just us, but everyone near us.

"God damn it." I chuckle, ducking down to scoop my princess up before throwing her over my shoulder.

"Hey! Where are you going with the birthday girl?" Rose calls as I push through my many club brothers and the barely clothed Cunts and Sweet Butts as the celebration amps up.

Zoe giggles, not even bothering to fight me as I head out of the main room, beelining for the stairs.

"You aren't even going to wait until the orgy starts up?" she asks, trying to shove her hands unsuccessfully down the back of my jeans.

"No way, Princess. I want to give you your presents." I give her ass a slap to stop her from trying to get into my pants, but it only makes her try harder as she squeals.

Getting her into our new apartment—which is Rocco's old one and a lot bigger and more homely than the last one—I lock the door and swing her back off my shoulder, planting her feet on the floor before the couch.

"Whoa." Zoe presses her hand to her forehead and sways as her head spins, and I grin, keeping hold of her hips to steady her as the blood rushes away from her head.

"Doing okay?" I ask, my eyes dancing between hers as she blinks up at me and nods.

"What was it you were saying about my presents?"

Chuckling, I release her hips and point to the plush couch behind her. "Sit."

She moves so fast, more fucking obedient than usual, eager as fuck to get her birthday gifts.

Her blue gaze is wide with excitement as I move to the cupboard by the door and open it, getting out her present as I remember her last few birthdays and how much she loves surprises more and more as each year passes.

Things over the last couple of years have been more peaceful than I knew how to handle. Our only real threat these days is getting caught by the cops doing our somewhat illegal business activities. There haven't been any other MCs trying to claim our territory, and in fact, most of the Cali ones have a lot of respect for us for ending Rusty Hunt and the Reapers' reign.

It took some time to get used to figuring out our new normal, and the money the club has been bringing in has helped us prosper, but also benefited the community.

Instead of going to the hospital every Fourth of July, we go monthly now, Zoe and the Cunts spending extra time in the burn unit.

"Oooh. What is it?" Zoe asks, her eyes glued to the wrapped gift in my hand while she rubs her hands together.

"I'm not telling you, Zo. You just have to open it and see."

Bouncing her ass on the couch as I get closer, she holds her hands out, desperate to open it already.

"I'm ready." She beams, but I hold it out of her reach.

"You are very greedy, Mrs. Black." I snicker at her pout and wait until her hands drop to her lap in defeat before I reach forward and pass it to her. "Hurry up and open it, then."

She doesn't hesitate, tearing into the paper like a woman starved and the item wrapped is a meal.

Sitting my ass on the coffee table in front of her, I keep my eyes trained to her face, gauging her expression.

"Oh my..." she trails off, holding up the leather jacket to see it better. "This is beautiful, Gray."

"Check the inside back panel." I suggest, and her blue eyes dart up to mine briefly before dropping back to the jacket as she lays it out on her knees to reveal the interior panel that I had put into the lining.

"Oh," she whispers as her fingers dance over the embossed Cruz Kings' skull head.

"I know it's not the same as having your own cut, but at least you can still wear the club skull in secret."

Blue glassy eyes dart back up to me a moment before she launches herself to wrap her arms around my neck, squeezing me tight.

"Thank you, Gray." She pulls back. "I love it."

Her lips claim mine then, and I hold her close as we get lost in the way our tongues dance. My hands wander over her, tugging at her clothes, peeling what I can off as I stand, her leather jacket forgotten.

Lifting her in my arms, she winds her legs around me as I carry her, peeking through my cracked lids as I go so I don't trip, and the moment we are through the door to our bedroom, I hurry to the foot of the bed and lower her to the mattress.

"You know we've already fucked like three times today, right?" She giggles, laying back on the bed as I loom over her.

"I do know." I agree, grinning at the way she drags her top over her head, tossing it to the side where it disappears out of sight. Probably on the floor. "You enjoyed having my fingers inside you while you woke up this morning." I remind her, picturing how ravenous she was when she finally roused. "Then there was the parking lot outside the lawyer's office. Apparently, getting your trust fund signed over to you turns you on." She beams, nodding, not in the least bit shy about it. "And then there was the hour before your party started that you tied me up and took advantage of me. I have to say, bringing out that fucking whip was uncalled for."

She snickers, pulling her own shorts and panties off and kicking them over her head. They land in a tangled heap on top of the bedside lamp.

"Well, it is *my* birthday, Gray. It's become tradition that you let me take away your control, and I think you secretly like it."

I curl my lip playfully at her before snapping my teeth. It's all for show though. She knows I love everything we do, including giving over my control.

"Since it's still technically your birthday for another," I check the clock on the wall, "seven minutes, I have one last gift for you."

"You do?" she asks, propping up on her elbows, her smile wide and eyes dancing with excitement.

"I do... well... maybe it's more of a gift for me." I take way too long pretending to think about that before her foot lifts off the bed and playfully kicks the side of my hip.

"Don't tease me." She pouts.

Fuck, I love those plump lips. She even makes pouting look sexy.

I start undressing myself, quickly ridding myself of my clothes, loving the way Zoe's blue gaze heats and travels over my body as I walk to the chest of drawers and quickly get out what I need.

When I turn to her, those blue eyes shift to the bottle of lube in my hand, and she bites her lower lip as she presses her thighs together.

"Tonight's the night, Princess."

"Tonight?" She pants, her voice breathy as I approach.

"Yes. I've been a patient man, prepping you for a few years, and now it's time."

She swallows thickly, even as her hand slides down her front to press her fingers to the apex between her thighs.

"O... kay." She breathes.

I growl in approval, reaching the foot of the bed and resting the lube on the mattress next to her feet before I grip her ankles and quickly pull her closer.

"I'm not going to be gentle." I tug her legs wide apart and hover over her as I drag my hand up the inside of her thigh. "It may even hurt, Princess." Knowing she's already slick from the thought of what's going to happen, I roughly shove three fingers inside her tight cunt. She cries out, her lips parting as she surges closer, making it sting even more. "But I promise, it will hurt really fucking good."

"Gray." She pants, accepting everything I give her, and I proceed to work her cunt into a gushing mess, edging her and pulling back before she reaches her release.

When she's practically begging me to fill her with any-thing, she doesn't care—her words, not mine—I flip her, pressing her face into the mattress as I lift her ass in the air and spread her knees wide.

"Fuck, Princess. Look at that ass." I press my thumb to her puckered rose, applying a bit of teasing pressure. "It's aching to be stretched. Filled."

"Yes. Please," Zoe begs, her voice muffled as she pants into the mattress.

Taking the lube, I lather my straining cock before pouring a generous amount over her winking hole.

"Rub your clit for me, Mrs. Black."

Doing as I say, Zoe's hand slides between her legs, and from where I stand, I can see the tips of her nails as she starts working the needy bud with vigor.

"Gray." She pants. "Stop calling me Mrs. Black. You haven't asked yet, and we aren't married."

Her reminder spurs me on, and I press the tip of my cock to her back passage and start to press forward.

"Relax, Princess." I grit out, forcing the first inch of my hard cock into her virginal passage. "Remember how much you want this," I tell her. "Remember how much you want to be filled in the most intimate way."

When she moans, I feel her relax a little more, and I clench my fucking teeth as I squeeze my dick in deeper.

"Fuck, Zo. You're so tight. Do you feel how big I am inside you?"

She whimpers, and even though there's a bite of pain to the sound, there's also want.

With one hand guiding my cock, I press the other to the mattress beside Zoe, holding myself up.

"Open more for me," I rasp. "Give me everything, Zoe."

At those words, any tension she had falls away, and I slide my cock all the way in.

We both moan, the sound a mix of pleasure and pain, and with my other hand now free, I reach forward and sweep her blonde hair back off her face to reveal her flushed cheeks, her eyes squeezed shut and lips parted.

"Are you still rubbing your clit, Princess?" Even though I already know she is because I can feel her fingers tickle my nuts, I still ask, because I need to make sure she's still with me.

"Yes." She moans.

"Tell me how it feels to have me take your ass virginity?"

A grin spreads her lips wide as her lids flutter open. "It feels full."

"Yeah, I bet it does. My cock has been dreaming of this moment, Princess. It's harder and bigger than it's ever been right now."

She moans, pushing back against me, and I chuckle.

"You ready for me to destroy this ass?"

"Yes."

"Hmmm. I do love that fucking word, Princess." I reach out to her hair again, tugging it back from her ear to reveal the word tattooed there. "I love that it's right here for me, too."

She's known for a while that I knew it was there, and at first, I had no fucking idea what the meaning behind it meant, but my princess has a tell, and sometimes, when I call her Mrs. Black, her fingers subtly brush her hair over her ear right where the ink is hidden. It wasn't hard for me to figure out that it was the answer to the question I kept refusing to ask her.

I start moving then, slowly dragging my dick nearly all the way out before easing back in. Each time I do it, it gets easier, her muscles getting used to the size of my dick, opening her passage for me.

I get a good pace going, my eyes glued to where I disappear inside her as small animalistic grunts slip past her lips every time I hit deep.

"Feel that, Princess?" I ask. "Feel the way I'm claiming you completely?"

"Y-yes." She stutters in a husky tone, nearly lost to the pleasure.

"I can feel you squeezing me." I grunt, sliding one hand around to her front and pushing her rubbing fingers away. "How wet are you?"

We both moan loudly when I sink three fingers into her tight cunt, and the combined fullness sends her over the edge.

Her scream is loud, probably the loudest it's ever fucking been, and it pulls at something in me. Something primal.

I pick up my pace, continuing to work my fingers inside her as she shatters, my dick pumping in and out of her ass faster as I chase my release.

"You're mine!" I roar, hitting her hard and deep before the pleasure washes over me and I stiffen, pumping my hot cum into her ass.

It takes a fucking minute for my hearing to come back and when it does, our panting breaths meet my ears.

Sliding my fingers from her dripping cunt, I straighten and twist her long locks around my fist, dragging her up with me.

"Princess," I rasp against her ear as I hold her flush against my chest, my dick starting to soften inside her.

"Yes," she pants, relaxing into me.

"Every part of you belongs to me now."

She tries to giggle, but her exhaustion cuts it off so that it's nothing more than a squeak, before her husky voice rasps. "Not every part."

I nip at her lobe before running my tongue up to the top of her ear and over the word forever inked into her skin.

"You will be my wife, Princess. Mark my words."

A few years later.

I stand on the wrap-around porch of the place we now call home as my club brothers wait at the bottom of the stairs, beers in hand. There are so many Kings now. My men tripling in size over the last few years meant we could no longer stay at the clubhouse in Santa Cruz, and short of some of the married men, I prefer to keep my brothers close, giving them a home and a purpose.

I'd already been scoping out a new place for us when Zoe insisted on using some of her trust fund to help. It was fucking hard for me to say yes. There's still a part of me that doesn't want a cent of her money, given how she was traded for it in the beginning, but she pointed out that there's just so much, and her portfolio is continually making income, so she simply didn't know what else to do with it.

She has been putting that income to good use, though, and Santa Cruz is thriving because of her and our contribution to the community. The detectives that once chased us just tend to steer clear these days for the simple fact that we've made their lives easier as well.

A yell from inside the large ranch style house reaches my ears, and I'm not the only one to chuckle at the sound as the Cunts and Sweet Butts do my bidding inside.

"She's gonna fucking kill you." Slasher smirks, his smoke hanging out of his mouth as he shakes his head.

"Probably. But fuck, she'll make it hurt so good."

My brothers laugh, even as something crashes inside the house.

"Are you sure she won't kill us, too?" Munroe asks. "Maybe we should go and hide in the clubhouse." He juts his thumb over his shoulder to the large farming shed that we gutted and renovated into our new clubhouse. There are some bedrooms off the back, plus the old farm hand quarters that've been renovated to hold twenty of our men, while others shack up in small cabins spread throughout the back of the property.

This house though, I glance at the ranch style farmhouse behind me, and light up a cigarette. This house is a real fucking home. Not a shitty apartment with basic appliances. This house is filled with welcoming warmth, partly because of the design thanks to the previous owners, but also thanks to my princess and the decorative touches she's added.

I wonder if it will still seem as warm after this is over. It sounds like my princess is trashing the inside of our home that we share with Alana and Slasher. Maybe I should have insisted the Cunts take Zoe to their quarters behind the house for this part.

"Grayson Black!"

My men 'oooooh' behind me while I fucking smirk as Zoe bursts out the front door, her long blonde hair flowing behind her as her feet stomp on the timber of the porch, heading straight for me.

"What is this?" She sneers, gripping the skirt of the black dress and shaking it like I can't fucking see what she's wearing.

"You look fucking beautiful," I say honestly, and her rage falls from her face for a beat.

Then it returns. "I fucking know I do. I chose this fucking dress, Grayson. So why the hell did *my* Cunts hold me down and force it on me?!"

"You know why."

Her eyes turn to slits. "Let's fucking pretend I don't, and you spell it out for me, hey?"

My brothers chuckle behind me again as the Cunts and Sweet Butts quietly move past their Mama and join my gathered men.

"Come here," I mutter, taking a deep drag of my smoke, and by the time I'm blowing it up over her head, she's closing the distance.

"Start talking," she sneers, her hands on her hips.

With my cigarette gripped in my fingers, I gesture to her dress.

"You chose that dress to marry me in." I remind her as I take a step forward, using my free hand to brush back her hair over her ear, making sure I graze my fingers slowly over the ink hidden there. "And you wrote your answer here for me."

"So?" she snaps. "You still haven't fucking asked."

Shaking my head, I sigh and drop my hand away. "You would think after all this time, you would know better." I drop my smoke on the porch and use the toe of my boot to stub it out. "I don't need to ask for what's already mine."

The rage that contorts her face falls away as I quickly dart forward and tug her flush against my front, fisting my hand in the back of her hair.

"No more fucking around, Princess. We are getting married now, and you *will* take my name."

"You know, King-Jack-High is in my name. I could just move into the studio above it." She shrugs, like her threat will deter me.

I fist my hand tighter in her hair.

That little fucking brat.

King-Jack-High is a dive bar we own in town. Zoe wanted to own a business, and she needed a way of giving her Cunts a job so the ones that didn't want to do anything on their fans' page could earn a legit living. She came up with the name, a poker term, and with the help of her Cunts, they decked it out with a poker theme. Most of her newest Sweet Butts have been recruited from the bar, and it's become a popular location for those who don't want anything fancy when they want to have a drink.

Jerking Zoe's head, I lean closer and sneer in her face. "I'll burn that fucking place to the ground before I let you leave me."

My words are quiet. I doubt anyone else but her can hear them and as I stare at her demanding her compliance, her bravado falters.

"Why won't you just ask?" she whispers. "You already know what my answer is, Gray. All I want is for you to ask for once, instead of taking."

Fuck.

She's the only human walking this earth that can make my fucking cold heart defrost.

Releasing her hair, I cup her face between my large hands, staring into her blue pleading eyes.

"Be mine? In every fucking way, Princess. Please?"

And just like that, the hardness in her eyes falls away, and the blue pools dance from one of my eyes to the other, before gazing at my lips. Then she looks back to my eyes.

"Is there room for negotiation?" she asks, snapping me out of the trance she had me in. "I still think it would be better if you change your name to mine. Grayson Miller has a nice ring to it."

Her face contorts to a shit-eating grin, and I grit my teeth as my hold on her face becomes rough.

"There is only one way this goes, Princess. Zoe Black. Mrs. Zoe Black. Mrs. Black. Fucking say the word I want to hear and let's finally do this."

"You're such a romantic." She giggles, her words loud enough that everyone hears, pissing me off even more.

"Say the fucking word," I snap, pressing my nose to hers.

"Fine." She shoves me back. "Yes, I'll marry your stubborn ass."

Everyone cheers at her words, and the next thing I know, Alana is jumping around like she has fucking ants in her pants, scurrying up to hug Zoe, while Slasher nudges me with his shoulder and Tex comes to stand before us.

Any fight Zoe had about me forcing this moment has completely vanished, and I realize I'm actually the one that was manipulated into giving in.

I'll punish her for that later.

Naked.

Writhing.

Begging.

I hardly hear what Tex says as he goes through the process of marrying us. I repeat basic vows, and watch Zoe's lips move as she recites hers, before we are announced as husband and wife and my lips are claiming hers in a bruising kiss.

We celebrate in true Kings style. Loud music. Lots of drinking. And a fucking brilliant orgy that Zoe insists we are the centerpiece for.

"In the old days," Zoe unzips the corset top of her black dress, letting it fall off her, the full skirt bunching around her calves, "didn't a king have an audience when he fucked his wife for the first time so there was no doubt the marriage was consummated?"

My brows shoot up. "That's what's happening here?" I ask. "Because I'm pretty sure most people have seen me balls deep inside you before."

She laughs, stepping out of the fabric of her dress, pointing at me. "Get naked, my king. Your princess is waiting."

I don't fucking hesitate.

My clothes are off, and I hoist her up, impaling my princess on my cock in a matter of seconds, before lowering her to the closest table in our new clubhouse.

My lips are on hers and her hands are in my hair, and while I can hear the sounds of everyone fucking around us, the loudest sound is Zoe's moans that fall into my mouth as we consummate our marriage.

Finally, Zoe is irrevocably mine.

"I fucking love you, Grayson Black," she pants, breaking the kiss to lock her blue eyes with mine as I pound into her.

"I fucking love you too, Zoe Black."

Finally, my princess had truly been claimed by a king.

"I SWEAR MY ALLEGIANCE TO OUR PRESIDENT, GRAYSON BLACK, AND THE CRUZ KINGS MC AND ITS MEMBERS, BOTH PATCH, AND PUSSY. I SWEAR TO UPHOLD THE CLUB VALUES WITH HONOR AND PROTECT EACH MEMBER WITH MY LIFE."

TRIGGER WARNING

Please note this is book 3 of 3 in a dark MC contemporary romance series. The book ends with a HEA, and contains a swoon-worthy alphahole MMC.

Age-gap | Blood-play | Death (graphic) | Dormaphilia | Graphic sexual content | Graphic violence | Grief | Kinks | Morally gray MMC | Rape (not h and H!) | PTSD | Sex trafficking | Somnophilia | Trauma Torture (mentally and physically) | Unaliving